P9-EMH-744

"Schrieve's queer vision of a monster-infested '90s is rich in metaphor and rife with meaning."

— KYLE LUKOFF,
librarian and author of *When Aidan Became a Brother*

"*Out of Salem* is the best urban fantasy I've ever read. Hal Schrieve refurbishes old-school world-building sensibilities into a note-perfect dysphoria metaphor that feels fresh and classic at the same time. Simultaneously nostalgic and forward-looking, this book should set a new standard in the genre. Terrifying, beautiful, exhilarating."

—APRIL DANIELS,
author of *The Nemesis* trilogy

"*Out of Salem* is the genderqueer, undead, anarchist *Harry Potter* replacement we have all been waiting for. Queer teen readers will fall in love with this gang of misfit magical monsters—not so much chosen ones as outcasts—and if you know a queer teen you should definitely buy it for them. However, in its political acuity, its sadness and, ultimately, its hope, Schrieve's book is much more than just a good YA read. It is also, in the best possible sense, an educational experience."

— CAT FITZPATRICK,
editor of *Meanwhile, Elsewhere: Science Fiction and Fantasy from Transgender Writers*

OUT OF SALEM

OUT OF SALEM

HAL SCHRIEVE

Seven Stories Press
New York • Oakland • London

A Seven Stories Press First Edition

Seven Stories Press
140 Watts Street
New York, NY 10013
www.sevenstories.com

College professors and high school and middle school teachers may order free examination copies of Seven Stories Press titles. To order, visit www.sevenstories.com or send a fax on school letterhead to (212) 226-1411.

Book design by Jon Gilbert

Library of Congress Cataloging-in-Publication Data

Names: Schrieve, Hal, author.
Title: Out of Salem / Hal Schrieve.
Description: New York : Triangle Square, 2019.
Identifiers: LCCN 2018029438| ISBN 9781609809010 (hardback) | ISBN 9781609809027 (ebook)
Subjects: | GSAFD: Science fiction | Horror fiction
Classification: LCC PS3619.C4643 O98 2019 | DDC 813/.6--dc23
LC record available at https://lccn.loc.gov/2018029438

Printed in the USA

9 8 7 6 5 4 3 2 1

1

The morning of the funeral, Z's Uncle Hugh made eight pots of bitter coffee. He circled the house holding the silver coffeepot, pouring cupfuls into different cousins' Fiestaware mugs.

"Are you taking her back to New York with you, then?" It was one of Z's aunts. She was talking to Uncle Hugh outside Z's room. Z could see his shadow on the floor.

"I suppose I have to," Hugh said. "The other option is to sign her into state custody. I asked about that. I called the hospital, and they said that meant they'd send her into the foster care system with a note. We know they wouldn't have wanted that. I don't want that."

"That's a lot of pressure." The aunt shifted her weight and the floorboards creaked.

"I'm going to have to get through all of this stuff in the house in the next couple weeks and then just leave the rest up to the lawyers," Hugh said, and sighed. Z could picture him wringing his hands. "I don't know that I'm ready to deal with her. My life isn't set up for that."

"It'll only be for a little while, though, won't it?" the aunt asked very quietly. Z strained to hear more, but couldn't pick out Hugh's reply.

Z chose not to go to the wake, the funeral, or the reception afterwards. Instead, they sat in their room with their science fiction books spread around them on the bed. Folded into the cover leaf of one of the books was a printout of the web page Z had visited at the computers at the public library. The page described the results of the online quiz Z had taken on a website called transsexual.org four months earlier. The pink background of the site had not translated well onto the library's black-and-white printers, so the letters were a little hard to read.

COMBINED GENDER IDENTITY AND TRANSSEXUALITY INVENTORY (COGIATI)
Your COGIATI result value is: -40 Which means that you fall within the following category:

COGIATI classification THREE, ANDROGYNE

What this means is that the Combined Gender Identity and Transsexuality Inventory has classified your internal gender identity to be essentially androgynous, both male and female at the same time, or possibly neither. In some cultures in history, you would be considered to be a third sex, independent of the polarities of masculine or feminine.

LAST UPDATE DECEMBER 19 1996.

Z threw the book to the end of the bed. The printout fell onto the floor and lay there, in the heap of trash and clothes. Z turned over on their stomach with their face pressed to the sheets. The printout's text, which had seemed so important a few days ago, now seemed stupid and useless, like something from an imaginary world. Z lay on the bed for several hours and let their hands go numb. When Hugh and the others returned from the funeral, Hugh stuck his head into Z's room. His face looked like a bald cat's.

"Hey. Susan, I don't mean to intrude, but if you aren't going to talk to anyone, you might start packing. You got stuff all over the place here. I know it's sudden, and very hard, but I don't have a lot of time. We're going to need to be out of here in the next couple weeks. It might be good to start putting together what's important to you to take."

"Oh," Z said.

"I pulled one of the suitcases out of the garage. It's outside your door." He paused. "Here, actually, you probably can't move it on your own." He opened Z's bedroom door and pushed the suitcase inside with his foot. "If you want to come down for dinner, you can. Otherwise I think it's fine for you to stay right here. Uh." He made eye contact with Z, swallowed, and looked over at the wall, where an Oregon Ducks pennant hung against the dusty plaster. "Oh, you, uh. You like the Oregon Ducks."

"I follow them, yeah," Z said.

"You know I used to go to games all the time, when your

dad and I were in college. I never played football but my friend Joe did."

"Oh. Cool." Z rolled off the bed and moved a pile of laundry from the floor into their suitcase, then looked up at Hugh. He made a strange bald-cat grimace and walked away from them down the hall. Z sat for a minute and then leaned over and shut their door.

Z stared at the mess in their room and, after a long time, moved the Oregon Ducks pennant from the wall to the floor. They looked around the room. They couldn't focus on any of the books or papers. Z's pen pal Chad's last letter to them was still on the dresser. He hadn't written because he was on the road. Z picked it up and carried it with them through the house, sitting in rooms with nobody else in them and rereading the note until the words lost their meaning. When the streetlamps came on in the neighborhood, Z was still curled in the nook between the kitchen and the living room, mumbling the text aloud, though their voice was barely audible over the noise of the radiator. *Dear Little Brother/Neutrois Sibling,* the letter began. *You're going to be totally okay. I can't, like, take you in and be your godfather because I have one backpack and eight cans of Spam to my name but I want you to know that we're out here and we love you and are waiting for you.*

But waiting where? And what did it really matter?

After the funeral and memorial service, the relatives left casserole dishes behind, stacked in the refrigerator like bricks: *Mexican, Pork Mint, Green Bean, Dill and*

Spinach. Z wasn't eating. Hugh packed the Chilworth family's things into boxes or threw them into black trash bags. The house grew emptier. Z let Hugh throw most of their things away rather than try to speak to him about what they wanted to keep.

"I think we should go to your father's church this Sunday," Uncle Hugh said one day. "To say goodbye to your father's congregation." He was standing in the kitchen cleaning out the coffeepot with a dirty sponge. Z was sitting at the kitchen table, in the same place they had been sitting for five hours.

Z had gone to church less than once a month before the accident. Since they had gotten home from the hospital, Z had trouble concentrating on anything and wondered if it was because they hadn't left the house once.

"You can go," they said. "I'll stay here."

"I think you should go too," Hugh said, rubbing at the coffee stains on the marble countertop with a dish towel.

On Sunday morning Z got up and dressed in new clothes for the first time in a week, pulling things out of the drawers Hugh hadn't already emptied. The pants were clean and the shirt had no stains. When they heard Hugh get up they moved into the kitchen and sat near the coffeepot.

"That's no good," Hugh said, looking at Z's corderoy pants. "Wear a dress. There's a dress over in one of the suitcases that'd be nice." He moved into the hall where the suitcases were piled on top of one another, and rummaged inside the plastic dry-cleaner wrapping. He returned to the kitchen and laid the thing out on the table.

Z looked at it. It was purple with long sleeves and a fake belt. Z had worn it for thirty minutes the previous Christmas and then fought with their mother about it.

"I'm already dressed," they said.

"I'll be wearing dress shoes," said Hugh. "I think you should try it on. Sunday is for dressing up. You get home, put on pajamas for all I care." Z noticed he did not look them in the eye as he spoke. He poured himself a cup of coffee and turned away.

"I'll wear dress shoes," they said. "Not a dress."

Their dress shoes were slightly too small, but their smallness did not seem to hurt Z's feet like they had before the accident. In fact, Z could not feel their feet at all, though they could still move them.

Beads of ghostly rain broke across the window of the car. In the lobby of the church, there was coffee. Z did not drink it; they stood instead on the scratchy short-haired carpet and watched their uncle. Hugh drank two cups of coffee and ran his tongue against his teeth.

The sermon was about the joy which was mankind's natural state of being, the basis of connections between people and God.

"I would also like to take a moment to mark a great sorrow," the pastor continued. "As many of you know, we lost four members of our congregation last week, when Darren and

Suzanna Chilworth's car hit a patch of ice out on the highway. Their three children were in the car at the same time. I know many of us knew Darren and Suzanna extremely well. Darren and Suzanna and their daughters Mary and Lucy were interred here this past week and I saw many of your faces at the funeral. I think a lot of us have really rallied in supporting Suzanna and Darren's daughter Susan and Darren's brother Hugh in this difficult time, but we can never do too much for each other. Susan, Hugh. I want you to hear from all of us how lucky we are to have you here alive."

A few people turned around and stared at Z. Z began to pick at the skin on their hands.

"May we keep now three minutes of silence and pray for their peaceful rest, thank God for Susan's life, and ask ourselves how we can make her feel cared for and safe in this time of grief," the pastor concluded. He asked everyone to close their eyes. Z stared blankly at the floor. Their contact lenses itched and Z was worried they would get blurry if they blinked. Z realized they should put on their glasses instead of continuing to wear contacts, since there were probably all sorts of microbes growing on their eyes, but Z hated the way their glasses made their face look round.

"Stop fidgeting," Uncle Hugh said.

"I'm not fidgeting," Z said loudly. Their right eye suddenly really hurt. They reached up to touch the contact lens and pull it out, but they couldn't find where the lens ended and their eye began. They began poking at their eye, aware that several people were still staring. Z recognized several of their mother's friends. Their necklaces and styled hair contrasted sharply with Z's disheveled appearance. I am a charity case, Z thought. They poked their finger into their eye. The contact lens would not move. Z scraped at their eyeball with two fingers instead, hoping to gain purchase on the small rubbery lens.

Suddenly, Z's right eyeball came out into their hand.

They stared down with their left eye—it took a moment to figure out what it was. There was some black gooey blood on their palm.

"Oh no," Z said. A few people looked around and saw them. There was a hysterical, horrible humor to the situation. They began to laugh, a low, humming, electrical noise that made the pew shiver. It was the first time they had laughed since the accident.

Uncle Hugh looked over and made a high-pitched noise in the back of his throat. He spluttered. He looked around frantically; most people who were looking did not seem to realize what had happened. He reached over and pushed Z's head down below the pew so nobody would see the eyeball, leaning over as if he was concerned for their safety.

"What the hell are you doing?" he demanded.

"I didn't mean for that to happen."

Uncle Hugh grabbed Z's shoulders and lifted them forcefully from their seat on the pew, steering them rapidly to the doors of the church. A few people watched them exit. Nobody intervened.

The connective tissues were still there, trailing back into

their eye socket, Z realized, as they tried to blink. Z could see blurry images out of the detached eye. The carpet in the church hallway was a dark musty shade of green and was dotted with spots where stains had never really been washed out. Black fluid dripped from Z's eye socket onto the green carpet, leaving small splotches. Uncle Hugh steered Z to a chair in the hall near the entryway, throwing them into the chair with such force that the back of the chair slammed into the wall with a loud thump.

"Hey," Z said. "That was unnecessary." They looked at Hugh's strange bald-cat face and laughed again. The situation was so macabre. They waited for some sign that Hugh thought it was funny.

Uncle Hugh looked horrified and angry. "Why did you do that?"

"I don't understand it," Z said. "Just the way this works now, I guess." They were trying to focus their left eye on their right one, to see if they could figure out how to put it back in.

"Trying to terrify people—everyone is looking at me—what are you doing? Can't you stop?"

"I wasn't trying to terrify people!" Z turned their eye in their hand. Why on earth would they take out their own eyeball in church on purpose? "I was trying to get my contact lens out. It was itching me."

Uncle Hugh wasn't listening. He was standing over Z, sweating and staring at Z's empty eye socket. "Do you know how terrifying it is to live with you?" he asked.

The question surprised Z. "No," they replied.

"Every moment I wonder when you'll snap and eat my brain. You pull out your eyes and you make that awful humming noise. It's like a demon. It's terrifying."

"I just—I don't know, I just talk." Z thought about the humming sound.

"I don't deserve to put up with this!"

Uncle Hugh was so large and looming that they decided to proceed cautiously. "I suppose not," Z said.

Uncle Hugh grabbed Z by the collar. Z had not been expecting this. They couldn't lift their hands against their uncle, because one hand still held their eyeball. Z shrieked, and it sounded a little like a generator exploding. Uncle Hugh lifted them so they were standing on their toes.

"Let me go," Z said. They tried to turn their head, to see if there was anyone in the hallway. Their vision was blurry and lopsided and they couldn't see anything clearly.

"You don't understand," Uncle Hugh hissed. "I have worked all my adult life to ensure that monsters like zombies are dealt with cleanly, efficiently, and present the minimum risk to the public. You know what kind of cases I have done. Prosecuting those who fail to contain monsters in their custody, lobbying to get them off the streets, and to incinerate those which present a criminal threat."

"My eye fell out on its own. I'm not terrorizing anyone."

"I don't deserve to put up with this. This isn't fair. This degeneration will reach your mind too. You know how much the legal work of the last few decades has made a difference?

But the monsters keep coming." He paused and wet his lips. "If people in there saw you with your eye out . . . In taking you on I am going to have to watch you disintegrate until you're beyond help, hungering for blood. I don't know what animates you—the hospital wasn't able to identify a curse—but I know you must have one inside you, and I don't know what it's going to do to me." Hugh's neck wrinkled upward toward his eyes along the creases in his cheeks. He looked hysterical, red, pulsing. Z could hear his heart.

"Let me go," Z said. The mass of tissue that connected their eye to the socket stretched; their head bobbed back and forth. They tried to remember the self-defense spell their mother had taught them. It had been a long time ago, when Z was six or seven. They remembered Suzanna Chilworth's face, alive, smiling. But something was wrong. Z couldn't feel the magic under their skin like they used to be able to. They hadn't thought about it during the week in the house because they hadn't seen the point in trying to use magic, but now that they needed it the absence felt like the absence of a pulse. They concentrated. Focus your magic at the point of contact—think of a wave, a surge, lean into your attacker. Let them take the heat of your fear. Release the spell. Z leaned into Uncle Hugh, throwing him off balance. They felt the magic going through their body now, but it was at a distance, as if it was coming from somewhere else.

"You deranged—" Uncle Hugh began, but then he stopped as an electrical current surged through his body.

He let go, looking puzzled and alarmed. A second current surged through him and he doubled over.

"Sorry," Z said, getting up. They walked quickly away to the women's bathroom. Uncle Hugh made no attempt to follow them.

There was nobody inside, because everyone was at the service. Z squinted and made their way to the sink. They knew they needed water for the eyeball. Saline solution would be best, but water would do. They turned on the tap and let the hot water run until the stream was lukewarm. Then they rinsed off their eye, carefully, hoping nobody would walk in. They gently pressed their eyeball to their socket, slowly increasing the pressure and hoping for the best. Their eyelid got caught, so they held it open with their other hand. After a few seconds, the eye slid back into the socket. Z blinked a few times, and the contact lens they had been trying to get out fell into the sink. Z took out their other contact lens. Their vision was blurry now, but at least they had eyes.

Z returned to the service and sat down in the back, far away from Uncle Hugh. They watched the weak gray sunlight come in through the windows. Z wondered why everything, everywhere, seemed so gray.

After the service, as always, there was sour coffee and dry ginger cookies. Z stood in a corner. Children stole sugar cubes from the bowl by the coffee and dropped them on the floor or ate them. Z was thinking about what they would do when they got home with Hugh, and how to avoid Hugh, when they noticed a small, wrinkled witch in a bright orange sweater standing nearby, staring at them avidly.

"Mrs. Dunnigan!" they said, with the first real feeling of relief they had had in the last week.

Mrs. Dunnigan was an old friend of the family and godmother to Z and their sisters. She ran a bookshop in downtown Salem. She had short, well-kept hair. Z had not seen her in over two months, and didn't know if she had gone to their parents' funeral. They forgot she attended church services weekly. As she approached, her manner intent and gregarious, her knees cracked. Z braced for the inevitable condolences.

"You still look just like your mother," Mrs. Dunnigan said. Her brown wrinkled face had not changed since Z was young. Mrs. Dunnigan was the same as when she had babysat for the Chilworths.

"Ah," said Z. They reached up and ran a finger through their hair. They thought there might still be some blood clotted in it. Z had not taken a shower since the accident. Their skin was discolored slightly, whether from not washing or something else, Z was not sure. They did not think they looked remotely like their mother.

"It's the worst thing that could have happened. I'm only happy you're still here."

"For now. Hugh is taking me back to New York with him."

Z glanced around. Uncle Hugh had disappeared into the men's bathroom. They felt a question rising in their chest, but weren't sure what it was.

"Looking for your uncle?"

"Yes."

"Come on, let's go sit out in the garden and avoid him. I want to chat with you."

"It's raining," Z said.

"I have an umbrella," Mrs. Dunnigan said. She brandished a monstrous hot-pink umbrella hung with water-repellent charms. Mrs. Dunnigan's entire person seemed to pulse with bright colors.

"I missed you," Z said. They and Mrs. Dunnigan went out, the huge umbrella clanking against the doors to the church. The rain was coming down much harder now. Mrs. Dunnigan led Z through the wet grass outside the church. There was no garden, only a few raised flower beds near the sign at the front of the parking lot.

Mrs. Dunnigan turned to Z when they reached the row of wet cars farthest from the church doors. "How have you been?" she asked Z.

Z wondered where to begin. There were no feelings to dredge up. "Well," they said, "I've mostly been just at home since it happened. Tomorrow Hugh and I leave for New York."

"New York. And you've been staying with him since the crash? How has that been?" Mrs. Dunnigan looked, for a second, very fierce and concerned.

"It's . . . I've been all right. We don't, you know, talk very much. I stay out of his way. He's, uh. He's dealing with stuff."

"Of course, of course," Mrs. Dunnigan said, rocking back on her heels. The rain pattered more softly on her umbrella.

She looked at Z very intently. "I am very worried about you, dear. I saw what happened in the hallway earlier."

"Oh," Z said. "Yeah."

"How terrible, Susan. Did your parents leave you with him on purpose?"

"It wasn't clear, in their will. They didn't think I'd be . . ." Z looked at Mrs. Dunnigan to see if they could trust her. "I'm undead now."

"I'm sorry?"

"In the crash. I died and came back."

Mrs. Dunnigan bent forward and looked at Z more closely. "Those scars," she said. "Good lord."

"Yeah," Z said. They studied Mrs. Dunnigan's face. She looked uneasy. "That's why it's so rough with Uncle Hugh. He's nervous I'm going to end up the kind of zombie who eats people. And he does legal work around that, so he knows how bad it can get, I guess."

"This is worse than I thought," Mrs. Dunnigan said.

"I mean, I'm fine. I'm me."

"I know, dear. I mean worse for you. Living with him."

"We're leaving tomorrow. I thought it was going to be all right, but now I don't know. Maybe I'll run away when we're in New York."

"That's not a good idea. I'm saying that as someone who has run away before." Mrs. Dunnigan reached into her pocket and pulled out a container of mints. As she opened it and popped two small mints into her mouth, Z kicked at a wet mushy place in the grass.

"Stay with me instead," Mrs. Dunnigan said suddenly. She proffered the silver case of mints.

"What?" Z took one, but didn't put it in their mouth. They clutched it in their palm like a penny.

"If I'd known sooner, I would have offered sooner," she said, putting her hands on Z's shoulder. "I've been asking about you and no answers. I think it makes sense. People don't like to talk about this, though it does happen. But it's not right to treat you like Hugh just did. We can leave here together now, if you want to. I mean it." Mrs. Dunnigan leaned forward. "He should not be near a child if he thinks it is appropriate to hurt you like that. I've liked you for a long time, Susan. It would be an honor for me to have you in my house. And I have to say I am worried about you in his."

Z said nothing for a moment. They felt a little dizzy. The incident in the hallway had changed things, and staying with Uncle Hugh no longer seemed like a remotely good idea. There was something wrong with him, something beyond his fingernails and fish breath.

Z made a quick decision. "That would be lovely, thank you," they said with as much sincerity as they could muster. Their voice rasped like a grave opening in dry earth.

"Let's go catch a bus," Mrs. Dunnigan said. "My car broke down in November, so I'm afraid that's all we really have to work with."

Mrs. Dunnigan's apartment was in a complex where the buildings looked like very long two-story suburban houses smashed together. The upper stories had a stairway up to a locked door, and the lower stories had front doors shadowed by balconies. It was close to the bus stop, and although it was very small, there was an extra bedroom. It once had been the office of the other Mrs. Dunnigan. It was only in the last year that Z had noted the meaning of the lesbian symbol on Mrs. Dunnigan's refrigerator and on the pin on her brown overcoat. The Dunnigan couple had lived together for over forty years. Z remembered the apartment from childhood, when the Chilworth children had sometimes stayed over for long weekends. Mrs. Dunnigan had more cats now than she had then.

Mrs. Dunnigan phoned Uncle Hugh at the house and left a message saying that Susan would be living with her now.

"He'll come and try to find me," Z said.

"Let him try," Mrs. Dunnigan said. "We'll sort it out. Have you met my cats? There's Millicent, Carlos, Pamela, Antonio, Isadora, Angelina, and Marceline. I originally named all of them Angelina but that got very confusing for everyone very quickly." Mrs. Dunnigan laughed. The cats took an interest in Z, nipping at their fingers.

The old office had a small bed and was papered in bubblegum-pink and acid-yellow stripes, which peeled slightly at the corners.

At four in the evening, five police officers appeared at the door. Uncle Hugh was just visible behind them, his white forehead spotted with sweat. Mrs. Dunnigan answered the door and then looked around at Z.

"We have received a report of you illegally harboring a dangerous, rabid zombie," the tallest policeman said to Mrs. Dunnigan. He looked skeptical of this claim as he scrutinized the pastel clutter of her domestic space.

"Nonsense," Mrs. Dunnigan said. "Susan is undead, but she's perfectly lucid. I'm her godmother, I should know."

"Can you provide evidence of that, ma'am?"

"She's right as rain, ask her yourself."

Uncle Hugh bristled. "The zombie's eye fell out today and she attacked me."

Z felt compelled to rebut this lie. "I'm okay," they said. "I promise I won't hurt anyone. He was grabbing me and shaking me. That's why I left."

"It is true, officer," Mrs. Dunnigan said politely. "I saw it and I was alarmed, and I thought, as a good Christian and dear friend of Susan's mother, I have to take this child away. I know Hugh is very concerned about monsters but it just isn't right to hurt a child."

"I have custody!" Uncle Hugh said. He looked at Mrs. Dunnigan. "Ma'am, we haven't met, but I promise I am more capable of handling this situation. I know you still see Susan as who she was, and she is that, sort of, but there is something else there and it will be too much for you." He reached inside the door and tried to grab at Z's arm.

"Don't touch me," Z said, and stepped back. Hugh fell in through the door and landed on all fours.

"Sir, please calm down. Escalating this isn't our policy," said the second-tallest policeman.

"Officer, I'm leaving tomorrow and traveling to New York," Hugh said, looking over his shoulder from the ground before standing. "I have to settle this tonight. Susan, come and get in the car." Z saw his car was parked outside. "You're my niece. I have custody of you."

"Do you?" Mrs. Dunnigan asked. She looked at the policeman. "Does he?"

Z looked at the officers, and felt a weight in the center of their chest plunge into their stomach. "Mrs. Dunnigan is my godmother," they said. "I've known her all my life. She knows me better than Uncle Hugh. If I'm a danger, she'll tell you."

The policeman turned to Uncle Hugh. "Unfortunately, sir, though the deceased is a minor and your relative, in Oregon State there's no kind of law that says you have custody. If she wants to live with this woman and this woman wants to take her on and can contain her until she disintegrates, that's legal. It's the Benjamin decision. Nineteen eighty-nine. The state can neutralize threatening undead, but has no authority in family disputes over nonthreatening undead relatives."

"I'm the only family in this conversation," Hugh said. "The zombie is only related to me."

"Look," the policeman said. "The only action we can take on zombies is shooting them or incinerating them when they present a danger. We take that very seriously. You told us she wasn't lucid and that's why we're here. But she's lucid. The kid's not dangerous at this point. That means we're not in the picture. She's undead, so it's not a kidnapping, it's not a custody battle. It's more like a dog, who gets custody of a dog." He looked at Z. "No offense."

"As the dog," Z said as clearly as they could, "I'm expressing now that I would like to stay with Mrs. Dunnigan."

One of the policemen smiled.

"Of course, you have to sign on as a custodian," the tall policeman said to Mrs. Dunnigan, scratching his nose. "And allow for an investigation to confirm that no illegal necromancy is being performed and that the deceased's state is the result of a preexisting curse or condition. Without a custodian, any member of the undead is eligible for incineration as part of the anti-necromancy act. That's if anyone reports them traveling alone in public. And you have to prove she's lucid and psychologically well every six months. I think it's within a week, you have to sign the papers. Up at the courthouse, that'd be. Get a registration card. All that."

"I'll do that," Mrs. Dunnigan said.

Uncle Hugh spluttered, "This woman is not competent. She may be fine, personally, but this is an undead creature. I work in monster case law. I know what I'm dealing with."

"Sir, look, the state will work to evaluate her competence. And if there's any trouble, we'll intervene." He looked back at Mrs. Dunnigan. "I have to say, though, ma'am, this was a rather sudden move on your part. Do you know what you're getting into? At your age, and all."

"Absolutely," Mrs. Dunnigan said.

The police went away, and Uncle Hugh stood for a moment outside and then got into his car and drove away as well.

"The impudence of that man," Mrs. Dunnigan said bitterly as they got onto the bus to go and buy Z replacements for all of their clothes the next morning. "Just because you're dead. It isn't like you aren't awake."

Z didn't say anything. The people in the bus stared openly at Z's scars.

They went to the courthouse with Mrs. Dunnigan on Thursday and signed the papers. There was a test that involved a civic spellcaster, who had a long sharp nose and cystic acne. Z stood inside a machine. The machine identified the location around Z's heart as the source of a necromantic spell. Z pulled up their shirt and sports bra and showed Mr. Sindul the nine-pointed star that had appeared on their skin after the crash. He took them to a different room, where another machine with a bulb like a camera was pointed at Z's heart.

"It's a spell cast by someone who is now deceased," the spellcaster said. "A protection charm to guard you from death and restore you to life if you perish. It's one of a set. Did you have any brothers or sisters?"

"Yes, but they're dead."

"It's not very well cast," the spellcaster said, looking at the sheets of film being printed out of the top of one of his gray machines. "It's disintegrating rapidly. It could be that the other loci were dissolved immediately with the death of the spellcaster."

"Do you think my mom could have cast it?" Z asked.

"Perhaps. Was she a dissident?"

"I don't know," Z said. "I didn't think so. But it couldn't be my dad, he couldn't do spells much."

"We'll assume she was the caster, given the lack of other evidence. Based on the looseness of the magic, I doubt she had access to necromancy books when she cast it, so there doesn't seem to be any reason to investigate further. The spell seems to be undoing itself fairly quickly. I would say in under a year it will unravel."

"What does that mean for me?" Z asked.

"You may gradually lose control of your body and also may be driven toward violent or cannibalistic acts," the civic spellcaster said. "Or you may simply lose consciousness."

"Is there any way to not have that happen?" Z traced the slightly raised lines of the star.

The man looked at them seriously. "That would be illegal necromancy, unfortunately. You are already dead. Physically, there's nothing that a doctor could do. Necromancy beyond what has already been cast is going to just prolong your disintegration in any case."

Mrs. Dunnigan had the people at the courthouse call the hospital to get another copy of the note saying Z was lucid, since Uncle Hugh had taken the first one back to New York with him. She filled out a form stating her income and listed all potential factors that could complicate her ability to care for and control an undead being.

"I may have fibbed about the income part a little," she confessed to Z on the bus home. "Nobody makes the amount I put down, running a bookstore in this town of illiterates."

"That's okay," Z said. "Money isn't everything."

Every evening after she took her vitamins Mrs. Dunnigan would make a strong-smelling salve out of various powders from the jars of herbs on her shelf and tell Z to put some on the bruises, but all that seemed to do was to keep the cats from getting as close to Z.

"It's about all we can do," Mrs. Dunnigan said. "But that's what I do when I have joint pain." Mrs. Dunnigan kept some of the salve for herself every night.

On the eleventh day after the accident Z realized that they were starting to smell. They hadn't showered since getting out of the hospital, and their hair was tangled, except for the patches where it had been sheared away from their scalp as doctors tried to stop the bleeding in their brain. Their sense of smell hadn't been very good since waking up, and it was possible the odor had started much earlier without noticing. Z took a long, hot shower in the yellow bathtub while Mrs. Dunnigan was out grocery shopping. They scrubbed hard oatmeal soap into their skin. It had taken on a faint gray-yellow color in some spots and a kind of funny mauve in others, and parts of it peeled off when scrubbed hard. Z wondered if the hot water would actually do any good or whether it would somehow hurt them, now that their body was different. As Z dried their hair and rubbed most of a bottle of clove oil every place that still smelled odd, they made a mental note to check Mrs. Dunnigan's library.

Z still had Chad's last letter to them. They kept it in their sock drawer, which was half filled still with things left behind by the other Mrs. Dunnigan. Chad had survived a lot. He'd been homeless for years, after running away because his parents kicked him out for wanting to live as a boy. His life seemed impossible, but it was real. For better or worse he was alive. Z wanted to email or send a letter to him, but they didn't know where he was. His forum account was still down. They couldn't tell if he had deleted it or someone else had gotten him blocked from the forums where Z had met him. Besides, Mrs. Dunnigan didn't have a computer except at her bookstore, and she used that one for sales.

Z finally went back to school. Z's mother, Mrs. Chilworth, had worked at the Integrated Academy of Lower Salem as a calculus teacher for six years. Z used to dread the day when their mother would be teaching them higher mathematics. When Z and Mrs. Dunnigan went into the school, Z saw that their mother's name had not yet been removed from the door of her old office.

Mrs. Dunnigan and Z had a hard time trying to convince the school to allow Z back. Though the meeting with the secretary in the hallway had initially gone well, the principal glared suspiciously at them both over his desk as he explained the school's policy concerning the dead to Mrs. Dunnigan.

"Our policy is to provide a safe learning environment to living students," Mr. Bentwood told Z when they and Mrs. Dunnigan went to the office to explain the long absence. "Susan was, when alive, a proficient student and a powerful young witch. I am sure she is still capable of great things . . . if she is as you say fully conscious. If she isn't, you understand that we have much to lose."

Z stared at Mr. Bentwood over the top of the desk, feeling they needed to speak up on their own behalf. "Trust me, I'm right as rain," they said in their scratchy, whispery paper-voice. They realized as they spoke that their voice sounded less than convincing; their voice was still raspy, deep, and ominous.

Mr. Bentwood turned to Z and glared at them. "Other schools have had undead students in the past that have been less than completely in control of their own actions, and I have no desire to repeat those incidents. The last thing I need on my record is an outbreak of necromancy. Pardon my vigilance, but we just can't take too many chances. Especially with an elderly guardian. Pardon me, ma'am, but Susan would have had four more years here, and who knows what health issues might come up for you in that time."

"I'm perfectly capable of child care," Mrs. Dunnigan said with a hint of ire.

"I'm not a necromancer," Z said. Their left leg hurt, painfully, and so did their head. It was aching and burning. Their head twitched on their neck in a brief spasm that was very difficult to conceal. Horrified, Z clutched their chair tighter. The ache in their leg got worse. "I'm really not." Z thought about what Mr. Bentwood would think if he knew the real necromancer had been one of his employees.

"We'll have to get a written document from you to ensure that you don't. A precautionary measure," Mr. Bentwood said. "I understand that this is a difficult time and I don't mean to place undue stress on you, but we really cannot let you attend classes unless you confirm in writing that you won't use any form of death magic on the campus."

"I'll sign whatever," Z said, staring at the ceiling.

"It's just our policy. We don't want any more zom—undead roaming around. Not all of them are as well-mannered as you."

"I sort of wish I had stayed dead."

Mr. Bentwood frowned. "How did you wake up?" he asked, flipping through the papers on his desk. "I don't have any records of you being the seventh daughter of a seventh daughter, or having any prophecies associated with your childhood or adolescence. Did your parents ever place any protective spells on you?"

Z and Mrs. Dunnigan exchanged a glance.

"The test at the courthouse said it was a spell cast by someone who's dead now," Z said. "It might have been one of my parents, but the origin wasn't totally clear."

"Hmm." Mr. Bentwood pushed a sheet toward Z. It was already filled out neatly in blue ink; the only blank space left was next to the x at the bottom where Z was meant to sign. "This confirms that you will only use approved forms of magic and will not raise any deceased persons or animals while on this campus."

"I don't think I could do that even if I wanted to," Z said, taking a ballpoint pen from the table and clicking the button on the bottom.

"Not that pen," Mr. Bentwood said, his tufty ginger beard quivering with nervous laughter. "It's a permanent promise." He held out a fountain pen. "A blood oath."

"Oh." Z rifled through their pockets and pulled out a short penknife, making a cut along their index finger. No blood came out; the wound stayed gray and dry. After all, Z was dead. It was so unexpected that Z started to laugh shrilly, still staring at their hand. The laughter echoed and bounced off the walls. Mr. Bentwood laughed nervously too, sounding like a panicked goat.

"I wonder if you can be bound by something other than a blood oath," he eventually said, sounding slightly unsure.

"No, hold on, something's coming out," Z said. A little drop of red-black viscous liquid had bubbled up at the cut. Z dipped the pen into the droplet and signed Susan Chilworth on the dotted line. I wonder if that still counts if I don't think of it as my real name, Z thought idly.

"Beautiful," Mr. Bentwood said, his yellow teeth showing. "You can go to your next class while Mrs. Dunnigan fills out the rest of the paperwork." He pulled at his mustache. "I'll write you a note."

Z stood up and grabbed their bag. Mr. Bentwood handed them the little yellow note and watched Z as they crossed to the door. The hinges creaked as they opened it and then slowly shut it behind them.

Z's locker was exactly as they had left it. Z picked up their history book and crammed it into their bag. The bag felt much heavier than it had felt before. Z wondered how long it would have taken for their mother's body to decompose if it had not been burnt. Z wondered how long it would take for the rest of their body to fall apart, or for their skin to fall off.

"Susan! You're back in school! You look terrible." Bethany Black appeared next to Z as they turned to go to class. Her braces glimmered in the fluorescent lights of the hallway. "So skinny, though. Did you lose weight?"

"I bet I did. I'm exhausted." Z tried to smile and then stopped, realizing that was probably inappropriate. It occurred to them that Bethany's comment probably hadn't been in the best taste either. Bethany must have realized it, as she also made a nervous smirk and then hastily rearranged her face into a concerned expression.

"I heard that . . . I mean, I heard about what happened with your family. We had a vigil for Mrs. Chilw—your mother last week here at school. I am so sorry."

"Yes," Z said, unsure of what face to make. Bethany was their best friend, but suddenly that didn't seem like it necessarily meant she needed to know everything that had happened.

"Were you in the car too?"

Z pointed to the stitches across their jaw. "Yes," they said again.

"Oh. Oh! I'm sorry, I'll stop talking about it."

"It's okay," Z said. "But thanks."

Bethany walked next to Z as they went upstairs to history class. She didn't seem to know what to say, but it did not stop her from talking. "Sam and Ginger got back together," she said.

"Isn't Ginger such a dumb name?" Z asked, relieved to be in familiar conversational territory and to be talking about a subject unrelated to death.

"Her real name's Agatha. I'd prefer Ginger too. She's got that nice hair, so it works."

"She's so mean. She did push Tommy Wodewose off the roof last year. Did you forget?"

"If Sam likes her she can't be that bad. And Tommy's weird. He wears sticks in his hair."

Z shrugged and went into class. "I don't know."

Bethany hesitated at the doorway for a moment and then walked away. Z wondered if they should have said goodbye. They suddenly didn't remember if they had used to say goodbye at the end of conversations with Bethany. In fact, Z didn't remember much of anything of their old conversations with Bethany. The blurry spot in between dying and waking up seemed to have expanded over Bethany and any knowledge of why Bethany and Z had ever become friends to begin with. Z wondered if it was temporary but that made them wonder if their existence as a resurrected life form was temporary in general, and that was frightening to think about. Z opened the textbook to the page named on the whiteboard and waited for class to begin.

Mr. Holmes was one of the few nonmagical teachers at the school. It was a condition that caused adults some embarrassment. In the last thirty years, there had been more and more programs to teach adults basic spell-casting, and the number of magically stunted adults had been reduced in America by ten percent, but Mr. Holmes was apparently beyond help. He wore a large, shiny amulet at all times. As he entered he rapped on the wood of the door three times and threw a salt packet over his shoulder, a ritual he pretended was an elaborate joke but which everyone else suspected was at least half-serious. It was a little sad, since every one of his students knew that salt only worked against fey—who were not allowed at the Integrated School or anywhere else in America—and that knocking on wood didn't do anything at all, besides maybe give one splinters. It was widely believed that Mr. Holmes had an endearing personality, though, so none of his classes were too hard on him.

"Today we will be covering the Second Undead Uprising of Portland," he said. Z looked up with a start. The page listed on the board corresponded to the beginning of a chapter on magical participation in the Civil War.

Cecil Pritchett noticed as well. His hand shot up. "Mr. Holmes, the board says—"

"I've decided to switch focus for today, Cecil," Mr. Holmes said. "We haven't focused on the West Coast very much in our studies, and I figured it was time to pay the sturdy pioneers a little attention." He laughed jovially.

Cecil lowered his hand, his brow furrowing.

"Can everyone turn to page 675?" Mr. Holmes asked.

Z flipped the book open to the page. There was a large woodcut of a skeleton with flesh falling from its arms sprinting down a muddy street, under the heading "Filthy Sewers, Walking Dead."

"Can someone read the first paragraph?"

Z started to bite at their fingernails before realizing with a jolt that their fingernails probably wouldn't grow back.

Cecil raised his hand, and Mr. Holmes called on him.

"The late nineteenth century," Cecil drawled, "was a time in which many towns along the Western Coast expanded at unprecedented rates. The towns often did not have access to resources which would ensure consistent infrastructure like paved roads or sewer systems. The town of Portland, Oregon, for example, was called 'the most filthy city in the Northern States' in 1889. Nevertheless, the population at the end of the century was expanding. The First Undead Uprising of Portland, discussed in Chapter Six, had been very small by most standards, and was an isolated event most likely caused by a lone necromancer." Cecil paused as Mr. Holmes gestured for him to stop reading.

"Does everyone remember that? Chapter Six? Do we remember what the identifying characteristics of the undead were?"

There was a long silence.

"Susan, can you tell us?" Mr. Holmes was suddenly standing directly in front of Z.

Z looked up sharply at Mr. Holmes. He had always seemed perfectly decent, but Z could swear there was something rather cruel in the way he was staring at them with his little smile.

Z looked down at their hands. They were cold and gray and dry. "The undead were at first mistaken for victims of cholera, because in dying they lost most of their body fluid. The people—the living ones—could only identify them as . . . you know, dead . . . because of the gray and greenish tone of their skin and the fact they had no pulse." Someone behind Z snickered. Z resisted the urge to touch the place where the vein in their neck used to mark their heartbeat.

"Very good, Susan," Mr. Holmes said, smiling. "Now, could you read the next paragraph?"

Z swallowed, to no effect. There didn't seem to be much water in Z's body anymore. Could Mr. Holmes already know they were dead? Why would he want to let Z know that he knew? "Okay." They took an ineffectual breath. "However, in 1891, three hundred warlocks of Irish and Chinese descent employed by Northern Pacific who had assisted in the construction of the railroad through Stampede Pass went on strike after their wages were withheld. Their numbers were not significant enough to prevent the use of the railroad, so they raised a group of forty dead former citizens who were buried in the cemeteries of Portland and Clackamas."

"Terrifying, isn't it?" Mr. Holmes asked nobody. "The dead, walking."

The class stared at him, puzzled. Mr. Holmes did not usually behave like this. Cecil glanced at Z sharply and Z realized that no matter how confused everyone else in the class was, Cecil had noticed something rather off about their skin and the stitches on their wounds.

The bell that rang at the end of history class sounded dull and tinny in Z's ears. The din of zipping book bags and chairs being pushed back drowned out the little pathetic noise of relief that rose up from Z's throat. Z stood and left the classroom as quickly as possible, but they didn't move quickly enough. Mr. Holmes followed them into the hallway and stepped in front of them. His soaplike pale face looked down on Z. They could smell his warm garlic breath and hear the blood pumping in his heart. Which was odd, Z thought, since their senses, particularly their sense of smell, had otherwise been so dull lately.

"Susan, I understand if you're upset."

Z squinted at him.

"As you know, I am preoccupied with safety," he added, making a little uncomfortable chirruping noise and clicking his teeth on the last word.

Z tried to move around Mr. Holmes, but he moved again to block their path. Other students, going to lunch, glanced back at both teacher and student curiously.

"All your teachers have sworn not to inform students about your new condition, but I felt that it was in the best interests of everyone if I provided my students with more information on the living dead." The loud whisper Mr. Holmes was using had a theatrical resonance. Z would have been astounded if any of the students passing by didn't hear him.

"Mr. Holmes, I don't know if you were told of the details of my new circumstances," Z said, struggling to keep their voice low.

"I have been told you aren't dangerous, Susan, and I am sure that they are right. However—"

"I mean the part where my entire family is dead." It was the first time Z had said this to anyone, and it sounded hollow and false in their own ears. Z didn't even care that much. But it had the desired effect.

"I'm very sorry," Mr. Holmes said.

Z pushed past Mr. Holmes' shoulder and stomped down the stairs. They were faintly aware that they left a slight smell of decay behind, hanging foully in the air.

Bethany had started sitting next to Catherine James while Z had been away. Z sat down at the table near the two quietly and smiled awkwardly at them. Catherine and Bethany were having a conversation about hair color, and as Z sat down the girls continued to talk.

"I heard that the store in the mall is having a sale on Charmed Pink dye this weekend," Catherine was saying. Her hair was short and bleached blonde with imperfect magic.

"I don't want pink though, eww," Bethany said. "I wish I could get my mother to fly us out to the city for a day so I could get some Midnight Blue."

Catherine looked over at Z. "Have you ever dyed your hair, Susan?"

Z blinked. "No. And, um. About my name. I like going by Z. Instead of Susan."

"It's because she's like, such a tomboy," Bethany said. "Nobody calls her that, though, don't worry."

Z looked over at Bethany. Bethany dropped eye contact and invested attention in her fruit cup.

"I can call you Z if you want," Catherine said, laughing.

"I just like it better than Susan," Z said, shrugging. "I don't feel like I'm a girl, and Susan is a girl's name. And it's too much like my mother's name."

Across the room, Tommy Wodewose was standing on his plastic chair and chanting quietly. In front of him on the cafeteria table was a bowl of salt, a bowl of water, and a tall black taper. In his hand he held a black stone about the size of his fist. A group of gawky ninth-graders had gathered to laugh at him.

"Doesn't he usually eat lunch outside?" Catherine asked.

"It must be too cold. Yikes, that kid is weird. Who the hell uses candles? It's the digital age. Did he get lost in a fairy ring or something?"

"He's only trying to be thorough, I guess," giggled Catherine.

Purification rituals were supposed to happen before every meal, especially in a place like the school where so many types of magic were gathered and where magic was constantly happening. In theory, not performing purification would result in mixed magic, which supposedly attracted spirits that might tamper with spells.

"Nobody really performs purifying spells according to the old method, though, do they? Not seriously. Like, what reason is there to draw pentacles and stuff when you can just wash your hands?" Bethany pointed over to where Tommy was now carefully blowing out the candle. "He's just doing it for attention."

"Maybe," Z said.

Z wasn't yet sure if they could eat or not. Since Z had not eaten a meal since the accident, *not* eating did not seem to be a problem. Mrs. Dunnigan had packed Z a lunch, and Z took it out of their book bag now and arranged it neatly on the table. The sandwich on white bread was cut into four equilateral triangles. Z tried to eat a little bit of the sandwich, but it had no taste and seemed very, very dry in their throat. They spat it out onto the table.

"Honestly, you made the right choice, Susan. White bread is so bad for you," Bethany said.

2

Aysel's glasses had gotten broken again during gym class, so she went to the art room between classes to get tape. She carried the pieces of her glasses in one hand and held the other over her nose, in case it hadn't stopped bleeding.

"What happened, dear?" Mrs. Hall asked when Aysel marched smartly in and asked if she could get into the supply cabinet. Aysel's nose had dried blood crusted underneath it and she suspected her hair had mud in it from when she hit the ground.

"Charley Salt kicked a soccer ball at my face," Aysel said.

"Oh no!" Mrs. Hall blinked several times.

"Yeah."

"He must feel terrible," Mrs. Hall said hopefully, standing up and getting the keys to the supply cabinet. In addition to crumbs, her smock had paint stains in an array of different colors all down the front.

Aysel pulled a chair out from a table with a loud screech and sat down in it heavily with the two halves of her glasses, a roll of purple duct tape, and a pair of scissors. She set about cutting a narrow strip of purple tape and affixing one half of the frames to the other half. Her hair fell in black frizzy strands across her face. She spat and brushed them out of her face in annoyance.

"You'd think," Aysel said after a minute, interrupting the silence, "that if someone kicked a soccer ball at your face, they'd be sorry about it. But you know how it is. The big fat girl gets hit with a ball and falls over, it's funny."

"Oh dear," Mrs. Hall said. She looked fretfully at Aysel from her perch on a stool behind the desk.

"Like when a roly-poly bug rolls over." Aysel stared down at her glasses. There was a crack across one of the lenses; she knew it would distract her for the rest of the day. "You wouldn't happen to know a spell for mending glass, would you?" Aysel asked.

"Are the lenses broken, too?"

"Just one. It's not a big deal." Aysel scraped at the dried blood on her upper lip.

"I'm not much of a witch. Spaced out in those classes when I was in school. Maybe try Ms. Glock. You have her for Woodshop, don't you? She may know something."

"No, she hates me." Aysel shrugged. "It's okay, I can cope. Thanks for letting me use the tape." She put her glasses back onto her nose. They dug into the spot where the ball had hit. Aysel knew she would have a mark there until her mother could do something about it.

"Have you been to the nurse?"

"My mom will fix my nose when she gets home from work. She's pretty good with that kind of thing."

"Okay," Mrs. Hall said, looking doubtful. "Maybe get a washcloth from the infirmary, though, and clean off the blood. You don't want it to get infected." She looked so genuinely, comically worried, her large watery yellow eyes round as golf balls, that Aysel nearly laughed aloud, despite how horribly everything was going.

"Thanks, Mrs. Hall. I'm fine. I think I am just having a bad day. I'll go."

"See you later, Aysel. I hope, er. Have a good day."

The first-floor girls' bathroom always smelled of bleach and bile. Aysel took off her haphazardly mended glasses, leaned over the sink, and splashed water on her face. She dried herself with a paper towel. Her face still looked blotchy when she was done, but it no longer looked like she had been crying, which was good enough.

Charley Salt was in Aysel's English class. When Aysel came in, he looked at her and grinned at his friends.

"Sorry for PE, Tay-her." he said.

"It's Tahir," Aysel said.

"Oh, I see. I'm sorry for PE, Ms. Tahiiiir," Charley said, drawing the word out slowly and lifting the syllables into his nose, which made the name sound ridiculous.

"Fuck you, Charley," Aysel said. She felt like spitting on someone. A witch's spit can give someone bad luck for seven years, and she thought Charley probably deserved this.

Charley laughed and looked at his friends, who all looked surprised. Other students who had overheard Aysel looked up in shock. A few began to laugh.

"What's her problem?" Aysel heard a girl say quietly to the person next to her.

"It was just an accident, Jesus," Charley said. He was still smiling.

"You meant it and you know it," Aysel said, but she realized the more she talked, the more everyone hated her.

"You're crazy." Charley laughed.

Aysel stalked to her seat and sat down. The chair was too small for her. She felt her hair begin to fluff up around her with static electricity. Something bad was going to happen if she got any angrier, she knew.

Mr. Bell finally entered. "Who has read the article I assigned?" he asked.

Everyone went quiet at once.

Aysel closed her eyes and breathed deeply. The light above her head stopped flickering. She rummaged in her bag for a notepad.

Mr. Bell's class was not so bad, when he was teaching. About halfway through the lesson, he went down the hall to print something out, and everyone began, once again, to talk.

"Everyone knows she just acts up because she's mad she's a dyke and nobody wants to get near her big smelly ass. It's sad, really," Charley said to one of his friends across the room.

"God, she does smell. She's got BO that smells like . . . what's that Vietnamese soup with all the fish in it?"

"It's 'cause her legs rub together all day."

Aysel gritted her teeth and closed her eyes.

Eventually the day ended. It was drizzling. A fog had come down after noon, and now settled in between cars in the parking lot, blurring the lines of items more than fifteen or so feet away. After her last class was dismissed, Aysel waited at her desk until the rest of the students had left the room before she slowly stood up. At her locker, Aysel unloaded her books carefully. The inside of her locker was neat and orderly; all Aysel's books were borrowed from the school library, and she didn't want to damage them. Aysel pulled on her raincoat, tugging her hood over her long soft hair and stuffing loose strands behind her ears. She knew her raincoat made her look like a gnome. It was purple and bulky and had a ridiculous peaked hood. To compensate, Aysel scrunched her face up into a severe scowl as she made her way toward the doors and braced herself for a walk to the bus in the cold afternoon.

As she walked through the parking lot to get to the sidewalk, Aysel heard a hushed commotion. A small group of students was clustered near the door of the school, talking. As she approached, she saw Ginger Lewis in the middle of the group. Aysel stomped solidly through the mud. The group did not get any quieter as Aysel approached, which was good, Aysel thought. It indicated that the talk was not about her. The rain tapped at her hood as she got close enough to the group to hear what Ginger was saying.

". . . and Cecil told me that in class Mr. Holmes was acting weird around her, too, and he tried to tell the class by assigning something to do with zombies."

"So the teachers know," someone said.

"Yes. But they probably aren't allowed to tell the rest of us directly." Cecil, his name having been included in the canonical account of events, felt obligated to speak up. "Mr. Holmes was trying his best to work within whatever magical contract the teachers were made to agree to. He probably can't directly accuse her outright or even suggest directly that we suspect her of anything. So he had us learn about a zombie massacre in Portland and made her read about it."

"Crap, Mr. Holmes is a hero," Sam said. There was a general murmur of agreement.

Ginger shrugged. "Yes, I guess so." She was miffed that Cecil had center stage. "Anyway, just be on the lookout I guess. And if she does anything weird—"

"Who are we talking about?" Aysel asked. Several people turned to look at her, and Aysel felt defensive. Usually when people looked at her, she felt the need to protect herself or snarl at them. At the moment, however, nobody seemed to particularly care about Aysel's unpopularity. Every person was eager to spread the news.

"Do you know Susan Chilworth?" Ginger asked Aysel. "Mrs. Chilworth's daughter?"

"The one who only wears the blue sweatshirt all the time?"

"Yes. Well, she came back to school today." Ginger exchanged a knowing glance with the group. Everyone basked in the honor of being looked at and appreciated as a fellow conspirator. "She's . . . different."

Aysel began to be annoyed. "Well, her mom died." As she said this, someone giggled. Aysel remembered why she hated everyone. "Her whole family died. I don't see what's surprising."

"Well, yes." Ginger smiled at everyone deviously. She paused and drew a deep, suspenseful breath. Aysel realized that the presence of a naïve audience was exciting the other students. "The thing is, we think that Susan is dead too."

It was obvious Ginger wanted Aysel to ask more questions, to hang on her every word. Instead, Aysel blinked, angry and befuddled. The air around her was chilly, but her coat made her torso too hot and a prickle of sweat had turned into a little uncomfortable dribble down her stomach. "Whatever." She turned and began to march away across the grass.

The buses rarely ran exactly on time. Aysel jogged to the bus stop and found that she had missed the bus by a few minutes. It would be another half hour before the next one pulled up to the sidewalk, so Aysel decided to walk home. She set off with her hood pulled down around her nose and her hair spilling out in little fluffs to blow across her face. The sidewalk was covered in dying earthworms which Aysel tried not to step on as she walked. Cars' wheels spun through puddles and splashed her intermittently with muddy water. Halfway home she pulled her hood back and tugged her hair back into a bun so that it would stay restrained.

When Aysel reached her house, she stepped through the wet garden gingerly. There was a path to the door, but it had been overgrown with squash plants and kale and the branches of Japanese maples. She let herself in with her mother's key. She took off her coat just inside the door and dropped it beneath the blue and white nazar bead that hung just inside the door. Aysel and her mother had lived in many houses through the years, but the nazar always hung in the same place. It was meant to ward off *cin* and other demons. Aysel wore another around her neck under her shirt. The blue glass bead had not guarded her particularly well, but it was always possible that things would be even worse without it. Aysel pulled the bun out of her hair, and the dark frizzy mass floated across her line of vision. The mail was lying on the table where her mother had set it down before going to work. Aysel crossed into the kitchen and put the kettle on. She examined her nose in the mirror that hung over the little table where her mother always left her purse. It was decidedly askew, she thought. It hurt a lot and was probably going to get all weird as the swelling around it continued.

She went and sat down on the couch and turned on the television. It was an infomercial for a special kind of cake pan. Without deciding to, she closed her eyes and fell asleep.

When she woke up again, it was almost seven in the evening, and the streets outside were dark, the lamplight shining on the puddles. Her mother was still not home. Her nose hurt, but a little less so. The television had been murmuring quietly as Aysel napped, and now she sat up and looked at it. The news was on.

"... last thought to be in Los Angeles, has now been sighted in Salem, Oregon. Police this morning advised citizens to stay home after dark and not to walk outside alone. The search is ongoing and will concentrate on the areas where detectives say Morris is likely to hide, like here, in Silver Falls Forest."

It was a story about someone on the run from the police, Aysel realized sleepily as the park ranger came on and began to talk cautiously to the camera. As the story continued, Aysel began to sense something odd about the familiarity of the forest behind the park ranger. She realized with a jolt that the man the police were chasing was not far from Salem. She sat up and watched the television, blinking blearily. Photos appeared on the screen of large paw prints in the dirt—dated to the previous month— and a mug shot of a pale man with a broad nose, thick, fluffy brown hair, and very wide eyes, staring in a startled way first at the camera and then off to the side. These photos were labeled: *Timothy Morris. Confirmed Werewolf. Arsonist and Suspected Murderer.* Aysel's throat suddenly went dry; she felt her stomach get heavier inside her. Her lunch seemed to be trying to escape from her throat.

A heavyset red-faced policeman with a roundish nose appeared on the screen. "Morris was last seen at a truck stop south of Salem. He may be in the area. We don't know if he is armed, but it is suspected that he is. Morris is a dangerous werewolf arsonist and has been seen in the company of gang members. Police are doing our best to secure the perimeters of forests and other places he may be hiding or planning on spending the night."

A reporter in a studio appeared onscreen, folding her hands in front of her awkwardly. "That was Sergeant Ford from the Salem Municipal Police at a press conference this morning. Since then, police have been patrolling the interstate and back roads. The search will continue tonight, even as the full moon makes it more dangerous for the officers involved. Meanwhile, many citizens wonder about why and how Morris managed to get from Southern California, where he was last seen, up into Salem, or why he is here. But it may be that he has been here longer than anyone believed." The reporter pressed her thin lips together in a line. "We go to Alisha Spencer to hear more on how Morris may be associated with another unsolved murder—this one here in Salem—after the break."

Ticker tape announcing the new Dow Jones Industrial

Average slid across the bottom of the screen, and then disappeared as a commercial for a new brand of decongestant began. Aysel watched it, mesmerized, swallowing painfully. She dry-heaved and gagged on her tongue as the commercials continued noisily.

The news returned. The screen switched over to a blonde reporter in a pink raincoat who wore a sad expression.

"On the full moon last month," said the reporter in pink, "Archie Pagan went for a run and never returned. His death has, until now, been ruled a freak accident. However, since Morris has been sighted in the area, inspectors have reason to believe that it was foul play. Before Pagan retired to the West Coast, he worked with werewolves in a reschooling center in southern Virginia, where Morris was born. Detectives believe there may be a connection—and that a murder once thought to be a freak accident could have been an act of revenge. Members of Pagan's family are not reachable for comment."

The camera cut to more photographs of Archie Pagan, with the newscaster's voice playing over them. "With the enhanced Werewolf Restrictions, werewolves have been prevented from easily moving around the countryside. They can't leave their state of residence legally without filling out paperwork and agreeing to be monitored at all times by an agent of Monster Affairs. No werewolves have been allowed into Oregon in the last four years. Morris may have been here illegally.

"Police are stationed across the national parks and are,

they say, prepared to search the forest throughout the night until Morris is found. For now," the waterproofed reporter said in a tinny grim voice, looking meaningfully out at the woods behind her and back into the camera, "the residents of Salem will have to be on their guard." She pronounced this last sentence with the finality of all newscasters, pressing on the last four words and making them sound serious and important. "We will continue updates on this story as the night goes on. And now, traffic."

Aysel glanced at the phone. Should she phone her mother? That was childish, and it wasn't as if her mother would know what to do anyway.

Azra Tahir arrived home thirty minutes later, looking frazzled, a sheaf of damp manila folders in one hand, her hair frizzing out in all directions from her ponytail. She muttered the first few words of the *ayet-el kürsi* under her breath and hummed the rest as she moved into the kitchen. Like the nazar beads, the verse was a protection charm—a passage from the Quran that was supposed to scare away evil. Azra made fun of herself for her superstition, but Aysel knew her mother believed that it genuinely protected them. For all she knew, it might. Most unregistered werewolves were discovered by the authorities quickly, but in the four years since her first transformation, Aysel hadn't attracted the attention of the police.

"Aysel, your nose is broken," Azra said. She took off her coat and moved briskly toward the kettle. Azra was skinny and small, and had been full of a constant, unceasing physical energy as far back as Aysel could remember. She was moving constantly, her hands fluttering at her sides when they had nothing to do. Azra's entry into a room gave the impression of a whirlwind when all she had done was taken a few steps and shut a door.

"Mom," Aysel said, not wanting to waste time, "did you hear about the news story?"

Azra froze and turned. "In passing. Timothy Morris, the man who crashed that car into the police station in Los Angeles. Now they are saying he is behind the animal attack last month." She looked at Aysel very hard, and the bags under her eyes suddenly seemed very dark. She looked old.

"They definitely seem to think it was werewolves," Aysel said. "And it looks like it was. Those tracks were huge. It was probably an adult, maybe a guy in his twenties. And the police are all over. I don't know if there's any in Salem, but they're at Silver Falls. Everyone's freaking out."

"Yes. The people at my office, they were all talking about how dangerous he is. The police are going to shoot him."

"Do you think they'll get him? Could he get away?"

Azra looked at Aysel and shrugged helplessly, looking pained. "I don't know, Aysel*cim*."

Aysel felt a pang of shame. "I'm sorry," she said at once, without anything to apologize for.

"Things like this happen. And keep happening. The world is like that. It always will make me worried."

"Do you think it's safe for me to even be out there tonight?"

"Obviously you have to. Maybe you can get far enough away from town." Azra put the kettle on automatically and took two mugs down. "We don't have much time before the moon rises."

"I hate this," Aysel said.

"Thank god I never registered you. Your father wanted me to." Azra mentioned this bitterly from time to time. It was why Aysel's parents had separated.

"Do you think they'll have investigators in the woods by the winery?" Aysel asked. Her mind was racing.

"If you can keep it in your mind that you have to stay far from town, you should be all right . . ."

Aysel's heart sank. "I'll try," she said. Azra, for all the reading she had done, had never seemed to grasp the idea that it was very hard to remember anything once the transformation happened. Aysel knew she would forget everything except sensation until 6:19 the next morning, when the moon set.

"I should fix your nose before you go, *yavrum*," Azra said, her voice high and fast. She was trying to make the evening routine again, and think of mundane things.

She walked over to Aysel, and laid both her hands on her daughter's temples. "*Acıyı bırak, iyileş.*"

The mild throbbing in Aysel's head receded until it was only a slight fogginess. She felt her nose shift back into place and snap to its normal shape. Electricity crackled off her eyelashes.

"Why do you never use Latin spells?"

"It doesn't work as well. Your Anneanne used this spell, so I know it best. You should know Turkish too, and Arabic. If you were around your uncles in Seattle more, you would have picked it right up. It's a shame."

"Lots of things are a shame," Aysel said. "Good riddance to Dad and everyone else. They treated you like shit."

"Language," Azra said. "How did you break your nose, anyway?"

"I got hit with a ball in gym class. Charley Salt kicked it at me."

"That boy again. You should tell someone," Azra said.

At eight in the evening, Aysel put her rain jacket on, pulling it over her shoulders carelessly, not bothering with the hood. They got into the little blue car Azra drove to work and pulled out into the dark rain, exiting the neighborhood and driving out of town. Azra had a chain of nazar beads that swung from the mirror, casting shadows on the dashboard. The nearest national park was forty miles away, and anyway Azra had always worried that Aysel would get lost in such a large forest, so instead they always went to a mile-wide forest about ten miles out of town. It was probably owned by a logging company—Azra wasn't sure—but there were never many people in the forest, so as long as Aysel stayed out of the fields where people might see her, she would be all right.

The trees were black as pitch in the night and the space between them only visible when the headlights of the car shone on them. Azra pulled the car up along the edge of the road. The headlights shone into the gaps in the trees. They had not spoken on the ride there; now Azra kissed Aysel on the forehead. The inside windows of the car were steaming up and the defroster was turned up all the way so that Azra would be able to see the road. It was raining more than ever now.

"Don't forget, stay clear of anyplace exposed, where someone might see you," she said.

"Okay," Aysel said. She scowled, to hide her misery. She thought of the police again.

"Give me your glasses, you'll lose them again."

"I found them last month. It just took a while," Aysel said, taking off her glasses and handing them to her mother.

Her mother handed her a flashlight and a duffel bag, and Aysel got out of the car. "Good night," Azra said. "Remember where to catch the bus home in the morning. Don't get too far from the road or you'll never make it to school on time."

Aysel set out into the woods, the ferns scratching at her ankles. She heard the car drive away into the night. Her hair was drenched with rain. The path she had cut through the ferns last night was still there, but spiders had strung webs across the gap which clung wetly to Aysel's cheeks as she stomped into the dark. She kept walking away from the road, her flashlight glowing a dim yellow against the deep blue of the nighttime forest. Time passed. Rain ran down her face and cooled her hot skin.

At nine, the moon rose. Aysel felt it in her blood. There was lightning flashing in her heart. At first, it was wonderful, like it always was. She felt warm. She took her coat off and removed her rain boots, and stood barefoot on the pine needles, looking up at the sky. One usually couldn't see the moon behind the clouds in Salem, but always felt its pull when it rose. It took a few minutes, but soon Aysel felt she was starting to change.

The lightning buzzed through her veins, searing her flesh like ants. Her legs felt like they were being pricked by thousands of moving pins, sticking her flesh again and again. The pinpricks moved up her thighs and belly, reaching toward her head. It stung—magic, and energy, and electricity. Aysel shook as the moon shone on her face, and rose and fell with tremors that consumed her and let her forget everything. Aysel felt her bones begin to stretch, and the hair on her legs got longer and denser, itching as it accumulated against the inside of her jeans. Hastily, she pulled off her pants and sweatshirt with hands that were getting large and clumsy, shoving them into the duffel bag and zipping it shut so the rain could not make it too damp in the night. She would pick up the duffel bag tomorrow morning, when she turned back. Aysel hoped that the wolf would decide to go somewhere and sleep a little.

Aysel felt herself begin to cry, her newly large eyes

sending streaks of salt water over a face which was rapidly changing form. All the emotion that built up inside her when she was human required a lot of effort to conceal, and during the transformation holding back tears or swallowing roars took more energy than she had to spare. Her skull rattled with the noise of the forest around her, and her nose suddenly could smell the birds sleeping in the bushes fifteen feet away. The world shuddered and shifted as her eyes changed, and jolted with the coldness of winter into her. Thoughts anchored in her mind began to fly away, as they did every time. She lost the memory of the homework she had to do, and of the gossip from earlier in the day. As her hands grew claws, Aysel momentarily forgot her own name.

The wolf rose and loped away from the place Aysel had stood. It was calm. The wolf's thoughts were tighter and simpler than Aysel's. Run, the wolf thought, and ran, at a pace which should have broken branches, with faint joy. The wolf's size and weight seemed to have no bearing on the sound she made as she traveled; the only noise that someone, standing a few feet from her path, could have heard was the deep breathing and the noise of displaced air and rainwater. The wolf was larger than a bear and could easily have taken down a horse, and her large black eyes and long black nose and tall black ears saw and smelled and heard almost every moving thing around her. The flush of sensation excited her, and she let herself be overtaken by the scents of animal tracks not yet washed away by the rain and by the noise and scent of smaller nocturnal beasts. The night air was cold and sweet. At the crest of the first hill, the wolf stopped and let out a great, throaty howl.

There was a deer close by, and the wolf smelled it. Aysel hadn't eaten dinner, and even if she had it would not have been enough for the wolf. The deer were not yet asleep and moved through the misty night in small groups. There were at least six. The flicker of Aysel left in the back of the wolf's mind worried about waking up with a stomach of full of raw venison, but that was tomorrow, and tonight the wolf was excited by the scent of the deer scat and the sound of soft moving creatures ahead. The black branches of the trees were wet and cold; the pine needles underfoot were damp and moved faintly with beetles and worms. The black wolf saw a flash of white through the trees: the deer were unconscious of her presence. Their tails reflected light as they bobbed along ahead of her slowly through the low trees and salal.

In the distance, Aysel heard the howling of other wolves. She followed the noise but could not find them. They were in the hills, traveling away from her. Eventually the noises faded into the night. Aysel forgot them by the time she woke up in the ferns the next morning.

In the morning, Aysel never remembered much. She didn't really try.

She heard on the news they'd killed Timothy Morris in the night.

3

When Z got home from school they found Mrs. Dunnigan sitting on one of her small, heavily pillowed chairs. She was watching television and drinking tea, her lap well covered with her cats. They meowed at Z as they entered, shaking off their hood. The apartment was dry and hot inside. Z could see on the oven clock that something was baking. Waves of yellow light seemed to fill the apartment.

"What time did you get back from the bookshop?" Z asked.

"I left at noon today. It gives the younger cashier something to do. Besides, my knee was bothering me again," Mrs. Dunnigan said. "And I got a little woozy. I've been making pies," she added, more brightly.

"You know, I don't think I can eat now," Z said.

"Nonsense. The undead can eat anything. It becomes incorporated into your essence. That's how you keep going."

Z looked at Mrs. Dunnigan in surprise. She was still watching television. "Really? Is that true?" The prospect of still eating—of even possibly having to eat—was slightly terrifying in its inconvenience. Z felt that death ought to be a kind of static state. Maintenance should not be required. The one benefit of their condition seemed to be its permanence.

"Biological matter similar to your own is ideal, naturally, since that's less transfigurative work, but you can certainly manage pie." Mrs. Dunnigan cackled in a very traditional way. She took a long slurp of tea and set down the cup and saucer on the windowsill. Her third-fattest cat, Isadora, noticed, and began to stealthily approach the abandoned dish.

"I tried to eat the sandwich you made me for lunch today, and I didn't taste anything. It got stuck in my throat. My taste buds don't work anymore."

"I'm sure with a good wizard we'll get your taste back in a while. I hear Mr. Weber at your school is a seventh son of a seventh son. We'll get him to help."

"The chemistry teacher?"

"He's supposed to be very good. He helped sort out that golem last spring."

"That was because the city asked him to," Z said. They had read about it in the papers, when it happened. It was national news for a little while, since golems were so rare on the West Coast and usually the military had to be brought in to dismantle them. Mr. Weber had received an award for his ingenuity and heroism. Z was not clear on exactly what spells were involved, but everyone at Lower Salem Integrated School had talked for weeks about how the chemistry teacher had managed to trap the golem within a circle before undoing the original life-binding spell by climbing up its body and reaching into its mouth himself to pull out the *shem* as it tried to crush him in its hands. This was probably rumor. Mr. Weber had taken three weeks' vacation afterwards. "I doubt he'd be very interested. He'd be breaking the law," Z added, the last part with some uncertainty as they were not completely certain about what the law did and did not say about zombies. "Anyway," they continued, sitting down on a cushion across from Mrs. Dunnigan in order to force the old woman to look at them rather than the television, "does this mean that I can starve to death like anyone else?"

"I'm not going to let you do that," Mrs. Dunnigan said, very seriously in an even tone. She got up and moved into the kitchen.

On the television screen, the news was playing a story about a werewolf on the loose. The man's face appeared onscreen, looking startled, his teeth white and eyes cheerful and large. Z remembered the photo from a Wanted ad they had seen in the newspaper a few months ago. The news said that the man was an arsonist and wanted for murder. The police thought he'd killed someone near Salem who had been out jogging late at night.

"He should know better than to jog about like that when it's a full moon," Mrs. Dunnigan said to Isadora and Angelina as she scooped two slices of what seemed to be apple pie onto mismatched plates and put one into a bowl for the cats.

"What, you think it's the werewolf?"

"Of course it's a werewolf." Her glasses slid down her large nose as she sat down and she pushed them back up with a buttery finger. It left a smear of grease on her sand-colored skin. "Eat your pie."

Z compliantly took a bite of their pie. It was still hard to get anything down their throat. It felt like trying to swallow a marble or a stone. "My throat is dry."

Mrs. Dunnigan took a moment to finish chewing, looking at Z contemplatively. Marceline the cat had crept up onto her lap by this point and she patted the large gray feline's head absently. "I'll get you some milk or something." She stood up, her chair creaking, and waddled into the kitchen. "Oof, I hurt all over. I think I have a cold or the flu coming on." She touched her clammy forehead with a hand and swayed for a moment. "We both have to work hard to stay alive, don't we?"

Early in the morning, after lying staring at the ceiling for five hours, Z heard three cats trying to get out the door. They got up to let them outside, flicking on the dim yellow light in the front hall. Mrs. Dunnigan had hung a mirror in the hall for some reason, so when you were moving in the dark it always appeared that there was another person next to you. It creeped Z out.

As they waited for the cats to come back in, they looked over at the clock. It was six. Almost time to get up anyway, Z thought, and turned on the television.

“Late last night, police cornered Timothy Morris at his campsite and, after Timothy threatened the police by baring his teeth, he was shot. After resuming human form he was taken to Salem Hospital, where he died of his wounds.” The reporter who said this tried and failed to look concerned. “Police who searched the site report that the tent had evidence inside it of a conspiracy of werewolf terrorism. Police advise the public to stay calm, as there is no indication that there are any plans for attacks in the area, and werewolves are usually not dangerous except at the full moon.”

A cat outside meowed. Z turned the television off. Something in their stomach felt unsettled.

Bethany was growing increasingly distant. Their lockers were next to each other so they exchanged words with Bethany, but the conversations were brief and Bethany seemed guarded. They would stand next to each other long enough for Bethany to grab a jacket, or get her books, but then they would part. Z greeted Bethany in the hallway and Bethany did not reply. So much for friends supporting one in one’s time of loss, Z thought grimly.

Mr. Holmes continued to drop hints about the undead. By the end of their second week back, Z noticed graffiti in the bathroom that said, *Susan Chilworth Is a Zombie.* Underneath, someone else had written, in blue, *To the Incineration Station.*

Z tried to eat lunch, but often ended up going to the restroom to spit everything out again. The food was too dry to swallow, or too tough to chew, or too difficult to keep from vomiting. Several times they had thrown up in the toilet. They imagined their sinews coming unraveled as no sustenance strengthened them, imagined their face sunken and rotten and gray, covered in spots where blood had pooled beneath the skin.

What made it worse was that that week, Mrs. Dunnigan also got sick properly. She had been coughing a little for a while, but then was struck low by a flu. She came home in the afternoon on Tuesday and said that someone had thrown a rock at the window of the shop, because the bookstore had a poster about a werewolf support group and a section on werewolf rights. Mrs. Dunnigan had put up a board over the broken window and put a Closed sign on the shop door. When she got home she went straight to bed. It was probably partly psychological, she told Z, but Z gave her a thermometer and the thermometer said Mrs. Dunnigan also had a fever. She stayed in bed for two days straight drinking orange juice and tea. Z had to figure out how to change the cat litter. Z stopped eating without Mrs. Dunnigan feeding them. When she finally got out of bed and announced it was time to go back to work, the apartment looked as if it had been home to two corpses, not one, for several days.

Z began to wonder what would happen if Mrs. Dunnigan died. Which she was bound to do, Z thought, at some point. What would happen to them if they started really decaying then, with no legal custodian? They remembered the policeman saying that a zombie without a custodian could be legally incinerated.

They decided to ask Mr. Weber for help.

Mr. Weber's classroom was used for both biology and chemistry courses. Z, who was taking environmental science, didn't see him much. Mr. Weber, who was more enthusiastic than many other teachers, had gone to great lengths to personalize the space. The room was ringed with tanks containing living amphibians and fish, who watched anyone who entered through the glass panes of their watery prisons. The filters in the tanks burbled constantly. The windows were partially obscured and shaded green with interesting potted plants Mr. Weber had brought from home. Tendrils of one enterprising vine plant had begun to grow along the ceiling.

Z had waited fifteen minutes after the last bell before entering the classroom, as they did not want to talk to the other students or be jostled by anyone else as they exited. Z had not taken a class with Mr. Weber since the previous year, but his room was mostly the same. He sat marking a student's test with a red pen and chewing pink bubble gum, blowing small sticky bubbles as he scratched corrections onto the paper. He looked the same as Z remembered from when he taught eighth-grade biology, though he was maybe a little heavier. His light yellow shirt contrasted with his deep brown skin and the empty whiteness of the room behind him. The room was mostly empty. There was a fat girl hunched in the corner, working on something and tapping on a calculator. She did not look up as Z approached Mr. Weber. Her dark hair formed a veil around her paper, hiding it from view.

"Mr. Weber?" Z said.

Mr. Weber glanced up from the paper, snapped his gum, and tapped the tip of the pen on the desk. "Susan? I haven't seen you in a while."

Z shifted awkwardly in their shoes. Z didn't like being called Susan, and somehow it felt worse coming from Mr. Weber than from other teachers. Z cleared their throat. "I'm going by Z now."

"I see." Mr. Weber looked politely at Z.

"Yeah, uh. I don't feel like a girl, so I shortened it."

"That's a cool nickname. Sort of skater punk, huh."

"Not really."

"What brings you here?"

"Could you ask that girl to go out in the hallway? I need help with something personal."

Mr. Weber frowned. "Are you sure I'm the best person to talk to about it?"

"I don't want to talk to the counselors about it."

Mr. Weber looked over at the girl in the corner, who was watching them now. "Would you mind moving the desk into the hall, Aysel?" he asked her. She shook her head, and rose with a great creak and squeaking of metal desk legs against linoleum, the cry of sad birds. She pushed the desk with some difficulty through the door, and Z and Mr. Weber could hear her settling back into her chair in the hall. The door stood open, still, and Z moved to close it. Mr. Weber held a hand up for them to stop. "I have to have the door open. School policy," he said. "Obvious concerns."

"I understand," Z said, though they wished the door could be closed.

"What did you want to talk to me about, Z?" Mr. Weber asked. He kept his voice low and confidential, and Z wondered if he was patronizing them.

"Well, I know you know a lot about animation of inanimate beings," Z began. They wondered if this was the right way to phrase it.

Mr. Weber shifted in his chair. "Relatively speaking, yes. I'm no expert." Mr. Weber pushed up his large glasses and smiled as if he was sharing a joke with Z.

"I was wondering if you could give me . . . um, well, some references or something on the undead."

Mr. Weber looked surprised—or pretended to look surprised. He scrunched up his nose to keep his glasses from slipping. He was motionless, his position in the chair casual and open but frozen. "I see," he said.

"You know what has happened with me, right?" Z glanced back at where the girl had been sitting, wondering if she was eavesdropping. "The teachers all seem to know."

"I do. We were told." Mr. Weber paused. "I personally think it was a breach of your privacy, but school policies, you know." He sighed. Z glanced again around the room nervously, their eyes lighting upon a purple toad stuck to the side of its tank. It glistened unnervingly in the fluorescent lights.

"And I know you know about that kind of thing. I don't know any other adults who have any grounding in that who would want to help. So maybe you could give me some books to read. I haven't been like this very long, and I'm not even sure what I can eat, or how much, or whether I'm going to . . ." Z lowered their voice. "Whether I am going to fall apart and turn into a skeleton or just disintegrate into black goo with no warning."

"I'm curious as to why you think I know any more than you do about this," Mr. Weber said.

"I don't. I was just hoping." Z gnawed at the inside of their cheek.

Mr. Weber breathed in deeply. "I really don't have much information to offer." He seemed nervous, and glanced anxiously at the door and ran a hand over his hair. Z looked at the door. Nobody was there.

"That's all right." Z pulled up a chair and sat stiffly in it. They wondered if they should lower their voice. "Just tell me what you know. I want to know more about why—or how—my body is staying alive. Mrs. Dunnigan . . . the woman I live with has some books, but it doesn't go into the technical rules of necromancy, since that's illegal and all."

"It is. Z," Mr. Weber said, sticking his gum in the inside of his cheek with his tongue, "I have to tell you that I could get in trouble with the school board for sharing any information with you on school grounds."

"Oh." Z sat, uncomfortable.

"Don't misunderstand me, Z," Mr. Weber said quickly. He glanced again at the door. "I want to help you, but I want you to know beforehand the professional problem that presents for me and the danger it puts you in."

Z studied him. "What do I do, then?"

Mr. Weber sucked in his cheeks and furrowed his eyebrows. "How about this," he said, slowly and quietly. He got up and grabbed a pad and pencil on his desk, and stood by his desk as he began to draw. "The Willamette library has detailed information on this sort of thing, in the Censored Materials Division. Behind a spell barrier. I have tried to get in a few times, for personal research reasons, and one time I had an old friend who worked there show me how to get past the barrier. This was back when all the restrictions were new and I thought I might still be able to pursue some of the stuff I studied in college as a career someday. I can draw you the rune. I don't think they'll have changed it. They don't have funding for that. There are tons of books in there. I don't know what about, you get me? I have no idea what you're looking at in there, and you did not hear this from me." He tore off the sheet of paper and handed it to Z. There was a complicated rune on the paper.

Z raised their eyebrows and felt the skin crack. "How do I use this?" they asked.

"Set it on fire," Mr. Weber said. "Blue fire, not too hot. You've already learned that, in eighth grade, right?"

"Yeah," Z said. "Though my magic's been hit-and-miss lately." Nonexistent, really, they thought, except for the time with the electricity and Uncle Hugh. Which hadn't even felt like their own magic.

Mr. Weber nodded. "You have a guardian, right? Ask them to go with you."

Z shook their head. "She can't go. She's sick. And old. This weekend she stayed in bed for two days. She's back at the bookstore today, but she gets tired really easily."

"Oh," Mr. Weber said.

"That's part of why I want to know this stuff. In case she doesn't get better and is declared incompetent. I have to know how to survive alone."

"Oh," Mr. Weber said, looking more unsettled.

"But I can go alone," Z added quickly. "What bus route do I take to get to the campus? I can go like, this Friday or Saturday. I can like, take a cigarette lighter in case my magic doesn't work."

Mr. Weber frowned again, and bit his lip. "That won't work," he said. "Nonmagical fire is just going to set off the smoke alarm. If you get caught, police are going to be involved." His brow furrowed further.

Z nodded. "Okay," they said. "Well, then I'll try to use magic. Thank you," they added. They stood and turned to go, but at that moment their foot turned numb and they fell over. They knocked over a chair and sprawled onto the ground.

"Are you okay?" Mr. Weber asked, leaning over to help them up with a look of concern.

"I'm fine," Z hacked. One of their eyelids was sort of turned inside out. "Sorry." They rose unsteadily, balancing on the edge of the desk. They shoved the rune into their pocket. "Thank you for all your help. I'll let you know how it goes." They tried to put weight on their foot, to see if it would hold. "I'll let you know next week."

"No, no no no." Mr. Weber shook his head. "I was stupid. I don't know what I was thinking. You're fourteen. You're . . . You can't . . . I'll go for you."

"You said it was dangerous for you. I can do it," Z said.

"I'm sorry for being so cold at first," Mr. Weber said. "I really didn't mean to imply that I don't care about your safety. I do care."

Z looked at Mr. Weber. He still had bubble gum in his mouth.

"Well, thank you," Z said. "But that's okay. I'll manage somehow. If I'm going to stick around I have to learn how to take care of myself sometime."

Mr. Weber scowled at a lizard in the corner, snapping his bubble gum. "I'm sorry," he said again. "Look, I don't want to talk to you too much in school, but I'll give you my number in the parking lot when I leave. We'll work something out. But not here."

Z nodded, tried to smile, and prepared to walk out the door into the hall.

"So, you're really undead?" The voice startled them

both. The girl who had been out in the hall was back, and was now craning her neck staring over at Mr. Weber and Z. A necklace with a blue glass bead that looked like an eye hung down over her black sweater. Her dark, frizzy hair hung down her back. Two eyes glinted fiercely through bottle-thick glasses. "Like, really undead?"

Horror flooded Z's body. "None of your business," they said, their voice catching on the words.

Z and the girl stared at each other for a long second.

"Aysel," Mr. Weber said. "Have you met Z before?" Mr. Weber looked at Z. "It's okay, she's a friend of mine. Fellow nerd."

"We have a class together, I think."

"Z was just asking me some questions. Come in, though, we're done now." Mr. Weber was pretending he hadn't heard Aysel's question.

Aysel stood up and walked across the room over to the desk. Z felt her radiating sweaty heat as she approached, her rubber-soled sneakers squeaking on the bright linoleum.

"I'm sorry for eavesdropping, Mr. Weber," Aysel said. Her voice was low. "That was rude to ask. I can leave. I won't tell anyone."

"No need to leave. I'd really actually like for you to meet Z," Mr. Weber said, seeming not to notice that Z was trembling with discomfort. "Z, this is Aysel Tahir. She's the president of the science club here. We're trying to recruit more members. There's a pretty cool paper airplane contest we have planned that's coming up."

"Hi," Z said quietly, making eye contact with Aysel's stomach.

"Hi," Aysel answered grimly, looking at the newt tank on the opposite wall over Z's head.

"Aysel is taking a test she missed last week in my class."

"I'm actually done with that," Aysel said. She thrust a paper forward at Mr. Weber. "I really can leave right now. I'm sorry."

"If you've got a minute, stick around. Z was going to leave in a minute, I believe, and I am almost done. I think I should give Z my contact information. We can all leave when I lock up and you could both help me carry Leo to the car. He's sick."

"Who's Leo?" Z asked. The discomfort had not disappeared, and they imagined that they felt Aysel's returning malicious energy in the air around her.

"The big bearded lizard," Aysel said, and pointed to a fat gray scaly creature skulking in a large sunlit tank behind Mr. Weber's desk. His legs were splayed unhappily on the rocky floor of his tiny glass room.

"I think he doesn't like my sixth period and is trying to make himself ill on purpose," Mr. Weber said. "I'll make him a remedy tonight and maybe let him take a break from the academic world awhile. But I can't carry his tank on my own. My Transportation Spell jostles him and makes him drool." Mr. Weber stood up and, slipping Z's paper into his pocket, set about stuffing various items into his large canvas bag and his coat. Aysel and Z meanwhile struggled to look each other over without actually making eye contact. Z noticed that Aysel's heart rate had increased: they heard it pumping loudly, far noisier than Mr. Weber's or any of the lizards, frogs, newts, or fish.

"Aysel, can you get the door?" Mr. Weber asked. He clapped his hands and the lizard's tank shook and rose a few inches off the floor. Leo the bearded dragon looked distressed and began to paw the glass with a petulant tapping.

"Z, grab the far end of the terrarium," Mr. Weber said. Z walked over and stooped down, feeling the skin of their back stretch uncomfortably with the stooping. The muscles in their arms seemed very weak, and were numb as they tried to heft the tank upward. They tried to focus on lifting, flexing, but the lack of feeling continued, as if there were a great distance between Z's arms and their brain. Z felt frustrated. The light on Mr. Weber's desk went off abruptly. He looked from the lamp to Z as they walked carefully, slowly toward the door that Aysel held open.

Aysel and Z shuffled awkwardly across the parking lot carrying the lizard in its dry, sandy terrarium. Mr. Weber followed behind, whistling, despite his heavy load of bags and papers. Mr. Weber's car was small and old and indestructible-looking. The terrarium barely fit into its trunk. As soon as the car door had shut, Z looked at Aysel with a glare meant to communicate to her that she should go. Aysel seemed to understand at least part of Z's intent, and moved away. She hesitated about fifteen feet away from the car as Mr. Weber gave his contact information to Z on a small sheet of yellow paper and Z, in turn, wrote down Mrs. Dunnigan's phone number and the name of her bookshop.

"I'll call you before Saturday," Mr. Weber said. "I need to think about what the best plan is. I do want to try to help you with this." He got into his car and started it. It clunked and came to life, and he drove down the street.

Z looked at Aysel suspiciously. They turned on their heel and began to walk away. It was almost a minute later when they realized Aysel was following them. Z hoped that she would go away if Z seemed entirely uninterested. Aysel's confidence did seem to falter as she approached.

"Hey," she said nevertheless. "Hey, uh, Susan. I mean Z. What name do you want me to call you?"

"Please call me Z," they said, mustering a firm tone of voice.

"Okay. And uh, while I'm at it, sorry, actually, what does it mean that you're not a girl? I heard you telling Mr. Weber."

"I'm just not a girl," Z said.

"Yes you are," Aysel said, though she sounded hesitant.

"Maybe I was born looking like one, but I'm not. I'm like in between a boy and a girl. An androgyne. I'm transgender. I'm genderqueer." The word felt funny in their mouth, not pretty like when it was on the screen of the library computer.

"Oh," Aysel said. Z was not sure Aysel understood at all. Her face was scrunched up.

"Do you know what that is? It's someone who's outside of men and women. Something else."

"Yes," Aysel said defensively. "I mean, I know about people who are transsexual."

"Right," Z said. "I'm not quite transsexual. Transgender."

"Like gay." Aysel looked hopeful.

"It's neurological. I did a test online. I'm *almost* transsexual but I'm not. I'm right in the middle. There's a lot of people like it."

"Oh. Well, I know about that. I know there are lesbians who dress like boys." Aysel shrugged. "And gay men who dress like women. I relate to that."

"It's this whole thing where you're *not* a boy or a girl. Even if you dress like a boy or a girl. Lots of societies in history had them."

"Yeah. Okay. Yeah."

"There have always been people like that. Like"—and here Z paused to remember—"Claude Cahun." That was from a website called DragKingForum. Or Sphere. They couldn't remember. "Who go by new names and live weird lives."

"Yeah, totally."

"I want people to call me *they*. Instead of her, or she. That's something people do. In other places. A neutral pronoun." Aysel was the first person to let them talk long enough to even mention the concept.

"They?"

"English only has neutral pronouns when it's plural. And I want to be neutral." Z paused. "Nobody calls me *they*, though. I guess you could also switch back and forth between he and she."

"I can say they," Aysel said.

"Don't do me any favors."

"Turkish has gender-neutral pronouns for everyone. It's just *o*, no matter whether you're a boy or a girl. It's not so weird to add the same thing to English."

"Oh." Z was a little taken aback. "Thanks." They felt that they were smiling, even though they had been determined not to smile at Aysel. Then Z remembered they were meant to be on high alert. "Why are you following me?"

"I'm not following you," Aysel said. "I just wanted to, uh. I think you should know that, uh." Aysel paused, scrunching her eyes up. Her voice sounded much more hesitant than it had in the science classroom.

"I should know what?"

"I think you were worried about me telling people that you were a zombie. So, uh, I thought you should know. I heard Ginger talking about you." Aysel stopped again. She seemed frustrated with herself. "Anyway, I think people know."

"Who knows?"

"Most people by now, probably. Though," Aysel added, "you don't look alive, honestly, so it might not be hard to guess."

Z set their chin and walked faster. They felt conscious of the stitches on their neck and pulled their collar up.

"Look, I don't know if you care," Aysel continued, "but I figured I would let you know, as Ginger is a . . . well. She pushed that kid off the roof last year just because people said he's descended from a shapeshifter or a troll and because he's sort of girly. Who knows what they'd do to you, you know. And the teachers aren't very friendly either. You know that. So I guess . . . just be on your guard. I'm on your side," Aysel finished loudly, trying to make eye contact. She continued to walk alongside Z.

"I know you don't really know me, or anything. But I feel like we're sort of the same."

"I don't think we're the same," Z said.

"You're right. I mean, whatever. If you want me to watch your back, though, I can."

"I don't see what it has to do with you," Z said.

"It doesn't have to do with me," Aysel said quite calmly, though she seemed a little disgruntled at Z's rudeness. "You're right. If you want me to watch your back, though, I can."

Z turned and looked at Aysel with trepidation. The fat girl looked depressingly earnest for some reason.

"If you want to watch my back, you can," Z said finally.

The bus arrived, splashing both of them as it pulled in.

The rain continued. The blank trees and earth soaked in the downpour and grew soggy. The windows of Mrs. Dunnigan's apartment all faced the road, and from their room Z could see cars driving by, their wheels spinning through mud and throwing up arcs of water along the sidewalks.

Mrs. Dunnigan was late coming back from the bookshop; she returned with arms laden with groceries she could barely carry.

"I'll make a stroganoff tomorrow," she announced. "I don't have the energy tonight, I hope you understand. All I can do is take my brittle self to bed and read. I found a really vital book on the great beast beneath the ocean and the end of the world."

Mrs. Dunnigan and Z had toast and pickles for dinner. Mrs. Dunnigan dripped dill-garlic brine on the pages of her book as she ate. After they were done, Z went back to their room.

The clock in the pink room was broken, so they kept time by the buses passing each half hour. At 10:30 p.m., the last bus drove by. Through the water-streaked windows Z could see that only a few people were on board.

They went over to the bed and sat down and turned on the reading light. They picked up the book they had checked out for themselves at the school library. *Everything You Need to Know About Monsters*, it was called. The author was called Dean Goldsmith, and he grinned unflappably from the back of the dust jacket, his hair coiffed into a style nobody had worn since before Z was born. Z had found the book in the section of the library dedicated to expository nonfiction intended for teenage readers writing reports. Its cover showed a colorful, airbrushed photo of a young woman with a torn shirt brandishing a head of garlic at a recoiling vampire. The summary on the back was extremely peppy. *You may think it's boring to learn about monsters,* the back cover read, *but it's actually pretty sweet to know facts that may save your life!*

The inside jacket, too, was a collection of upbeat phrases with a lot of exclamatory punctuation. Z laughed when they had first looked it over in the library.

Did you know that one in thirteen high school students will encounter a monster before they turn eighteen? That's pretty "wack"! Here's the source for the real truth about monsters. No rumors or myths—we play it straight.

Z had checked out the book as a kind of last resort. After all, they needed something to fall back on in case they didn't get any help from Mr. Weber. However, as Z began to read, it became clear that despite the book's promises to be helpful, it was not. The page on "Zombies and Enchanted Undead" had very little in the way of useful facts.

Most monsters are like people, but with a huge personal supply of magic they can't control, which drives them crazy or makes them violent. Zombies are different: most have no magical power of their own, since they are the product of other people's spells and their own magic is gone with their life force. They can, however, leach magic from other people around them and direct it back at their attacker, making them difficult to bring down without nonmagical weapons like fire and guns.

Goldsmith spent most of the time recounting anecdotes about famous zombie massacres. Toward the end he mentioned, briefly, the fact that some zombies seemed to be capable of "some limited cognition, maybe equivalent to that of a mentally ill living person." Z supposed that Goldsmith must not think very much of "mentally ill" living people, because he still recommended either cutting off the head of a zombie and burning it or putting a tire around the zombie's neck and then covering them with gasoline.

Z thought about what they would do if someone tried to cut off their head. Probably bite them, Z thought. And then stab them, maybe, and run or stumble away and then—what? Set everything on fire. Z looked at the picture of Dean Goldsmith again. This man wants people to cut my head off and throw it in a river, they thought.

They got up and grabbed a red pen and colored the picture on the dust jacket so it looked like Dean Goldsmith's eyes were bleeding. The ink glistened in the dim light of Z's bedroom and got on their hands. It didn't look like blood, really—it was too close to pink, especially because of all the pink and rose and fuchsia and magenta already in the room. Everything seemed too warm so Z tried to walk across the room to the window, where rain was still coming down. Z looked out into the night at the silent street. The rain made noise on the pavement.

"I'm going to eat Dean Goldsmith's eyeballs for breakfast!" Z yelled out the window. Their voice was cold and hollow and dead-sounding, like a rasp that comes from something at the bottom of a cave. A dog in the backyard of the house across the street barked.

4

Choir was always the worst hour of the day. She only had it once a week. Aysel could have elected to have a period of silent reading on Thursdays instead, or chosen to play piano for the band, as she had last year, but at the beginning of the school year she had been very attached to the idea of getting out of school when she was eighteen and starting a band.

The alto section was composed of Aysel, Tommy Wodewose, a girl named April Kua who never spoke and who seemed to whisper instead of sing, and Abigail White, an overly tall tenth-grade girl who tried several times to convince the choir teacher, Ms. Coulter, that she was really a soprano, with no success.

Today, they were singing a chorus number from *The Music Man*, an obnoxious musical about a con man and a noble woman librarian. Tommy was singing enthusiastically and the people around him kept elbowing one another and giggling at him. He seemed unaware, but Aysel had learned that his hand twitched when he knew people were making fun of him, and his fingers were dancing against the side of his leg. Tommy had braided two twigs of rosemary and a length of black ribbon into a plait on the top of his head.

"Tommy is the only one of the altos who is singing," Ms. Coulter said loudly, over the music. "Come on, you three, listen to him sing the part once and then sing it with him. Take out your music, Aysel."

Last year, just before they had taken him up to the roof and thrown him off, the rumor had been going around that Tommy had been seen talking to birds there. Talking to birds was supposed to prove that you had fairy blood. It was all made up, naturally.

Aysel squinted through her hair and her glasses as Tommy's skinny shoulder bumped past her out the door and down the pale white hall as the bell rang loudly.

Aysel spent lunch poking at a pimple on her neck while sitting in the science room. Mr. Weber always kept his classroom open during first lunch, but he wasn't always in the room. Today he was somewhere else. Aysel thought about Z, and wondered how they were doing, and where they were. Azra had stopped packing Aysel's lunches in the eighth grade. Nowadays Aysel ate mostly toaster pastries and bananas. Since she had gotten her braces off it was okay for her to eat hard foods, but she'd fallen out of the habit.

Crumbs fell down over her black cotton T-shirt and onto her lap as she ate and stared at the purple toad in its tank and did her math and Magic Application homework.

This week they were learning Detailed Summons and the quadratic formula, and there were at least four problems in each subject that had symbols Aysel was mostly but not entirely sure she understood. She hadn't caught up on the homework for either class and was falling behind. The pentacles and parabolas started to get mixed up in her head. The toad stared at her uncomfortably. Aysel decided she would try again later. She got up and went looking for Z, her shoes flapping on the linoleum floors.

Aysel was not sure what it was about Z that made her feel so dedicated to becoming friends. Before the accident, Aysel hadn't noticed Z very much, because their name had been Susan then and they had been friends with Bethany, who had once asked Aysel rudely how many Pop-Tarts she ate every day.

Z was nowhere to be found. Aysel stomped upstairs and looked into the library, but there were only a few boys in the back by the photocopy machine, working on something for a class. Z wasn't in the lunchroom, either. So Aysel sat down next to the door to Mr. Holmes' room and hummed to herself until class started.

Mr. Holmes scratched under his nails, which made awful clicking noises as he pushed his hands together. Aysel thought about what she had heard, about him trying to give Z away. Mr. Holmes had never been one of Aysel's favorite teachers because of the way he talked about monsters—once he had spent the whole lesson talking about how immigration from Southern and Eastern Europe had worsened the United States' werewolf problem in the early decades of the twentieth century, and made it clear to everyone that he was one of those people who believed that werewolves were better dealt with during the fourteenth through eighteenth centuries, when they were burned. Most people seemed to like him.

"The Eastern Warlock Union made inroads toward workers' rights in the 1880s in the wake of the Great Fire of Baltimore. Who knows what started that fire? Anyone?" He looked around. Nobody had been paying attention enough to answer, but Mr. Holmes wasn't really looking for audience participation. "It was, of course, caused by poorly supervised dragon slaughterhouses." Mr. Holmes snuffled loudly.

Ginger was in the very middle of the middle row, discreetly coloring a detailed pattern of stained glass on the cover of her notebook, her long straight red hair falling elegantly to one side. Mr. Holmes either did not notice her or chose not to reprimand her. Aysel was certain that if she tried to draw in class she would be called on it immediately.

It was after fifth-period Magic Application, as Aysel was walking down the corridor, that she heard Mr. Holmes talking to one of the janitors.

"A window broken in Town Hall, and you know it's werewolves, Morris wasn't the only one—they've been having this happen in Portland too—"

"They're saying it's werewolves," the janitor was saying, "but you can't know that. It could be anything. It could be bears. Don't worry so much." Aysel looked back over her shoulder. Mr. Holmes was rubbing his amulet between two fingers.

"Of course it's werewolves, Mike," he said nervously. "It's the breakdown of law and order, I swear. We'll be overrun. Anarchists burning things down and opening the way for the monsters. A werewolf attack once a month—just think of it. We'll all be overrun. And that bookstore downtown with a themed display about *accepting werewolves as part of society,* without electroshock. What the hell are they playing at?"

Mike the janitor shrugged. "Well, don't let it get to you," he said. He began to walk away with his cart of mops. Mr. Holmes was left standing alone, staring at the other side of the hall like it was about to attack him. Aysel felt, momentarily, sorry for him.

She stepped into the bathroom and pulled her hair into a ponytail and poked again at the pimple on her neck. Behind her, one of the stall doors opened. It was Z. Aysel started and looked around, hoping that Z hadn't noticed her touching the pimple. They hadn't seemed to have noticed Aysel at all. Z looked worse than the previous day. Their eyes were watery and yellowish and tired, and there was a dark spot under the skin on their cheek. They smelled slightly acrid as they approached the sinks. It wasn't enough to notice unless you were close, but Aysel had a very good sense of smell. Z wore a black shirt and black pants and had a black wool hat pulled low over their eyes.

"Hello," Aysel said, drying her hands on a paper towel.

Z did not answer at first. They looked apathetically at the mirror, and for an instant Aysel had a horrifying impression of a hollow, unmoving body, a corpse propped up. It only lasted a moment. Z turned toward Aysel and seemed to recognize her. "Oh," they said. "Hello."

Aysel had a strong impulse to hug Z, or to rip them apart. She stepped backward instead. "What's your next class?"

Z stared into the mirror again. They touched their face gingerly. "Do you see that spot?" they asked.

Aysel tried to decide whether to be truthful. "Yes," she said. "A little."

"The book I got on forensic analysis," Z said, "says that those are formed by blood clotting under the skin. Or sometimes by gases that are given off in decomposition."

Aysel looked with polite interest at Z's spot. "Oh," she said.

"After a while, they burst."

"Well, I have spots," Aysel said. "Zits and things. They all look worse than that, too."

Z stared at Aysel. "I guess," they said.

"Look, you just have to not think about it for now and you can sort it out later," Aysel said helplessly. She felt this was the opposite of good advice, so she amended it by saying, "Maybe. Sorry."

"My next class is Spanish," Z said.

"Me too," Aysel said, flustered. She and Z left the bathroom and walked down the hall together. Most people were already in their next classes, so the halls were empty.

"I like your outfit," Aysel said, a little timidly.

"Thanks. I'm in mourning." Z smiled a little. "Also, my uncle threw away my favorite sweatshirt."

"It's a good look," Aysel said. "I want to dress like that—I don't know what you'd call that style. It's not goth, just minimalist maybe. Goth is overdone."

"Yeah," Z said.

"Except I might end up being a goth. I also want to dye my hair a bunch of colors."

After the last class ended, Z and Aysel walked out of the school and crossed the lawns. The clouds still hung thick in the sky. They passed a few groups of people; Aysel imagined she felt people staring at them. It was almost four in the afternoon and the sun would set soon—midwinter was all short gray days and long nights. Aysel's feet made slipping noises on the pavement.

"Oh hell," Z said suddenly, and stopped walking. Aysel looked over.

"What's wrong?"

Z stood there, looking ahead with wide eyes. They made no noise. Aysel saw again how much Z resembled a corpse but tried not to let it faze her.

"What's wrong, Z?"

Z made a long, low rasping noise. It did not sound like human speech—it resembled the noise wind made at night. Their eyes rolled back into their head for a second, yellow watery orbs. Then they bent over and began to cough loudly.

Aysel began to panic. "What's happening? What can I do?" She moved a little frantically and held Z's shoulder. Z was stiff and cold and shook with each cough, as if whatever they were coughing up was from a very deep part of their body.

Z spat out something soft and black onto the pavement and stood up again, clearing their throat. Aysel looked at the thing on the pavement and wondered if it was an organ. Z didn't seem very concerned. They rubbed their eyes and smiled. "Sorry," they said. "That was probably really weird."

"It was scary. What was that?"

"It's been happening lately. I'm not sure what it is."

"Does it hurt?"

"When it starts it hurts, but then I go all numb. I think my pain cells must be dead. Neurons." Z began to walk again, stepping carefully over the thing on the sidewalk.

"When are you going to go to the university for the books about necromancy?" Aysel asked.

"This weekend, I guess," Z said. "Saturday or something."

"You're going alone?"

"Mr. Weber is going with me."

"He's a great teacher. He helped me start the science club last year. He's not like other teachers."

"I know he isn't," Z said, "but I don't know if he'll do anything for me. He does have to stay safe." They turned to Aysel, who blinked at the unexpected eye contact. "You know what it's like. Adults always say they'll do something nice or protect you, but they don't know what you actually need."

"I know what you mean," Aysel said. "I'm sure Mr. Weber's not like that, though."

"Okay," Z said doubtfully. They reached the bus stop.

"What are you doing this afternoon?" Aysel asked.

Z shrugged. "I'll probably go home and sit in the house alone and try not to get eaten by cats and do homework." They smiled. Aysel was still getting used to their weird, supernaturally low voice.

"Who do you live with?" Aysel was suddenly curious. She realized that Z must have had to deal with a lot lately on their own—there didn't seem to be an adult in the background helping them through anything. Who was there for you when your parents died?

"This old lesbian witch from my mother's church. She offered to take me in because my uncle is a terrible person." Z said it matter-of-factly. "She owns that bookstore, The Reading Circle, in town. It hasn't been doing too well lately. Some people threw something through the window and broke the glass because she has a section on werewolf rights."

"Oh," Aysel said. She had been inside the bookstore, but she hadn't known it was run by a lesbian.

"It's pretty okay. I mean, if I have to choose someone to live with, Mrs. Dunnigan's all right. We don't have a lot of money for groceries and she's kind of messy, but she's really cool."

"She sounds that way."

"For a while she was into acting like a mom," Z added,

"but it finally stopped this week. She's too old to juggle everything. She's got an event at her bookstore. Some author coming in to read about his time working with at-risk werewolves. So she's out tonight."

"Do you want to come to my house?" Aysel asked suddenly. She heard her voice shake.

"Why?"

Aysel floundered. "Well, just because. I don't live too far from here. My mom isn't working today, either, so she could make dinner."

"Okay," Z said.

They walked the rest of the way to Aysel's house. When they got there Aysel realized for the first time in months how messy their yard looked. It was a garden in the summer, but in the winter it was just kale and squash plants and dirt mounds which hid potatoes. The earth was still damp from the rain, and their shoes were both muddy.

"Could you take off your shoes? Sorry," Aysel said, as Z walked into the hall.

"Oh, right," Z said. They slid off their shoes, and Aysel got a glimpse of a grey, dry ankle between the edge of Z's pants and their sock. Z looked up at the nazar bead, hanging on the wall. "What's that? It's the same as your necklace."

"A charm to protect us against evil. Demons and monsters and shapeshifters and *djinn* and stuff. It's a Turkish thing."

"Didn't do anything to me," Z said.

"You must not be the kind of monster it's set up for."

Azra was asleep on the couch, dressed in purple pajama pants and a thick black sweater that was too long for her. Aysel was embarrassed when she saw her mother like that. Azra woke up when the door clicked open. She looked groggily up at her daughter and Z.

"Hello, Aysel*cim*. Who's your friend?"

"This is Z, Mom," Aysel said.

Z waved timidly. "Nice to meet you, Mrs. Tahir," they said.

Azra ran a hand through her hair, which had gotten messy while pressed into the couch pillows. She was not wearing any makeup, and looked sleepy and puffy. "It's Ms. Tahir, actually," she said, "but please, call me Azra. I'm sorry for my appearance, I have today off and was catching up on sleep. I had a big court date yesterday and I haven't slept much for a while."

"Oh! It's um, it's all right." Z looked over at Aysel as if expecting her to say something or guide them. "Um, thanks for having me over, Azra," Z said.

"You don't need to thank her," Aysel said. "It's fine."

"It's nice that you have such a polite friend, Aysel. Don't reprimand her for just being decent." Azra turned to Z. "It's a pleasure to have you, dear. Zee, you said? What is that short for?"

"It's not short for anything," Z said, at the same time that Aysel began to tell her mother Z was short for Susan. Aysel was glad afterward that she hadn't finished saying that.

"How unusual," Azra said.

"You can go back to sleep, Mom," Aysel said. "Z and I are just going to do homework for a while."

"No, I'm up—and look, it's nearly five, I should start making dinner. Are you going to eat with us, Zee?"

"I—am I invited?" Z asked.

"Sure, of course!" Azra said. "Go with Aysel and dig me up some potatoes before you start your homework." She went over to the sink and began washing her hands. "I'll make tea."

Z and Aysel walked back outside. The light shifted from the yellow glow of inside to the cold blue light of winter.

"My mom enchants the potatoes and kale to grow year-round," Aysel said. "It doesn't work on things like strawberries—too much work—but she manages the boring foods."

"Your mom seems cool," Z said.

Aysel felt a wisp of hair at the end of her nose and scowled. "Not really," she said. "Help me dig up the potatoes."

Z stared at the cold earth, at a loss.

"Here," Aysel said, and bent down and began to part the earth with her hands. It was cold around her fingers, and soft. She reached down, moving the earth with sweeps to the side. She lifted up a grubby potato and handed it to Z. A worm crawled away from a pile of dirt that had been overturned, and Z was staring at it.

"The food just comes out of the ground," Z said a few minutes later, their hands full of small potatoes.

"Well," Aysel said, maybe a little crossly—which she felt was fair, seeing as Z had done nothing but stand there while she dug in the dirt—"you have to tend them and then go and dig for them."

"Still, though, it's a miracle," Z said.

"Okay, it's a miracle. The circle of life."

Z giggled unexpectedly as Aysel pulled the door open. "I bet I'd make good compost," they whispered.

After dinner they went into Aysel's room and listened to music and did homework. Z showed Aysel how the quadratic formula worked after Aysel fried her calculator with frustrated magic, twice, and had to put in new batteries. As it turned out, there was no quadratic formula button on the calculator. Aysel thought there should be. Couldn't one thing in mathematics be easy?

"You have to learn to use math if you're going to be a scientist," Z said. "Isn't that what you want to do?"

"I want to work with animals, not anything that needs math," Aysel snapped. She felt friendly, though. They were both writing papers about their weekends for Spanish class, and Z joked that they could write about accidentally pulling out their own eyeball while trying to take out a contact lens. At least Aysel thought it was a joke. It was meant to make Aysel laugh.

Azra was watching the news in the front room. She had been tuning in to the evening news regularly since the police killed Timothy Morris. The coverage of the story as it developed, and the police's growing case against the dead werewolf, put Aysel's teeth on edge. She had not been able to pay attention. She jumped and looked warily at Z when Azra called out from the front room.

"Aysel! This news story is about the Pagan murder."

Aysel stuck her head around the corner and gestured behind her to where Z sat studying Spanish adverbs. "Mom," she said, "I can't right now." But she looked toward the television and stood halfway in and out of her room as blurry ticker tape announcing the story scrolled across the twenty-inch screen.

"New evidence has come to light that Archie Pagan did not stop working with werewolves when he moved to Oregon," the reporter onscreen said. "The murdered man had previously cooperated with a nonprofit on the East Coast that helped provide electroshock to wolves. He claimed that his new practice in central Salem was devoted to traditional psychoanalysis and family therapy, but an anonymous source claiming to be a relative of a local patient says that Pagan continued to secretly provide electroshock therapy to werewolves inside the state of Oregon. The source described an underground operation that had continued for over a decade, through which potentially thousands of unregistered werewolves were rendered nonmagical. Pagan's wife was not reachable for comment, but police have obtained an initial warrant to search his old office for evidence of illegal werewolf treatment."

Z stood and came to stand behind Aysel. "What's this?" they asked her.

"It's about that guy that was murdered," Aysel said. "By Timothy Morris, the werewolf. The news says he was treating unregistered werewolves, giving them electroshock so they didn't transform."

"Fuck."

Azra looked over at Z. "Hey, watch your language," she said. Aysel knew the tone of her mother's voice meant that she was distracted.

"What will they do if they find out that he was really doing this?" Z asked. "They can't try him if he's dead."

"They could track down the werewolves that he helped," Azra said. "Unless they were smart and used assumed names. But that's only if Pagan was stupid, and didn't hide his files."

They finished their Spanish homework and sat around listening to Aysel's Şebnem Ferah casettes, because Z wanted to know what a Turkish girl rock band was like. It was dark outside, but Aysel didn't turn on any more lights. She lay on the floor with the desk lamp's pale glow against the window, the only source of illumination, looking at Z.

"You should see the video we have for this song," Aysel said. "She's got these platform boots and is wearing this amazing halter top and she leans back really far when she hits the high notes. My mom likes her too."

"We could watch it now," Z said.

"No, my mom's out there still and she would try to give us a history of the whole rock scene and be really goofy. But sometime we should."

When Z had to go home, Aysel offered to walk them to the bus. Azra smiled and said goodbye to Z and tried to help Aysel put on a coat. They both went off into the dark, hurrying from streetlight to streetlight. The last bus was due to run soon. Aysel was wrapped in her mother's coat and was still cold; Z wasn't even wearing a jacket.

"Can you feel anything? It's freezing out here," Aysel said.

"I can't really tell it's cold out at all," Z said. "It's just numb. I can't feel a lot of temperatures very well. I only feel really hot things, like fire."

"How do you know that?"

"I've experimented a little. Just to see what happens."

"What if your toes freeze off?"

"I don't know," Z said.

"Sorry. That was awful of me. Thanks for coming for dinner."

"Thank you for having me," Z said. Suddenly they were stiff and formal again, a cardboard cut-out. "You don't have to wait for the bus with me. It comes in ten minutes."

"Okay," Aysel said. She didn't want to risk saying anything else wrong. She turned around and walked away. Halfway down the block she realized that she should turn and wave or something, so she spun around—but Z was gone. Maybe they had realized they wanted to walk home, Aysel thought.

Azra was up watching reruns of a show about ghost hunters in the Canadian wilderness. Aysel sat and watched it with her. They didn't speak; eventually both of them fell asleep curled in different positions on the same couch.

5

Z left the bus stop and went into the woods across the street. Something about being in Aysel's house had felt like an escape—homey and with a mother ready to care for her daughter, who grew food in the yard like witches long ago had. When Z had gotten up from doing homework to go sharpen a pencil in the office, they had glanced into the kitchen and seen Aysel's mother stirring a rice dish with one hand and holding a cigarette between two fingers of the other. There had been something so profoundly amazing and entrancing about Ms. Tahir in that moment. Z figured it had something to do with grief. They touched the place on their chest where the spell was burned into their skin and wondered how and when Suzanna Chilworth had cast the spell, and what she was thinking when she did it. And why she had never told Z about it—or even that she knew how to do necromancy. Z couldn't remember the last time they had talked to their mother about anything serious, and now they never would again.

Z didn't want to take the bus back to Mrs. Dunnigan's

apartment, so as Aysel turned to walk back home, they spun around and walked through a hedge into the nearest backyard. They distantly felt the branches scratch at their face. Z's feet slid on the wet grass. A few dogs barked at them as they ambled along in the shadows. They walked through people's backyards until the yards started having fences, and then they moved to the streets. Z looked through the bright windows onto the scenes inside—everything seemed so small from outside the houses. There was a dog sleeping on a couch, a woman at a sink, a man playing video games. They stood staring in one yard for a few minutes, watching two children run around each other in a living room. Above them, the sky was completely black; no stars were visible. They reached the end of Aysel's suburban neighborhood and tried to figure out where they were. They vaguely recognized the strip mall they were facing from when they had seen it out of the window of a bus. They walked across the street without looking for the crosswalk. Behind them, a car rushed by.

As Z crossed the parking lot next to the grocery store, they saw two people walking toward them. Z squinted at them. Both of the strangers looked messy and were wearing large backpacks. They both had patched jeans stiff with mud and heavy sweatshirts.

"Hey," one of them called out. Z stopped and turned around. Both of the approaching strangers looked ragged and clumpy and strong. As they got closer, Z realized that they were just teenagers. One of them was a girl, which made Z less nervous. Z wondered what they could want. Not money, hopefully. Z did not have any money.

"What do you want?" Z asked.

"Chill out," the girl said. She was missing a front tooth. "Do you have a cigarette, kid?"

"I don't smoke," Z said.

The boy laughed. "What did you think, Elaine? He's like eleven."

Z's ears pricked up. People usually didn't think they were a boy.

"What, I mean, could be a small adult."

"I told you."

Z grimaced.

"Okay," the girl said. Her face looked greasy and she had a zit on one side of her chin. She looked tired. "I shouldn't really be smoking either. It's so bad for you. Hey, kid, do you know how to get to the Union Gospel Mission from here?"

"I have no idea," Z said. The wind blew and Z felt it very slightly. The boy shivered and hugged himself. Z felt sorry for him. Living people felt so much.

"It's this meal thing we heard about. We're hitchhiking and we haven't got any money, you know?" He paused. "You know? We're staying at a friend's place but they haven't gone grocery shopping and we need dinner."

"Yeah," Z said, realizing that they were actually expected to answer. The boy grinned, encouraged.

"I'm not asking for money," he said. "You're a kid, I don't

ask for money from kids. Anyway, we just need to get to this thing. Apparently it's kind of close to Riverfront Park, on Commercial Street near the bridge."

"Oh," Z said. They had to think for a minute. "Well, that's . . . that way." They pointed north. The boy and girl both turned and looked in the direction Z had pointed. "I don't know how far it is or anything," Z added hastily. "I think it's like two miles to the bridge. But if you walk north on Liberty Road you should get onto Commercial Street."

"Oh, okay," the girl said. "We couldn't get a bus there or anything, could we?"

"I . . . I am not sure," Z said. "Maybe the 08? I don't know how late the bus runs. But it wouldn't save you much time. It has like a million stops." Z felt very grown up, giving this advice.

"Thanks," the boy said. "Means a lot, man."

"Yeah, thanks," the girl agreed. The two walked off. Z watched them. They looked smaller the farther away they got. They couldn't be that old, Z thought. Maybe eighteen or nineteen. The boy had one of those mustaches that meant he couldn't grow a beard yet.

Something felt odd in their heart.

Z walked on, thinking about how scared they would have been of two strangers in the dark before the crash. They wondered if they had forgotten how to be scared of things.

A few blocks away from the street where Mrs. Dunnigan lived, Z stopped. They looked up at the street sign and across the road—they were close to the cemetery. The bus didn't come this way. Z stopped for a few minutes and wondered whether to go find their parents' graves. They decided not to. It would take too long in the dark.

Mrs. Dunnigan did seem glad that Z had gone to Aysel's house.

"What are her parents like?" she asked. "What did you do?"

"We didn't do much, just homework. And her mother and father are separated, or maybe she doesn't have a father. Her mom's nice." Z thought of Ms. Tahir's cigarette and her smile again and of the warm, protected feeling she gave Z. Z felt a little guilty about it.

"It's good that you're making new friends," Mrs. Dunnigan said.

"How was the bookstore event?"

"It went all right for a little while," Mrs. Dunnigan said. "The man who came to read is a friend of an old friend of mine. Not a werewolf, but he was married to one. But then two or three angry people came in and tried to start an argument about this business with the Archie Pagan murder. I don't know if you heard, but apparently Pagan gave electroshock to unregistered werewolves. It's a very controversial thing. There are people who think that's fine, since it makes werewolves safer to be around, and there are people who want all werewolves to be registered with the state and get treatment through those avenues, and there are people like that Morris fellow who think electroshock hurts werewolves more than it helps. It does cause things like memory loss and different allergic conditions."

"Who were the angry people?"

"These people were the people who want all the wolves to get registered and get shock therapy. They said I was a monster activist. Sometimes with those people you can talk them down, but they were looking for a fight, so I had to ask them to leave, and right after that it looked like time to close up shop for the night."

After her dinner, Mrs. Dunnigan and the cats watched the news and Z sat behind her, looking at the television and sort of absorbing what was happening. A new farmers' market was opening, and a street downtown that was currently inhabited by homeless people was going to get cleaned up and made safe for businesses. There had been no new werewolf attacks; an initial search of Archie Pagan's office had not turned up any evidence to show that he had treated werewolves there. All the reporters seemed tense.

Mrs. Dunnigan fed the cats and turned off the television.

Outside, it was dark and cold, though not cold enough to freeze. Mrs. Dunnigan tried to talk to Z about the book she was reading, but it was about something Z found very hard to pay attention to. Some of it had to do with sea monsters.

In the shower that night, Z was washing their hair, humming, when a large clump came out in their hand. They stared at it. Bits of wet skin clung to it, gray and disgusting. They felt their scalp, where the hair had come from. It was bald. There was no blood, but then that might just be because Z was dry of blood.

"I'm losing my hair!" Z shouted, as if there was anything anyone could do about it. The shower was loud and the TV was on and Z couldn't hear if Mrs. Dunnigan responded.

Z released the clump of hair and watched it float toward the drain. They sat down, clutching at themselves as if their whole body might disappear, just dissolve and diffuse down the drain, so many particles of carbon. Their legs felt thin and bony. The skeleton inside them moved visibly. Z didn't turn off the water; they were wishing in some part of themselves that if they didn't act the water might destroy them right there at that moment. That would have at least been an effortless and probably painless end. The water was hot enough that for once they could feel something—the sensation of burning. Their fingernails were torn and scratchy. They sat down in the shower, the hot water sloughing over them in waves, steaming up the mirror and the frosted glass window high up on the wall. Nothing was okay. Nothing was okay. Everything was going to fall apart, Z included. Worms were going to shred their body and make it into mulch and Z was going to remain conscious for all of it. I wish I could just get it over with, Z thought.

Eventually the water went cold. Z wasn't sure they wanted to self-preserve, but they still turned off the tap and wrapped a towel around their shoulders. Then they curled up and lay with their heart not beating and their lungs not working and their skin the temperature of a cool windowpane on the floor of the shower, as the night grew thicker and colder outside. They weren't sure where Mrs. Dunnigan was.

The phone rang, and Z got up to get it before Mrs. Dunnigan could leave her room and reach the phone.

"Hello?" they said into the receiver.

"Hello? Z?" It was Mr. Weber's voice on the other line. "I think I figured out a plan for Saturday. I think I can put an invisibility hex on you and get you inside the room alone to look for the books. I'll try to create a distraction or just keep watch outside, depending on who is in the area."

"Aren't invisibility hexes dangerous to put on people?" Z asked. "I could suffocate . . ." they trailed off. "Oh."

"I think that's not a danger in your case," Mr. Weber said. Z could hear the gum snap between his teeth. "It's still going to be dangerous, though. I don't have any idea what the staff schedule is like or if we will run into trouble. I'm going to try to minimize the danger for you as much as possible, but I can't promise that this is safe. If there were other options, I would say try those first. But there aren't."

"Thank you," Z said. "I do really appreciate it. I didn't think you'd like . . . end up helping me. Everyone else has been so weird to me."

"If you can get over to my house Saturday morning, we can drive over to the library together."

"Oh," Z said, trying to hide their excitement. "Great. Where's your house?"

Mr. Weber gave Z his address, and Z wrote it down in green ink on a yellow Post-it.

"I am so worried about everything," Aysel said to Z as they waited for Spanish to start on Friday. "The test is this Monday and I still haven't caught up from last week."

"What were you sick with?" Z asked. They felt ill and their eyes were puffy. They pulled their knit hat lower on their head, to hide the balding spots and the red and purple patches of skin that showed through.

"Nothing really awful," Aysel said elusively.

"Mrs. Dunnigan's been sick too," Z said.

"I think I want to go shopping," Aysel said. "That sounds so dumb, but it'd be fun I think. We wouldn't be dumb about it. Will you come with me this afternoon?"

"Where would we go?" Z asked.

"I don't know, Goodwill. The mall. I want some black clothes."

They sat out by the dumpster during sixth period. Aysel ate Pop-Tarts and Z sat and threw rocks at crows. Aysel told Z about her crush on Kathleen Hanna, the singer.

"When you say a crush, do you mean a crush crush?" Z asked.

"I don't know any other kind of crush," Aysel said.

"Well, like, a gay crush, or a crush that just means you really like the band?"

"I am gay and I like the band," Aysel said.

Z stewed in surprise for an instant, and then smiled. Aysel didn't look as terrified of Z's smile as she once had. "You're gay?" Z asked.

"I've been told it's very obvious," Aysel said. "I also have a crush on Şebnem Ferah. She's like the Turkish Kathleen Hanna, or maybe the Turkish Joan Jett. Or something. She's more of a real rock star than Kathleen Hanna is. I also have crushes on Olivia Newton John, and Winona Ryder, and Julie Andrews. But they aren't punk."

"I sort of have a crush on this singer my mom likes," Z said. "Joanna Newsom. I like her voice. And I think I had a crush on my swim coach when I was ten."

The custodian came around the corner with a garbage can, humming. When he saw Aysel and Z, he shouted for them to go back inside. Z's joints hurt whenever they tried to stand too fast.

The rain that had been so intense the previous week became deep mist.

Z and Aysel went to the department store downtown after the final bell. They both had homework to do, but because it was the start of a weekend they lingered under the fluorescent lighting, counting dimes and figuring out what they couldn't afford. Aysel's mother made an okay amount of money, Aysel said, but a lot of it was going back to repay her debts for law school, so things were still tight. Aysel was pretty good at shoplifting, she had told Z before going into the store. Z pretended not to be fazed by this information, even though they had never known a shoplifter before and were worried about what would happen if Aysel got caught. It didn't end up being that dramatic. Aysel shoved things into her backpack while Z bought black eyeliner and the palest foundation the store had.

When they got outside and went down the street, Aysel started dumping the things she had stolen out onto the sidewalk. Z was sort of horrified by all the junk Aysel thought would be useful.

"Why did you steal pink mascara?" Z asked, picking up the little tube from where it had rolled off the sidewalk into the grass.

"It was the smallest, most expensive thing there," Aysel said.

Z didn't know what hours the library at Willamette University was open. When the sun came up slightly over the edge of the horizon, they were sitting at the window of Mrs. Dunnigan's front room, looking out at the foggy street. Mrs. Dunnigan was up early even on Saturdays, and Z could hear her moving in her room, closing and opening drawers.

"Mr. Weber gave me a spell to disable the security on the Censored Materials room at Willamette," Z said when the old witch opened her bedroom door and stood for a moment to put on her slippers. "We're going there today together if I can get to his house."

Mrs. Dunnigan blinked. She looked for a second at Z uncomprehending, and then her face settled into a smile.

"Well, I'm glad that worked out," she said. "Where does he live?"

Z showed her the address.

"That's a ways across town from here, but it's not terribly far from the bookstore if you take the bus," Mrs. Dunnigan said.

"Do you think you can go there with me?" Z asked. "Or do you have the bookstore to take care of?"

"The bookstore is open today and I've sworn to myself that I'll stay open in spite of the people who want to close it. You can come with me downtown if you want and I can send you on your way from there." She cleared her throat and folded her bathrobe more tightly around her small body. "I wish it was the seventies so I would have the kind of thing you needed on the top shelf of the back room ready to give you, but they burned all my rare books about that kind of magic years ago and they do the same to anyone nowadays who tries to get at the ones they keep locked up." She moved past Z into the kitchen and began making tea.

Z didn't say anything, and stretched their arms above their head, listening to their own bones crack.

The bookstore had not been badly damaged by the rock or by the angry people who had shown up to protest the werewolf rights display, but there was a long, uneven line of splintered glass down the length of the front window that had been patched up unevenly on both sides with layers of clear packing tape. Z had carried the spell Mr. Weber gave them in their pocket.

"Okay," Z said at the door of the bookstore. "I think I'm going to head on my way."

Mrs. Dunnigan studied Z. "Do you think you can stay out of danger?"

Z shrugged. "I'll wear a sweatshirt or something so people can't see my scars."

"Wear a hat too. But let's see. You can wear my friend Sal's baseball cap and sweater with the Oregon Ducks logo."

"People hate the Ducks here."

"If anyone asks you can say you're from Eugene and you're visiting your brother at school and showing your allegiance for the Ducks to spite him."

Z nodded. "Okay."

As they closed the door of the bookstore behind them, the bell chimed so loudly that it almost covered Mrs. Dunnigan's goodbye. They caught the bus at the corner.

Mr. Weber's house was low and small. It was close to the center of town, but in one of the older, more dilapidated neighborhoods of tiny bungalows. His yard was neat and his car sat outside, brown and bricklike. He was sitting on the stoop waiting for Z.

"All right," he said as Z approached from the road. "Go Ducks." He looked tired. At school Mr. Weber always dressed neatly, but today he was wearing baggy gray denim pants and a loose vest over a T-shirt.

"Are you sure you want to do this?" Z asked.

"Well, I haven't missed Shabbat morning service for years," Mr. Weber said. "But I can today."

"You're Jewish?"

"Sure," Mr. Weber said, standing. "It makes for dangerous living in central Oregon, especially when you're black at the same time, but I guess I just like to live on the edge like that." He stretched over and touched his toes, and Z heard his shoulders pop faintly. "Let's do this, huh?"

Z looked at him to see if he was annoyed with them, but they couldn't tell. "You really don't have to. I know I'm here, but if—"

"I felt terrible about leaving you to do this on your own. I never wanted to be that kind of person. I thought about it all yesterday and realized I had to help you. I get scared sometimes, but this is something I need to do."

The ride in the car on the way to the library was pitted with bumps from Mr. Weber's car. Though it looked solid on the outside, it seemed to stagger along like an old dog.

"How is Aysel?" Mr. Weber asked.

"She's okay," Z said. "She was pretty sick the other week, I think."

"She may get sick again. She misses school once in a while. Look after her, okay? I'm glad she has a friend. She's a cool kid. She reminds me of my friend Sam who studies dragons."

"You have a friend who studies dragons?" Z asked.

"Yeah, at the fossil fields out in Montana and Idaho and stuff. It's fascinating stuff. You know, lizards are mostly descended from them."

"Yeah, you told us in class," Z said. "I meant more that it's weird to think of teachers having friends."

Mr. Weber laughed. "I have friends," he said. "Mostly they got sick of Central Oregon, but there's a few who are still around here."

"Where does your family live?" Z asked.

"They're down in the Bay," Mr. Weber said. "Three of my brothers work in computers, one is a glassblower, one is figuring himself out and working in a pet store, and one has been directing a reality television show about narcissistic personality disorder for six years running."

"Why do you live here, then?" Z asked.

"I mean, who knows, really," Mr. Weber said drily. "I've gotten attached to teaching, though. It's something I like doing."

The library at Willamette had been built in the later eighties and was still fairly new. It was made of brick and glass and had a clock tower in the front that looked like it had been built more to represent the idea of a tower than to fulfill any real function.

"Originally it was going to be named after a US senator from Oregon, but once the senator was investigated for affiliation with dissident magical groups, the committee in charge decided to call it the Wells Library instead. After the Boeing guy," he said.

"That's sad," Z said flatly.

"I didn't like the senator much either," Mr. Weber said.

It was made of brick and glass and had a clock tower in the front that looked like it had been built more to represent the idea of a tower than to fulfill any real function.

You could not climb into it, though it was true that if you stood in its shadow it blocked you from the rain. Z passed under the clock on their way to the sliding doors that opened into the building. As Mr. Weber and Z passed the front desk a bored student employee looked up and then back down at the book they were reading.

"We're going down to the basement," Mr. Weber said in a low voice to Z.

The only other people in the library early on a Saturday were students who looked harried and sleep-deprived and carried with them large stacks of books or papers. Z's feet made little noise on the thin blue carpeting as they made their way to the elevators. The elevator doors opened onto a flat, fluorescent expanse of shelving and computer banks, labeled in a way that Z couldn't make heads or tails of. As the silver doors closed and the chain inside the elevator mechanism lowered Z and Mr. Weber to the basement, he cleared his throat. Z looked over at him, but he seemed to have decided against saying whatever it was he was going to say.

The elevator reached the basement floor and the small chime rang out as the doors slid open. Mr. Weber gestured for Z to stay where they were, pressed into the space on one side of the door.

"Invisibility," Mr. Weber said.

"Oh," Z said. "Right." They squared their shoulders.

Mr. Weber pressed one hand lightly to Z's forehead and muttered a rapid-fire incantation. Z recognized part of it from basic invisibility lessons the previous year, but it went on far longer. Z felt a sensation along their spine and in their fingers and toes as if someone had just wrapped them in a thin, sticky bedsheet.

"The archives are at the end of the hall to your right," Mr. Weber said. "It's all in cabinets and lockers. You're looking for the last four cabinets on the right side of the hallway. I know from having broken in once before. You can probably unlock them easily once you're through the outer security spell."

"How will the invisibility work with me holding things?" Z looked down at the bag they were holding, trying to see if it was invisible.

"Whatever you touch and hold to your chest will be invisible until you get out of the building and probably to the other side of the quad. Duck behind a bush or something for a few minutes. Tap your foot three times when you're on your way past me to the elevator so I know you're leaving with books. Tap twice if you didn't get what you came for."

Z didn't know what to say. "Thank you," they said through the plasticky invisibility hex, their words muddled.

Mr. Weber nodded. "Go as fast as you can," he said in a low voice. "I'll talk to the librarian to buy you time. Hopefully there aren't too many staff." He turned and walked slowly out toward the open office door a few yards from the elevator. Z followed behind him, unsure if they were really invisible. They looked down at their own hands and body and could see just fine where everything was, though at the same time there was a kind of mauve cloudiness around the edges of their elbows and knees and fingers. They felt as if they were encased in a spiderweb as they started down the hall toward the large black metal door with the inscription *Authorized Staff Only*, fumbling in their pocket for the spell Mr. Weber had given them earlier in the week. The paper was crumpled and torn on one side. Z tried to remember the incantation for fire. Z glanced behind them and saw Mr. Weber standing near the open door of the librarian's office, looking at them.

"Incendi," they muttered at the paper as they neared the black door. They felt at a distance the magic, as if it was entering their head from behind and shooting through their arms. It was a shock like a lightning bolt. The edge of the charmed scrap caught fire and began to send up a ribbon of smoke. When the red ember reached the sigil scratched in the middle of the paper, it sent up bright white fire. Z pressed it to the door, unsure if this was what they were meant to do. All at once, a bolt of brilliant blue emanated from their palm and an acrid chemical smell surrounded Z. They pulled back their hand, and the door swung open.

Inside, the cabinets looked at first just like the ordinary filing cases that filled the rest of the basement. There were no windows, though the room stretched farther than Z had expected. It seemed to be organized in a different way than the rest of the library. Some cabinets were stacked one on top of another, and narrow ladders on rollers hung like long ship's beams down the length of the walls. Z began to walk down the aisle of metal cabinets, looking for something about death, or necromancy. They remembered Mr. Weber's directions and walked quickly to the back of the expansive room. The subject listings stood out on their small white placards, written haphazardly in a way that contrasted with the orderly university shelves outside the black room. *Cohens, Hattie Mae. Commune, Paris. Druidic Rites. Fey, American.*

Then, at the end of the long room, Z heard the sound of someone closing a drawer and the noise of footsteps. They froze in place.

"Augustine?" a voice called out. "Did you reorganize this section?" A woman's head peered around the corner, wearing a surgical mask and glasses that had a slight tint. She was otherwise dressed with exacting plainness, in a brown sweater and corderoys. "Augustine? Are you here? Is this door open?"

Z edged past the woman as she made her way rapidly toward the open door, looking at the labels on the shelves. They were at the N section now. They opened the nearest cabinet, where the slightly peeling label *Necromancy, Practical* shone in the fluorescent lighting. It squeaked on rusted hinges, and Z froze before edging it open the rest of the way.

The drawer was empty. Z's heart plummeted into their stomach.

Outside in the hallway, Z heard a shout and a sudden

loud high-pitched screech that continued to drone on in a pulsing monotone. The lights above them in the room of censored materials began to flash red. After a moment of horrified paralysis they realized that it was an alarm. The noise was followed by the noise of running footsteps. Z frantically opened the remaining drawers in the cabinet. They were empty—folders divested of contents, and spaces where the books should have been. They moved in on the next one, which was empty too, and then desperately opened the drawers labeled *Naiad, Nazis, Nigerian Exorcism*, and *Nostradamus*. These drawers had volumes and folios inside them, but from what Z could see they all had to do with the designated subjects.

The noise of the footsteps got closer. Z heard a shout and realized that the voice was Mr. Weber's.

Z had only moments to react. They shut the drawers with a bang and raced back down the corridor to the black door. Two people were standing near it, and Z slowed to look, their legs aching. It was a large security guard in a dark navy uniform, standing pressing something into the back of Mr. Weber's neck. Z almost cried out, but at the last second remembered to stay silent. About ten feet away, the woman Z had seen in the Censored Materials room stood, mask off, next to another librarian, watching.

"We had a notification that an unauthorized person disabled the security spell on the Censored Materials Division door," the guard said. "You're the only non-faculty personnel in the area. Hands above your head, sir."

"You have the wrong person," Mr. Weber said. He looked to and fro as if he was seeking out Z, but he could not place where they were. Z tapped their foot twice, as loud as they dared. Mr. Weber jerked his head toward the elevators and nodded in their direction. The guard pressing him into the wall didn't notice.

"We're going to have to take you to the campus police station and conduct an inventory of the room, unfortunately," the guard said. "Willamette staff takes the security of their federally protected censored materials very seriously. I need you to remain still and not perform any magic. Any failure to comply will be interpreted as assault of Willamette faculty."

"I swear I was just down here to look for a volume I need on lizards," Mr. Weber said. "I can't find the oversize books in the public library, and this university has such a fine collection."

"I'm going to need you to remain silent," the guard said.

"Well, *get a move on*, whatever you're going to do," Mr. Weber said. He nodded again in Z's general direction.

Z ran for the elevators, and then at the last moment decided to use the stairs instead. They hauled the door open. Racing up the stairs, they stumbled, and began to feel the sticky spiderweb feeling lifting from their face and limbs. Z grabbed the railing to right themselves and scrambled up to the ground floor. They tried not to run for the exit when they left the stairwell and limped as carefully as possible toward the door.

Out in the foggy morning, Z threw themselves down on a bench across the quad from the library and held onto the wood on both sides of their legs as tightly as they could. Their heart was not pounding and they were not breathing, but the muscles that remained were pulled as tight as a string about to snap. Z didn't know how long they sat motionless under a drooping bare black tree and the shadow of a square concrete lecture hall. As they sat and tried to think about what to do next, they heard a wail of police sirens approaching. Z did not want to run or move more than they already had, and so hesitated, frozen, watching a black-and-white cruiser pull slowly down the wide footpath to the library. They did not wait to see the people inside get out.

When Z told Mrs. Dunnigan that Mr. Weber had been arrested, and that Z had opened the door to the Censored Materials Division only to find the books on necromancy gone, Mrs. Dunnigan did not say anything at first, and then stepped forward and enveloped Z in a bony embrace.

"At least he turned out to be brave," she said finally. "He did the right thing. And at least you're all right."

"Will he be all right?" Z asked. "I feel like I did the wrong thing, asking too much of him or something. He's been arrested. He's so nice."

"We'll check up on him," Mrs. Dunnigan said. "But

you didn't do the wrong thing. You were protecting yourself. And he's a grown man. He chose to help you." There was such a tone of conviction in her voice that Z almost believed her for a moment, until they remembered the stance of the security guard and the thing pressed into Mr. Weber's neck.

Z felt a deep ugly sensation in the pit of their stomach, and pushed Mrs. Dunnigan away.

A story appeared in the Sunday paper. *Local Man Apprehended; Materials on Necromancy Found Missing from Willamette,* the headline read.

"The books really were missing, then," Z said. "Not just in a different place. But then someone else must have stolen them. Why didn't the people notice before we showed up?"

Mrs. Dunnigan, who was in the living room, did not seem to hear Z.

Before school on Monday, Z told Aysel what had happened. They sat outside together with Aysel underneath the awning. It wasn't raining, but there was mist. They watched people trudge into school, looking weird and eerie under the yellow lamps that were turned on before sunrise. Aysel was already eating her lunch because she had forgotten to eat her breakfast.

"I can't believe that he went through that and you didn't

even get the books," Aysel said. "I read the story. I had a sinking feeling."

"I know," Z said. "He could have stayed home and then they would have got me instead, which would be fair anyway."

"They won't let him go," Aysel said.

"How do you know?" Z asked.

"My mom is a paralegal," Aysel said. "She went to law school. I know about this stuff. If someone is suspected of holding censored materials they can be held indefinitely, especially when they have known exceptional magical abilities. And Mr. Weber's a sorcerer."

"Not indefinitely," Z said. "That's against the rules. And he doesn't have anything. Even if they search his house."

"Maybe he'll get out of it. He's kind of a genius."

"Yeah," Z said. They felt like Aysel was judging them. They wondered what they could do to make her understand that they felt guilty. "Aysel?" Z asked. "This is all my fault, isn't it?"

"I mean, yeah. He was going there for you. And it's because of him that you didn't get caught while he did."

Z swayed weakly in the morning breeze.

The second bell rang. Aysel turned around and walked off to class.

At lunch, a rumor had started that Mr. Weber was the one suspected of having the stolen books. It spread very fast. Aysel wasn't anywhere to be found. Z had to walk around alone. They wondered where Aysel was.

Tommy Wodewose was being harassed again because he had worn a long black cloak to school. It had silver clasps and billowed out behind him as he walked. He had worn his hair loose and long today, and it must have hurt when Charley Salt reached out and yanked it as Tommy sat reading and eating alone at a table in the cafeteria.

"Ouch," Tommy said. His voice was reedy and high.

"What are you doing today, Tommy?" Charley asked.

"Nothing," Tommy replied.

"What are you reading, Tommy?"

"It's a book on ancient druids. It's very interesting."

"Do you want to be a druid, Tommy?" Everyone laughed again. "Make friends with the feys who change shape into monsters?"

Tommy just got up and wandered vaguely away down the hall. Z wondered if he even knew it had been a real insult. He must know, they thought. He was thrown off the roof.

Charley and his friends just turned around and began making fun of Danny Xu's glasses. Danny Xu took it in stride and pretended he was in on the joke.

Z went looking for Aysel after school. They looked by the dumpsters, which were deserted, before making a slow circuit of the rest of the school. Finally they found her. Aysel was sitting on the floor of the girls' bathroom near the entrance to the school, her backpack and coat on the floor next to her. Her face was turned away toward the wall, and she looked like she was crying.

"What's wrong?" Z asked. "Have you been here all day?"

"You don't understand," Aysel said. "You just don't get it."

"I get it, Aysel. I'm sorry. But I don't think they'll burn

Mr. Weber or whatever. They will figure out that he's innocent and they'll let him go."

"You've never thought about this. You just think police protect people."

"Well, not all the time. It was scary to see the guard—"

"Or you don't care. He was just someone for you to use to stay alive. A black guy the cops would pounce on so they wouldn't look at the fucking zombie stealing government secrets."

"No, Aysel."

"*No, Aysel*," Aysel said, imitating Z's voice. She looked angrily up at Z. "You're dead, don't you get it? They hate you. You can get burned in a big furnace now as easy as anyone else, easy as any of the rest of us monsters. You're not a person anymore in their eyes, just a thing. Mr. Weber protected you and they're going to hurt him and you don't even seem to think you're responsible!"

"I don't understand what you're talking about," Z said. They felt scared and also angry. "Who's them? Who's 'us monsters'? I'm the only monster here."

Aysel only made a gurgling sound.

Z felt angrier and they felt their voice get meaner. "I don't understand what you think you're talking about. I know people hate me. My whole family is dead! My mother is dead! I lost my friends. My uncle hates me and I'd be homeless if it wasn't for Mrs. Dunnigan." Z paused. "And you have a mom and a house and you feel like a monster, but really it's just that people don't like you. My hair's falling out. You just have pimples and are sad because people call you a lesbian. Well, you *are* a lesbian, so what does it matter anyway? You're going to get out of this stupid town someday and I'm going to be rotting somewhere with my eyes open."

"Go away," Aysel cried out. "I don't have to listen to you."

Z scowled. "Aysel, I thought you were on my side."

Sobs shook Aysel and made her face red and blotchy. She looked dangerous, even crying, Z thought. They sat down on the bathroom floor with her. Eventually Aysel's crying stopped. She began to make little hiccupping noises and then sat up. Z wasn't sure what they should do.

"Do you want any water?" Z asked.

Aysel shook her head, then nodded. Z went to the sink and emptied out the thermos Mrs. Dunnigan had filled with soup. The bits of beef got stuck in the drain. Z rinsed out the container and filled it with water and gave it to Aysel, who drank deeply.

Z felt like they had run their mouth off, but they didn't want to say anything else, even if it was to apologize.

They got up together without talking and left the bathroom. Both of them looked really awful, Z realized. They wandered out of the school and went out into the parking lot. There were still cars there, because of various sports practices happening. Aysel dropped her bag on the cement so she could put on her coat.

"I hope we're not enemies," Z said.

"No," Aysel said. "I'm mad at you because you're dumb, that's all."

"I'm sorry." Z paused. "I know it's my fault Mr. Weber's in jail. But that doesn't mean the police are after you."

"It gets to me more than most people. All this stuff with the werewolves and then the Pagan thing and now Mr. Weber getting arrested."

"Why?" Z asked. They walked to the bus stop and waited for the bus. It was a long time before Aysel answered.

"I guess I *should* trust you," Aysel said, but then she didn't say anything else. Z didn't want her to cry again so they didn't press her. The bus came.

"I have to go home alone today, I think," Aysel said.

"Okay," Z said. They were sure that Aysel was never going to speak to them again.

But then Aysel scribbled something on a piece of paper against the wall of the bus stop and handed it to Z. Then, unexpectedly, she lurched forward and hugged Z hard. Z was sure they felt one of their ribs crack, but they didn't want to spoil the moment, so they hugged Aysel back.

After Aysel was gone, they looked at the note.

I'm a werewolf, the note said. *Sorry and stuff.*

6

Aysel felt open and weak and empty. Resting her head against the frosty window of the bus, she watched as Z and the bus stop retreated into the distance.

At least Z knew now, Aysel thought. Whatever else happened, Z would know they were in the same boat, and that Aysel had been in it before Z's parents had ever driven over an icy patch.

Aysel was worried about Mr. Weber. She remembered when he had first guessed that she was a werewolf, when she was sick at a full moon and came to school late with pine needles in her hair. He had taken her aside after school and had a very long, kind conversation with her about how life was going to be hard for her and how he would protect her secret with his life.

Aysel pulled at her sweater and at her hair. Across the bus from her, an old man was staring at her. Aysel turned away so she didn't have to make eye contact. He was old and had pale dry wrinkled skin and pale blue eyes. Couldn't anyone tell old men not to stare at fat girls on buses? Couldn't anyone just leave her alone?

Obviously not.

"What day is it?" someone asked the old man across from Aysel. Aysel glanced over. The person talking was an anxious-looking teenager with a huge backpack and greasy hair. The old man ignored him.

"Hey man," the boy repeated. He had an awkward, greasy mustache. "What's the date?"

The man looked up. "Please don't bother me," he said. But he wasn't doing anything, like reading or listening to music. He had just been staring uncomfortably at Aysel before the boy spoke to him.

"I just asked the day." The boy started to move toward a seat near the front of the bus.

"It's the eighteenth of February," Aysel said loudly.

"Thanks," the teenager said. He laughed nervously. "There's going to be a supermoon on the eleventh of March." He paused, as if waiting for someone to ask what it was. "It's when the moon gets closer to Earth than other times. It gets really big in the sky. It's going to be intense."

Aysel looked at him with interest. "Oh, you know about it too?"

"Yeah," the boy said, looking surprised. "I'm really into that stuff. Really into like, the uh, the energy."

Aysel smirked, feeling very hollow. "Yeah. Me too."

"Nice eye makeup," the boy said, smiling. "You look like you're too cool for this town." Aysel wasn't sure if he was being sarcastic.

"I was crying all afternoon because someone I know is dead and someone else might die soon," she said.

"I know how that is," the boy said. "I'm sorry."

When Aysel got home she made herself a cup of tea and watched the pigment diffuse through the hot water and refused to watch the news. She painted her fingernails black instead. She wanted to cut her hair. She touched the split ends and curled them around her fingers. Aysel took a pair of scissors and held them near her hair, hesitated, and put them back. She felt like it wasn't the right time for some reason.

She lay in her bed and wished she had a cat.

"What's wrong?" Azra asked when she got home.

"Mr. Weber is suspected of stealing from the Censored Materials Division of the Willamette University library. He didn't do it. He's in jail."

Azra's hands shook a little but she went to Aysel and tried to comfort her. Aysel felt like clinging to her mother but didn't because she knew it wouldn't accomplish anything. She sat up and moved away instead.

"I think it'll be okay," Aysel lied.

"I heard about that case today. It sounds like the police take it very seriously. They've even put the search of Archie Pagan's house on hold."

"I know," Aysel said. "Mr. Weber's the only good person at my school. He was going to help me enter the robotics competition."

"It just shows what a racist mess this place is."

"I want to leave Salem," Aysel moaned.

"The place I mean isn't Salem. It's the whole country. Maybe Earth."

At seven, Aysel heard her mother turning on the stove top with a click and a hiss and setting down the heavy pot onto the grange. After a few minutes, the smell of onions frying filled the air.

"Can you go get some kale from the yard?" Azra called from the kitchen. "I'm making *Karalahana çorbası*."

"Couldn't you make the chicken dish?" Aysel yelled back. "We have that chicken in the fridge."

"I know what I'm doing with the chicken. I'm going to make it this Friday. We have to use the kale."

Aysel went to put on her shoes. She braced herself against the cold and tripped down into the dark garden with the big colander and a pair of scissors. The porch light came on as she moved down the steps into the mud. She cut the leaves from kale plants until the bowl was full. When she went back inside, Azra had added the tomato paste and peppers to the onions.

"I got the kale," Aysel said.

"Now chop it up. Remember, fine little strips."

"I still wish we were having the chicken," Aysel said, but she pulled the cutting board out from behind the dish drainer and took a knife from the drawer.

Azra shrugged. "I cook for you and I make sure you eat good things. It's a stew night. Pretend you're in Trabzon with my family. Pretend you're going to cook this to impress your *anneanne.* She would like it if she knew you could cook so well."

Aysel almost started to cry then, but she managed to stop herself. She felt the tears stinging her eyes.

Azra frowned. "Your eyes are all red." She brushed her hair out of her eye and reached out with a smooth soft dry hand and did the same with Aysel's hair. Aysel swallowed hard to keep from sobbing.

"I'm fine, Mom."

They ate dinner on the couch, Aysel trying not to drip onto the red fabric upholstery. They rarely used the table, except on weekends. They usually watched TV, but Azra didn't want to, so they just looked at each other. Aysel ate slowly.

"How is school going?" Azra asked Aysel. "Besides Mr. Weber."

"I got an A on the Spanish test."

"That's good. I still wish you had taken French. It would be so much more useful if we ever visited my parents."

"Well, I'm taking Spanish and I'm getting A's. I don't know what you have to complain about."

"So school is good? You're doing well in everything?"

"I'm doing well, but everyone hates me," Aysel said.

Azra looked upset. "Does your friend Zee hate you? She seemed nice."

Aysel began to cry into her dinner.

Azra looked distressed. "Oh no, Aysel. Aysel," she said, "I didn't mean to upset you. Oh dear." Her hands fluttered. "Be strong, Aysel. Stop crying."

Aysel sniffed loudly and blinked hard. "Mom, I did something really stupid. I—I'm really sorry, Mom. I'm really, really sorry, but I did something really stupid."

Azra settled back like a cat into the pillows on her end of the couch. She set her bowl on the table behind her. "What is it?" She looked tense and nervous suddenly.

"I told Z." Aysel made an odd snuffly noise in her throat.

"Told her what?" But Azra had already guessed, Aysel could see.

Aysel sobbed loudly, for a long time. Her wail crested up toward the ceiling.

"Aysel, what did you tell her?"

"I told Z I'm a werewolf."

Azra's eyes went wide. She sat frozen on the couch.

"I told—I'm sorry, Mom. I just thought I should. They're my friend. They needed to know why I was upset today, and I was upset because Z didn't understand how I felt like a monster."

"What?" Azra's voice was almost a yell, which was odd because Aysel had spoken softly. Azra's face was drawn and pale. "What?"

Aysel started to cry again.

Azra took a few deep breaths. "Aysel, you told her—Zee? You told Zee?"

Aysel choked on her own spit and coughed. "I'm sorry, Mom. I had been really mean to them because I was worried Mr. Weber would be hurt, especially if they got it out of him that he'd been protecting me. And Z thought I was mad at them, so I had to explain . . ." Aysel felt herself swallow a sob and her eyes clouded with tears.

"What happened when you told her?" Azra asked intently.

Aysel paused. "Nothing."

"Nothing? What did your friend say?"

"I ran away after I told them. I didn't want to see."

Azra put her hand to her face. "Of course you ran away," she said.

"What? I was scared!"

"With all this nonsense with the police happening, it's not a good time for anyone to find out about you. I'm not mad at you," she added, again touching Aysel's shoulder, "but *think*."

"I mean," Aysel said, "I don't want to get all paranoid." She was trying to talk herself down.

"People think werewolves are dangerous, Aysel. You are dangerous in their mind."

"I know."

"The police who take you won't give you back to me. I could go to jail for hiding you from them. You'll go into a treatment facility until you are eighteen and be under probation for the rest of your life. With all this happening right now, it couldn't be a worse time. The police think there is some kind of werewolf radical cult that killed Archie Pagan. They're looking for unregistered wolves to blame. I never wanted that for you. I wanted you to be safe. I wanted to protect you. We've worked so hard to do this."

"I know! I said I'm sorry! You've told me a million times already. I don't need to be any more scared than I am!"

Azra looked away and made no reply. Aysel felt embarrassed of her anger. She got up and made tea and brought it back without speaking. They turned on the television and watched a competitive housecleaning show. The television distracted from the fear both of them felt. Gradually, the atmosphere calmed.

"I'm sorry," Azra said, over the noise of a power saw on the television. "You're right. You didn't need that outburst from me. I'm being stupid, darling. I should be tougher than this."

"It's too late for that," Aysel said.

Aysel got up and walked past her mother. She carried her plate to the sink. Then she went into her room and turned on her music as loud as it would go. She didn't come out to brush her teeth until after she was sure Azra was asleep.

In the morning Aysel did not want to go to school. She covered her head with the pillows and sat and felt the comforter curled around her. Her room was dark and she could hear the wind outside rattling the trees against one another. Her alarm went off twice and so she arose, scowling.

Azra had already left for work and Aysel dressed in a hurry.

The gym teacher hadn't arrived and Tommy was getting shoved into the big trash bin by the art room when Aysel finally reached class, ten minutes late. Nobody was helping him; the other students were gathered near the doors to the gym, talking among themselves like nothing was happening.

"What are you doing?" Aysel demanded, running over. Tommy's feet stuck out of the bin. The rest of him was submerged in wood scraps and old charcoal drawings.

"We're showing him what kind of treatment he's going to get when Fey Regulation comes for him," Charley Salt said, turning around. "They take fey and put them in these big silver boxes so they can't get out and destroy society."

"Why is it always you?" Aysel asked. "Can't you stop picking on someone for maybe two seconds?"

"He's a fairy," Charley said. "In more than one way," he snickered. "I heard his granddad was born in this Celtic circle and changed into five animals a day."

"Oh, okay, yeah," Aysel said loudly. A few students who were waiting by the gym looked over. "Harassing him because of his relatives and because you think he's gay. That's really cute, Charley." She wasn't scared of Charley today. She was too tired and too angry.

"I think it's realistic. He needs to know what the world has in store for him. I'm only helping."

"Maybe you want to tell the nurse how realistic you thought it was after I break your nose. It's only fair that I get a shot at yours, since you did mine." Aysel rolled up her sleeves and felt the hair on her arms and head rise with crackling electric current.

"Chill out, Tay-her."

"You chill out, you toad!" Aysel said. She stepped forward solidly and swung at him. Her fist made contact with his temple, and his head swung around sideways. She kicked him in the gut and he doubled over. His friends rushed over to him and tried to haul him to his feet.

She went over to the bin where Tommy was. "Are you okay, Tommy?"

"I'm fine."

Aysel was too short to lift Tommy out, so she tipped the bin over as gently as she could. It clanged against the ground.

"Jesus," she heard Bill Oswald say behind her, as she and Tommy turned to head back to the gymnasium. "If Tommy's a fairy, she's a troll."

"Is she a dyke?" Neil Trotter said. He laughed nervously.

Aysel wheeled around to face Bill and Neil. Her hair flew out behind her, a black frizzy wave of sparking static. She stormed forward, her fists ready to hit something again. Punching Charley had been the most fun thing she had done all month.

"Oh shit, here she comes," said Neil.

"Yeah, here I come. What did you just say about me?"

"I said you were a dyke. You don't even look like a girl. You look like a whale with eyebrows."

Aysel grinned. "Well, Neil, joke's on you. I *am* a dyke and I think it rules."

They all stared at her, then laughed dumbly.

"Are you serious?" Bill asked. "You're a lesbian?"

"I am serious," Aysel said. "I am a big mean whale dyke!" She shouted this last phrase loud enough for the people by the gym to hear it. "I'm hairy and fat and have huge fists and I will break your jaw if you mess with people I care about!" She shook her head to get her hair out of her eyes and her mouth. She felt like she might start shooting fire out of her eyes.

"You care about Tommy Wodewose?" Bill asked incredulously.

Neil laughed. "Do you lick each other's"—he held up his fingers in a V and stuck his tongue out of his mouth.

She launched herself at Neil and punched him in the teeth.

That, of course, was the moment the substitute gym teacher chose to appear from inside the school with his coffee and keys, and of course the only thing he saw was Aysel trying to pin Neil on the ground and punching him in the face.

"This is the earliest in the day I've ever seen anyone be sent to the principal's office," Mr. Bentwood said thirty minutes later.

Aysel stared at him and did not speak. She had a bruise near her eye and a split lip, but was otherwise whole.

"This is the first time you've been in here for disciplinary issues, Aysel," Mr. Bentwood said, sighing a little as if he regretted that Aysel had gotten into a fight. Aysel knew he didn't care.

"Sorry, sir," she said as politely as possible.

"What possessed you to get into such a fight, Aysel? You're not a stupid girl."

"Charley and his friends were harassing Tommy Wodewose, sir. I stepped in because they shoved him in a trash can."

"Let's not talk nonsense," Mr. Bentwood said quickly. "I'm sure they did nothing like that. Don't spread rumors, Aysel."

"I'm telling the truth." Aysel sucked on her split lip, tasting the blood.

Mr. Bentwood looked seriously down at Aysel, his skinny face hollow and dour. "Charles Salt and his friends are good boys," he said. "I'm sure they and Tommy were only having fun, like boys do."

Aysel scowled up at him and stayed quiet. She knew better than to contradict Mr. Bentwood directly. He had a grisly expression and tiny crumbs of something in the grasslike red fur on his chin.

"Perhaps you misunderstood the situation, Aysel," Mr. Bentwood said slimily. "After all, maybe it looked as if Tommy and Charles were fighting. No adults were there, after all. It must have been very upsetting."

"Maybe," Aysel said, sensing an out.

"In that case, I won't suspend you. This is the first time a disciplinary situation with you has involved violence, and I admit that it is partially the fault of our faculty for not being present to supervise."

"Thank you," Aysel said, looking at her shoes. The early morning light shone through the window. The streetlights outside still hadn't gone out. The day had barely begun.

"I still have to call your mother," Mr. Bentwood said. He smiled primly and shuffled the papers on his desk.

"She's at work, so she won't be able to come talk to you," Aysel said.

"Well, it's school policy." Mr. Bentwood shrugged at Aysel apologetically, but he was smiling. He reached over and dialed the phone. Aysel made her face as blank as possible, because she didn't want to look scared. What would her mother think?

Azra was indeed busy, and did not pick up her phone. A crackling voicemail message sounded distantly on the other end, and then there was a beep.

"Hello?" Mr. Bentwood said. "Mrs. Tahir, I am calling about your daughter, Aysel. She got into a fight today with some boys before first period. I'm calling to let you know that this has happened so you can speak with Aysel, as it was her first offense and I am choosing not to suspend her. I have to inform you that if this continues to happen, she will be suspended and you may be obliged to attend a hearing before the Court for Magical Juvenile Affairs. That's all. Have a nice day. Goodbye."

Aysel knew the message would horrify Azra.

"Are you all right, Aysel?" Mr. Bentwood asked, his yellow teeth showing.

"I can't really go to court, can I?" Aysel asked.

"Not for this, Aysel. But be careful how you deal with conflict in the future."

"I can't help getting into fights that other people start," Aysel said, trying not to make this statement sound too contrary. There was something tricky about using polite tones of voice and Aysel wasn't sure she had gotten the hang of it yet.

"Careful, Aysel. Charley doesn't see it that way."

Aysel looked blankly at the principal and then turned and looked blankly out the window.

"Aysel, is there anything going on at home?" Mr. Bentwood tried to make his voice soft and sympathetic.

"What?" Aysel asked. The question had come from nowhere and it surprised her.

"Well, is everything okay at home?" Mr. Bentwood asked. "Sometimes when children have trouble dealing with their anger, it means that their home situations may not be the best. I want to let you know I won't tell anyone what you say to me here. You can trust me."

"My mom is a great mom," Aysel said angrily. "There's nothing wrong with her or with my home."

"I'm sure she is," Mr. Bentwood said. He looked taken aback by Aysel's immediate and intense defense of her mother. He drummed his fingers on the desk. "Still, uh, Aysel. If you want to talk about anything, I'm here, and uh, the school counselor Mr. Peach is also here if you want to talk to him. I can make you an appointment with him, if you like. He's here Wednesdays and Fridays from eleven thirty until one, and you can talk to him about anything. Your feelings, your family . . ."

"Are you going to make me have an appointment with a therapist?" Aysel asked.

"No, of course not," Mr. Bentwood said carefully.

"I won't then," Aysel said.

"Okay," Mr. Bentwood said, trying to sound accommodating. It did not work. He tapped both hands firmly on the desk. "Well," he said, "if you're sure you don't need to talk, Aysel, you can go back to class."

"Gym class is almost over," Aysel said. "I can just wait in the hall," she added as a worried expression passed over the principal's face.

"Yes, all right," Mr. Bentwood said. "You can do that."

Aysel got up and left. She let the door shut loudly behind her.

It was then she remembered the other reason she had been grumpy this morning: she had told Z her secret.

Aysel looked for Z after second period. She couldn't find Z in the bathrooms or the library, though, and the bell rang before she could check back by the dumpsters, so she went to third period.

Aysel didn't think that Z would outright reject her. Or—maybe she did. She wasn't sure what she thought. Everything was so convoluted. Aysel knew how people thought about werewolves. They thought werewolves were sick. Z was a monster too, and so should understand that not all the prejudice against werewolves was based on fact, but they wouldn't understand everything, and they might say something awful. Aysel didn't know how she could stand it if Z did that.

Aysel's pen shook in her hand and she could barely write during class.

By lunch, Aysel didn't feel like looking for Z anymore. She also didn't feel hungry.

At the end of fifth period, after forgetting to draw the sigils from the board in her notebook, Aysel tried to get up but was shaking too much. She sat down hard on the lowest step of the staircase and stared at the frosted glass window and the wall. It took her a few minutes to pull herself up enough to go to Spanish class. She walked down the halls, pulling hair out of her face and lint off her sweater.

Z was in class, staring straight ahead. Aysel froze in the doorway and almost turned around again, but made herself take the few steps to her desk. She sat down and stared resolutely at Z.

"Hi," she said grimly.

Z turned and half smiled. Aysel had a hard time figuring out if there was anything odd about the smile or if she was just being paranoid.

"How are you?" Aysel heard herself ask from far away.

"I'm glad you're in school today," Z said.

In Spanish class that day, they all had to walk around the

room with little cards that had Spanish present progressive verbs on them and define them for each other. Z couldn't really stand up and walk around easily, and so would lean on one desk or another and wait for someone to approach them. Nobody did except for Aysel and Mrs. Cortez, the teacher. Z didn't seem to mind too much.

After class Z and Aysel went into the hall with everyone else. People bobbed around them, hurrying to their next class, not paying attention to the way Z leaned against the wall or Aysel's black eye. Z turned to Aysel and hugged her abruptly. Is this weird? Aysel wondered. She realized she had hugged Z yesterday, so maybe it made sense that Z would hug her back.

"Wow, okay," she said aloud.

"I just—I'm glad you're here. I'm glad you're my friend," Z said.

"Why?" she asked.

"Because you're great," Z said, rocking back onto their heels. Their yellowing eyes shone and they smiled with teeth that were too long because their gums were receding. "I hope I am friends with you for a long time."

Aysel felt tears coming to her eyes. "You too, buddy," she said, trying to make it sound sarcastic so it wouldn't sound too soppy.

They went to Mrs. Dunnigan's place after school that day.

"Is it all right if I tell her?" Z asked as they and Aysel walked toward the house. Aysel and Z had decided not to take the bus so they could talk privately.

"That I've got problems with the moon, you mean?"

"Yeah."

Aysel considered. Azra had made Aysel promise that she would never tell anyone about her lycanthropy. This secret was the backbone of her life. She remembered how many times they had moved because her mother had thought someone knew about her. "No," she said. "I told you because I trust you. I'm sure Mrs. Dunnigan is great, but even great people don't act so swell around werewolves. I don't trust her yet. She might not be okay with it."

"I guess so. I mean, she had a rock thrown through her bookstore window because she has a werewolf section that has books by werewolves, and she had a werewolf author come speak once," Z said.

"Oh," Aysel said. "Well, cool. I'm still not going to tell her."

"Do you ever think that you could change someone's mind about werewolves by telling them?"

Aysel laughed.

"Why are you laughing?" Z asked.

"Well, I mean, it doesn't work like that," Aysel said.

"Like how?"

"One time when we were living in California after my parents broke up, there was this guy who started dating my mom. He was from Texas. My mom liked him. But I remember one time he was at our house, and I heard him tell my mom that she wasn't like most Muslim women. He told her she was smarter than them. Like that was a compliment."

"Oh," Z said.

"So it's kind of like that with werewolves, too. Even if you prove that you're human," Aysel said to Z, "they just think you're the exception, and it just allows them to contrast you with everyone else. Someone might say, 'Oh, sure, you're a good werewolf, you aren't like the other ones.'"

The trees were icy and their branches were silver spears against the sky, except for the pine and conifer trees, which were black and prickly. Aysel tracked pine needles into the apartment. Z turned around and gestured for her to remove them. Aysel felt smaller without the rubber soles giving her an extra half-inch in height. The apartment smelled like cats.

Mrs. Dunnigan was sitting and crocheting something which looked like a very large potholder in black yarn.

"Are you dears all right to study quietly for a while?" Mrs. Dunnigan asked them as they came in. "I have a terrible headache. I don't think I could possibly watch the news or listen to music."

"That's all right, Mrs. Dunnigan," Z said. "We'll just be in my room. Thanks."

They sat on the floor and stared at the ceiling in Z's room. There were mysterious flecks of blue on the ceiling, and Z had never asked Mrs. Dunnigan where they were from or what they were made of.

They lay in reverent silence, a tribute to the blue spots. They did not do any homework.

Aysel volunteered to cook when she saw that Mrs. Dunnigan was sitting on the couch with a compress on her head. Rice and corn and salt and tomatoes and carrots fried in butter. It was all right.

"So, Aysel," Mrs. Dunnigan said at dinner, "Z tells me you're gay?"

Aysel made a small coughing noise. She looked up at Mrs. Dunnigan cautiously. "Yeah," she said. She looked at Z. When had that come up?

Mrs. Dunnigan smiled. "That's so nice that you folks today can come out so young." She looked very friendly, Aysel thought, very motherly.

"Mmm," said Aysel. She looked at Z sternly, and Z looked away with an expression of embarrassment. Aysel's mother still didn't know Aysel was gay, and Mrs. Dunnigan knowing made her feel like it was only a matter of time before that uncomfortable conversation with Azra had to happen. Word would surely get around.

"When I was a girl it was hard. Lesbians weren't supposed to have happy lives. It's so nice that they can now."

"I'm not so sure my life will be that happy," Aysel said.

"New legislation is being passed all the time. That anti-gay bill last year failed. In ten years you may be able to get married."

"Aren't—I mean, weren't you . . ." Aysel trailed off. "I mean, your name's Mrs. Dunnigan, right?"

"Hmm? Yes, it is, dear. My first name's Alondra, though, and you can call me that."

"She wants to know why your name is Mrs. if you're a lesbian," Z said. Aysel glared at them.

Mrs. Dunnigan laughed. "Oh!" she said. "Well, that's because I married a shapeshifter in Ireland." She paused to laugh some more. "That was back in the fifties, and Ireland was getting sorted out, you know."

Aysel didn't know. "Right," she said.

"What a story it is, when I think about it!" Mrs. Dunnigan grinned. "I had just moved to Ireland, and I met Cassie and fell in love. She was very attractive. Since she was a shapeshifter she couldn't get very many jobs when Ireland was under British control, but the new government was very eager to hire people they thought represented Gaelic magic, and she helped scientists with some of the deep-sea diving work by becoming things like seals. All the people in the ecology department knew how useful she was so they paid her lots of money."

"I never knew that," Z said. They looked at Mrs. Dunnigan as if they were reevaluating her.

"I don't talk about it much. Americans are a lot like British in how they look at fey," Mrs. Dunnigan said. "Irish are better."

"I didn't realize they hired fey anywhere, especially back then."

"Because of how new the Irish government was, and how much druidic magic was valued there as part of the

Republic's nationalism, they were passing some very progressive laws. People like selkies were getting citizen rights, you know."

"Selkies?" Aysel asked. "What are those? I've never heard of them."

"Like werewolves, in a way. Related to fey but not as powerful as shapeshifters. In reverse, though," Mrs. Dunnigan said. "They live as seals most of their lives but come ashore and take on human forms and take off their sealskin. Usually only long enough to mate or to bask in the sun—once or twice a month or even less. If a human hides the sealskin from them, they can stay human the rest of their lives. If they get the skin back, they have to return to the water. It does of course make for a very complicated bureaucratic situation. Some selkies like to come ashore, and some avoid people and don't want to be included in legislation. Selkies can live a very long time and come ashore for only a little while. Anyway, the Irish government tried to make it easier for them to live as humans if they wanted to."

"Wow," Aysel said.

"So you see it was very different than here. One of those things that sort of got thrown in with a lot of other things like that was that shapeshifters could marry either male or female people. Cassie and I just screamed when that one got through."

"People approved that?"

"Well, yes. Shapeshifters can be male or female, you know, biologically, whatever that means to you, so even though Cassie spent most of the time living as a woman, the law said, oh, well, she could be a husband if she felt like it, so they let me marry her."

"That's so cool," Aysel said.

"They don't even have that in America, do they?" Z asked.

"Definitely not after Reagan," Mrs. Dunnigan said. She had finished with her dinner, and stood up. "No, definitely not. They don't even let shapeshifters walk around in the sun."

"What happened to Cassie?" Aysel asked, looking over at Mrs. Dunnigan as she cleared her plate.

"Oh, well, we moved here to study the water dragons in the Pacific. We hid her past so she wouldn't be incarcerated as a fey, even though things weren't as bad then as they are now. She lived to be quite old. And then she passed. When we lived here we weren't officially married, legally, but I still had her name because my passport from Ireland had it on there and we called ourselves Mrs. and Mrs."

Mrs. Dunnigan stood at the sink looking sad for a few seconds, and sighed. Aysel thought she was just preparing to say something, but then the silence dragged on a moment too long, and Aysel realized there was nothing more to be said on the topic. There was something that couldn't be talked about. Mrs. Dunnigan eventually turned the faucet on and began washing dishes.

Aysel helped to clear the table.

"Did the situation with Mr. Weber get sorted out, dear?"

Mrs. Dunnigan asked Z as she pumped rosemary-scented dish soap onto the sponge.

Aysel turned away so that nobody would see her facial expression. She was worried she wouldn't be able to control her face. She looked out the window instead, at the dark cold yard where several cats still circled, waiting until the last possible second to show humility and ask to be let in.

Z frowned. "He's still not in school," they said.

"He could be dead," Aysel added in a monotone.

"Or he might have skipped town," Mrs. Dunnigan said brightly.

After they cleared the plates, Aysel and Z finally started their homework. Aysel had gotten out her notebook and was looking at a page about Magical Summons of minor objects. She had to copy out the pentacle and practice summoning pencils from across a room. Magic homework was always just about the dullest thing in the world. Sometimes it seemed like school didn't teach students magic so much as slow them down and mire them in busywork so they would never move on to the good stuff. Aysel tried to draw the pentacle. Her pen jittered and left splotches on the paper. She set it down, frustrated. Z was also having trouble.

"I can't hold the pencil hard enough," they said. "My handwriting's barely legible."

Aysel looked over. Z's handwriting was indeed very faint on the page. "Maybe use a darker pen? A fountain pen?"

"I'd just spill ink everywhere."

Aysel drew the pentacle again and tried to practice the spell they were learning in class. She summoned pencils and hair clips and bottles of clove oil from the bathroom. They made small buzzing noises when they appeared in the middle of the inky circle. A cat nestled on Aysel's lap, and she smelled the clove oil. For a moment she was calm.

"They say they found evidence that Archie Pagan treated werewolves after all," Mrs. Dunnigan commented nonchalantly. She was reading the paper.

Aysel spluttered, "I didn't know they were still investigating that." She wondered if Mrs. Dunnigan knew about her. How would she have found out?

"It was covert, I suppose," Mrs. Dunnigan said. She squinted at the newsprint. "Something too about a werewolf terrorist ring they're pretending exists. Some kind of house of anarchist werewolves. Which is nonsense."

"Wow," Aysel said. She felt herself begin to sweat.

"It's really going to put everyone on edge," Mrs. Dunnigan said. "There haven't been any new werewolves in the state for years because of the controls on that kind of thing. Nobody knows how to deal with it. They just shoot them all."

7

"Where are the police going to be, though? The national parks, right?" Z asked on Saturday March 2nd, a week or so before the next full moon.

"Yeah, that's what they're saying," Aysel agreed. "They said that they're going to monitor the parks, and the patches of forest out by the winery and the archery range."

"But that's private property out there, right? The police can't do that without a warrant."

"I guess." Aysel looked doubtful. She drummed her fingers on the hard ground next to her. They were sitting on Aysel's mother's back porch, looking out onto the garden, in which kale poked green leaves up despite the frost which had overwhelmed the ground. Azra was out somewhere doing errands and wouldn't be back for a couple of hours, so Aysel had dug up a pack of Azra's cigarettes and she and Z were trying to smoke them. Z was mostly using the cigarettes to burn marks onto their hands and lips.

"It'll be okay," Z promised, patting Aysel's hand gently

and then pulling it back, worrying it was more disgusting than comforting. Z's skin flaked off in patches now.

Z felt themselves growing more and more tired every day. It seemed to take more energy to do things, and their joints were always stiff. They tried to sit down and rest as much as possible. They sometimes felt like something hot was leaking out of the spell mark on their chest, and was sure it was the spell unraveling. Mrs. Dunnigan also had them drinking huge amounts of salt water with garlic, in the hopes that it would pickle them or kill bacteria, but this made Z feel bloated and dehydrated and ill. They weren't sure Mrs. Dunnigan really knew what she was doing. They looked at themselves in the mirror each day and every time felt more distant, more removed.

On the next Thursday morning, though, Aysel came up to Z with a look on her face that said something terribly important had happened. When Aysel's moods were very strong, she did that to you. You could sense the magic coming off her in bright waves of heat that shot out right at your eyes and heart.

"Mr. Weber's back," Aysel said breathlessly. "I haven't seen him yet, he must be in the staff lounge or something. But his car's in the parking lot."

Z leapt to their feet and hugged Aysel. "That's fantastic," they said. "Oh my gosh."

Aysel seemed exhilarated and nervous. "I have to go talk to him right away," she said.

"We have class," Z said.

"I don't care," Aysel said. "I'm going to his room to wait until he comes in."

"Aysel, he has class."

Aysel looked disconcerted. "Well—I'll talk to him anyway," Aysel said. The bell rang as she started off toward the science room. Z watched her go. They hoped she'd be able to find him and talk to him and satisfy herself that he was okay and not dead.

But at lunch, Aysel looked morose. "He was on the way to his car. He's gone already. He looked really bad. He said he just came to get papers. He barely said anything and he told me he couldn't talk to me. He's not teaching today. I wish I knew what happened to him."

"Well," Z said, "at least we know he's alive. And you'll see him tomorrow or whenever he comes back."

Aysel made a face. "I don't know," she said. "It's a full-moon week, and it's worse than usual. It's because of the supermoon. I feel like I'm getting sick right now. Cramps and . . . I don't know if I can come to school tomorrow."

Sure enough, Aysel wasn't there the next day. Z waited until lunch in case Aysel had just stayed home for the morning, but at eleven she still wasn't there.

Mr. Weber was at his desk, grading student assignments he was slowly going through, moving papers from one pile to another as he went.

"Hi," Z said. Mr. Weber looked up, and started. Z wasn't sure if it was because he didn't want to see them, or just because they looked exceptionally terrifying and dead now.

"Z. How are you?"

"I'm tired," Z said truthfully. "Aysel wanted me to say hi for her."

Mr. Weber gave a nervous, exhausted smile. "Tell her I say hi too. I'm looking forward to the robotics contest in June."

"She wants you to call her. She's worried about what they did to you."

Mr. Weber looked up and frowned, and did not reply.

"I am too," Z said. "I'm sorry for what happened. I never meant for it to. It's why I tried to go on my own."

"Shh," Mr. Weber said. He looked around nervously, as if someone in the room might be watching him. "We can't talk here. Z, I understand. I don't blame you."

"What did they do to you? Did they torture you? Are you hurt?" The questions spilled out of Z before they could think about what they were asking.

"I can't tell you that, Z." His voice sounded like it was coming from a great distance, from some cold pit in his belly. He was weaker-looking, too, his dark skin dry and unhealthy-looking. He was not chewing gum, for the first time ever that Z remembered. He no longer looked like he could survive anything, as he had the last time Z saw him—in fact, it didn't look like he was strong enough to survive much at all. There were no fresh bruises on his face, but there was a long pink gash diagonally across it, from forehead to the left corner of his lip. It was healing, but still deep and nasty-looking. Z felt a profound terror the longer they looked at it.

"Why not? They let you go. They must know that you're innocent. If they tor—"

"Please be quiet, Z. I'd rather not talk about this." There was that nervousness again, as if Mr. Weber thought that one of the lizards in the cages around the room was a spy.

"Mr. Weber, what did they do to you? What happens when they arrest you?"

"I can't talk to you about this, Z." Mr. Weber's voice was louder now, firm.

"Mr. Weber, tell me. Please." Z felt a little hysterical but made themselves speak calmly. "You have to tell me. You owe me that much. I'm going to be taken eventually. I'm losing it, I'm going to go crazy."

"Don't talk like that, Z," Mr. Weber said unconvincingly. He looked deeply pained. Somewhere in there is the nice teacher who'd do anything to protect me, Z thought.

"Are *you* okay?"

"I can't speak to you, Z," Mr. Weber said. "Things have changed. I'm being watched. It isn't a good idea to talk to each other." He got up and walked to the door and down the hall. Z watched him go and then got up and limped after him but couldn't keep up. Mr. Weber walked quickly, as if he was escaping a monster. They thought of the long gash across Mr. Weber's face again. It looked like it had been made by a single long, hooked claw. Z felt a pang of guilt.

Z had to go to the bathroom. They felt like they were going to be sick. They knew that all the bathrooms would be full of people, though, since it was lunch hour and lots of older girls would be gossiping and fixing their makeup and lots of the younger girls would be fixing their hair or hiding from friends. Z didn't want to walk past them all to get to the stalls. They thought of the places in the school they could run to instead, and decided on the nurse's bathroom.

Z turned around to walk back down the hall toward the nurse's office, and was suddenly face to face with Mr. Holmes.

"Sorry," Z said, and tried to walk around him, but Mr. Holmes advanced slightly on Z and they found themselves backed into the hallway that led to one of the janitor's closets.

"I couldn't help but overhear that exchange with Mr. Weber," Mr. Holmes said.

"You were eavesdropping," Z half asked.

"Anyone in the hall could hear you," Mr. Holmes said. This wasn't really true, Z thought. If you were in the hall, the din of the distant lunchroom echoed down the linoleum floors and stopped you from hearing anything.

"I'm a student here like anyone else," Z said. "I was just talking to Mr. Weber because he'd been gone. I was hoping he was okay."

Mr. Holmes leaned one arm against the wall. "What concerns me about this, Susan," he said, "is that you seem to be pulling people in positions of power onto your side to defend you, and involving the faculty of the school in your personal life. This feels deeply inappropriate to me, and I may have to discuss this with Mr. Bentwood. You have already managed to get one rather gullible member of the staff arrested on charges of attempted necromancy. This seems to go against your promise—your blood oath—to not practice necromancy while enrolled in this school."

"He hasn't been charged with attempted necromancy," Z said angrily.

"Susan, I overheard your conversation just now, and it worries me," Mr. Holmes continued. "What you said in there, about feeling as if you are going to lose it, go crazy, decay—if that really is the case, I do not think you should be coming to school. That really does present a risk to other students."

"I'm not a risk. I'm just worried because the police do stuff like what they did to Mr. Weber to people who aren't even monsters."

"Susan, you have already begun to decay. I can see that. Everyone can. If you really are concerned with the welfare of humans surrounding you, you will remove yourself from school and seek institutionalization to control what's happening to you."

"I'm not dissoluting," Z said loudly.

"Okay," Mr. Holmes said. "I may still voice my concerns about this to Mr. Bentwood. My job as a teacher is to protect students. What I just heard, and what I have read concerning the library incident, suggests you may present a danger to other students. Now, perhaps that danger is not apparent yet, but you seem to already know it could grow."

"I'm worried about falling apart, about losing my mind, not about killing anyone," Z said. "I'm worried about my physical disabilities. I'm not going to eat anyone."

"The undead when they lose their minds are murderous, or at least very unpredictable. It's like asking if it's okay for us to ignore someone on cocaine or heroin. It's unsafe. If I see that you are decaying, losing lucidity—then I will contact the police. If I become aware that your guardian is so incompetent that you need to ask teachers at the school to perform her task for her, then I will contact the police. That is my duty."

Z set their chin. "Do what you want," they said. "I'm not doing anything illegal. I'm not doing anything wrong."

"I would advise you to not bring the faculty of this institution into your private troubles, then," Mr. Holmes said. "You and your guardian can handle your medical condition alone."

Z felt like they were about to fall over from shaking so hard. They tried to hold eye contact with Mr. Holmes, but his face was contorted with such intense, dispassionate hate that they couldn't bear to keep looking at him. They looked away behind him, toward the main hallway, trying to think of how to get away from him. It was then that they saw Mr. Weber standing there, watching. Z didn't know how long he had been there, but it must have only been a couple of seconds. Behind him, people passed back and forth on the way to their lockers or to the bathrooms. The light from the hallway illuminated him from behind, so his face was half shadowed. His expression was unreadable. He had a cup of coffee in one hand.

"What are you doing, Jules?" Mr. Weber asked. "What's going on here?"

Mr. Holmes turned around and gave a slight start. "I was just talking to Susan about not pulling you into her . . . precarious situation."

Mr. Weber sipped his coffee and looked at Z very briefly. Then he looked back at Mr. Holmes. "I didn't notice you outside my classroom when I left to get coffee just now."

"I happened to hear," Mr. Holmes said shiftily, "from Rebecca's classroom, where we were meeting. It's my opinion that Susan's matter should be referred to the administration. We are mandated reporters."

"Of abuse, neglect, and self-harm, yes," Mr. Weber said. He pulled himself up and seemed taller. "None of which this student is currently suffering to my knowledge. There's only a medical condition, which is for the moment under control."

"I am concerned," Mr. Holmes started again, but Mr. Weber cut him off.

"Jules, if you want to ask any questions of me, you're welcome to, but please don't pull this student into it."

"Magical beings like her—"

"Are pretty common, on the whole," Mr. Weber said, raising his eyebrows. "I think you know as much as anyone about that, Jules. Anyway, please do not threaten students in the halls. It doesn't really help anyone learn."

Mr. Holmes spluttered, and turned his body away from Z toward Mr. Weber in a gesture of indignation.

It was at that moment that the bell for the end of lunch rang.

"Excuse me," Z said, "I have to get to class." They edged around both men and walked down the hallway, back down toward the front entrance and the lockers. If Mr. Holmes had wanted to grab them and stop them, he could have, but he made no attempt.

But Z did not really want to go to class. They thought of walking and getting their bag, and going up the stairs toward the geometry classroom, and felt like passing out. Their throat was all dry and they were still shaking from what Mr. Holmes had said. They didn't want to stay at school and risk seeing him again before the end of the day. They passed their locker and hesitated. They had to go to class, to prove that they were well. Their hands fumbled with the combination and they pulled out their bag and hefted it onto their back. But then they paused again. No, Z thought, I just can't do it.

At the front office, Z could tell the desk ladies that they needed to leave school, that their head hurt, but then the ladies would look at each other in horror and think Z was about to unhinge their jaw and turn rabid on them, and the news would make its way to Mr. Holmes and Mr. Bentwood by the next morning, and Z would never be allowed to go back to school. Or possibly the police would show up at their door with gasoline and matches.

Z left through the door of the lunchroom, and wasn't noticed. Some classes were held outside in the portables, so some people were walking outside the main building after lunch. Z walked like they were going toward one of the portable buildings until the last second and then turned and walked out between two of the chain-link fences that wound their way around the back of campus. They stumbled down the sidewalk, not sure where they were going.

It was kind of right, what Mr. Holmes said, Z thought. Z was going to fall apart sometime. Everything kept getting messy in their head and they couldn't sleep, and even living people go crazy if they can't sleep. Their legs were stopping and their gut was stopping and they vomited out organs and they couldn't think straight or remember anything. Z didn't have any friends except a werewolf who needed to lie low. Z was messing up Mr. Weber's life and Mrs. Dunnigan's life. And—

My family is dead. My family is dead. My family is dead.

Z looked and saw there was a bus stop on the other side of the road. They didn't see any cars coming, so they started to shuffle, slowly, across the asphalt to the other side. Their foot caught on a stone and they stumbled in the center of the road over the yellow strip and nearly fell over. Z thought for a second that it might be kind of cool to get run down by a car, or a bus. But gravity didn't totally knock them over and they didn't feel like lying down on purpose in the middle of the road, because it wouldn't really be cool to have their skull run over, that wouldn't be a cool way to be truly dead.

They finished crossing and sat on the little bench in the bus stop. The glass in the bus stop had been busted and nobody had fixed it so the wind blew through Z.

What would be—? Z thought. What would be a good way to actually permanently exit? They tried to think. They literally would not be able to hang themselves, or cut their wrists, or anything.

The bus came and Z got on and paid with quarters and rode it for a while without really thinking of where they were going to get off. But then they remembered that this bus line ran sort of close to the cemetery where their grandma was buried, and where their family was buried too—though Z's parents and sisters had been cremated and put in little jars first, so it wasn't really their bodies in the cemetery, just the little dirt jars. They couldn't exactly remember what stop it was, so they pulled the yellow cord too soon and had to stumble-walk aimlessly for a couple of blocks until they recognized a street name. The backpack on their back felt heavy and leaden. They felt a pounding in their head that was solid like a drum or someone tapping the base of their skull with a hammer. It traveled all the way down their spine and up again.

The gates to the cemetery were open during the day and there was a path you could drive down if you were in a car, and Z walked down this path toward the middle of the cemetery. It wound around in this very inefficient way, though, so eventually Z walked off into the wet grass. The sky overhead was overcast but not totally raining. Z looked down at the graves they were walking over. Most of the graves in the graveyard were old-people graves, and a lot of the men had little flags to show they'd served in the military.

The Chilworth family grave site was near one of the corners of the cemetery, near the iron railings that divided it from the surrounding neighborhood. Behind the iron railings, between the cemetery and the sidewalk, was a screen of rhododendrons that didn't belong to anybody. As a consequence you couldn't see this corner of the cemetery from outside, because of all the leathery green leaves in the way. There were eight total Chilworths in the site. Two were relatives Z had never known. Z's grandfather and grandmother had a big stone that they shared, with a picture of an angel on it. Z's father, mother, and sisters had little flat rectangles of stone laid into the grass and dirt, with the little cups of ashes sealed into the stone in bronze or brass or whatever the metal was. Z sat down and looked at the row of stones.

They reached into the dirt with their hands and started to dig. They pulled up the grass bit by bit and then scraped at the matter underneath, which was cold and packed hard. For a second they did not know what they were doing, and then they did. Z wanted to be in the earth. They wanted to lie down next to their family and and pull dirt over themselves and stop doing anything at all, forever. Eventually the worms would eat them entirely through and they would stop thinking, even if they had some kind of magic holding them together. If anyone came to check on them in the dirt when it was discovered they were missing, Z would just hold really still and pretend they were truly dead, and people would leave them alone. More dirt. More dirt. Z used their hands like shovels and raked it aside. A mole, Z thought, I'm like a mole. I'm never coming up, though.

Their fingers were numb and they didn't feel how hard the dirt was at first, until they looked and saw that one of their fingernails had half broken off. Z figured it didn't matter. They wouldn't need their nails anymore. This was an all right thought, but then they realized the finger with the broken nail wasn't useful for digging, and at this rate they weren't going to be able to dig a big enough hole before all their nails broke off. They would be shoveling up dirt with soft rotten stumps. Z sat still for a second, thinking about this, and then decided the solution was to use their shoe. They pried it off their cold foot and started to scrape with it in the dirt, pulling up half-diced earthworms. The heel of the shoe was more effective than their hands had been, but it still wasn't a shovel. Their arms ached and got tired. Z kept going, desperately, and a little hill of earth began to come up around Z's knees. Their hole was only big enough for their shoulders and head, so far. Their hands trembled with the effort of holding the shoe. Z tried to rest for a second and found they could not unclench their brittle fingers.

"Fuck," Z said, and surprised themselves with cursing. They fell into a heap with their head on their mother's headstone, next to the hole. Their whole left side was pressed against the loose dirt and they knew their clothes were already filthy. Z started to cough again, and felt stuff come up in their throat. They let it, and spat a black thing onto their mother's name. It was wet and slimy. Z reached up with their right hand, the one with the broken nail, and touched the slime gently, trailed it across the word *Died*, and then pressed it into the engraved lettering of their mother's first name. *Suzanna.* The slime made the word look like it had been printed in black ink on fancy paper, but the printer ink had bled and made blots. Z rubbed the black sludge out around the edges of the letters with the heel of their palm.

"Fuck," they said again. "Fucking kill me."

They rolled onto their back and looked at the overcast sky. The earth was cold against their spine and they felt the dampness of the grass and the earth seeping into their skin. Z thought about the corpses that got disfigured on one side due to being immersed in mud from the moment of death. Their faces turned purple and swollen, or else their back did and got green and inhuman. Z closed their eyes and tried to stop thinking. Another cough rose up, but they swallowed it.

In the cold, with the overcast sky over them, Z did not initially notice that the shadow that fell over their face and blocked out the sun wasn't just because more clouds had drifted over the sky. It wasn't until the voice spoke that they realized they weren't alone.

"Susan?" a voice asked.

Z opened their eyes. Over them squatted Tommy Wodewose. He was wearing a black sweatshirt and his hair hung blond like corn silk in two braids on either side of his face, woven in with rosemary and dried plants that Z didn't know. His face was all peaky and worried-looking. His shoes, near Z's nose, were wet and dirty, like he had been shuffling through mud.

"What the fuck," Z said, swearing again.

"What are you doing?" Tommy asked.

"I'm trying to bury myself," Z said. "Fuck off."

Tommy stood and silently looked down at them.

"What are you doing?" Z said. "You're not dead. Go to school."

"Why are you trying to bury yourself?" Tommy asked.

Z rolled over onto their back and looked up at him. "Why the hell not?" they spat, and then coughed again. "Ugh." They sat up, or tried to sit up. They ended up propped up on their elbows. They couldn't get their spine to do the thing where it acted like a lever and helped them roll over onto their knees. They couldn't seem to make their spine do anything.

"Here," Tommy said. He reached down and grabbed them under their armpits and pulled them up. He was surprisingly strong. Z yelled out a little syllable of protest. Tommy let them go but hung onto their shoulders.

"You're covered in dirt," he said.

"Yeah," Z said.

"Don't bury yourself," Tommy said. "You'll just get

underground and then be claustrophobic and getting eaten by worms and stuff."

"Why the hell are you here?" Z said again. "Are you following me?"

"No," Tommy said. "I was here by myself and heard you yell and looked over and saw you freaking out and falling over."

Z reached down carefully to grab their bag. "Okay, whatever. I wasn't freaking out. Why were you here in the first place?"

"You're not the only one who has dead people to skip school to go see."

"What's that supposed to mean?"

Tommy turned and pointed to a spot a few yards off. "You know the guy who got murdered by werewolves?" he asked.

"Archie Pagan, yeah," Z said.

"He was my therapist. He's over there."

"Oh," Z said. "Small world." They weren't sure what tone their voice had.

"Come on, I'll show you," Tommy said.

They walked together over to the spot of earth, which was raised in the shape of a big rectangle. Archie Pagan, unlike Z's parents, had not been cremated. He was just a body in the earth. The headstone read, underneath the name and dates of birth and death, *May His Soul Be at Peace in the Hereafter.*

"Is his soul at peace?" Z asked. "You think?"

"No," Tommy said, pulling a weird face. "He was murdered."

"Hmm," Z said.

Tommy looked at Z. "What's it like to die?" he asked.

Z stared at him.

"Like, does it hurt?"

"I mean, I was in a car crash and that hurt," Z said. "Then I just fell asleep. It probably depends."

"What about coming back?"

Z realized that if Tommy knew they were a zombie, literally everyone in school must know. "I don't remember anything except waking up."

"It must have been your mom or something. Some maternal protective thing."

"Yeah, that's what the guy at the courthouse said. It's like a mark on my chest. It's fucked up, though. It's coming apart already, since she's dead. The dude said it wasn't very good to start with."

"So you feel hopeless." Tommy dropped to his knees by the gravestone and reached behind it, and for the first time Z saw he had a whole bag of stuff there with him—bells and candles and stuff. Chalk.

"Tommy, what's . . ." Z trailed off as Tommy turned and made eye contact with them. His eyes were very bright. "Uh, what's all that stuff."

"I'm going to try to bring him back from the dead," Tommy said, leading into the sentence with a hesitant, breathy noise, and finishing it with a nervous glance at Z.

This took a second to sink in.

"What?"

"I want to bring him back to life," Tommy said.

"Why?"

"Because he was my therapist," Tommy said. "I've been going to him since I was eight. There's nobody else in town who practices."

"That's dumb," Z said immediately. "Let the poor man die. You can drive south or wherever to find a therapist."

"No," Tommy said. "Not for me. I'm like, super crazy." He was laying out the candles in a circle.

"Well, you can't bring him back from the dead," Z said.

"Why not? You came back from the dead. It can't be that hard." Tommy fumbled with the large stone bowl meant for ash. "I mean, I know it's hard. But I'm good at this and I'm going to get it right. I have to get it right."

"Let the dead be."

"One book, right, this one from 1890, says you have to lay out candles on the grave, and a different one says you have to have a salt circle. I'm trying to figure out what would work better."

"You can't just try to resurrect this guy in the middle of a cemetery in broad daylight. You heard about Mr. Weber, right?"

"What about him?"

"He got arrested when he was trying help me steal these books on necromancy. Not even big stuff. Just how to preserve me. And he got arrested because someone else had stolen necromancy books a while ago and he got blamed for it, just for being there, in Willamette's library. It's a big crime, and the cops are racist."

"What?" Tommy asked. His voice was high-pitched.

"Which is why I'm going to bury myself," Z said. "It's basically illegal for me to try to live so I'm going to go over there and lie down and just stay there. That's where people want me. A cemetery is where people want dead people. Don't try to bring Archie Pagan back, you'll just make his life suck."

"Mr. Weber got arrested?" Tommy asked.

"Yeah," Z said. "And beat up. Have you not—he just came back today. He's all smashed up."

Tommy was silent. "Ugh," he said. "Shit."

"What?" Z asked.

"Look, Susan, I'm telling you this because I trust you," Tommy said as if it were all one word.

"Don't trust me. I don't even know you."

"I took those books. I stole them last month. I went to the Willamette library at night just when they were closing. I figured nobody would miss them."

"Well," Z said after a second of being very quiet, "probably don't trust anyone else with that information." They were wondering: How the hell did Tommy take the books when Mr. Weber and I couldn't?

"It's my fault he got arrested," Tommy said. "Shit shit shit."

Z shrugged ambivalently. "Mostly my fault. So you have books now."

"Yes," Tommy said. He gestured to his bag.

"Can I have one?" Z asked.

Tommy looked at Z. "You're not going to turn me in?"

"I mean, my body is falling apart. If you give me one, I won't tell anyone you're trying to resurrect your therapist." They bent down and looked into Tommy's bag.

Necromancy in the Twentieth Century. Franz Boas's Demon Anthropology. Summoning Great Old Ones for the Absolute Beginner. Necromancy and You. Z felt an ecstatic high build in their chest.

"Can I help?" Tommy asked. He leaned over again and looked over Z's shoulder to the book. "What are you looking for?"

"Anything that would keep me around longer. Preferably something that would make it easier to walk," Z said. They were looking at the beginning of the Preservation chapter.

"I think there's a spell for like, an eternal undead guard that doesn't rot," Tommy said. "It's probably got something you could use."

Z flipped to the page and examined the text. Most of it was in Latin, so it took a second. "This spell is all about controlling the guard, though. I don't want to be controlled."

Tommy shrugged. "You could modify it. I've tried a couple of these spells—"

"A couple of spells from a necromancy book?" Z asked.

"Just on rats and toads," Tommy said quickly, as if that made it any less dangerous or illegal. "Anyway, I mean, like, you can change some of the words around and change the way the spell applies to the thing. So you could, uh, you could try that." He looked very nervous suddenly. "Right now, I'm just practicing—just setting things up for when I really do it. I come here maybe once a week and practice setting things up. I want to be careful. I'm not being crazy about it."

"I think I'd prefer a potion," Z said, ignoring him. "Something I could take like medicine that wouldn't feel as dangerous."

Tommy's face screwed up. "I wonder if there is anything like that." He paused. "Wait. We could try to find the spell your mom did and do it again, right? Do it over?"

"I don't think that'll work," Z said.

"You could try. What do you know about the spell?"

"Uh, the mark is shaped like a star," Z said. "That's it."

Tommy flipped through the pages of the book. "See, I found this spell called the Familial Protection Hex, where anyone in the spell system won't be able to die because the magic is shared between members. Moms use it to keep their babies safe. It's like, if your baby dies, your magic brings it back. As a zombie. But if you're dead, like the mom is dead, I guess there's only so much magic and then it runs out maybe."

Z looked down at the page Tommy had turned to. There was a column on one side of the page which showed stars of various shapes, next to a series of complicated instructions.

There was a subtitle on the yellowing page, printed in

black-green ink, which read: *This spell is for the necromancer who wishes to protect beloved companions and who wants a tasteful way to keep away the odors and signs of the crypt. Initial casting requires blood rites from all members of the spell system. Up to twenty people may be protected. Blood of the unicorn and the fruits from exotic lands help to preserve the heart and mind of the drinker and keep your companion as fresh and lively as the day they died.*

CAUTION: If four or more members of the system die, or the caster dies, all remaining undead protected bodies will gradually disintegrate after absorbing the magic of the caster. Some undead bodies will be able to access magic belonging to someone else, but it cannot sustain them without a new system.

"That does look promising," Z agreed. They looked at Tommy. His face was very close to their own—awkwardly close. They scooted farther away from him, to show him what distance was appropriate. "I guess I could recast this. Or could get help." Their ankle cracked inside their shoe as they put it back on and rose to their feet, stumbling a little before they realized their foot was twisted sideways. "This is like too perfect. You showed up at exactly the right time with exactly what I needed. I think I'll go home and try to do some illicit necromancy."

Tommy grinned at them awkwardly. "I'm glad I could help," he said. He looked down at his books with a new, unsettled expression. He looked around, and then looked back at Z. "Please keep it secret."

"*You're* not very good at keeping a secret," Z said.

Tommy shrugged. "I would want someone to help me if I was in your situation. And I know what it's like to be on your own. People never stick up for me. You and Aysel do, I mean, but nobody else."

"They're jerks." Z's fingers were waxy and white in the cold.

"They say I'm gay. They tell everyone I look at boys in the locker room. And that's the worst because I don't." He said the last part with a kind of forced laugh. He looked at Z. "Aysel's gay, though, isn't she?"

"Yes," Z said.

"And you. So you don't mind if people are."

"Why should I?"

"Are you gay?" Tommy asked. "I said that but I was assuming."

"I . . . uh," Z said, "I guess."

"It's okay, you don't have to say," Tommy said quickly.

Z took that as the OK to leave.

Z arrived at Aysel's house an hour later, carrying the book in their backpack. Their knees were weak and unexpected snow was coming down now, so the walk couldn't have been easy. There was a gap in their memory. It was just that suddenly they were on Aysel's porch. This kind of thing was happening more lately. Aysel answered the door.

She looked sick. Z really hoped that being around a dead person wouldn't make Aysel's moon-illness any worse. Z swayed. Behind them, the street was going pale gray as snow settled on it and became slush that gradually piled up. Aysel let them in.

"You got a book?" Aysel asked, her nose sounding stuffed up, as Z showed her excitedly, unable to speak because something was happening in their lungs that made it hard to expel air.

Z coughed. "Yes," they rasped. "You'll never believe what happened. It's a necromancy book."

Aysel looked at Z, eyebrows raised. "I really hope you didn't like, kill someone for that, Z. You look really messed up right now."

"No," Z said.

Aysel squinted and swallowed. Her eyes were puffy. Z felt bad that she was having to take all this in while sick.

"I went to the graveyard to visit my parents because I felt really bad, and Tommy was there," Z said. "He, uh, he was doing some kind of thing over Archie Pagan's grave. He had a bunch of books with him. You know how Tommy is. He said he took them from the library last month, before Mr. Weber and I were there. He's trying to bring back Archie Pagan or something, because he was his therapist. And I was like, hi, can I have one of those?"

Z felt very tired when they were done explaining. They got up to make more tea and fumbled at the handle of the pantry door with their numb arthritic fingers. They were thirsty lately; it felt as if their throat was made of cement. Aysel was staring into space, scowling, as the water heated.

"Wait," Aysel said, "so it's his fault that Mr. Weber got arrested?"

"Well, sort of," Z said. They touched the hot kettle with one hand, trying to feel something. They didn't really want Aysel to get mad at Tommy. "I mean, it is still my fault. Tommy took the books because . . . he's Tommy. He's weird and wanted to learn something, or do some kind of weird magic."

"Dangerous weird magic. Why would he bring back Archie Pagan?"

"He wasn't thinking of hurting anyone," Z said, not making eye contact. "Nobody would have noticed the books were gone, and nobody would have gotten hurt."

"Hmm." Aysel looked disgruntled, but it was clear she was too stuffed up to do anything about it. She gargled the last of her lukewarm lemon tea and stared at a spider on the ceiling.

"We can recast the spell my mom put on me that brought me back," Z said. "He helped me."

"So what's in this spell you found?" Aysel asked.

"Right!" Z looked down at the book again and squinted at the ingredients. "The main thing is unicorn blood, it looks like."

"That's so expensive!" Aysel exclaimed. "Shit. They probably want it to be organic, too. I guess we have to go to the store."

"You should stay here," Z said hastily. "You're sick."

"Not so sick," Aysel said, grinning and snuffling. Her nose was bright red.

Z made a face. "Let's make a list of the other stuff we need," they said. They went over and got a notebook and copied down the rest of the ingredients. It took an obnoxiously long time because of how long it took to move their hands. "We'll need a lot of bananas for some reason," Z said.

Aysel came over and looked at the recipe. "That's just for flavor, probably," she said. "And to make it seem exotic. When this came out it was probably the nineteenth century and bananas were très chic."

"Do you think we still need them?" Z asked. They could not imagine their mother mixing a bunch of bananas into unicorn blood.

"It wouldn't hurt," Aysel said. "We have bananas here, though." She tapped her finger on the paper. "We have some of the other stuff, too, like the ground licorice root and ginger. It's mostly just the ground Himalayan enchanted turmeric and all that nonsense that we'll have to go looking for."

They went out to the grocery store and somehow found everything except for tiger milk yogurt. Aysel managed to steal most of it in her coat. The cashier watched them suspiciously but didn't say anything when they came through to buy just the turmeric and applesauce. Then they went to the health food store for the yogurt. The health food store was too small to get away with stealing something straight out, but the tiger's milk yogurt was something awful like eighteen dollars for a big tub of it. It was a bit of a dilemma, and they kept pacing back and forth talking about what to do. Eventually Z sighed and dug the money out of their wallet and paid; it was almost the last of the money Z had saved up the previous summer walking dogs. Z wasn't sure what they would do when it was gone.

Z and Aysel brewed the potion on the floor of Aysel's garage. When Azra got home, they told her it was a health potion to cure Z's eczema. Azra still didn't know Z was dead, or if she did she was too polite to say anything.

After preparing the initial spell, the caster(s) must send a small energy pulse containing a drop of their own blood into the potion, the text read. *This will allow the caster's magic to be diverted into the companion's body in a reliable way. It should be noted that once made, the seal can NEVER be broken, or the entire supply of the caster's magic will be diverted through the body of the companion at once, causing magical tremors to disturb reality and potentially destroying both companion and caster, as well as anyone else around.*

"I guess I'm the caster," Aysel said.

"Is that okay?" Z asked.

"Blood drinking, sharing magic, a bond that can only be severed by ripping apart reality . . . Pretty punk rock. This seems like it's probably *haram*."

"What?"

"Against Islam. Probably against a lot of other religions too. It's chill, though. Either God's cool with me saving my friend or he isn't. Not gonna let that stop me."

"I don't want you to do anything that's against what you believe in," Z said.

"If God exists and is good, I know he's cool with this. Saving a life is the most important thing. Don't tell my mom, though. She's a hippie but she would want to at least have a heartfelt discussion about consequences and smart life decisions and commitment and I'm so not ready to engage with that."

"Are you *sure* you're okay with this?" Z asked. "It's like, you're sharing your magic with me to keep me alive. That might be a literal drain. And what if you get sick of me? Then I'm like a parasite."

"I have too much magic energy to begin with." Aysel pricked her finger with a safety pin she had been wearing as an earring, and opened her hands to cast the energy pulse. Z watched her and felt a burst of something bigger than love in the middle of their stomach.

The brew smelled really rank until the licorice and bananas were added. It turned an odd purple color in spite of the orange turmeric and bubbled sluggishly when the unicorn blood was poured in.

When it was all done they realized they had to let it ferment for at least two days in a sealed glass container. Then a sigil was put into the body of the companion and the companion drank the brew four hours later. Z wondered how their mother had done it the first time, and when they'd been given the potion.

A massive pulse of energy is sealed into the sigil at the moment of casting. If this energy is released at any point it will have an enormous destructive force, the text warned. *Additionally, if the spell is tampered with by a third party and the seal breaks, the companion runs the risk of becoming a magical sink, draining magic from any immediate source around them and channeling it outward; the companion may not be able to control this magic, and it will either cause self-destruction or massive external chaos.*

"We should do it on the full moon," Aysel said. "Then you'll get a super huge dose of magic from me while the moon's hitting me. You can be somewhere else, I think."

"It's a good thing the full moon is this coming Monday," Z said.

8

Aysel could feel that it was going to be a supermoon. Even though the clouds hung low and thick over the trees, Aysel could feel it pulling at her in the morning and the evening, tugging at her brain and her eyes and her stomach and arms and legs and hair, setting her teeth on edge and setting her shaking. She was sore in her bones. Her eyes did things to the light that made everything seem brighter than it was. When she watched TV it was bright, too bright. That usually only happened about thirty minutes before or after transformation. The perigee moon drew everything out. She tried to read, but everything in her felt like it was snapping and popping and buzzing and waiting. There was so much energy in her ready to sizzle out in a million directions.

For the sigil on Z's skin they used a temporary tattoo shaped like a moon. Aysel said the spell over it, and they both waited for something to happen, but nothing did.

"I hope it works," Aysel said. "Drink the stuff just when the moon rises."

Azra dropped Aysel off the night of the full moon just by the road, as she had the previous month. It had been warm during the day, so the snowfall of Friday was mostly gone.

"Be good," Azra said as Aysel got out and grabbed her duffel from the back. She seemed solemn instead of frantic, and this made Aysel even more scared. The car drove off down the road, gravel popping under its tires.

In her sweatshirt and jeans, Aysel felt almost as if she didn't have a body. The moon was just beginning to rise, and though it was freezing outside she was breaking into a sweat. She knew her temperature had been high for days; now it was burning hot. She staggered into the woods, loping in a way that even to her did not seem human. The dusk set in, cold and misty and wet, and the last rays of light faded fast from the blue-gray sky.

Something else was happening, and Aysel felt sure that it had to do with Z and the spell. Whenever she moved, she felt a little spark like a fire left outside of her body, pulling vaguely at her back in the direction of town. She hoped that the spell would work even if she was not there with Z.

Aysel saw something move out of the corner of her eye, and spun around fast, shining her flashlight on the ground and on the black branches of the trees above. She thought of the police. There was nothing—or whatever it was had moved. Aysel tried to tell herself that she was imagining things, but she couldn't shake the feeling that there were huge things moving in the shadows. She walked on for a little before she heard, again, a cracking branch behind her.

"I know there are other wolves out here," she cried out loudly. "I am not hunting you. Just please, tell me who you are. I'm one of you."

There was a crackle of leaves and a thump in the distance, maybe a hundred yards away. Aysel was not sure whether to run toward it or away from it.

It was about then that the moon came out from behind the clouds for an instant—or maybe the clouds just thinned enough for some streak of it to come through and stick to Aysel and her magic. Aysel felt the low shiver in her spine and the cramps. It was starting. The air was chilly and her hair frizzed and stuck to her face. She spat to keep it out of her mouth.

Aysel could not keep track of her thoughts or which way they were spinning anymore. The moon radiated through her, transforming her up and out. Fur grew in billows from her forearms and thighs. Aysel forgot the things she had been worrying about before, and her mind cleared as if a cold wind was blowing through it. Everything became about the fur, the teeth, the claws, the hot blood in her boiling and transforming. Aysel cried out with something that was almost joy as her ears grew and her skull stretched into something alien. Her tongue grew long and the elated cry became a keening howl that was not human in tone. She rose up in the moonlight and then collapsed.

It felt like a bonfire burned through her brain and then

yanked her backward toward the road and town. Everything was distorted but Aysel could swear she saw light leaving from her body and moving away, flooding like water down a drain toward the river below. The river was Z. Make them okay, Aysel thought.

Aysel lay on the ground longer than usual after this transformation, trying to grasp at her human mind. The wolf's thoughts were almost completely dominant, but some strain of the girl remained. Gradually, as she caught whiffs of other creatures on the breeze, Aysel the wolf became aware that she was not alone.

It was there on the edge of her vision at first, moving subtly in and out of bushes. It was very large, though, and even the most shadowy and quiet of shapes is eventually seen if it is very, very large. Within a few minutes, Aysel realized that there was not just one other wolf—there were two. One was large and black and scruffy, like Aysel except with more hair. The other was sleek and brown-red.

As Aysel shook with the pain of the transformation, her eyes watering, they watched her for a second, and she looked back. The wolves were huge, and their eyes glowed deep soft colors in the darkness between the trees. Both of them slid in and out of the shadows around Aysel as she finished her transformation and curled up on the floor of the forest, waiting for the pain of the change to subside.

Aysel had never seen another wolf on a full-moon night before. She had always been alone. She had never met other werewolves in their wolf form, she realized—and in fact, Aysel suddenly thought, in the conscious part of her mind which still formed words, I haven't met any other werewolves at all, except when my mother is with me—like at that support group. Sometimes Aysel had doubted the existence of other werewolves, just because she didn't see any of them around.

She looked around for the wolves. They were gone.

Aysel was conscious in a way that she hadn't felt on a full-moon night in a long time—she had a goal. She needed to find the other wolves. She wanted to be with them, not alone. It occurred to her faintly that they would be safer together, though by this time she couldn't remember what it was they would be safe from. The memory of the existence of police was distant, inconsequential, lost. Smells and the forest and the night were real. Aysel's heart beat very fast.

As she began to follow the scent trail left by the two wolves as they brushed against trees and left pawprints in mud, Aysel felt more aware of herself in her wolf body than she ever had before in her life. She was on the edge of something, pushing hard, hoping somehow to remain aware and not lose herself in the drive for sensation. There was a mission here. Aysel the wolf had never had a mission before, and it was exciting. The scent in the mud got stronger. Aysel was filled with a longing, a pining scream. She wanted to cry out. She wanted closeness, and other soft pelts against her own, and she wanted speed, and the things were wrapped up together in the way the wolf could not untangle. She had to run with the other wolves. She felt the worms move in the leaves beneath her feet as she paced quickly through banks of brambles, following in the wake of larger paws.

The wolves did not want to lose her; it was not long before they let themselves be found.

She came to the edge of the river and looked up. The large black wolf was watching Aysel from just a few yards away, where it stood looking down on her from on top of a fallen tree. Greens and browns all became black in the night, but they were different kinds of black. In the dark Aysel could make out the wolf's eyes, the tapetum lucidum reflecting moonlight back at her. The second wolf, its red fur shadowy rust in the dark, stood a ways farther up the hill. Aysel couldn't see its face, but she could hear its breathing and smell the blood in the fur around its mouth and the musky smell of its body and breath. Aysel drew near, and the wolves turned and raced off into the darkness. She followed them, feeling warm and happy that they had stopped and waited. They wanted her around. The air was cold and she could hear the owls and bats overhead. In the back of her mind, Aysel the witch, the human, was concerned, but as a wolf she was braver than when she was a girl. She wanted to be with other wolves. She wanted their protection and their affection.

The wind rushed against Aysel's eyes. The moon hung high and large in the sky, swollen and heavy behind the clouds. Aysel could smell the frost in the thick misty air.

Eventually the wolves let her catch up. She smelled them. The other wolves took Aysel's ears in their mouths and smelled her and leapt into her, jostling her. Then they ran together, their feet sometimes dipping into the prints made by the wolf ahead of them.

There was a deer, in the night, and they all saw it from a distance. The creature bolted, unwise, and they pursued her. The wolves were very hungry, after all. They ran and were like dogs tearing through the underbrush, nothing stately or graceful or too overtly magical about it. Branches broke in their wake. The wolves were not delicate things, and they were new to the forest and still carried with them a frightening human scent. The deer realized soon that she was being pursued. She ran; it might have been that the deer knew then that she was not going to escape. From the long mouth came a cry of warning to any other creatures who might be nearby. Then the deer paused for a second to try to look behind her, and her leg caught in brambles, and she fell. The deer had fur which was sleek in the day. Her fur was dark in the night because the moon was still behind the clouds. Her breath fogged the air. She scrambled to her feet, but it was too late at that point.

The black wolf leapt first, mounting the doe from behind and bringing her down. The red wolf tore into her belly. Aysel leapt into the fray at the scent of iron and salt and bit hard on her neck, which killed her so she stopped feeling the pain. Aysel fell back once the deer was dead and allowed the other wolves to eat, their noses dipping into the steaming body and coming up red. As they finished they watched her.

Far away, distantly, there was the sound of a police siren. Aysel barely registered it.

The black wolf ran into the night, out of the forest and into the surrounding fields; the red wolf stayed and with Aysel finished the deer, and Aysel and the red wolf took a long time eating. Their bodies were huge and needed nourishment. They sizzled with heat and magic and ran together in the dark.

The impressions of the latter part of the night ran into one. There was the scream of an owl, the magic crackling like flame inside Aysel's head—and what was that, oh, what was that noise? She was so tired.

The morning came, and was cold.

Aysel woke up human in the woods, her hair tangled in ferns, her body covered in crusted blood and dirt. Her eyes were half stuck shut. She tasted the iron and salt of blood in her mouth as she tried to wet her dry tongue. Alarmed, she clawed at her face and hair and hugged herself, looking around. Sticks cut into her thighs as she sat up. There was blood everywhere, and that panicked her for a second.

Who had she killed? Flashes of wolves' teeth bared themselves in her memory. After a few moments, though, she noticed the feathers. Aysel was relieved. That meant it was just a bird. On Aysel's wrist and above her eye were scratches from the dead bird's talons, scabbed over and dry under her fingers. They would heal in a week, but Aysel had read somewhere that when scars healed it wasn't really the same as normal tissue. Aysel thought she remembered the article saying that if you stopped eating vitamin C, then the collagen would break down and your scars would eventually reopen. If that ever happened to me, Aysel thought, I would be nothing more than a series of open scars. A net of open wounds inefficiently enclosing the organs inside, like an envelope that's been opened and inexpertly resealed.

The morning air was cold on her skin and she got goose bumps all over her back. Aysel stood up and saw the dead barn owl lying on the ground a ways off, its heart and organs torn out and its head at an odd angle. It was messy and red. She felt a pang of guilt, but it evaporated as the cold wind blew against her. Who cared about barn owls, anyway? Aysel realized she had no idea where she was in the woods. She remembered, vaguely, running far and fast, after the other wolves. Her duffel bag must be over a mile away. She felt at her nazar necklace and sat down, drawing her hair around her, hugging herself, breathing hard. How was she going to get home without her clothes? The moon still rattled around in her head, shaking her body from the inside out, the echo of the supermoon.

"Hell," Aysel said. "Hell, hell, hell." She tried to stand up, but then she couldn't figure out how to do that without getting very cold, so she sat down and screwed her eyes shut and began to rock back and forth. She was not sure how long she stayed like that, panicking very quietly, hoping that someone would come and fix it for her. Nobody did, and she began to stand up again. Nervous energy radiated off her in sweaty waves. She took a few short steps, feeling the cold mist against her bare skin and shaking, her cut feet getting cut more by jagged branches.

Suddenly Aysel felt a heavy warmth envelop her from behind. She couldn't see anything. It was soft. Aysel pawed at the thing covering her. She realized after a moment that it was a very large flannel sheet; she pulled it off her head, fluffing her hair, and looked around. There was a noise coming from somewhere. Someone was laughing, long and high. Aysel shivered and whirled around, clutching the sheet to herself, looking for the voice. Aysel had to push a lot of hair out of her eyes and squint before she saw who it was. Eventually her eyes focused enough to pick out the shape of the girl standing near the base of a tree a couple of yards away.

"I figured you might be needing that. It sucks to walk home naked," the girl said, and laughed. "Sorry I didn't find you sooner. I just woke up myself."

"Aah!" Aysel hugged the flannel sheet around her, terrified. She stood up shakily and stumbled backward, tripping over her own feet. She felt her hair warming and crackling with panicked magic. A few sparks shot in all directions, flakes of dried blood frying against her scalp. She tried to get up, but her knees were weak and wobbly. Run away, she thought, I have to run away. There was a sizzling as Aysel hastened back toward a clump of dark trees. She looked down to see that her foot had burned a hole in the layers of leaves that cover the ground, leaving a blackened footprint.

"Whoa there," the girl said, rushing over and standing in Aysel's path. "Hold it, friend." She was wearing about three sweaters and a pair of pants patterned with hunting camouflage—prints of leaves and sticks in earth tones. Her feet were bare. She had a brown face covered in freckles. There were deep rings under her eyes. Aysel could see that one of her teeth was missing as she laughed. "No need to set the forest on fire. You met me last night, remember? When we were wolves. It was a hell of a moon. I'm still sore all over."

Aysel's mind went blank for a minute, but slowly her memories began to come into focus a little. She wasn't used to trying to remember things from full-moon nights. Usually she tried to forget. Faintly, she recalled the red wolf, the way its eyes were the same as this girl's eyes. "Oh," she said weakly.

"I'm Elaine," the other werewolf said. She extended a hand. Her reddish hair was very long and curly, curlier than Aysel's, but in a different, less frizzy way, the ringlets tight and tangled loosely. She didn't look as if she had combed her hair in a long time. Her complexion was several shades darker than Aysel's, and her outstretched hand was much browner than her face.

"Aysel," Aysel said, extending a hand while clutching at the sheet with the other. Elaine shook the hand lightly and then, loudly, laughed again. It was not a mean laugh.

"Hell of a moon," she said again. "Whenever the moon

comes out like that I feel like I switched into a totally different universe where everything is made of like streetlamps and lightbulbs and sparklers. You just feel it all over your whole ass. You should put on some real clothes before Chad gets back," she added. "You don't want him seeing you naked." She paused. "I hope he hasn't gone far. Kind of scared about that. Especially after Tim got it."

Aysel laughed weakly. "Is Chad the other wolf?"

"He's my travel buddy, yeah, you know," Elaine said. She talked very loudly, like she was trying to get your attention from across a street, only Aysel was very close to her and they were in a forest with no sound but the birds.

"Where is he?" Aysel looked around, hugging the sheet to her, trying to make sure it was bundled to hide her body.

"He's out someplace—I'm not sure exactly. He was probably hunting on his own. He took off last night, remember? But he knows where our camp is. He should be back soon, probably."

Aysel squinted at Elaine. "Your camp?"

"Yeah, our camp," Elaine said.

"Your camp out here? In the woods?"

"Later we're moving in with some friends, but we couldn't until the moon was past. I hate this town already. It's a pit of fascist scum and then, just like, boring shit. There's not anything to do even, unless you want to watch all the people driving to Portland stop and eat at Subway or ride the carousel by the freeway."

"I live here," Aysel said.

"You'll know all about it, then," Elaine said. She turned and began to walk away, and Aysel followed, as she had the night before, dragging the sheet in the dirt behind her. "It kind of reminds me of like, those little dirt towns in the Rust Belt, except no mines or anything and probably less drugs."

The camp was not much. There was one tent, a battered two-person with holes in a patched tarp roof. In the trees around the tent there hung bags, presumably containing food. On a stump near the tent sat a huge water jug, a kettle, and two small mugs. The ground on the campsite had been cleared away roughly and a trench dug around the tent for irrigation. The black earth was swollen with moisture and Aysel wondered how you were supposed to sleep in the tent without getting wet.

"Oh, also I think I found your glasses. I found your duffel, too, but it's all wet. I can dry stuff out and give it to you later."

Elaine pulled out a pair of glasses which were definitely Aysel's, then dug through a bag and threw Aysel a baggy black sweatshirt and pants, which were damp and smelled intensely of wolf-musk. She put them on quickly behind a tree.

"Much better, right?" Elaine asked Aysel when she was done dressing. Aysel agreed that it was more pleasant to be in the woods on an early morning in March when one was wearing clothes. She tried to comb her hair with her fingers.

The trees were light and their tops hidden in the morning mist. Aysel began to wonder about the campsite. It's not permitted to camp on this land, she thought. Elaine was building a fire. She had firewood and lighter fluid and everything. There was a pit with ashes in it and old bits of charcoal that Elaine poked at as she set the fire alight. She had been here awhile.

"Make sure nobody sees the smoke," Aysel said. "We're not even supposed to be in this forest. I don't know who owns it."

"I'm camping out here," Elaine said. "I can't cook without a fire, and it's March."

"I just said, make sure nobody sees the smoke," Aysel said anxiously. "I come here every month, I need it to stay safe. You mean you don't hide it when you make fires out here?"

"What else are we supposed to do? Smoke is smoke. It goes up when you have a fire." Elaine shrugged and pushed her hair out of her face.

Aysel gestured with her hand and thought of the incantation for invisibility, and the smoke became invisible. It was still there—the smell would tell anyone that—but it was entirely hidden from view. If Aysel was good at one kind of spell, it was illusions. She had been using invisibility for years.

"Hey, that's a neat trick. How did you do that?" Elaine looked at Aysel, apparently impressed.

"It's an invisibility charm. It's not sustainable for a long time, but smoke is just little particles of things, so you only need to make it invisible until it disperses."

"How do I do that?"

"I don't know, you just think the incantation."

"What's the incantation?" Elaine asked.

"It's just . . . you know, a standard Latin incantation." Elaine stared at her blankly. "Just like, *invisibilia*, and you think it and think about what you want to happen." Aysel tried to figure out how to explain. "Do you know *any* illusion spells?"

"I know how to make it look like I have makeup on when I don't," Elaine said, grinning, the hole between those teeth a distracting void. She scrunched up her face. Suddenly her lips were pink and her eyes larger and lined with thick lashes. It was startling and slightly unnerving.

Aysel laughed aloud with surprise. "Okay, well, you think about the basic incantation for that—did you learn it with a Latin base?"

"I didn't learn an incantation, a woman on a bus in Minnesota showed me how. You just scrunch up your face and think about models in magazines." Elaine scowled again and pulled the corners of her mouth down. Her lips got redder and her forehead seemed to shrink.

"Stop that, ugh," Aysel said.

"Well, excuse me," Elaine said. Her face relaxed and all at once appeared unwashed and normal again.

"I've just never learned a spell that way. I learned the invisibility spell in school. For things bigger than smoke you start out by chanting the incantation—*non videbo vos, et videre non possumus, et latitant*—"

"Oh jeez, I don't want to know anymore," Elaine said. "Fancy Latin shit makes my brain go numb."

"Didn't your school teach magic?" Aysel asked. Elaine couldn't have gone to a nonmagical school. The last of those closed in the 1980s, when the Reagan administration was concerned that dangerous and uncontrollable new kinds of magic would spring up unless every student learned the basics of Latin spellcasting.

Elaine laughed loudly. "I didn't go to school after I turned twelve."

"Oh," Aysel said. She scowled at the fire. She hoped that she hadn't been rude, though she imagined she had been. "Why?"

"I decided I wanted to be a beautician," Elaine said with an absolutely solemn face.

Aysel couldn't tell if she was serious or not, so she said nothing.

Elaine smiled at Aysel and poked the fire with a long stick. It shot up an array of sparks. "What do you think, dummy? They kicked me out. I became a giant wolf one day and the whole town knew and everyone at my house said no way, don't want that one back. Happens to everyone eventually, you know? I was eleven. "

"Oh," Aysel said.

"Do you go to school? Like, still?" Elaine asked.

"Yeah," Aysel said.

She turned to Aysel with an expression of some shock. "Like, a normal school?"

"Nobody knows I'm a werewolf. If they did, I'd be kicked out or sent to get electroshock treatments."

"How does nobody know? The registry would . . ." Elaine trailed off, squinting at Aysel in confusion.

"My mother never told anyone I was a werewolf. She doesn't believe in regulating werewolves. So I'm not registered."

"That's nice of her," Elaine said. "My parents dumped me at the police station the second that my first moon was over and I was strong enough to stand up again."

"Why were they allowed to do that?" Aysel asked. "I thought it was Child Protection Services that dealt with . . ." Aysel trailed off when Elaine grinned and started laughing. Her laugh was a wheezing, throaty thing, like a hyena.

"I don't know what world you've been living in. I mean, it might be different out West, I guess. CPS doesn't have much to do with werewolf kids where I come from."

"I don't know any other werewolves," Aysel said apologetically.

"For most of us it's like, a little hospital, a touch of juvie, and then more hospital till your brain turns black and your magic curls up inside your muscles and dies. I ran away before I was old enough to get shocked more than twice a year, and even then my magic got pretty messed up. I still have like magic arthritis and a bunch of pain problems."

"In newspapers you only read about electroshock as helping people," Aysel said.

"Yeah. It doesn't help. Or like it eventually makes you stop transforming but your body hates you. It makes you go crazy.

I almost joined a cult for a second in 1992 and then squatted in this house for four years with some anarchists until they got super into drugs and I was like, oh wait, this place is gross."

"Oh," Aysel said.

"We got diseases, you know! We're all little scummy babies running around and they wanna shock us until we turn into regular babies but we aren't regular."

Aysel nodded. "My dad wanted me to get shock treatment. My mom divorced him."

"Tell your mom she's cool for not registering you."

Aysel had never met someone angrier than herself. She couldn't figure out what to say in response to this. She tightened her mouth, tasting her hot morning breath against her tongue. She wanted to ask about Elaine, find out everything about her. She felt her stomach do a strange slippery flop inside her. "Where do you live now?" she asked. "Like, when you're not here in the woods."

"Nowhere," Elaine said. "I'm a travelin' soldier."

"Yeah," Aysel said as if she understood. She blinked and, embarrassingly, yawned loudly. It was one of those yawns that come on with an irrepressible force, and she couldn't stop herself.

"How old are you, anyway, little puppy?"

Aysel scowled. "I'm fourteen."

"A puppy," Elaine said again, giggling. Her face grew serious. "But hey, really, are you really fourteen?"

"Yeah," Aysel said. She felt like she should leave soon.

"You're really young."

Aysel wasn't sure whether to feel flattered. Mostly she felt as if she'd missed a chance for something. "How old are you?"

"Nineteen," Elaine said, throwing another log on the fire.

"Wow, nineteen, that's so old," Aysel said. She meant it to sound biting but instead it sounded whiny.

"It is, compared to fourteen," Elaine said. Suddenly she looked up, tensing. "Someone's coming."

"Hello, good morning, is anyone alive?" a boy's voice called from the trees. There was a rustle in the bushes behind the tent.

"Oh hey," Elaine said, her shoulders relaxing. "Chad's back. Chad, do you have pants or do you need some?" Elaine reached over and covered Aysel's eyes with a grimy hand. Aysel felt the heat of her palm against her thin eyelids and shuddered. It was only partly because of how dirty Elaine's hands were.

"I have pants," Chad called back. "I ended up pretty close to camp when I turned back. My clothes were right there."

"Your clothes? *Your* clothes? Whose pants are those, Chad?" Elaine yelled, uncovering Aysel's eyes. She was laughing again. Aysel turned around to look at Chad.

"Okay, yes, they're your pants," Chad said. He emerged from behind the tent. He was not wearing a shirt, and his chest was striped with scars: two, cutting bilaterally across his chest, looked straight and sharp and surgical, white and faded, but others were like bite marks. The scars intersected with a pattern of wobbly home-made-looking tattoos. He had on a pair of acid-washed jeans which looked as if they had been made for someone with broader hips than either Chad or Elaine. Chad rolled up the cuffs and hitched the pants up around his hips. They fell down again, showing the waistband of blue boxer shorts. His curly black-brown hair was tangled in one large mat on the top of his head. He had a slightly greasy mustache. Aysel recognized him as the boy who had spoken to her on the bus, the one who had known about the supermoon.

"Hey, Lane, do we have a rope?" Chad held his pants up with one hand and gestured to them as a way of indicating that he was having a hard time keeping them up. The clean pants contrasted with the rest of Chad's grimy body. His pale skin was smeared with dirt and as he approached Aysel could smell a strong odor coming off of him—sweat and blood, for the most part. Aysel knew she didn't smell too great either, so she couldn't hold it against him.

"In the tent," Elaine said. Chad went into the tent.

"He's such a loser," Elaine said, loud enough that Chad could probably hear. "I love him so much."

Chad emerged wearing the pants with a rope and a sweatshirt. He looked at Aysel with interest. "So who are you?" he asked. "Are you new?"

"No," Aysel said. "I've lived here for a long time."

"She's not with the House," Elaine said matter-of-factly. "She's enrolled in school. She's like fourteen."

"Hey, I've met you before," Chad said. "Cool necklace."

"I saw you on a bus," Aysel said. "You asked what day it was."

"Yeah," Chad said, grinning. "You knew about the supermoon. I was like heyyyyy this kid's somehow . . . You're in school? How'd you work that?"

"Her mom lied to the school people," Elaine said.

Chad raised his eyebrows. "That rocks," he said. "I mean about your mom. School sucks."

Aysel shrugged. "It pretty much sucks."

"Yeah, I bet," Chad agreed.

"School is important, though," Elaine said.

Aysel remembered again it was a school day, and she needed to get home and get ready—if she wasn't already late. She stood up anxiously and almost tripped over her own feet. "I have to leave, actually," she said. "I need to get back to the road and get to class. Do you know which way it is?"

Chad laughed. "Uh-oh, poor little werewolf can't find its way out of the woods."

Elaine looked like she was also struggling to contain a smirk. "How the hell have you survived this long?" she asked Aysel.

"I just don't go over the hills," Aysel said. "I stay close to Zena Road and the Maple Mound reservoir. That way my mom can find me if anything goes wrong. I've never been this far out."

"That ruins all the fun," Chad said. "We get to run through all the fields, too."

"Ruins all the excitement to hide all night," Elaine added. "Anyway, it's misty a lot this time of year. There's nobody looking, except maybe the odd cow. Police don't come out this way."

"Well, okay," Aysel said. "But my mom has rules. And the cops . . ."

Both of them laughed, the fire crackling between them, and Aysel flushed.

"You have to learn to navigate sometime," Elaine said.

"Hey, I'm a puppy, remember? Can't you just tell me where to go?" Aysel asked. She was beginning to worry that if she was marked absent her mother would find out and think that she'd run into trouble as a wolf and gotten shot or captured—or that she meant to skip school. Aysel wasn't sure which was worse.

"That way," Elaine said, pointing. "But there's no trail."

"It's not that way, it's that way," Chad said, pointing the opposite way. He smiled.

Aysel pursed her mouth. "Please just tell me where to go," she said.

"I'm right, Chad's messing with you. Just stay and have breakfast with us," Elaine said. "You need to eat some human food. You need energy."

"It's Spam and bananas," Chad said. "How exciting, right?" He rolled his eyes. "There's instant oatmeal too."

"Spam tastes okay when you fry it," Elaine said.

"I should go right now," Aysel said, though she was hungry. "I can hang out with you all sometime, that would be cool, but I need to get to school. I can't start missing first classes after a full moon when everyone's so worked up about werewolves."

"Whatever," Chad said. "I have to pee." He stood up and went into the bushes.

Elaine looked interested in what Aysel had said. "You mean like, hang out not on the full moon? You'd want to do that?"

Aysel looked at Elaine. She wondered if Elaine had friends who weren't werewolves or who didn't live in the woods. "Sure," she said.

"Like—could we go to the movies?"

Aysel was surprised by her enthusiasm. "Yeah, we could go to the movies," she said. She took a deep breath. "But not right now."

"Oh my gosh. Could we go to the movies this Saturday?" Elaine asked.

"Um. Sure?"

"We should go to a matinee."

"I guess, yeah," Aysel said. "That sounds fun."

"What time should I meet you? We can go see *The Crucible*. Wait, is that still out? Probably not, huh."

"I . . . have to ask my mom. Maybe the afternoon?" Aysel said, wondering if she was going to be able to leave soon. Elaine and Chad didn't seem to understand that she had everything to lose if anyone realized she was always sick the week of the full moon. They had already lost everything, or hadn't had it to begin with. Aysel knew that meant she should be sympathetic toward them, but it made her feel even more alienated. She couldn't even empathize with them.

"How about two?" Elaine asked. She was still caught up in the details of the movie. "I'll wait around for half an hour and if you don't come I'll know you're a liar or your mom's a jerk or something," Elaine said.

"Okay," Aysel said. "Let's uh, let's do that."

"This is great," Elaine said. She was grinning. She opened a can of Spam. "I'm so excited we're friends now."

"I'm really excited about meeting other werewolves, I really am. I just . . . really have to leave now, okay?"

Elaine shrugged. She was smiling goofily. "That's real," she said. "I'm still worried about you not eating breakfast."

"I get lunch at school," Aysel said. "I'll be okay."

"Okay." Elaine brushed her hair back from her greasy forehead. "The path we cut to the road is through those trees." She pointed. "That's not very far. Not too much brush."

Aysel set off walking. The sun was still low overhead, but she couldn't be sure that she would make it to class on time. As the wind stung Aysel's toes, she realized she still didn't have any shoes on. Elaine hadn't had any extra to spare, apparently. This was going to be very hard to explain, Aysel thought.

By the time she walked into the office—without her backpack and with pine needles still sticking to her clothes—it was past ten in the morning.

"I'm really sorry," Aysel said to the woman at the front desk.

"What did you do, dear, roll down a hill in the woods?" the woman asked her, sniffing. Her hair was frosted and fluffed up on the top of her head. Aysel looked at the name tag in front of the woman. It said Crystal Bell. It took Aysel a moment to realize that this was the woman's name. "Are you barefoot?"

"Yes," Aysel said with automatic impudence.

"Excuse me?"

"I am barefoot."

"Are you all right? Were you in the woods?" Crystal's voice was rising in pitch, like a thermometer shooting up. She looked very distressed.

"Not in the woods, exactly. I, uh, I rode my bike to school," Aysel invented wildly, looking as earnest as possible.

"A bike?" the woman named Crystal Bell asked, looking down her nose at Aysel. Aysel knew she was trying to say something about Aysel's weight as well as the fact that Aysel had no shoes on.

"My mom just got it for me," Aysel said quickly. "She wants me to exercise more." That should satisfy her, Aysel thought. She had referred to her own fatness. Adults liked it when she acted insecure about her body. Now Crystal Bell the secretary wouldn't have to poke at her about it.

"Oh, I see," said Crystal Bell. Her eyebrows looked like thin needles.

"And, uh, there's this stretch of the road with no shoulder, and a truck drove by and I had to go off in the ditch to avoid getting hit. My bike's tire popped and I had to leave it there. I uh, I lost my shoes when I fell." Aysel wasn't sure if this was entirely credible, so she said it with a helpless smile. "I had to take a city bus the rest of the way to school. My mom's already at work." It reoccurred to Aysel that Azra would be worried about her. She would be worried that Aysel wouldn't be able to get to class. "Could uh, could I call her so she knows what happened?"

Crystal Bell stared skeptically at Aysel but gestured with a manicured finger so that Aysel could see where the phone was. Aysel rang her mother and left her a voicemail saying she had had a mishap but was at school. She hoped Azra would remember to check her messages. If she didn't she would be in a state of absolute panic by the afternoon. She'd think that Aysel was dead or had been captured by police.

"Can I just go to class now?" Aysel asked Crystal Bell.

"You can't go to class barefoot," the secretary said. "You should go to the nurse's office and get some shoes there."

"I don't need to. I have some extra socks and shoes in my locker for gym class," Aysel said, wincing at the idea of putting some unknown pair of smelly extra nurse's office shoes on her feet.

"All right, well, go get those." The secretary tapped her fingers on her desk. It was clear that she wanted Aysel to go away.

"I will," Aysel said.

"All right, dear. I hope the rest of your day isn't as unusual and stressful as this morning must have been."

"It won't be," Aysel said with bright ferocity.

"Good luck with the bike," Crystal Bell told Aysel in a saccharine tone. As Aysel walked out into the hallway and headed to class, she made a mental note that she would never in her life learn to ride a bicycle.

9

After two days in the Tahirs' garage, the potion was no longer the original deep purple; instead it was an odd opalescent lavender color. It had the consistency of a thick milkshake, and it wobbled as Z walked home with it on the night of the supermoon, moving shakily. The sky above was slate gray and mist covered the ground and slid between the trees. Z imagined that a living person would be able to feel the mist pressing against their skin.

One of Z's eyes couldn't see properly; something had gotten into it, and because the eyeball was so dry, Z had not been able to get it out again. The eye was the same one that had fallen out in church. Z was afraid to touch it too much, in case it fell out again. They closed their eyelid over their eye on the walk home, which left everything a little skewed and off-kilter, and made it even more difficult to balance.

When Z was a block and a half away from Mrs. Dunnigan's apartment, they paused and set their bag down on the cold sidewalk. They weren't sure if they should hide the potion from Mrs. Dunnigan or not. They knew they would have to explain where the necromancy books had come from, and even if Mrs. Dunnigan wanted to protect Z, they weren't sure she would want to protect Tommy too. Z wrapped the potion bottles carefully in their sweater and put them in their bag. They walked the rest of the way to the apartment.

The sun set early in winter, and the misty afternoon became the misty night. It was very dark. Z pictured Aysel in the woods at night.

Lately Mrs. Dunnigan had decided organ meats were probably very good for Z. Because money was tight, she didn't buy much else. There was rice in the cupboard, and meat in the refrigerator, and cat food, and some tea, and that was almost everything. She had almost bought cow's brains at the supermarket until Z convinced her that this was a bad idea. Z wished fervently that they could be vegetarian.

They didn't watch the news that night. Mrs. Dunnigan had decided she didn't want to.

"All the news lately is so bad," she said.

Z did their homework to the noise of hissing cooking meat in a pan and the sound of cats endeavoring to be in everyone's way at once.

After dinner, Mrs. Dunnigan was tired and went to rest on the couch, so Z cleaned up, trying to scrub the black marks off the pan and the plates. Z looked out the window. The sky was very black and because it was so misty one could barely make out anything at all in the space between the houses.

The phone rang. Mrs. Dunnigan could not hear it over the sink, so Z slouched over and picked it up. The thick white plastic cord bumped against the wall.

"Hello?" Z asked.

"Hey," said a high voice on the other end.

"Who—"

"It's Tommy," Tommy said quickly. "Is this Susan?"

"I go by Z," Z said.

There was a moment of confused silence.

"You have the right person," Z said, "I just go by Z, not Susan. I had to tell you sometime."

"Oh," Tommy said. "Well, uh, can I talk to you? Are you free?"

Z looked over at Mrs. Dunnigan. She had picked up one of her books about the history of Irish independence. "Why? What do you want to talk about? Does it have to be now?"

"I just felt like talking to you," Tommy said. His voice sounded odd, like he had been crying.

Z did not explain to Tommy that they were not really friends with him and therefore it was not odd to not speak to him. It felt a little too cruel. "Sorry," they said instead. "I can talk."

"Who is it on the phone?" Mrs. Dunnigan asked quietly.

"Someone from school. Tommy Wodewose," Z rasped. They wondered suddenly how Tommy had their number.

"How nice," Mrs. Dunnigan said.

"Yeah," Z mumbled. "Hey, I'm going to take the phone into my room."

"Okay," said Tommy on the phone.

"All right, dear," Mrs. Dunnigan said, and picked up the nearest cat.

Z picked up the receiver and the phone and carried it as far from the wall as it would go. If they stretched the twisted cord all the way and set the receiver on the floor, they could just manage to sit inside the door to their room and, tilting their head a little, speak on the phone. The cats watched curiously as Z arranged all this.

"Okay," Z said when they had hunkered down just inside the door to their room. "What do you want to talk about, Tommy? Is something wrong?"

"No." Tommy giggled, and it sounded a little weird. "Nothing's wrong. Nothing."

"Okay," Z said slowly. "You sound like it is."

"My dad's just being weird tonight," Tommy said. "He's like, mad at everyone. He gets weird sometimes."

"That sucks," Z said. "I hope it's not like"—they paused, unsure how to ask—"I hope it's not like, dangerous."

"No! No, it's not like, a hitting-people thing."

"Oh," Z said.

"It's not like that," Tommy repeated edgily.

"Okay."

"He just snaps at my mom and then locks her out of their room and I don't know, lifts weights or reads books about the coast of Spain or poetry or whatever he does. But then she can't get in to brush her teeth and she has to sleep on the couch. It stresses everyone out. This time it was because she had left a thermos and a candy wrapper in his car. He doesn't like messes."

"Oh," Z said. They held the phone close to their face with their shoulder and rubbed their hands together to generate heat. They felt cold all of a sudden.

"I don't want to talk about my parents," Tommy said.

"You don't have to," Z said, not pointing out that Tommy had been the one to bring it up. They hoped it came out in a kindly way. Everything they said was a kind of flat eerie rasp.

"I've been reading the books I still have, the ones not about . . . you know, your stuff. It's really amazing, all the things people have done with magic before the Censorship Act."

"Yeah?"

"It's really great. There's this spell here for summoning the thing that built the Eiffel Tower. It was this ancient afrit. You need about two hundred people to call it, and the book—this one's from 1930—says you need a special license from the French government, but really, it's amazing."

"Sounds like it," Z said, looking around the corner to see if Mrs. Dunnigan was listening. They couldn't see her.

"Did you make the potion?" Tommy asked, surprising Z. "Did it work?"

Z paused. "Yeah," they said hesitantly, not sure if they wanted to talk to Tommy about it. "I mean, I've made it. It's not done yet. Aysel helped cast it but I have to drink it tonight. Something with the full moon."

"That's cool. Wow."

"Yes," Z said.

"I wonder—" He stopped. His voice was high and wheedling, and Z felt sure he was going to ask something of them.

"What?" they asked, in a voice that immediately felt too snappish.

"Can I see you when you drink it?" Tommy asked.

Z furrowed their brow and stared at the opposite wall. "Why?"

"I don't know, it just would be—I mean, it's pretty intense magic. It would help me when I bring back Archie, to see it."

"I guess so."

"Forbidden magic like that might get sort of crazy. You might want a friend," Tommy said, his voice softening. It was as if he realized he had scared Z and was trying a different tactic. "And the spell can have multiple casters, right? I could be another caster."

"How would you know?" Z pressed the plastic phone into their head, feeling it scrape against their jaw through the skin of their cheek. They did not want any lights or flashes or bangs inside them.

"I just remember from reading."

Z was quiet for a moment. "Tommy," they said, "don't try anything."

"I'm not even thinking about Archie Pagan right now," Tommy said. "Just helping you."

"I'm not saying you can't," Z said. They paused. "Although maybe you should consider not trying anything else. That isn't an especially brilliant thing to do."

"I won't. I'll be careful," Tommy said. "So can I see you tonight when you take it?"

"I guess so," Z said.

"Where are you going to do it?"

"I don't know. By the bus stop. Or the park down the street."

"I can meet you there," Tommy said. "I'll bring . . . like, I don't know. I can bring snacks or something." He laughed. "What do friends do? Should I bring something?"

"I'm fine," Z said, not interested in explaining to Tommy that they didn't eat much. "You don't have to bring anything."

"What time should we meet?"

"I don't know," Z said. A cat licked them with its rough tongue. "The moon rises soon. Forty minutes?"

"Okay," Tommy said.

There was a long silence. The cat crawled into Z's lap and began to gnaw at their hand. Z petted it, and it meowed loudly.

"What was that?" Tommy asked.

"One of Mrs. Dunnigan's five million cats. They try to

eat me whenever I sit still." Z smiled as the cat bit them again. They didn't mind it anymore. It wasn't like they could feel it.

"If I leave now I can get there before the moon is up, I think," Tommy said.

"Okay." Z told him their address, and said they'd meet him by the side of the house.

Z put the phone back and went into their room again. They opened the window and peered out at the foggy night. It didn't look like the moon was going to come out. Z walked back into the kitchen, thinking vaguely that they needed something to stir the potion with. Mrs. Dunnigan watched them get a spoon. Z made eye contact with Mrs. Dunnigan and slowly walked to the fridge, took a carton of yogurt to make it look as if they were eating something, said good night, and then returned to their room.

They pulled out the potion and put it on the windowsill and stared at it. It seemed to be glowing, but Z wasn't sure if that was just a trick of the light.

Fifty minutes later, a shadowy figure moved down the sidewalk past the bus stop and stood, looking around. Z glanced into the hallway, saw that Mrs. Dunnigan had gone to bed, and then moved back to the window and hauled it open. They tried to get outside quietly but instead fell loudly into the bushes. A cat meowed inside. The figure looked over and saw them. Its blond hair shone in the dim light of the streetlamp.

"So why do you go by Z now?" Tommy asked.

"It's my name." Z managed to stand, and reached back inside their room to grab the potion and shut the window. They turned around toward Tommy and fumbled with the cap on the bottle.

"It hasn't always been. What made you change it now?"

"I've been using it for a while but nobody has paid much attention," Z said. Their response was clipped. "I just prefer it. It's more gender-neutral."

"Oh. Why do you want that?"

"Well, I'm not a girl or a boy," Z said. They didn't make eye contact, concentrating on their slippery, feeble fingers and the reluctant cap. "I'm something else. I'm a third thing. I don't wear skirts or makeup but it's not just about that. It's like a deep feeling that I just don't want to be a woman. I could do stuff that women don't do and still be a woman, I know that, but I don't want to still be a woman because people will always see me in a certain way, and make me act a certain way to be more like a real woman, and I don't want to have all that in my head. If I'm a third thing I just refuse all that. And I don't think I could be a man, because I hate almost every man I've ever met."

"Oh." Tommy did not say anything else.

"Not that it really matters if my body falls apart." Z, feeling that was the end of that, struggled again with the bottle. This time they managed to open it.

"It looks weird," Tommy said, pointing at the potion.

"I prepared it just like it said to," Z said, giving the opalescent mixture a firm shake with their finger over the opening. It fizzed against their skin. It was the color of a smoggy sky at dusk now.

Tommy sat down in the dark grass to watch, expectantly. "So what was casting the spell like?"

"Aysel had to put blood into the potion in an energy pulse so I could access her magic to stay alive, and then we applied the sigil and she said the spell over it." Z opened their pajama top to show the temporary tattoo above the sigil their mother had made. "I think it'll work. The moon's just about out."

"Do you still have the book?" Tommy asked.

"Yeah," Z said.

"I could be a second caster," Tommy said. "I'm good at magic."

"I like, leach your magic to live, is what would happen if you did that," Z said.

"That's okay," Tommy said. "I don't want you to die. Where's the book? I'll do the spell."

"Uh," Z said, and looked back at the window. They were worried they had jammed it shut.

"I can open it," Tommy said. He went over to it and ran his hands along the sill. There was a slight blue glow and the window slid up silently. Z had not heard him say any spell, which was weird. He swung his narrow leg over the sill and scrambled in. "Where is it?"

"My bag," Z said as quietly as possible. They were worried Mrs. Dunnigan wasn't asleep yet, or would wake up.

Tommy climbed back out the window a second later, and a cat followed him outside, meowing.

"Get back in there!" Z said to the animal they thought was Angelina.

"Is it an indoor cat?"

"It's just dumb," Z said. "But she'll be okay till morning I guess, and I'll go back inside in a bit anyway if she sticks around."

Tommy opened the book to the page with the spell. He had to go over to the streetlamp in order to read it. Z watched him.

"You need your blood," they said. "Aysel used a safety pin."

"It's okay," Tommy said. He took out a penknife and made a cut across the skin of his wrist.

"I don't know if you need that much," Z said. Tommy held his hand over it and the blue magic crackled around the blood. He moved the energy sphere over and pressed it down into the potion, which hissed and changed color. Then he put his wrist to his mouth.

"Ow."

"I told you you didn't have to do this," Z said worriedly. They pictured the headline: *Undead Teen Tricks Local Boy into Blood Servitude.* Or something.

"No, it's cool, really." Tommy folded his arm to his side, holding the book with the other hand. He looked down and started to recite the sigil spell. Z felt the temporary tattoo do something as he read, or they thought they did. They also felt an echo of the feeling they had for Aysel earlier, though it felt more like physical warmth than the kind of emotional reflex Aysel inspired. Tommy finished and looked up.

"The thing on your chest is glowing," he said with a hint of pride. "I guess that means we're doing something right."

Z figured there was no point in waiting. They tilted the bottle back, opened their mouth, and swallowed the stuff down. It was colder in their mouth than the temperature outside really warranted. Z felt weird as they drank.

"How does it taste?" Tommy asked.

"I can't taste anything," Z started to say, but they realized that for the first time in months they were tasting. The potion on their tongue was sweet and bitter at once. There was something happening in their mouth. It started with a buzzing that filled the spaces between their teeth like mechanical bees, and a drumming sound in their chest. Then it spread. Their forehead ached with novel temperatures, icy and then hot. Their veins seared. Z suddenly felt their hands against the dirt of the ground; they had fallen over. It seemed like there was water seeping into them, like their flesh had become a sponge.

"Do you need help?" Tommy asked.

Z shook their head. They pushed themselves upright with difficulty and swallowed the rest of the potion, drinking deeply. A discomfort settled in their throat; the more they drank, the thirstier they felt. They coughed. Suddenly they felt for the first time since the accident how dry every cell of their body was, how full of salt. The air was cold, chilling; Z hadn't felt it before now. They breathed it in, uncertain if sensation was an improvement. It seemed as if every pore of their skin was aching for fluid. Z was a desert, parched.

"Water," they coughed.

Tommy had a water bottle in the side pocket of his backpack. He turned frantically, his shoes scuffing in pine needles, and went to get it. He held it out to them nervously, his pale fingers quaking. Z drained it. They felt the potion in their gut, and they were filled with burning and boiling. There was an uncertain moment and Z fell over again onto the grass. Their eyes went black. They did not breathe.

"I thought you were dead," Tommy said when they woke up again.

"I am," Z reminded him. But they felt less dead now than they had, somehow. Something was happening in their chest—not exactly a heartbeat, but a kind of presence. Z wasn't sure how to articulate that.

"How do you feel?" Tommy asked.

"I don't know," Z said slowly, honestly.

"You look a little better," Tommy said.

"Do I?"

"The skin on your face looks less like it's . . . it's less flaky."

Z reached up and felt their face. It was true. There was

something else, too—Z's fingers felt cold against their cheek. Z's cheek was warm—or at least warmer than the icy air which surrounded Z and Tommy in the cold night by the bus stop. Their bones ached more intensely than before, as if something in them was trying to mend.

Z almost felt like crying.

In the morning, Z heard Mrs. Dunnigan get up at a quarter to four and make two pots of coffee in a row. They stayed in bed awhile, to give her some time to herself. At five, they got up and walked out. They glanced over at the potion as they opened the door and realized a cat might come in and knock it over, so they put it on a high shelf.

Out in the living room, Mrs. Dunnigan was glued to the television set. This was very unusual.

"What is it?" Z asked.

Mrs. Dunnigan did not answer.

On the screen there were two paramedics hauling away the body of a young dead man. He was naked, and his body was riddled with bullet holes.

"Holy shit," Z said. "What's happening?"

Mrs. Dunnigan remained silent, jittering quietly in her chair. Her brow was furrowed. Z looked at the screen as a reporter appeared to speak about what was happening.

"The werewolves set upon Ron Hardeback by this Salem grocery store last night. He attempted to fend them off, to no avail. Luckily, a local woman, who has preferred to remain anonymous, tipped off police when she saw the two giant beasts moving quickly past her home. The police arrived and shot both werewolves. Both have since died. They are as yet unidentified. Hardeback has been moved to Salem Hospital, where he remains in stable condition." The reporter onscreen looked tired, like she hadn't had time to put on makeup after waking up this morning.

"Oh," Z said.

"This is very bad," Mrs. Dunnigan said very quietly.

The television continued to speak. "Hardeback had worked for years at a clinic for treating werewolves with electroshock therapy under the Werewolf Commission in Sacramento, California. His leg was bitten deeply, and he has significant nerve damage from bites. Police are looking into the possibility that the attack was revenge."

Z was still mesmerized by the repeating footage of the dead bodies. "Why are they showing the bodies?" they asked. "And they're naked. Is that appropriate? Shouldn't that be censored?"

"They're werewolves," Mrs. Dunnigan answered, her eyes wide as she peered over her glasses. Her teeth chattered faintly. "Werewolves are classified as beasts on full-moon days. Censorship rules don't apply to beasts."

"That doesn't seem quite fair," Z said. "Even if they were attacking someone."

"No," Mrs. Dunnigan said.

At a quarter past seven, the news was still playing, but

Z left to go to school. Cop cars drove by quickly in twos and threes. Z wondered if it was because of the werewolf attack. The sirens weren't on, but they still made Z jump. They thought of Aysel and worried.

Z met up with Tommy in the woods near the school. The trees hung low and thick and green with needles falling incessantly in fine waves on the ground. Tommy waited beneath a tall tree, submerged in shadow. He looked as if he hadn't slept at all. His backpack was on the ground next to him. It was too empty-looking to contain any books.

"Have you seen all the cop cars?" he asked Z. "It's insane."

"It is," Z agreed. They almost added that they were worried about Aysel before remembering Tommy knew nothing about Aysel. They bit their tongue.

"I heard they found more documents. There's a whole ring of werewolves," Tommy said. He laughed nervously.

"I wonder what the cops will do."

"Shoot more of them, probably," Tommy said. "And try to find out who was seeing Archie Pagan before he died, to track them all down."

Z didn't like to think about anyone meaning to hurt or kill someone. It made them think of Uncle Hugh, and what he had said while shaking them. They looked back up at Tommy, who was watching them with a frightening intensity.

"Thank you for what you did," they said.

"What are friends for," Tommy said, not making eye contact, but sort of smiling.

10

Aysel was eager to tell Z about what had happened. When she saw Z at lunch, she ran over to them at once and panted a hello. They were looking better already, Aysel thought. After only one dose of the potion, they looked much more whole than they had a few days before—the bags under their eyes were gone, and they looked less mottled and green and more like a pretty body lying in a casket. Their face was still pale and sickly-looking, and their skin still looked loose and weird, but it was all relative. Aysel, who hadn't been sure if the spell would improve Z's condition or just stop them from deteriorating, was glad that it seemed to be doing the former. Her friend's face was less emaciated and flaky, and it looked as if the cartilage in their nose, which had been rapidly vanishing, had partially regenerated.

Everything was going so well, Aysel thought. She could barely wait until they were safely out of the way in the hallway by the bathrooms to tell Z about Elaine.

"Z, there are other werewolves in the forest. I met them last night," Aysel hissed excitedly in a stage whisper.

"Oh no," Z said.

"Actually I think I have a movie date with one of them this weekend. A friend date. She's nice, her name's Elaine."

"Aysel."

"She wanted to go to the movies with me. I don't think her friend Chad's going. She lent me this," Aysel added, gesturing to the clothes she had on. "I couldn't find my duffel bag."

"Aysel," Z said, interrupting Aysel's enthusiastic, somewhat frantic exposition.

"What?"

"You haven't heard the news today yet, have you?"

Aysel frowned, a cold terror spreading in her legs and back and stomach. "No. I came straight to school from the forest this morning. I didn't get home. Why? What's happened?"

"It was on the news this morning," Z said. They pulled a crumpled newspaper from the pocket of their jeans and handed it to Aysel. "It was at the grocery store—the Cash and Carry, I think. I mean, that's not that far . . . It was really close to where you were. Wolves attacked him and bit his leg and his hand. The police came and shot the werewolves." Z's dry tongue came out of their mouth and traced their chapped lip. "If you saw other werewolves out there . . . Do you think they might know the werewolves who got shot?" Z asked.

"I don't know." Aysel paused. "They said they had friends in town."

They stared at each other. Aysel ran a few fingers through her hair, feeling for pine needles she was sure were still there. Z crossed their arms and looked down at the ground.

"This was covered on national news. It's not just a local issue anymore. It's Salem, Oregon's Werewolf Problem." Z flattened the newspaper with their hand. "It's crazy. I don't even know what's going on. It's so mysterious."

"I hope Elaine is okay," Aysel said.

"Me too."

Aysel almost forgot to ask how the potion had gone. "How did last night go for you?"

"Tommy helped," Z said. "He did the—the thing you did. Said the words. So now I have two casters. Which is probably why it worked so good. I feel better."

"Tommy?"

"Shh," Z said. "Yeah."

Aysel felt like she was losing track of everything that was happening.

Azra was home already when Aysel walked in the front door. The kitchen smelled like tobacco. Azra looked up with a panicked expression. Aysel froze in the doorway, feeling the beam of her mother's gaze as if it were a searchlight.

"How are you?" Aysel asked to avoid her mother asking first.

"How was the moon?"

Aysel looked at Azra. "Fine," she said. She decided not to mention Elaine. "I got lost and was late to school but there were no police where I was."

"Aysel," Azra said, her voice low, "have you heard—"

"I've heard about the deaths," Aysel said. "Some werewolves attacked some guy named Hardeback and got shot."

Azra nodded slowly. "What do you know about it?"

"Mom, I wasn't there!" Aysel said.

Azra walked quickly over and wrapped her arms around Aysel. "I know! Oh, oh. Aysel, I didn't mean that. I meant what have you heard about the case? Do you know the whole story?" She pulled her head back and looked in Aysel's eyes, her mouth drawing into a line.

"Oh. I don't . . . they attacked him and he was a part of the Werewolf Commission, right? Z told me. I haven't seen any news coverage, just heard what people said."

Azra sighed. She let go of Aysel and walked over to the counter. She picked up a packet of cigarettes contemplatively, then put it down again. She had been trying to stop smoking in the house. "Hardeback—the man the werewolves supposedly attacked— had a gun on him when they found him and the werewolves," she said. "They only mentioned it once all day, but I've been watching the news since seven this morning almost constantly. I kept going to the break room at work. They said it very fast, so nobody noticed."

"What does that mean?" Aysel asked.

"It means he was out there to kill werewolves," Azra said. Her voice was high, reedy, hushed. Aysel had only seen her like this a few times. Her nose was somehow narrower than usual, the skin stretched across her face in tight lines.

"Oh," Aysel said. Then: "Are you sure?"

"In the forest, you can hear a werewolf moving from a ways off. Believe me, I know. There is no reason he would have stayed if he had not planned a confrontation." Azra put her hands up to her temples. "Aysel, think about what I thought when I saw that, heard that he had a gun. Think about what I was thinking."

"I'm sorry, Mom," Aysel said. She felt awful suddenly.

"If one man was out with a gun to kill werewolves, there were probably many men out to kill them. And after what happened last night I feel there aren't many people on our side. Do you have any idea how dangerous it is to be wandering outside in this kind of environment? There are police cars all up and down the street near my office—"

"Nobody knows, though!" Aysel interrupted in spite of the fierce and terrified gleam in Azra's eyes. "Nobody knows I'm a werewolf."

"Tell me where you are going next time you go out when I am going to work," Azra said. "That way I'll feel better, like I'll know where to look if something happens. Someone might try to hurt you, and that scares me."

"Okay."

"And for now, I'm going to drive you to and from school.

No buses. If you want to go to Z's house, or somewhere else, I will drive you there. I need to know where you are."

"Okay," Aysel said. Then she realized this meant she probably wouldn't get to see Elaine again anytime soon. She felt the tears—all stopped up until now in the back of her eyes—spill over. How dumb, she thought, but a sob ripped from her throat.

"Oh, honey," Azra said. A hand touched Aysel's arm. Aysel wondered if she should tell her mother about Elaine. She decided against it. It wasn't worth the explanation. She closed her eyes and went into the bathroom to wash her face. When she came out, Azra was watching television, leaning forward, her eyes red-rimmed.

At lunch on Wednesday, Charley Salt and two of his friends were sitting at a blue Formica-topped table in the cafeteria with a clipboard in front of them. A large red poster hung on the edge of the table. A line of students were queued up and slowly approaching Charley and his friends. One by one, they went up and wrote something on the clipboard. Aysel squinted to see what was on the poster, but she couldn't quite make it out. As Z and Tommy moved through the cafeteria and out the other side toward the doors that led outside, Aysel went over to the line to investigate.

"What's this line for?" she asked one of the girls who was waiting.

"It's something Charley's come up with," the girl said. She had pink plastic glasses. Aysel vaguely remembered her from Spanish class. "The Youth Vigilante Squad. You sign a pledge to report any suspicious magical activity to the school or an adult. It's in response to the attacks and the stolen books at the university."

"Oh," Aysel said, feeling the prickle of terror already creeping up her arms like a fever.

Another girl turned to look over her shoulder. "Charley's also organizing a rally for this Thursday. Tomorrow, I mean. There's a bunch of people going to protest the lack of action over the werewolf attacks, so he's getting some people from the school to go."

"How thrilling," Aysel said.

"You should go, Aysel," the girl said. Aysel was surprised that she knew her name. "Even if you hate Charley, it's a good cause to be active about. It's something everyone can get behind."

"Not me," Aysel said. "I don't like crowds." She walked off and joined Z and Tommy outside. Tommy was performing a purification spell. Z was sitting on the ground watching him.

"Tommy, why do you do that?" Aysel asked. "It's really not necessary."

Tommy said nothing and finished the rite, then put the stone and candles back into his bag.

"What was the line about, Aysel?" Z asked.

"Something Charley's done," Aysel said. "Apparently

there's like, an anti-werewolf rally happening tomorrow, and Charley is recruiting the Youth Fascist contingent."

"That sounds terrifying," Z said.

"We should go."

"Why?"

"It'd be funny. It's bound to be a bunch of stupid people." Aysel smiled. Z looked at her worriedly. "I mean, like, it'd be ironic," she added.

"I know." Z still looked concerned.

They ate in silence for a few minutes. Tommy seemed to be eating only raw vegetables, cut up into little bite-sized pieces. Aysel had brought leftover rice and lentils in a plastic container. She had taped it shut because that particular Tupperware always seemed to spill in her bag, and now she spent a while peeling the tape off. She had kept the food hot magically all morning, and Tommy looked over at Aysel's food hungrily when the scent reached him. Aysel ignored him and watched Z. Z looked even better than the day before; they seemed more interested in food than a few days ago, too.

"How do you feel, Z?" Aysel asked when Z's mouth wasn't full.

"Surprisingly not dead," Z said. "I'm hungry."

"We did good with the spell, then," Aysel said proudly. "Not bad for two teenage shoplifters."

"Three," Z said, nodding at Tommy.

"Right," Aysel said.

Mr. Holmes announced that the class would be skipping forward in their history books significantly once more. This time, of course, it was obvious why he was doing it.

"The werewolf civil rights movement will give you all background on werewolves," he said to Aysel's class. There was a nervous twitch to the way he handled himself now. "I think we can all agree that this is pretty valuable information, considering how werewolf-prone our town seems right now. So turn to Chapter Twenty-Eight and we'll look at how that started, and where it went wrong. This week we'll be just reading out of these chapters, so I'm counting on you to stay on top of your research projects outside of class."

Aysel's paranoia was through the roof. She pulled her hair back in a ponytail then undid it again out of nerves. Mr. Holmes spoke of the Werewolf Riots of the 1920s and then moved onto how the 1960s had ushered in a new generation of furious radical werewolves which the government had, he said, rightfully put down. He studied the class with a grim eye during this lecture. At the end of it, Abigail Garcia raised her hand.

"Yes, Abigail?" Mr. Holmes asked, crossing his arms over his chest and leaning back against the blackboard.

"I'm sorry," Abigail said. "I was wondering if you knew—are there more werewolves than there used to be?" The class around her looked at one another nervously.

"Yes," Mr. Holmes said. He looked seriously at Abigail. Aysel sensed that he felt a connection with her and imagined that he was protecting her. "It is true. It isn't something that is widely acknowledged, but lycanthropy has been on the rise for over a century. Nearly tripled in occurrence."

"Why doesn't anyone do anything?" a boy asked in the back of the class, without raising his hand. Aysel did not know his name. "Why don't we kill them all with silver bullets?"

"Now, hold on," Mr. Holmes said. He raised a long-fingered hand and smiled with an odd little twitch of the mouth. "What needs to be remembered, of course, is that werewolves are not monsters to begin with. No," he said as the eyebrows of the class went up, "it is like any other mental illness. They are just sick, and in need of care. Their magical energy is concentrated and ferocious. It is hard to control. Too much magic in one person can drive anyone to extremes."

"Extremes like killing people," the boy said. Aysel thought his name was John, but it might have been Arthur.

"It's true that many werewolves become psychotic without treatment," Mr. Holmes agreed. "This psychotic tendency is why werewolves can be found at the core of all kind of extremist political movements. They lack the ability to think rationally."

Ginger Lewis giggled and made a small howling noise. The students around her giggled in response, though their voices were strained. Aysel could tell they were afraid. She felt her scalp start to prickle, and before she could think about what she was doing, she raised her hand.

"Mr. Holmes," she said loudly, "I don't think that what you're saying is true."

Mr. Holmes paused and looked at her with an expression of vague surprise, immediately followed by a cold look of suspicion.

"After all," Aysel continued, "Virginia Woolf and Ernest Hemingway were werewolves. And they wrote some of the best novels of the twentieth century. And they critiqued the war. And later, people knew the war had been bad."

"They also both killed themselves," Mr. Holmes said shortly, and somebody behind Aysel snickered. Aysel felt as if her lungs had shrunk. She slouched down in her seat.

"I still don't agree with you," she said, but quietly. She did not want to attract too much more attention.

"Werewolves left untreated suffer instability their whole lives, even if they are artistic or creative," Mr. Holmes continued. "Obviously, I think we all can agree that this doesn't mean that we should kill them. That may have been a practical solution in the past, when there was no treatment and they threatened communities, but with the rise of electroshock, lithium treatments and other anti-psychotics, there have been many cases of werewolves making complete recovery and becoming ordinary, if nonmagical. The issue we are seeing in our society is that many more people than in the past are, for unexplained reasons, suffering from lycanthropy, and often they are not getting treatment in time. Left alone too long, werewolves become dangerous, sometimes killers. Or, as Aysel has reminded us," Mr. Holmes added, as an afterthought, "they redirect their harmful urges within."

Aysel looked around at her classmates to gauge their reaction to this speech. They did not look as sedate as usual. Ginger was leaning forward in her seat, rapt, and did not appear to be doodling. Most of the students were studying the photographs in the textbook with deep interest. Aysel looked down at one from the 1960s. It was in black and white, and depicted werewolves with signs being beaten back by armed police. The signs once had slogans on them, but the slogans had been censored out into blurred gray areas. Aysel wondered what they had said.

Mr. Holmes ended the class by asking them all to write a paper on werewolves using primary sources from science magazines. Aysel could have predicted this, but Mr. Holmes now made her more nervous than ever during history class. His panic and jumpiness had been replaced with a terrifying look of grim resolve, which left little lines around his mouth and eyes.

"It looks as though he is about to condemn someone to being drawn and quartered," Aysel told Z when they met up with Aysel in the halls between classes and began to walk together.

"It's really unnerving," Z agreed. "He gave the same speech in my class." They paused and looked over across the hallway. "Hi, Tommy."

Tommy raised his head from where he was pulling books out of his locker. He saw Z and gave them a timid little smile. He closed his bag and walked toward Z and Aysel. Aysel wasn't sure what to think of Tommy; mostly she resented that she couldn't talk about being a werewolf with Z at school when he was hovering.

"It's like people think there's a war on," Aysel said carefully to Z, nodding to Tommy to show him she saw him. "I feel like Mr. Holmes wants everyone to walk around with bats or guns."

"Well, he's swallowed a lot of bullshit about it," Tommy said. "He's just saying what he thinks he has to say. It's amazing what people can make themselves believe. Mr. Holmes is shaken up because of the whole Archie Pagan thing."

"They don't even know that was a werewolf. Everyone just assumes," Aysel said. "It could be the dumb dipshit was just jogging near a bear den."

"Archie Pagan was Tommy's therapist," Z said in a sort of warning tone to Aysel.

"It's okay," Tommy said quickly. "He wasn't a great guy. I just feel bad that he died."

"What does that mean, he was your therapist?" Aysel asked. She looked over at Tommy, squinting. "Just regular therapy? Did you know anyone who went there because of werewolf stuff? Electroshock?"

Tommy swallowed audibly and frowned. "He was pretty confidential," he said. "He didn't talk about patients with other patients. But I knew he was doing electroshock for werewolves. He had a back room for it and everything. I think everyone who went to him probably knew."

"*You* aren't a werewolf, though," Aysel said very quietly. "I know it can have something to do with fey ancestry sometimes. Don't worry if you are, I won't tell."

"No," Tommy said, swallowing hard again. "I'm not a werewolf."

11

The students gathered outside the school on Thursday as soon as the bell rang, shoulder to shoulder in the basketball court. People pushed past Aysel and Z as they went out. Aysel and Z watched from the library window as the school emptied out. The teachers stood in a ring around the group of teenagers, looking interested and nervous at the same time. After about ten minutes of confusion, Charley Salt emerged from the group and climbed onto a chair, and began speaking to those assembled on the cement.

"What do you think he's saying?" Z asked. They tried to sound nonchalant. They held *Hamlet* in their lap and were flipping in a perfunctory way through the pages.

Aysel crossed her arms over her chest. "Probably talking about how terrible werewolves are or whatever." She let out a little laugh.

"Let's open a window. Try to hear what they're saying."

It took some time to pry the window open, and by the time Aysel had wrenched the pane up and propped it in place with a book, Charley was concluding his speech.

". . . a new future, with hope and unity, where none of us must live in fear," he shouted through the megaphone.

The students applauded. At the edge of the crowd, Aysel and Z could see Mr. Holmes clapping with a hysterical gusto.

"God, can you believe that guy?" Aysel said, pointing. "Look at the bald spot on the back of his head."

"He's pathetic," Z agreed.

"We need to brace ourselves for the storm ahead," Charley finished. "Whether or not we have magic, we can stand together against the dark, and keep this town safe for its citizens. Just because we are young does not mean we are blind, or defenseless. Let's show the people of Salem that we know what must be done!"

Out on the basketball courts, students cheered again. Aysel leaned out the window so her arms dangled out over the rhododendron bushes, and rested her head on the sill, scrutinizing the scene below. Z sat on the bookshelf next to her. Down on the ground, Charley smiled out at his audience through the applause and shrugged his shoulders humbly. He got down from the chair and raised a fist in the air—met with cheers— and then began to march toward the gates of the school. Other students followed him. As they filed out onto the sidewalk that led to the center of town, the teachers remaining in the parking lot looked after them. There was an eerie silence. Then the teachers, too, got in their cars and drove away, or returned to the building. The chair where Charley had stood was left standing in the middle of the parking lot, as if none of the teachers wanted to be the one to move it back inside.

"I feel like we should go and watch the rally," Aysel said. "Especially since we know all these idiots will be there."

"That sounds incredibly dangerous," Z said, smiling a little to show they were kind of joking. They picked instinctively at a scab on the side of their face.

Aysel shrugged. "Better than not knowing what's going on. And we'll take suspicion off ourselves by being there. Do you really think it'll be dangerous?"

"It might be."

"It'll probably just be some people with signs and stuff, don't you think? Nothing, like"—Aysel paused and took the book from under the windowpane, which shut with an enormous noise—"Nothing, like, violent. Right?"

"You tell me," Z said. They stood up and turned from side to side, listening to their muscles and bones pop with the movement. They felt much stronger than they had yesterday, but an immense soreness had crept through them. Every twist of their wrist or turn of their head was painful. It was better, Z supposed, than creeping numbness, but it didn't go very far toward convincing you that you were all right.

When the bus came, its doors opened with a hiss. Z and Aysel sat next to each other, looking out the window at the street names passing by. Aysel reached out and quietly took hold of Z's hand on the seat. Z froze for a moment, and then uncomfortably drew it away. Their hand was paper-dry and still had a weird greenish cast to it and they felt like it was repugnant against Aysel's soft, living warmth.

Downtown, unlike in the neighborhoods around the school, there were cars everywhere. People, too, crowded the streets in numbers Z hadn't seen since the last Fourth of July. The gray buildings and low brick-fronted shops that normally looked out on fairly deserted thoroughfares now were witness to an immense mass of people—young and old people, hurrying—and cars trying to park along the sides of the roads. Z watched as the bus passed a group of middle-aged men in suits carrying signs. They couldn't make out the words on the signs. They tried to steal a glance at Aysel to see her reaction, but her face was blank and unreadable. As the bus pulled into the transit center across from the courthouse, Z saw that the front lawns before the building were covered with people. They turned and looked back over their shoulder.

"Did you see that crowd?" they asked Aysel.

"Yes," Aysel said.

"Do you still want to go to the rally?"

"I didn't come downtown for nothing. You don't have to come if you don't want to. I'd understand." She stood up and got off the bus. Z followed her, their knees popping.

The front of the courthouse was overrun with people. The crowd spilled off the lawn and onto the streets, and traffic officers paced helplessly along the sides of the building, trying to keep the crowd out of the road, to no avail. Z and Aysel were surrounded by people as they moved into the crowd. They sat on the lawn or milled around as Z and Aysel were doing, as if they were waiting for something.

"Look at that stage," Aysel said abruptly, pointing. "That's probably for the people who are going to come up and talk. This is really organized." Z looked and saw that there was indeed a wooden platform that had been erected near the steps of the courthouse. Nobody was on it, but several empty plastic chairs with water bottles beneath them, a set of speakers, and a microphone all seemed to promise that speakers would soon arrive.

"Where did all of these folks come from?" Z said quietly. "I didn't even know there were this many people in Salem."

A family with five or six children passed them. Aysel moved out of the way to avoid being trampled. A little girl in a stroller craned her neck to look backward at Z, then turned her face up to her mother to say something. Z swallowed and pulled their hood up and over their head.

As they passed beneath one of the towering oaks that ringed the courthouse lawns, they were driven close to a group of college-age students gathered in a ring.

". . . this is why we need looser gun regulations," one of them, with a huge fluff of blonde hair, was saying. "I was trying to talk to Professor G about it on Monday and he just laughed at me. Now, you know, I'm going to go to class tomorrow and say, Who's laughing? Look what you get by being lax about these kinds of things."

"It's all this academic stuff that makes them think like this," another boy said. His hair was cut short in back. "Even with the censorship, all the universities are like this. They all want to be lax on monsters. Back in Texas nobody would have stood for this. Werewolves are practically extinct there. It makes you wonder if that's why a college town like this is so susceptible to these kinds of attacks. And organizations."

"It totally is."

Aysel pulled on Z's arm and Z realized that they had stopped, frozen in place, to listen. They hurried forward away from the college students, looking back over their shoulder.

There was a tent set up on one corner of the courthouse square with some people underneath it. A clot of people crowded around the tent and moved toward it and away. Some of them were carrying rolled T-shirts.

"Let's go see what's going on over there," Aysel said. She moved toward the tent with a heavy stride. Z followed her, afraid that if they got too far from her someone would accidentally trample them, or else realize they were undead and stab them on the spot with a wooden stake. It seemed like the kind of thing this crowd would do. But as they got close to the tent, Aysel disappeared amid a forest of broad and narrow shoulders, and Z lost sight of her altogether. They hugged themselves and stood as still as they could in the middle of the noisy masses of people, feeling the wet grass through their black canvas shoes. It was soggy and uncomfortable. Z looked down at their feet and realized they hadn't felt any sensation so vividly since the accident.

Aysel appeared at their shoulder. "I got a T-shirt," she announced, unrolling one of the white T-shirts that others around the lawn were carrying. It was screen-printed with an image of a ferocious wolf overlaid with something obviously meant to be the crosshairs of a gun's sights. Beneath the image, emblazoned in green, was the legend "Monsters Want to Destroy Human Civilization".

"It was this one or one that said 'Citizens' Vigilante Squad,'" Aysel said. "This one was more charming."

"I hope you didn't pay for that," Z said.

"Nah." Aysel grinned.

Suddenly there was the screech of speakers turning on and the loud sound of a microphone changing frequencies.

"It looks like the show is about to start," Aysel said, suddenly scowling. "Let's get somewhere we can see." She marched off through the crowd again, and it was everything Z could do to keep up with her. The crowd moved forward and pressed close to the stage, making Z feel claustrophobic. Eventually Aysel stopped at the foot of a tall maple tree with a fork in it close to the ground. She scrambled up and offered a hand to Z.

"I'm fine down here," Z said.

"You won't be able to see."

"Being in the tree makes me feel like they could set fire to it or something if a mob formed, you know? I'd rather not." Z didn't say that their arms were suddenly aching and they had a headache which they were fairly sure would increase a hundredfold if they did anything as remotely strenuous as climbing a few feet up a tree.

"Suit yourself," Aysel said.

Back onstage, someone was stepping up to the microphone. He was a short, broad man with a narrow face and sideburns. Z couldn't see him very well over the heads of the crowd. He was dressed in a suit. As he took hold of the microphone and tapped it, a few people clapped, and this sent a chain reaction of applause across the lawns until the whole audience—with the exception of a few bystanders like Z and Aysel—was pounding their palms together.

"Welcome," the man said. The applause was hushed. "I want to thank everyone who has come here today, whether you are local or have driven here to show your support. I see a lot of Washington and California license plates on the cars. If you've come a long way, I just want to say that we genuinely appreciate that time and energy. Let's give a hand to our out-of-state supporters."

There was a smattering of applause.

"We've come here today," said the narrow-faced man seriously, "to discuss the problem facing Salem." He paused and looked out at the crowd, his eyebrows lowering with concern over his deep-set eyes. "The things this town has been through recently has shocked the nation. We have seen," he said more loudly, "an unprecedented rise in the rates of werewolf attacks this winter." A few people in the crowd yelled their assent. The man raised a fat hand to silence them. "The police," he continued, "have attempted to respond to this problem, but their efforts have been unsuccessful. Each month, we find that yet another monster has done violence to Salem's citizens." The man made a gesture as if he were pounding a podium, though there was no podium. "This cannot go on."

"I just realized," Aysel whispered down to Z from her perch in the tree as the crowd responded noisily to this statement, "I've seen that guy before. I think he's Charley Salt's dad."

"Makes sense," Z said, looking up at Aysel.

"Probably where Charley gets it," Aysel scowled. She looked worried. Z crossed their arms and squinted at the stage.

"And yet," the man—Mr. Salt—said, onstage, more softly, "This is not the first time we have seen this occur." He moved the microphone closer to his mouth. "Those of you who, like myself, have lived in Salem your whole lives will remember older horrors. It is only recently that this town has been able to shed a little of its reputation as a site for dangerous and illegal magic, as a haven for monsters. What we are seeing now is a resurgence." He paused again. The crowd was silent. "The dark forces are testing us. They want to see if we really have the defenses against them that we say we do. They are coming to our gates. The police may be doing their best to stop them. I do not know. What I do know is that what is happening now is not enough. So here today we are organizing—the people of Salem—to collectively call for a needed change." He stepped back from the microphone and bowed, and then quickly bent to grab a water bottle from under one of the chairs. He paused and coughed into his elbow. "There are, of course, many solutions. This was one of the first states to implement werewolf-tracking programs and require registration. The fey regulations advocated in the 1980s were put into place here right alongside the establishment of institutions to house rehabilitated shapeshifters. Shapeshifters were impounded with a success rate seen in few other places. The citizens of this state have voted for decades to put more money into these programs wherever the opportunity arises, with the hope that the government and all the shades of bureaucracy could protect them from monsters, without the panic and violence earlier generations witnessed. Many times, programs tested in New York and then further developed on the West Coast have gone on to be models for nationwide institutions. You all have been at the forefront. You should be proud."

The crowd clapped again.

"But it is not enough," Mr. Salt said, glowering suddenly. He pounded a soft hand on the invisible podium, too lightly. In compensation, he raised his voice, which went up an octave. "You have seen that the government programs have failed to control monsters to the degree you require. You want security. But what do we see? Werewolf attacks, these last few months. Unregistered werewolves under our noses, being given inadequate treatments. A golem attack last year. Rumors of shapeshifters and the undead. Books on dangerous magic missing. You want security—you have not gotten it."

A few of the college students began to raise their fists and banners and cheer loudly. The rest of the audience looked more interested in what Mr. Salt was saying.

"What we need is discipline, not negotiation. No longer can these programs that you have put your trust in be said to protect you. A crackdown is needed. We must strike back with none of the ambiguity of current practices. Monsters do not deserve due process. Monsters are not citizens."

The crowd murmured at this, a positive kind of mumble, growing in volume. Aysel and Z looked uneasily at each other.

Mr. Salt continued. "In New York," he said, "the police force deal with this very simply. In all areas, monster misbehavior is not tolerated. New York has a big population to protect. I'll give you an example. Werewolves not confined to institutions have to observe a curfew on nights adjacent to the full moon and must remain inside for a full twenty-four-hour period on the day of the full moon itself. Many do this, as they recognize that in wolf form they pose a public menace. The ones who do not observe curfew on nights where they do not transform are taken into custody. If they fail to observe a curfew more than once, they are burned. Meanwhile, any werewolf out in wolf form is shot." He paused to let this sink in. "Now," he said after a moment, laughing with a small grin that looked obscene and creepy on his bald-catlike face, "I am not saying that this solution will sound good to everyone. Certainly it is a little brutal, particularly in New York, where there have been no werewolf attacks since 1986. But then we must ask—why have there been no attacks since 1986? Could it be that this approach sends, for once, a strong and definite message, one that actually sinks in?"

"God," Aysel muttered weakly, somewhere above Z, as scattered clapping broke out.

He sank back and rocked on his heels. "Today I am announcing my candidacy for the position of Chief of Regulations at the Salem Police Department. Our current Chief of Regulations, Samuel Warring, is a good friend of mine, and he has done his best for the eight years he has held the position. He has been held back on all sides by—let me say this politely—a kind of bumbling, good-natured bureaucracy and an apathetic or fearful populace who do not believe in the power of police. If I am elected, I hope you will all stand with me in demanding change, and moving our police department into a new era."

The crowd hollered its assent. Somewhere within it someone began to clap again, and the clapping spread, a heavy, pounding rhythm. It went on too long, increasing in intensity until at last Mr. Salt bowed and smiled and stepped away from the platform to chug deeply from a bottle of water.

At the front of the crowd, someone suddenly shouted, "Burn the wolves!"

Aysel dropped down from the tree next to Z. "Come on," she said. "Let's go. I don't want to watch any more of this."

"I thought you were all excited to see what they were about," Z said sarcastically. They faltered as they saw that Aysel looked as if she was about to cry.

Aysel and Z walked together away from City Hall and down a side road. The blare of the speakers and the noise of the crowd could still be heard distantly as they went down a side street. Aysel was rubbing her eyes behind her glasses, swallowing hard every few breaths. Z wasn't sure how to comfort her.

"Let's get something to eat," Aysel said eventually. She grabbed Z's hand and began to walk faster down the sidewalk. The streets farther away from the courthouse were less full of people, and the gray sky above seemed to muffle the noise of the crowds behind them. Aysel began to breathe easier. After a couple of blocks Aysel towed Z into a coffee shop. The bell jangled noisily as they entered. The woman behind the counter was watching the news on a tiny television perched on a shelf, her arms crossed over her chest. She looked around when the bell rang. There were only a couple of other customers in the shop. Aysel ordered herself and Z cups of coffee and two muffins, and they sat down near a window looking out into the afternoon street.

"All those people were agreeing with what he said,

though. I can't believe that." Aysel blew her nose in a napkin. She looked up at Z. "I got . . . haha, I guess I got really scared."

"That makes sense," Z said.

They sat there while Aysel ate her muffin. The woman behind the counter switched the TV station over to a soap opera, the theme song for which played loudly and drowned out any noise from outside.

Aysel used a telephone to call her mother and let her know where she was. Azra drove up fifteen minutes later, and Aysel gave her a guilty shrug through the window. Azra stood outside against the car in an olive sweater, crossing her arms over her chest and scowling. Aysel got in and the two drove away down the street.

Z thought that maybe Mrs. Dunnigan would still be at her bookstore. They wanted to go home with her if she was. The town didn't feel safe. On the way to the store, Z walked a little farther than they had to so they wouldn't have to pass City Hall again. Z wondered how many people were like Mr. Salt. The afternoon was cold and darkening to an ash color. Steam fogged up windows on the street. Far away, the noise of a crowd continued, almost louder than it had been when Aysel and Z left the rally. Finally Z reached The Reading Circle, with its cracked and taped-over window and the display of werewolf rights literature untouched in the display case. Z opened the door, their joints cracking. They trembled with relief to find the narrow stacks of books inside pristine, and Mrs. Dunnigan sitting peaceably by the register like it was a normal day.

"Darling! It's good to see you," Mrs. Dunnigan said from behind the counter. "I've been fretting all afternoon about where you were."

"Me too about you," Z said. "We should close up the store. I think these are the kind of people who won't like your display."

"I was waiting for Sal to come help me board up the windows," Mrs. Dunnigan said. "But I don't think he's coming. I think I want to stay here and protect the place."

"Did you see the crowd?" Z asked.

Mrs. Dunnigan looked about to answer, but at that moment the bell on the door jingled.

"Hello," Mrs. Dunnigan said brightly.

The man who entered was one of the people from out of town, Z could tell. He looked around with a mixture of confusion and something else. The expression was the kind people made when they were ready to be angry but had not heated up yet. He was wearing one of the anti-werewolf shirts from the booth Aysel had stolen from. He walked over to the counter and put both of his large hands on it, and stared Mrs. Dunnigan down.

"I've heard about this shop," he said to her.

"Well, that's very nice," she said, her eyes flashing.

"People say you hosted some kind of pro-werewolf get-together in here." He fumbled in his pocket and brought out a piece of paper, which he squinted down at. "You sell books supporting werewolves, shapeshifters, and monsters living without treatment," he said, reading from the paper. "That true?"

"We also have a section on LGBT rights and HIV education," Mrs. Dunnigan said, her voice steely. "As well as the Mexican labor movement."

"Look," the man said. He looked a little bit taken aback by the tone of her voice. "The folks I'm with think it's inappropriate to talk about werewolves not needing treatment just after someone's been killed. The Salem Anti-Monster Action Council wants to make this town a safe place for people who aren't monsters, not people who are."

"I'd like it to be a safe town for everyone," Mrs. Dunnigan said. "But speaking of town, you aren't from Salem, are you?"

"I'm from Eugene, ma'am," the man said. "Close enough for me to be worried about what's happening here."

"I'm just interested," Mrs. Dunnigan said, "in why they've sent you to tell me this. This Salem Anti-Monster Action Council."

"There are some others on their way," the man said. "In an hour or so. They sent me to ask you if you would like to issue a formal apology, or if you wanted to publicly state that you supported monsters."

"I won't issue an apology," Mrs. Dunnigan said. "I think

what you people are doing is very silly and wrongheaded and vicious."

The man cast his eyes around uneasily. As he was doing so, he saw Z. He gave a start. "Oh Jesus," he said. Z winced and turned away from him and edged around the corner of a bookshelf. They crouched, pretending to be browsing.

"Oh Jesus indeed," Mrs. Dunnigan said. "That's just what I thought when I saw you walk in." She looked down at her watch. "You said they would be coming by in an hour, your friends?"

"Once the rally winds down. I imagine they'll be pretty feisty."

"The shop will be closed by that time."

"They will still plan on coming by," the man said.

"Well, how about you all leave a nice little manifesto stapled to my door, then," Mrs. Dunnigan said.

"I don't imagine that that is what they have in mind," the man said. He turned toward the door, but then hesitated, and moved over toward Z. They were on their hands and knees pretending to look at the spine of a book called *Les Guérillères*. The man stood uncomfortably close for a moment, leaning over them. Z felt his eyes on their neck. They felt paralyzed. They heard Mrs. Dunnigan shift and start to come over, her feet tapping on the floor.

"Can I help you with something before you go, sir?" she said, resuming her customer-service voice with only a slight metal edge. "You're right on top of our sizable French section, there."

"I'm just going," the man said. Z glanced up at him, and at the same moment they felt a heavy weight come down on their left hand, and heard a pop. It was not exactly painful for the first moment—there was too much surprise. They looked down and saw the man's heavy boot lifting off their fingers. He walked toward the door and went out, striding heavily down the street away from the shop.

"Did he just step on my fingers?" Z asked slowly.

"Good fucking god," Mrs. Dunnigan said, and Z almost laughed in surprise. They had never heard her curse. "Your hand!"

"It's okay, I can barely feel it," Z said.

"It's mangled," Mrs. Dunnigan breathed. She wheeled toward the door. "I'll kill him," she said, and started off.

"Don't!" Z exclaimed. They lifted their hand and studied it. Several fingers were bent at an angle. "We should just board up the shop and go."

Mrs. Dunnigan put her hand to her forehead. "Yes," she said. "I guess you're right. We'll fix your hand as best we can when we get home. God, I want to kill that bastard."

"It won't do any good," Z said.

The bus was nearly empty, and filled with an amber glow from intermittent streetlights that lined the route. Mrs. Dunnigan sat next to them with her hand over their injured fingers. They had boarded up the shop with the plywood panels Mrs. Dunnigan had in the back. Z tried to become mesmerized by the passing lights and forget what had happened that afternoon. It did not work completely.

They glanced backward as the bus rounded a corner, and saw a thin pillar of smoke rising from the place where the rally had been.

"It's burning," Z said, their voice rising a little too much. "Something's burning."

"Shh," Mrs. Dunnigan said. "Let's not look back at it. We can worry later."

Z felt their chest draw inward painfully and clenched their good fist around Mrs. Dunnigan's hand. They submerged the panicked yelp that was swelling in their throat and stared at the scratchy upholstery of the bus seats. They tried to think of something to talk about that didn't have to do with the man from Eugene or the fire. They realized they hadn't spoken to Mrs. Dunnigan much in the last few weeks, beyond the daily routine speech needed to communicate. It wasn't the right time, or really the right place, but Z suddenly felt a question rise in their throat.

"Mrs. Dunnigan, I wanted to ask you about Cassie," Z said.

"Cassie?" Mrs. Dunnigan looked into Z's eyes. There was a little bit of fear there.

"Well, I mean, for one, she's the reason you have the views you have, isn't she?"

"Yes. One of the reasons," Mrs. Dunnigan said.

"Did you ever feel like maybe the other people were right? The people that say monsters should be locked up or sent away? That they're dangerous?" Z didn't say *we*. They were on a public bus.

"No," Mrs. Dunnigan said quietly. "It's about loving someone, and seeing them as part of your family. I think some people have the capacity to see different people as part of their family and some don't."

"With your marriage," Z said, "and the way she could change gender." They lowered their voice. "Did you ever feel like Cassie was both or neither? Or did she ever talk about not being sure about being a woman? It would have been easier for both of you if she were a man, right?"

Mrs. Dunnigan held Z's hand. "People often ask that about shapeshifters and fey and werewolves, you know. Except about their species. Trying to figure out where their allegiance is. Cassie could have shifted into any body, but she chose to be a woman, and to be a lesbian. She just liked it that way. There are other shapeshifters who choose to live in many bodies, though it's true that makes people afraid of them."

"Like people are scared of my body now."

"You're defying death. It frightens people who believe in death. People are worried that there will be a time when shapeshifters and fey overtake humans, overtake women and men, and make the whole world shifting or formless. When things like life and death will stop meaning anything."

Z closed their eyes. "I kind of wish that would happen." They looked at the colors on the back of their lids.

The town grew distant behind the bus. When the bus reached their stop the two stumbled on the curb and almost fell, and then shuffled as quickly as they could toward Mrs. Dunnigan's home. Z was thinking of Aysel and her mother, of fire . . .

The night seemed longer than usual. Z watched the wall. They realized they were waiting for mobs to come and break down their door. But the hours dragged on and the smoky night became a mist that shrouded the shrubs around the apartment complex at dawn. The road outside Z's room remained empty of cars. No mobs came.

Only an effigy of a werewolf was burned, everyone learned on the news Friday. Some students had made it out of socks and old sweatshirts and a Halloween mask and brought it out after all the speakers had finished. City Hall had not been notified that the effigy was to be burned, and now there were some minor felony charges being pressed against the people who had set up the bonfire. However, these all paled in comparison to what happened afterwards, when the crowd dispersed into the streets. *Three Salem Homeless Beaten by Mob; In Critical Condition,* read one headline on the cover of the *Portland Tribune. Bookstore Ransacked.* Z grabbed the paper and studied the story beneath it.

In the wake of the Thursday night protest, the copy went, *crowds fanned out around the metropolitan area of Salem. The crowds spread leaflets which explained their views. They also attacked three transients who were sleeping in the doorway outside a warehouse near City Hall, after proclaiming them to be werewolves. Those responsible for the attack were described by witnesses as young college students. These transients sustained bruises and two broken bones before being removed to the hospital. None are currently suspected of any crime, though policemen will make inquiries. The anti-monster activists sought, according to one anonymous informer, to look for people who might be werewolves. Additionally, they broke the windows of a bookstore, the name of which has not been disclosed. One source said the bookstore was targeted for supporting radical pro-monster views. Charles Salt, a candidate for Chief of Regulations with the Salem Police Department who spoke at the rally earlier in the evening, clarified that the activists do not generally see themselves as violent or want violence. "It is in self-defense," he said. "Citizens perceive themselves at risk, and take action to protect themselves." Charles Salt continued that his campaign platform was based on giving citizens a greater feeling of security, so that outbreaks of mob violence become unnecessary. The police department responded to the popular discontent by issuing a statement early this morning saying they would be deploying a full-scale investigation into recent werewolf attacks, and to possible connections with terrorist groups. Chief Fuller of the Portland police will be present at a more comprehensive press conference this morning to elaborate on this plan.*

Mrs. Dunnigan looked over the story, little puffs of

breath escaping from her nose intermittently. She was stirring her coffee with a fork in the Friday morning light that struggled through the windows and lit up the aloe vera plant next to the sink. The paper folded and made crackling sounds against the crumb-covered table. She looked up at Z. Her wispy white hair was illuminated from behind and resembled a halo.

"Well, it doesn't say they burned my place down," she said. "Nice way to find out about it, though."

"Are you going to close the store?" Z asked.

"Not for now," Mrs. Dunnigan said. "I've had this kind of thing happen before. Just after the '92 election, for one, a few years ago. I've never closed it before. Besides, your mother wouldn't have wanted me to."

"My mom?"

"She and I first became friends at the store," Mrs. Dunnigan said. "She was political."

"I didn't know." Z paused. "So if you aren't closing the store, what are you doing?"

"I'll get a concealed-carry license for my revolver."

"Are you sure? That doesn't seem like a good idea," Z said.

"I'm all right," Mrs. Dunnigan said. "It's you who needs to be careful. Make sure you bring people to protect you next time you go hang around in public. That Aysel girl is strong, but I don't know if she would be very good against a mob."

Z shrugged and looked down at their blue flower-patterned plate. Half a well-blackened sausage still sat uneaten in a puddle of runny egg yolk and rosemary.

"This sort of thing always makes me nervous," Mrs. Dunnigan added. She fiddled with the large silver hoop earring that nestled in the velvety brown skin of her right earlobe. The left earlobe held a pearl earring. "I expect they'll have stolen things. Sal will be nervous. We won't make any sales. Maybe I *should* just close up shop for a while."

"It makes me nervous, too," Z said. They ate the rest of their sausage and drank the milky coffee Mrs. Dunnigan had put in front of them. "People at school agree with what's going on."

"Of course," Mrs. Dunnigan spat. "They're all the children of these people, these violent nasty people. You stay clear of them unless you're with me and my revolver. Keep yourself safe." She brandished her coffee fork at Z, and dripped brown onto her newspaper.

"I already do," Z said. "I mean, I try." They bit their lip. "Do you really have a revolver?"

"Somewhere in the front hall closet," Mrs. Dunnigan said. She stood up and took her cup to the sink. "It's been a while since I've had to carry it. I used to in the eighties all the time, even though I didn't have a license then." She sighed. "I suppose I have to go in now. Take care of whatever they did to the shop."

On the intercom that morning, before the Pledge of Allegiance, it was announced that the police would be conducting a search of the school sometime next week. Z skipped second period and instead stood in a janitor's closet, swaying slightly but not sitting down on the cement floor. They smelled their wrists, their hair obsessively. Did they smell dead? They pulled up the collar on their shirt. The lamp in the closet flickered.

Tommy and Z walked to the cafeteria together at lunch. Tommy had cut his hair the previous night, and it was now shoulder length. The long yellow halls echoed with the noise of people and the screech of rubber shoes on linoleum.

"I like your haircut, Tommy," Barbara Walsh said to Tommy from where she stood in the lunch line, as Z and Tommy passed. Barbara was thirteen years old, probably no more than eighty pounds, and shorter than Tommy, but her voice carried.

"Thank you," Tommy said, raising his chin higher. Z could hear his heart begin to pound as Barbara's friends and the boys around them began to laugh.

"It really reminds me of a fairy I saw in a picture book as a kid. Is that what you were going for?"

Tommy swung his head haughtily around—his soft hair flipping— and turned away.

"Or was it a fairy princess? I can't recall." Barbara's voice rose an octave on the word *princess.* "I wonder if princesses are above the law around here. I wonder what the police will say."

Z felt a prickle of anger beneath their skin and in the

stitches on their neck. They turned to Barbara. "What's your problem?"

"I don't have a problem. I was saying I liked his haircut." She giggled.

"Oh, really." Z crossed their arms over their chest.

"Z, leave it alone," Tommy said softly, looking around uncomfortably.

"Tommy looks great and you all can go eat mud," Z said. They spun around and grabbed Tommy's skinny arm, hooking it around their own, and tried to move away. Behind them, Barbara laughed. Z felt like hurting her, but there were lunch ladies all around them, and Barbara wasn't the only one giggling. They bit their lip, feeling the skin peel.

Someone passing Tommy and Z abruptly stepped in front of them, their foot catching the end of Tommy's long cloak. Tommy gave a little gasp and stumbled into Z. The person in front of them—it was one of Charley's friends—spun around, quickly. The contents of their tray—a fish burger, a large container of runny ketchup, and carrots in ranch dressing—collided with Tommy in a heavy, wet thunk. It happened so fast that neither of them registered what had occurred for a few seconds. Tommy dropped his lunch box. Z, who had caught the spray from the impact, wiped their eyes. People around Tommy and Z were watching them, giggling. The container of ketchup had hit Tommy square in the face before spinning down his front. It was now oozing onto the linoleum at his feet.

One of the lunch ladies looked over from where she was

checking students into the system on a large computer. "Did someone have a spill?" she asked, her voice raised loudly enough so that everyone in the cafeteria could hear. Z was sure she did not mean it unkindly. The laughter around Tommy increased. Z saw Bethany laughing with a group of girls by the door. They turned away.

"Someone just tripped and fell into me, that's all," Tommy said to the lunch lady brightly. He turned to a table of boys who had stopped their card game to snicker at him and smiled broadly.

"We'll get some paper towels to help you clean it all up," the lunch lady said. She wiped her face with the back of her gloved hand.

"He shouldn't have to clean it up," Z said loudly. "It isn't his fault."

"Well, it isn't mine," the lunch lady said. She tilted herself off the stool she was perched on and marched heavily over to where the napkins were, next to the silverware. She handed a stack to Tommy. "It's too bad."

Z and Tommy scrubbed the floor with the dry napkins. Behind them, someone said something; Z heard Tommy's name, and then a laugh. They spun around and glared but could not tell who had spoken.

"Let's get out of here," Tommy said quietly, touching Z's arm. "I'm not hungry anymore."

In the hall outside the cafeteria Aysel was carrying her lunch box and grimaced at Tommy's spattered visage as if it was no better than could be expected.

"We have to get you cleaned up," she said, and Z heard the tones of Azra in her voice.

They all went to the girls' bathroom; Z thought it would be a good place to wash up. The strong acrid smell and graffiti would deter anyone from hanging around long enough to continue to harass them. Tommy looked over his shoulder as they went inside.

"I'm not meant to be in here," he said.

"It's fine," Aysel responded, wetting some napkins in the sink and pressing the soggy pile into his hands. Tommy shrugged and set to work getting the ketchup out of his eyebrows and off of his shirt.

"That was the dumbest prank in the world," Z said, watching him. "Like, what the hell do they want to say to you by doing that?"

"It's better than getting beaten up. This shit is going to smell like vinegar and corn syrup and tomato paste into the next century, though." Tommy scrubbed at the cotton with a napkin, which disintegrated from the friction.

"Do you want me to lend you a shirt?" Aysel asked.

Tommy lifted the hem of the stained shirt and picked a few pieces of wet napkin from the black cotton. "That would be really great," he said.

"I'll go grab a sweatshirt from my locker. Be right back." She hurried back out the door, nearly knocking over a girl who was coming in. The girl looked apprehensively at Aysel's retreating form and then glanced with trepidation toward Z and Tommy before going into a stall. Z and Tommy stared at each other.

Aysel came back and handed Tommy the sweatshirt. It was black and had zigzag green stripes along the chest. Tommy accepted it graciously and went into a stall to change. Aysel turned to the mirror and began to fix her makeup. She had been wearing more lately.

"I have to decide whether I'm going to go meet Elaine or not," she said to Z.

"Did you ask your mom?"

"No. She'll just say no."

"Who's Elaine?" Tommy asked, coming out of the stall and straightening Aysel's sweatshirt.

"Someone Aysel met this week . . . downtown," Z said, looking over at Aysel for approval. Aysel shrugged and nodded.

"I really want to go see her. I haven't met any other people . . . like her, like me, before." Aysel glanced shiftily at Tommy as she said this. Z knew she was still suspicious of him.

"Lesbians, you mean?" Tommy asked, looking at Aysel with interest.

Aysel and Z looked at each other and Z turned away to suppress a giggle. "Exactly," Aysel said. "Lesbians."

"Why wouldn't you be able to go? Is your mom like, homophobic?"

"No," Aysel said, barely containing her grin. "Or I don't think so, anyway. It's just that she is worried about me going anywhere on my own lately, never mind meeting new people. I got a lecture yesterday. I'm not supposed to go places on my own. She wants to keep me safe." Aysel pulled at her eyelashes where her makeup had made them clump together.

"I mean, at least it was only a lecture," Tommy said.

"I don't think she has too many other tools," Aysel said. "There isn't that much you can do if you ground your kid and they just keep going out, right? You just say that they're grounded again."

"I guess," Z said. They noticed Aysel seemed to be talking herself into going to meet Elaine. "It is still good to be careful, though."

"We're just going to the movies," Aysel said dismissively. "It won't be dangerous."

"That's cute. You should go," Tommy said. He grinned at the floor. His shirt was soaking.

Aysel looked at him and smiled. "Thanks, Tommy."

Tommy walked Z to the bus stop after school. He had pulled his hair—still a little sticky—into a ponytail. The sun had come out during the afternoon, and illuminated the puddles on the street left over from the rains of the night before. The bus was late, and they sat together on the bench waiting for it. There were moments when the clouds covered the sun, but then they would draw back and everything would flash into brightness again.

"I'm worried about you," Tommy said suddenly.

Z looked at him. "Don't be. I'm fine."

"I'm still worried," he said, turning his face away. There was a group of girls approaching the bus stop. Z didn't want to look at them too closely in case one of them was Bethany. They stared at their hands, and at the wet pavement.

"I can take care of myself," Z said. "You've already helped me a lot, and Aysel too. Besides, Mrs. Dunnigan is looking after me too."

"I really care about you, for some reason," Tommy said in a confidential way. He looked profoundly embarrassed, his ears reddening. "Not in a weird way," he added, looking up at Z. "Just . . . you know. Like you're someone who is important, and I'm lucky to know you."

The bus arrived, and the doors flung themselves open.

"Thank you, Tommy," Z said, feeling like they should add something. "You're a good friend. Take care of yourself, too."

Tommy smiled, and then turned quickly and hurried away.

12

Aysel walked to town from her house in the morning, hours before the time she and Elaine had agreed on. Azra was still asleep, and Aysel knew if she woke up she would absolutely refuse to let Aysel go out alone when the police were everywhere. Aysel knew there would be a fight when she came home; her mother would be worried sick, and would shout. Aysel pulled a sweatshirt on and shoved Elaine's clothes into a paper bag from under the counter, to return to her. She tripped over the doormat, sprawling loudly on the floor, and then stood up and set out into the cold day.

The first sign that things in town were still on edge appeared when three police cars in a row drove past Aysel on the sidewalk. They did not flash their lights at her or slow; none of them looked at what to them would seem to be an ordinary young girl with a shopping bag. Aysel still felt her palms start to sweat. What if Elaine had already been arrested?

She knew she couldn't go straight to the theater because

she would be waiting there for hours, so she walked instead to the library and sat down on the curb outside. Police cars drove by one after another. Aysel shivered and went inside the library. The man who sat behind the front desk looked up at her sharply with steely eyes and then waved brusquely. Aysel sat down in a chair. After a few minutes staring at the wall with nothing much going on in her head, she figured it might be a good idea to pick up a book, to make it look as if she was doing something.

Out of the corner of her eye, she saw a policeman come into the library. He walked up to the desk and spoke quietly to the librarian. The librarian spoke quietly back. Aysel strained her eyes trying to look at them around the corner of her glasses without turning her head. She could not hear what they were saying. The librarian shrugged and pointed in Aysel's direction, and Aysel felt a coldness creep from the base of her neck all the way down her spine as the policeman turned and stared at her. She chanced turning her head to look back at him, trying to put on an innocent expression. The policeman was tall and white and young and oval-faced. Aysel glanced only quickly at his face and then looked determinedly at his torso. She was worried her eyes might give something away—some sign, which policemen would surely be trained to recognize even from a distance, that marked the werewolf. The cop looked at her with a blank, neutral expression, nodded at her, turned back to the librarian, said something, and then left by the front door.

After reading cookbooks for a while, Aysel got hungry. She didn't have enough money in her pocket for lunch after the movie ticket, but she thought she might have enough to get a snack. She wandered up the street in search of options, carrying the grocery bag of clothes.

There were not many people out on the street shopping on a Saturday morning in March. Aysel looked around for someplace warm. None of the lunch restaurants were open yet. She paused and dug one of her mother's cigarettes out of her pocket and contemplated it. She held a lighter to it and looked around. Two officers in blue walked in the opposite direction on the other side of the street. Aysel hurriedly stuffed the cigarette and lighter back in her pocket. She picked up her bag and walked on quickly. The officers across the street spoke to each other in low voices. Aysel set her mouth in a firm line. She would not be afraid. She went into a café full of yellow light and bright people and bought a doughnut. She ate it standing inside the café, watching the barista behind the counter pour hot foaming milk into people's coffee. Then she returned to the counter and ordered another doughnut to eat while she was walking.

The pavement outside the movie theater was disgusting with layers of dropped gum, so Aysel couldn't sit on it. She stood awkwardly waiting for half an hour, eating slowly toward the middle of the doughnut with tiny bites. She cast her eyes round uncomfortably through the parking lot. There were, fortunately, more people walking toward the movie theater than there had been walking around town. Going to the movies on a Saturday was a perfectly ordinary thing to do. A large family of thin blond children and a mother passed Aysel and watched her reproachfully as she filled her mouth with the sweet.

Elaine was late. It wasn't easy for Aysel to figure out the time, but she would look over her shoulder periodically at the clock on the front of the ticket box. Elaine was twenty minutes late.

Part of Aysel was eager to conclude that Elaine had either been arrested or stood her up. Elaine was not her problem, this part of her told her. Aysel did not have to worry about what had happened to her; she should go home, face her mother, have the necessary argument, and then hide in her room until the whole thing blew over. The police would soon leave the streets. There was a larger part of Aysel, though, which was determined to wait for Elaine. This bit of Aysel, admittedly, couldn't figure out exactly how long a wait this course necessitated. Two hours? An hour? She looked at the clock again. Thirty minutes late. She decided she would wait for another half hour. Aysel leaned back against the cold outer wall of the theater and crossed her arms across her chest.

Out of the corner of her eye, Aysel saw someone approaching her. She resisted turning her head until the last second, in case it wasn't Elaine, but then the person spoke.

"Aysel!" Elaine exclaimed.

"Hi," Aysel said, feeling her hair fluff out around her. There was a warm crackling in her stomach and heart and she felt static electricity in her toes and fingers. The air around her did not feel as cold suddenly. How stupid, Aysel thought. "How are you?"

Elaine laughed. "Not dead yet," she said loudly, and lowered her voice. "The cops are crawling all over the forest. We had to move camp really quick last week after the moon. We're staying at a safe house right now—it's what we came to Salem for. Chad and I thought it'd be a good place to stay for a while; we have friends here. Practically every werewolf within a forty-mile radius is at the safe house right now. How have you been?"

"I'm fine," Aysel said. "Nothing's been too bad yet. There were people downtown last night, and that looked scary, but the police made everyone go home."

"The police don't want anyone to do their work for them." Elaine smiled grimly. Without warning she bent and hugged Aysel tightly. Aysel was too surprised to hug back. She inhaled against Elaine's warm shoulder. "I hope you stay safe," Elaine said.

"I will. Here are your clothes back," Aysel said, pushing her hair out of her face. She thrust the grocery bag at Elaine. "I washed them."

"Thanks," Elaine said. She looked inside the bag. "I'm running out of clean clothes. I smell like a garbage dump."

"No," Aysel said.

Elaine laughed. "Sure I do. Even Chad says so."

"You don't," Aysel said. "Trust me." She wondered suddenly if she was saying this because she had been spending so much time with Z. Z literally smelled like something dead, through the layers of clove oil; the smell was imperceptible to most people but strong to Aysel, with her doglike nose. It could be that anything smelled nice compared to that. Aysel didn't think that was all of it, though. There was something that smelled downright nice about Elaine, despite the body odor that hung around her. It was a friendly smell, salty and fragrant.

They went and bought tickets for the movie. Elaine stepped up to the window first and paid with a credit card. Aysel pulled out her wallet and was preparing to count coins onto the counter when Elaine stopped her and handed her a ticket.

"You didn't have to do that," Aysel said, spluttering. "I have money. And you should use your money to buy things like—" She stopped. She was going to say "like food," but that sounded too patronizing.

Elaine laughed again. "Don't worry about it," she said. Aysel stared at her, disconcerted.

They walked toward the theater and went through the doors. Inside, Elaine used the credit card again and bought a huge container of popcorn and a thirty-two-ounce cola, which was almost too much for her skinny arms to hold. She slurped at the straw, her lips curled around the purple plastic. Aysel tried not to watch, as it made the heat in her stomach grow.

"Can you afford all that?" Aysel asked. Movie snacks were expensive. Aysel realized she sounded like a jerk.

"I can right now," Elaine said, smiling.

"Right now?" Aysel repeated dumbly.

"I got the card from a dude I met in California. He hasn't canceled it yet. Do you want anything?"

Aysel looked at Elaine, skinny and tall and eating so much food, and thought of the doughnuts she had eaten sitting in her stomach. "No," she said.

"That's fine," Elaine said. She ate a handful of popcorn and grinned.

Aysel decided not to ask any more questions. She had a feeling Elaine was making fun of her. Why, she wasn't sure. "Right," she said.

They went into the theater. They had had to pick a later time because Elaine had been so late, so they were early for this showing. The theater was empty and the lights were on. Elaine and Aysel sat down in seats near the screen. Elaine clambered over each row of seats to get to the next, somehow balancing popcorn and cola in her hands as she went. Her long legs under her spindly body reminded Aysel of storks which strode through deep water. Suddenly Aysel realized she had doughnut crumbs down her shirt. She dusted them off hastily.

"So how's school?" Elaine asked with a mouthful of popcorn. "Did you make it back on time on Tuesday?"

"Not on time, but I made it," Aysel said.

"Good."

"People are all acting really weird," Aysel said. "There's one teacher at my school who used to be really great to me, but he's avoiding me now. He knows I'm . . . you know. He's the only one besides my mom and my best friend. I trusted him enough to tell him, and I don't think he'd tell the police, but I'm worried."

"Never trust anyone, is what I say," Elaine said dryly. "I mean, it's more stressful to do that, but you're never disappointed."

"Yeah," Aysel said uncomfortably. "I just . . . he seems like a good person, is why it's worrying. He's afraid, I think. I thought he was braver than that. Maybe it's just that I've been so protected until now. Nothing's happened recently to remind me that . . . what I am . . . means anything. But it does, really. It makes a lot of difference when something like this happens." She looked at her hands, her face grim.

"You're lucky it's only one guy who knows," Elaine said. "Only one bomb to go off."

Aysel shrugged. "Well, I mean, if I don't trust anyone, there's three bombs to go off. My friend and him and my mother." Aysel wrinkled her brow. "My friend Z and my mom wouldn't tell anyone unless they were being tortured, but still."

"That's true. You're beginning to think like a real werewolf now." Elaine picked up a piece of popcorn between her forefinger and thumb. "Want a piece of popcorn?"

"Sure," Aysel said miserably. She was suddenly thinking of all the ways she might not be as safe as she thought she was. Z and her mother would never willingly betray her, she knew—but if they messed up and somehow accidentally revealed her, she would be in for it. Danger suddenly felt very close.

"Open up and I'll toss it," Elaine said.

Aysel looked up, alarmed.

"Open up your mouth," Elaine repeated.

"That's stupid, just hand me the popcorn," Aysel said. Elaine looked at her, smiled, and then put the bag of popcorn behind her back. Aysel glared at her, blood rushing to her face in embarrassment. Aysel looked at Elaine and realized that the older girl was not going to move until Aysel allowed her to throw the popcorn. Grumpily, after a small pause, she opened her mouth. She felt like the stupidest person in the world. Elaine threw the popcorn kernel at her and it hit her on the nose. It left a small buttery spot on Aysel's skin. She wiped at it with her sleeve.

"Sorry," Elaine said.

Aysel said nothing. She felt humiliated and desolate.

"Here," said Elaine. She took a different piece of popcorn from the bag and put it in Aysel's hand. "A consolation prize. It was a good attempt."

"Thanks," Aysel grumbled.

"You're great, don't stress," Elaine said, and patted Aysel's hand.

This was too much. Aysel felt a spark shoot out into Elaine as their skin made contact.

"Ouch," Elaine said, looking down. There was a tiny white burn mark on her skin.

"Sorry," Aysel said.

"You're a hell of a witch," Elaine said, rubbing her hand.

"I'm just really—anxious today."

"I wish I could shock people when I was anxious," Elaine said. "That'd come in really handy."

Aysel shrugged. "I have a lot of magic, I guess."

"I wish I were you. I would have fried so many people's brains by now." Elaine sucked cola into her mouth and sloshed it through her teeth. "If the police get their hands on you, you can just—zap!"

"I'd be burned."

"Zap!" Elaine made an enthusiastic motion with her hands. "And they'd be all—" She shook her arms as if being electrocuted. "They wouldn't stand a chance. You could take out a whole police station."

Elaine's smile inspired confidence in Aysel, but Aysel also was horrified about the police beyond the point of being able to be confident. She felt scared and wanted to hug something to her chest—a pillow or a stuffed animal. She wanted to be nine years old again with nothing to be afraid of, in a world where she was still welcome.

"Sometimes I think there's something true about what they say about werewolves," Aysel said. "I think that maybe we are more crazy or more violent or something. I get mad so much, and I beat people up."

"Every werewolf I meet has some kind of issues."

"How encouraging," Aysel muttered.

"Werewolves can't get jobs or houses, so we're unemployed and homeless unless we do electroshock," Elaine continued—quietly, because people were coming into the theater now. "Doctors want to operate on us or feed us weird drugs or shock us, or else they worry we'll infect them, so we can't get health care. We get mad."

Aysel stared sadly at the blank movie screen. "God, I'm so scared to grow up," she moaned.

"Or," Elaine added, "we do get shocked, and lose our magic, and don't transform, and either we report to the Department of Regulations every month—that's if we did it legally—or we get illegal shocks and then live in secrecy pretending we can't do magic for some other reason." She swallowed a mouthful of popcorn. "My least favorite type of wolf is the kind that shocks himself out of his own magic and then spends his life being all anti-werewolf."

"What would you do if you weren't a werewolf?" Aysel asked Elaine.

"What?"

"If you were nonmagical, or just regular magical, and could get a job. Any job."

"When I was little I wanted to be a marine biologist. I'd never seen the ocean."

"The only grown-up lesbian I know had a wife who was a marine biologist," Aysel said. "Maybe it's a gay thing." She said it before she remembered that she didn't actually know if Elaine was gay.

Elaine let out a scream of laughter. "Oh my god," she said.

"I'm gay, so if it is I need to know," Aysel said.

"Ohhh my god," Elaine said.

"A lot of us must like science," Aysel said, pretending that her heart wasn't racing. "I'm literally president of my school's science club."

"Holy shit," Elaine said. "Solidarity."

Elaine reached over and took Aysel's hand from her lap and held it like they were on a union poster. Aysel didn't shock her this time—maybe she was more prepared for it. Elaine didn't let go; she held it lightly on the armrest between their two seats as the movie started. It was not a tight grip—Aysel could have taken her hand back if she had wanted to, moved it and put it back in her own lap. But this was far from her mind. Elaine's skin was hot and her palm slightly sweaty, and her fingers were thin and bony and long. Aysel knew Elaine only meant it as a friendly gesture, but she let herself get carried away anyway. Closing her eyes, she thought: small swallows. My hands are small swallows.

After the movie, they hesitated on the periphery of the theater, cautiously watching a cop car drive by on the street, the tires spraying mud up into the air in slow arcs.

"Want to see where I'm staying right now?" Elaine asked. "I can introduce you to some people. Other werewolves," she added quickly when Aysel's mouth pursed in concern. Aysel was thinking about her mother.

"Okay," Aysel said anyway.

The house was low and seemed to sag in the middle. It was painted black. There was an overgrown brown garden sprouting from the space in front of the porch and behind the sidewalk. Out on the front porch, three women sat looking out at the street. Aysel couldn't tell how old they were, though they were somewhere between seventeen and thirty. All of them were dressed in clothes that had a slightly ragged look—patched jeans and heavy sweatshirts. They still managed to exude a sense of solid confidence and beauty.

"Hey, Elaine," one of them said. Her face was heart-shaped, her chin pointed, and she wore lipstick that was coming off around the middle of her mouth. She had three piercings in her nose. The back of her head was shaved and bleached. She held a cigarette between two fingers and stubbed it out on the step she was sitting on.

"Hey, Alice," Elaine said. "This is Aysel."

"Uh, hi," Aysel said, lifting her hand halfheartedly and waving. Aysel wasn't good at making eye contact with new people, so she looked behind Alice to the house. She noticed that in the shadows of the porch there was a deer skull mounted over the window.

"Aysel, this is Alice, Carmen, and Matilda," Elaine said, grinning, gesturing to each woman. Alice grinned at Aysel. Carmen smiled. Matilda didn't seem to be paying attention. She was eating macaroni out of a Tupperware container.

"Hi," Aysel said again, feeling idiotic.

"Heyo," said Carmen. She was smoking a cigarette, too. Her hair was elaborately braided in a way that made Aysel think it must have taken hours. She had wide-set shoulders and a strong jaw and large eyes, and she stood to greet Aysel. "Is this the kid you were telling us about, Elaine?"

"I'm not a kid," Aysel said predictably, defensively.

"Yes you are, sweetie, but it isn't a bad thing," Carmen said. She blew smoke straight into the air.

"I'm fourteen."

"We know," Carmen laughed. "Elaine's been on and on about you for days."

Aysel blushed and looked at Elaine for confirmation. "Really?"

"I don't know, sure," Elaine said, smiling. "I just haven't met that many werewolves who are doing as good as you, you know?" Elaine reached around Aysel's shoulder and thumped her on the back. "It's cool to meet werewolves who are young and not dead and not messed up. Especially in this fucking town."

Aysel didn't know what to say to that.

"You smoke, kid?" Alice asked, relighting her own cigarette. Next to her, Matilda finished her macaroni and put the lid on the container.

"Not really," Aysel said quickly—too quickly, she worried. She sounded like a loser. But none of the older women seemed to care one way or the other.

"Did Elaine tell you what this house is?" Carmen asked.

"Not yet," Elaine said before Aysel could answer. "I mean, I told her it was where we all stayed, that it was a safe house. She hasn't met too many of us before, so I wanted to take her to talk to people."

Alice smiled, and Aysel saw she had a tongue piercing. "Man, I remember the first time I met some other kids like me. Aysel, right? I hope we get along." She held out her hand. Aysel reached forward and Alice grabbed her hand in a powerful handshake. It seemed like everyone's hands were bigger than Aysel's. Aysel wondered if her hands would ever be so large.

The interior of the house was a blatant, unrepentant mess, like one would expect a house of werewolves to be. The shelves that lined the room were crammed with books and loose papers and jars and empty paper bags. At first one's eyes were overwhelmed by the superficial chaos, but it became clear after a few seconds that there was a method to the spread of objects and scattering of nouns. Parts of it, true, were organic matter: half-empty teacups and beer cans littered a kitchen counter, a pizza crust sat on the edge of the sofa. Most of it, though, was paper. As Aysel looked around, she realized she was standing in the middle of an amateurish printing workshop. The smell of hot ink filled the air and in a corner a fat gray copy machine whirred like a storm, spitting out pages and pages of tiny text intermingled with images. In the corner, a small, fat man was kneeling and stacking each fresh page onto different piles. As everyone came in from the front porch, he stapled a pile together and folded it into a booklet. Aysel craned her neck trying to read the title.

Elaine looked horrified.

"Jesus, are you making a library?" Elaine asked. She glanced over at Aysel and back to the man. "You weren't doing this when I left."

"Josh thought it'd be best to go ahead and copy and distribute the zine now," Carmen said casually over Aysel's befuddled head. "Alice and her girlfriend are leaving tomorrow for Texas and can take a box of copies with them, leave 'em at safe houses along the way."

"Ah. Are there more safe houses than I remember?" Elaine asked. There was an edge in her voice. "Why do we need this many copies?"

"Calm down, Josh paid for the paper," Alice said loudly, stepping over a box of pens and assorted wires and disappearing around the corner into the kitchen. There was the sound of a fridge opening.

Elaine made a scoffing noise. "I don't care if we shoplifted all eight boxes of copy paper or whatever this is."

"Well, then, I don't see what your problem is," Alice shouted.

"Josh isn't even a werewolf, he's a white anarchist dudebro who doesn't know what the fuck he's doing," Elaine said. "And Alice, you are too. What the hell do you know about wolves besides the fact that you've been dating one?"

"I'm not a fucking dudebro!" Alice said. She said it loudly

enough that the people outside turned around. Carmen came up the steps and stuck her head inside.

"Chill out, Elaine, I know you don't like Josh but just because you don't like him doesn't mean we don't. It has nothing to do with him being a white guy."

"Go suck it," Elaine said. "Josh is probably with the fucking FBI. Don't say I didn't warn you."

"That's unnecessary," said the fat guy named Josh. "I know you don't trust me—"

"I don't," Elaine said.

"Oh, piss off," Alice said, and stormed out the front door.

Elaine turned to Aysel apologetically. "Sorry," she said. "It usually isn't this messy or this stressed out here." She glared over at Carmen and then toward the kitchen.

"It doesn't seem stressed out. What's the zine?" Aysel asked. She stooped over one of the piles and picked it up, turning it over in her hands. The cover had a picture—a scratchy woodcut—of a full moon and two silhouettes of wolves. *Wolf Guts #3*, the title read.

"It's a werewolf information journal we put together every once in a while," Josh said. "Mostly when there are a lot of us here at once to work on it. It's nothing special usually—"

"Usually, as if we've done more than three," Carmen laughed.

"Well, we try to put information in there that people can use," the man continued. He pushed his straight greasy hair out of his eyes and over to the side of his head.

"Where to get health care, legally or illegally, which doctors to see if you feel like you want to try experimental drugs, how to avoid cops, where to go during moons, that kind of thing. We also have essays and advertise shows and events," he added as an afterthought. "It's modeled on other community zines people give each other. Down in the Bay Area—"

"This is Josh, Aysel," Elaine interrupted. "He thinks the zine will change the world." Her voice was light and sarcastic.

"Hi, Josh," Aysel said. "I'm Aysel."

Elaine was trying to play the role of a good hostess, but it was clear to Aysel that this wasn't a role she was meant to play. "This whole thing is a mess," she said in a flat tone, looking around at the interior of the house. She picked up the pizza crust off the edge of the couch and crunched it between her teeth. "I hope you all haven't left any peanut butter open anywhere, or Craig's allergy is gonna act up like a bitch. You'd think we were like five years old." She turned and glared at Josh.

"I think it's pretty cool," Aysel said quietly.

"Look at this sweetie," Carmen said, smiling at Aysel. She reached up and tugged at one of the braids in her hair, took out a hairpin, and pinned the braid into place on a different part of her head. "I'm sorry, everything's just a little crazy right now with everything happening. Can I get you anything to eat? Show you around?"

"Uh," Aysel said, looking over at Elaine.

"Oh, go on," Elaine said. "It's not you I'm mad at, Aysel, don't worry. And it's a cool space, mess or whatever. Carmen will show you around."

Aysel followed Carmen into the kitchen and out into a long yellow hallway. The voices from the other room still projected clearly through the walls, and Aysel caught every word of the argument still under way in the front room. Elaine's voice was the loudest.

"Just can somebody tell me why the hell we are printing out copies of this like mad just when the police are looking for evidence that a gang of werewolf terrorists exists?" Aysel heard her shout. "It talks about how Archie Pagan did electroshock for people and has just died and so won't be doing it anymore! For the cops, that's tantamount to saying we killed him. And when we're planning a homeless encampment? Someone's gonna give 'em a tip that we're all wolves, and they'll come here, and they'll ransack every single fucking place we mention in this fucking trash and kill a million homeless people who aren't even wolves."

"Oh, 'cause this is the time to lie low, when we're being persecuted, good thinking," Matilda said. Aysel looked over her shoulder as Matilda strode into the kitchen and shoved past a pile of boxes to get to the sink. She filled the Tupperware container with water and shouted over the noise, "Best to stay silent, right? Maybe they will leave us alone."

"What else are we supposed to do, get killed? Do you like, remember last moon? Or did you forget y'all dated before the wacko shot him in the head? People are dead. It's time to stop." Elaine's voice, issuing from the front room, grew inappropriately loud. Aysel looked back over her shoulder. She could see Matilda through the kitchen door, gesturing in exasperation with a fork.

"We knew it was dangerous. It'll keep being dangerous. That's a risk we have to take. That's the price of liberation. We aren't going to win against them by shutting up."

"The price of liberation! They didn't get shot because of this shit. They got shot for being wolves out in the forest after dark."

"Come on," Carmen said. "They're gonna be arguing awhile. It's a hot topic lately." She opened a door at the end of the hall, and Aysel followed her through it.

They had left the house and were outside again, looking out at the backyard. Aysel paused and stared with incredulity. She was staring at a blooming garden. Under the gray sky green spread out thickly across the ground and up the tall fences that bordered the yard. High walls of fat pink climbing roses and sweet peas flowered, and bizarre rotund pumpkins and red cabbages nestled in the black earth. Aysel looked across the yard and saw chamomile flowers, lavender, and a mess of zucchini spreading into the paths that traversed the soil. And there, near the foot of the makeshift wooden ramp which led down into the midst of it—

"Strawberries in March?"

Carmen smiled and jumped over the railing of the

ramp to stand in the patch of strawberries. Aysel noticed a tattoo on the dark skin of her calf as she jumped, though she couldn't tell what it was. "Yeah. This is all Alice and Craig, they've got like, hella green thumbs."

"My mom's a garden witch too, but she can't make anything grow like this," Aysel said reverently, looking down at a plump red strawberry near Carmen's foot. "It's—it's amazing."

"Yeah. It's funny how magic power works. Some people have all the luck. Werewolves who've never gotten shocked are crazy good magicians." Carmen bent down and picked a strawberry between two fingers and held it out to Aysel. It looked so bright and odd against the gray of the early spring that surrounded it, redder than anything was supposed to be before May.

"So what is this place?" Aysel asked. "I heard Elaine say it was a safe house . . ."

Carmen shrugged. "I don't know how much I'm supposed to tell you, really," she said. "But yeah, that's one of the things the house is for. Werewolves come through here and can stay here if they want. Used to be some of 'em were coming for Pagan's stuff, like, they didn't want to transform any more. Others were just coming to wait out moons. Of course, it's not perfect, 'cause when it gets near full moon we all have to clear out and find a patch of forest, and we can't all do that together, 'cause it attracts attention. Such as the attention you've seen lately. Scary stuff, you know. But the rest of the month we can stay here, get hooked up with resources and all that. We don't always have food and stuff, but we do what we can."

"Do you all own it?" Aysel asked. The dilapidated house didn't look like it would be expensive, but it seemed as if everyone in it was otherwise homeless or traveling. She couldn't imagine them being able to buy it.

"Nah. It's just the landlord lives in New York or Los Angeles or somewhere, owns hella property here and in Portland, doesn't really care what's happening. It was abandoned for a while. The house used to be a bunch of college kids partying."

"How long—I mean, how long has it been here?"

Carmen shrugged again. "Few years. I came here the first time two years ago, when I was moving up from LA. It's one of the only places in Oregon you can like, hunker down if you're a registered werewolf. Otherwise it's backpacking. Unless you have a false ID."

"Do you stay here a lot?"

"As much as I can when I'm traveling." Carmen smiled and leaned against the rail of the ramp. "It's a good place. We're trying to set up this camp, because of what happened to the homeless guys after the rally. Not just for werewolves, just in general, to raise awareness of how many people here need housing and are persecuted not even for being monsters, just for being poor. The argument Elaine's having is about whether we should say we're werewolves while we do it."

"Yeah," Aysel said. She hoped that Carmen would

continue to talk, but she didn't, so Aysel went over and examined some chamomile. Carmen ate a strawberry and smoked a cigarette. Eventually the argument inside the house stopped. There was the slam of a door. After a few minutes, Elaine came outside. She looked very tired.

"Hey, y'all. We're done. Aysel, Josh and Chad want to know if you want to come back here when we have the meeting tomorrow. Get filled in on stuff. I talked to him, he says it's okay."

"Sure," Aysel said. She wanted to know what the meeting was about. She was burning with the very idea of a meeting, a place where other werewolves gathered and spoke to one another. She thought of her mother waiting for her to come home. "When's the meeting?"

"It starts at seven p.m. Is that okay? Can you make it?"

Aysel smiled a little at how earnest Elaine was. "I don't know. I'll try. I'll tell my mom I'm at Z's house." If she isn't enraged about me going out today, Aysel thought.

"Should she be coming to meetings without knowing what they're for?" Carmen asked, crossing her arms over her chest.

"Where do you want to start?" Elaine asked.

Carmen lit a cigarette and looked at Aysel. "Where do you want to start?"

"I don't know, wherever. I'm all ears," Aysel said.

"Well, basically," Elaine said, "we've all come here for the supermoon, but now shit has hit the fan and there are a ton of us in one place just as everyone goes all bonkers and decides to kill us all and also maybe kill all homeless people in general. And we have to figure out what to do about it. So we're organizing a homeless camp."

"And some of us think we can also use it to connect the homeless population in general with the same network of safe houses werewolves have been using, and get some zines out to help educate the public about werewolves," Carmen added.

"Which is such a great idea," Elaine added, rolling her eyes. "Not like the cops wanna know where wolves are or anything, or like, some homeless kid isn't gonna take the chance to nark on us for a couple hundred bucks or whatever reward the pigs are offering."

Carmen shrugged. "I mean, Chad's point is, we gotta stop running sometime. Though I gotta say he's more spoiling for a fight than anything else."

"I think resistance is a great idea, but we don't have the means. We got to be restrained. I think now is a good time to just try to make a space for some of the other people to hang out and be safe for a while, prove homeless people aren't dangerous, don't mention anything about wolves, and then when stuff dies down we can all get the hell out."

Carmen nodded and sipped at her mug. "No, that's all real," she said. She let out a little hiss through her teeth. "The best thing we can do a lot of the time is help each other escape and lie low. Down in the Bay Area and Los Angeles folks have been sabotaging police werewolf records and helping Mexican werewolves get across the border."

"Wait, the thing with the police in California, is that what the Timothy Morris thing—" Aysel stopped, looking from Elaine to Carmen. "The guy everyone said killed Archie Pagan?"

"Yeah," Carmen said. "He was with a werewolf group. But it didn't happen like the police said. We never attacked nobody. Timothy got shocked when he was younger a couple times, but he didn't fuck with Pagan. They spin it like we did so nobody asks why they shoot us."

"So Timothy Morris didn't attack that Pagan guy or anyone? That was made up?" Aysel asked, thinking of the body on the news.

"Nah. Tim lit a dumpster on fire once and got in a fight with a cop once and did time as a teenager for selling something that was supposed to be fairy dust when he was about thirteen, but he never hurt anybody."

"Who killed Archie Pagan then?"

"Dunno," Carmen said. "That's just how it goes, isn't it? Sometimes the cops get you when you haven't done anything at all. It wasn't anyone here that I know of."

"Why was he up here?" Aysel asked. "Morris."

"Couldn't pay rent, couldn't find a job. Supermoon. Same reason any of us are up here."

"Anyway," Elaine said, loudly, "the organizing and stuff's what happens at the House of Wolves. It's what the meeting's about tomorrow. A few homeless people from downtown are bringing their tents and we're putting up a fence around the house and just helping people settle in and talking about what to do next."

"I'll be there," Aysel said, though she wasn't sure if she would be. In the distance there was the noise of sirens.

Aysel walked home, fearing her mother's reaction. When she walked through the door she heard her mother in the garage doing the laundry. She sat down on the couch waiting for Azra to come back in, squaring her jaw and preparing for the inevitable.

Her mother walked in with a large box in her arms. "Oh, there you are. I thought maybe you'd decide to let me know when you went out this morning. I guess I was wrong," she said.

"I'm sorry," Aysel said.

"We talked about this before, didn't we, Aysel? I'm glad you're safe, but you can't keep doing this. You're grounded."

Aysel's heart sank. "Okay," she said. She still planned to go to the meeting later. She knew she had to get there somehow. It was just going to be more difficult now.

"I'm just scared for you," Azra said for what felt like the thousandth time. "There was a police report today. That Charles Salt man got voted in, in the local election. He wants to give the police more power to shoot on sight, to—I don't know what all."

"I'm as scared as you are," Aysel said, too grouchily. She knew her mother was not trying to make her hurt.

"So why do you do this? You didn't say, Mom, I'm going

to the library! You said nothing to me at all!" Azra banged a narrow hand on the table with an abruptness that startled them both. "Aysel, I am on your side."

"Mom," Aysel said, "I'm not saying you aren't."

"I want to protect you. I know it feels—suffocating—but this is the worst time for you to assert your independence. You are all I have, Aysel, besides my mother across the world and my work friends, and of them all you are the most precious thing in my life." Azra said this in the way she often said truly moving things: nervously. Her hand went to her cigarettes again, and this time she lit one.

13

Sunday Z woke with their tailbone pressing against the hard floor of the kitchen. It took a few moments before they put together that waking up meant they had slept. It was the first time since they had died that they had been unconscious. For a second Z had an ominous feeling of dread. They blinked and raised themselves up painfully onto their elbows, half expecting to find themselves in a prison or strapped to a gurney. Instead they opened their eyes and sat squinting and scrunching their pale wasted face against the weak sunlight. It was seven in the morning. There was a cat watching them. Z did not remember falling asleep. They sat and offered a hand to the cat, who walked over and cautiously rubbed against it.

Mrs. Dunnigan came out of her bedroom a few minutes after eight. Her hair was sticking up from her head in crazy directions. She had been sick lately, but she had gotten better over the last few days. She yawned and lifted a cat. Carrying it, she shuffled into the kitchen, her bare bony knees visible under the hem of her nightdress. She seemed surprised to see Z still sitting on the floor.

"What are you doing down there?" she asked.

"I fell asleep," Z said.

Mrs. Dunnigan looked at them but said nothing, and fried slices of bacon and scrambled eggs for breakfast. The coffee maker burbled. It was so odd to have slept. Z examined the bags under their eyes. Were the circles less dark? Z washed their face and felt the skin come away in places as it had before, but there seemed to be new skin underneath somehow. Z wondered if it was the potion. The rain made noises on the roof. It was clear that it was going to be a nice cold day.

After breakfast, with the greasy pan soaking in the sink and the dishes washed, Mrs. Dunnigan put on her coat to go out on a walk with her fourth-fattest cat. He needed the exercise, Mrs. Dunnigan explained, fastening the leash under his large resentful chin. Even if he was trimmer than some of the others, he was having digestive problems. She zipped up her pink raincoat and stepped outside. Z sat down on the couch to wait for her to come back, staring into space and listening for noises in the rain. After far too short a time, the door opened and Mrs. Dunnigan came back into the hall.

"There is an enormous box on the porch," she called to Z. "Do you know why it's there?"

"I don't," Z said, and got up from the table to go and look. They rounded the corner into the hall. Mrs. Dunnigan and the cat, which seemed to comprehend with some measure of joy that no walk was happening, were staring at a box the size of a small coffee table which was laid carefully across the front porch. It was made of a battered, mildewed-looking cardboard, held together with extensive duct tape. The daily paper was laid on top of it.

"Maybe it's a mistake," Z said, but when they examined it the box was addressed to Alondra Dunnigan, in a childish all-capitals print that left no letter or word in doubt. There was no return address. Mrs. Dunnigan stared at it for a few moments with her arms crossed over her chest.

"It's not a mistake," Mrs. Dunnigan said. "This is one of the boxes that disappeared from the bookstore after the break-in."

"Oh," Z said. "So they're giving it back?" They frowned. "That's weird."

"It is weird," Mrs. Dunnigan said. She looked deeply unsettled.

"What's in it?"

"I don't know," Mrs. Dunnigan said. "A lot of the organization of the back room was up to Cassie, and I haven't touched a lot of those boxes since she died."

"Do you think they left whatever was in it, or put something else inside?" Z asked.

Mrs. Dunnigan was quiet for some time. "I don't know if we should take it inside," Mrs. Dunnigan said at last. "Since those hooligans had their hands in it."

"We can deal with it," Z said.

"I suppose it isn't going away unless we deal with it in any case."

"Probably not," Z agreed. The mist of apathy that had been crushing them for weeks, and the fear that had recently replaced it, was gone now: they had slept, and were perhaps not rotting anymore, and could fight whatever the rioters had put into this box. They moved forward and tried to turn over the box with magic, half expecting to have new strength.

"Don't hurt yourself," Mrs. Dunnigan said.

The box shifted, but Z's magic had been coming in stops and starts. Sparks shot out and fizzled away. A corner of the box raised into the air, then fell back down, and that meant the task was possible. Eventually, with Mrs. Dunnigan's help, they wrestled the huge thing a safe distance from the porch, into the rain. Mrs. Dunnigan went and got a knife while the fourth-fattest cat, still attached to his leash, sat glaring at them. Another cat took advantage of the open door and walked outside, tail in the air to show it had no intention of returning. After a moment it seemed to realize it was getting soaked and ran back to the kitchen.

"This is exciting," Mrs. Dunnigan said nervously, emerging again and approaching the box with a knife that looked as if it was meant to slice through bone. Z wondered vaguely where one bought a knife like that. "A thrilling mystery. Maybe it's not a bomb at all. Maybe it's seventy pounds of anthrax. Best back up."

But there was something in her voice that told Z Mrs.

Dunnigan knew exactly what was in the box. They stood back and watched the muscles in the old woman's shoulders strain as she bent to slice through the tape. The box came open like a scab, ripping along one corner. Mrs. Dunnigan stepped forward and undid each cardboard flap while holding one arm over her face as if to protect herself. She carefully leaned over, and then closed her eyes and heaved a great sigh. She ran one hand through her short hair.

"What is it?" Z asked.

"It's another box," Mrs. Dunnigan said. "A crate."

Mrs. Dunnigan moved as if in a trance, back into the house to the kitchen where she kept her toolbox. The wooden box was nailed shut and each nail had to be pried loose individually. With her brittle bones and Z's fragile skeleton it was long work. Z didn't know if Mrs. Dunnigan expected them to help. She seemed singularly focused on her project as she wedged the back end of a hammer under each nail and pried up, moving the thing back and forth until the nail at last was freed, and fell, and rolled across the pathway.

She lifted up the lid of the box. Inside it was packed with straw. Mrs. Dunnigan felt through the straw with her hands, immersing her arms. The smell of the straw filled the air—sweet and farmlike. Underneath it there was a hint of salt. The box rustled as Mrs. Dunnigan drew out something from its heart. At first Z did not know what it was. It looked like a dead thing, dry and black and wrinkled and curled in on itself, and then Mrs. Dunnigan took it in her arms and stood up, and it looked like it might be a leather jacket. But Mrs. Dunnigan was holding it too close for Z to be certain. She folded her little brittle arms around it and folded her torso forward so she enfolded the thing, and stood there, half bent over, shaking.

"What is that?" Z asked, not expecting an answer.

Mrs. Dunnigan was crying now. It took a moment to see really clearly, but she was crying. There were large tears rolling down the wrinkled lines of her face. She stretched her mouth like she was smiling, but there was a deep tension in the muscles of her jaw. After a moment a little keening sound started coming from the back of her throat. Watching her welling up and shaking in her raincoat and boots, with this mottled black thing clutched in her hands, Z felt deeply afraid for the first time since they had died. A deep chill came over them and they stood there feeling it rattle around their bones and trembling as Mrs. Dunnigan trembled, wondering: What is happening? They stood that way for ten minutes, aching, watching.

"Mrs. Dunnigan?" Z asked again. "What's that thing you're holding?"

Mrs. Dunnigan made no reply, but suddenly lurched like she had been bitten and dropped the wrinkled thing back into the box. Turning quickly, she went inside and stumbled down the hall past the living room like she was going into the bathroom. Her feet shuffled against the carpet and made the faint noise of the rain more pronounced. Z watched her and waited for a few seconds, but realized she had left in order to be alone. They got up and shut the door so no more cats could escape and strand themselves in the rain. Then Z looked into the box at the thing Mrs. Dunnigan had held. There did not appear to be any sort of monster or poison or bomb. Mrs. Dunnigan's reaction made it all seem deeply private in a way that Z was nervous about, but they felt such a pang of curiosity that they reached out and pulled the leather thing up into the cold morning. As it came out of the box, a piece of paper fell to the wet cement with it. It was written on in red ink.

Shapeshifter Monsters Out
Go Back to the Ocean, Selkie
Close Your Harpy Bookstore
—Anti-Monster Citizen Action Committee

Eventually Mrs. Dunnigan came out into the rain again. It was obvious that she had washed her face, but her eyes were red. Z did not look at her longer than they thought absolutely necessary. It was embarrassing and horrifying. Mrs. Dunnigan crossed to the box and kneeled down next to them. She was still wearing her raincoat, and it made an odd swishing shuffle of every movement. Her hands shook as she lifted the note and looked at it.

"If it isn't too private, can I ask what the coat thing is?" Z said as quietly as they could.

Mrs. Dunnigan turned over the note and looked at the blank back side. She breathed slowly through her mouth.

She seemed like she wanted to answer, but when she opened her mouth, no words came out. It was unsettling. She was so old, and her eyes were black and deep in the dim morning. She took a deep breath and sighed. "When you're as old as I am you end up having a lot of dangerous secrets," she said finally, looking seriously at Z. "I thought I left all mine someplace safe, but I judged rather badly."

Z waited for her to continue. "I don't understand." They looked at the note again. "Why did they call you a shape-shifter?"

"When Cassie and I met, in Ireland, she was studying seals," Mrs. Dunnigan said. She reached out slowly and ran her hands over the leather of the thing in the box. Z saw her eyes were watery. "One day she found me when I was on the beach, and she had come back from the water. I'd been watching her swim as a seal, out near the point where my family was summering. I watched her turn from a seal into this beautiful solid woman who had the biggest arms I'd ever seen, and I thought, I want her to hold me and never let me go. I went up to her and let her see me."

"Do they have you confused with Cassie?" Z asked. "Since she was a shapeshifter?" They looked back at the note. "A shapeshifter isn't the same thing as a selkie, I thought."

Mrs. Dunnigan slowly shook her head. "They mean me," she said.

She lifted the thing in the box and brought it out completely, standing as she did so. What Z had thought was a coat fell the full length of Mrs. Dunnigan's body to the ground. It was a skin—but a skin which had not been cut open. It was somehow folded, opened, without there being any kind of cut or seam. It took you a moment, but you could see it once you knew. There were the odd legs, the eyes, there the tail. A sealskin. The deep chill cutting through Z got worse and an enormous tension shot through their legs and gut.

"Cassie told me she was keeping my skin someplace safe. She hid it so we could be together. I knew it was in the bookstore someplace, so I never went rummaging in boxes in case I found it by accident. I knew I would be able to find it again if I needed to go back to the water. This year I almost went looking for it when I was sick. I thought I might be dying. But I stopped myself, because you needed me."

Z stared at the old woman, bent low with the weight of the skin.

"Oh," they said finally.

Mrs. Dunnigan took a few moments to gather herself, and then she closed her eyes and opened them again and looked at Z with those deep black pupils and lids red with crying. "They took it from the bookstore. They could have burned it. If they had burned it I would have died."

"Now you have it back," Z said, worried. "They didn't burn it. Can I see?"

She lifted up the skin again and it flapped forward, toward Z, letting off a warm, musky, salty smell, mixed with the smell of the straw it had been packed in for who knows how many years. It hung there, dead and dire and unfathomable.

"It's beautiful," Z said.

"Do you understand?" Mrs. Dunnigan asked Z, leaning forward. "Look at it. This is the kind of skin that people in the North used to hunt. Look how thick it is, how smooth, how dark. There was such a huge trade in sealskin at the turn of the century."

"You're a selkie," Z said, framing it aloud and hearing their own voice crack. "A selkie, and this is your skin."

"Yes," Mrs. Dunnigan said, and two tears sped down her face simultaneously. She had embraced the withered leathery thing again. "Oh lord. My skin. My skin. They take it from you and you don't know what it feels like to be without— My skin."

Z watched her, unmoving. "Why didn't you tell me?"

Mrs. Dunnigan's eyes met Z's for only a moment. "You always have to be careful."

"I know."

"Z, darling, I love you," Mrs. Dunnigan said suddenly, and lurched forward with the terrible black thing around her shoulders. She threw her arms around Z. "I love you so much."

It felt like a goodbye. Z did not want to go too long without saying what they were thinking, so they braced themselves and clenched their jaw tightly and burst forth with it. "If you're a selkie, doesn't that mean you have to go back to the ocean now that you have your skin?"

Mrs. Dunnigan's smile faded a little at that.

"Doesn't it?" Z asked again, looking with determination out the window. "That's the rule, right? Selkies are brought from the ocean to live when a human takes their skin and hides it from them, and they return when they get it back. Ancient magic. So you getting your skin back, that means that you go back to the ocean."

"Yes, it does." Mrs. Dunnigan paused, and there was a thing hanging in the air then that felt heavy and wet like a body underwater. "That's why they gave it back to me instead of burning it or telling the police. So that I'd have to leave you alone."

"So now that they know where we live, and they know that you have to leave," Z said, "they'll come here . . ." They paused. "Who's the 'they'? The rioters?"

"Probably," Mrs. Dunnigan said. "The man who stepped on your fingers, maybe."

"They'll come here, then," Z said.

"I don't know how soon," Mrs. Dunnigan said. She scowled. "We should put the box back where it was so it looks like we haven't opened it. That'll buy us time, unless they're watching all hours of the day."

She busied herself for a few minutes closing the crate, and shutting the box over it. She told Z to go get tape and tape it closed again, and they did. They went inside. Then Mrs. Dunnigan started moving around the house as if she were shutting it up and preparing to go on a journey. But she packed no bags.

Z stood in the kitchen and felt their muscles spasm and their knees shake.

"You could stay just for a little," Z said. "Throw them off."

"You can't know the—the pain of this." Mrs. Dunnigan was speaking through gritted teeth. "They're bastards. I didn't think they could do this. I didn't tell Sal to move the box when I had time. Now I have to leave you here, and there's no time." Mrs. Dunnigan was pulling the curtains of the house closed. "There's no time for *anything* I meant to do."

"Is the ocean thing forever? Can you go in and then come back out?"

"That depends on a lot of things," Mrs. Dunnigan said. She turned away and Z saw her shoulders shaking. Z moved around the table and leaned against it, staring her in the face, trying to make eye contact.

"What am I going to do?" Z asked. "Go with you and walk into the water?"

Mrs. Dunnigan was quiet. She looked down at the floor and fumbled in her pocket for her keys. She found them and thumbed through them as if to make sure they were all there. Then she handed the ring to Z.

"Stay here until you can't. You have the checkbook. My savings aren't much, but it is a little. My bank card is here in the drawer."

Z watched Mrs. Dunnigan point to the drawer. They froze up and felt the world narrow around them. They took the keys from Mrs. Dunnigan, but their hands were stiff and they dropped the keys on the floor. Z's body was shaking. Mrs. Dunnigan finally looked at Z. She exhaled slowly.

"If I resist and I have the skin with me I'll get sicker. I'll waste away. Not a matter of weeks but three or four days. I'm old. You must have heard me coughing in the morning. I couldn't survive it. The doctor told me three months ago I didn't have much longer and I didn't believe him, but lately it's been getting hard to ignore. The water is the only thing that will save me."

"You're abandoning me," Z said abruptly. "I can't live alone, like this. I'm a kid. I'm just a kid. You said you would protect me."

"You will be taken care of. You have your friends. You'll get out of this town. I'll make sure you do. Once I'm in the water I'll have more of my magic. I'll do magic for you, for safety."

Z did not say anything. They looked at the blue teapot sitting on Mrs. Dunnigan's table and felt like sweeping it off with their hand, but they just stood there leaning on the table, staring at the pattern on the ceramic.

The light in the kitchen looked yellow against the blue daylight outside.

Z made tea for her and fed the cats. After the box had been opened they had begun to behave strangely, pawing at the doors. Mrs. Dunnigan opened the door a little and three cats departed, rapidly, as if there were a stench behind them. Mrs. Dunnigan called her friend Sal, from the bookstore. Z wasn't sure if it was the college student who helped her sometimes with stocking or the older man who worked on Saturdays. Z had been told and had forgotten the names of both. Mrs. Dunnigan spoke to Sal about the rain. Her voice was still shaky. Her narrow knees knocked and the black sealskin hung down her back as she stood there in the yellow kitchen. She curled the cord around her withered finger and said it would be nice to drive to the seaside today, wouldn't it? Despite the rain? Can't you humor an old woman? She could give Sal that month's check in person, too.

Sal agreed. Mrs. Dunnigan set the phone down and explained that she would be leaving in an hour. Z was glad that she did not try to look solemn for Z's sake; the brightness in her eyes was unconcealed and one could feel a sweaty buzz coming off her. She wrapped the skin in newspaper and held it on her lap, sitting on the couch by the door looking out at the road, and Z helped her pack a picnic to take with her. Sandwiches and carrot sticks and apples. It was probably unsanitary for a dead child to make food, but Z wore rubber kitchen gloves. The car pulled up outside just before one in the afternoon and Mrs. Dunnigan got into it, and then it drove away. And so Z was alone with the cats, who were pawing at the door. Z opened the door and the rest of them ran outside. Z could see none of them lingering in the yard and became worried for a moment, but then put out a bowl of cat food and thought, They will come back if they want to.

Aysel said over the phone that she had to go to a meeting across town for anarchist werewolves and she couldn't get out of the house, and for some reason she thought Z would have some idea as to how to resolve the situation. Sitting next to the phone in Mrs. Dunnigan's kitchen, Z tried to help.

"Tell her you're going to the store."

"She's grounded me."

"Go to the bathroom and climb out the window and when you get back say you went to the store."

"I can't do that."

"Can't, or won't?"

"Z, please. Can you think of anything—is there anything with school we might be doing? That I could come over to your house for?"

"I don't know," Z said. "I haven't been doing that much homework."

"That's it. You're going to fail out of school and I have to help you study. There's a paper tomorrow that you didn't know about. I am trying to help you and you're doing your best, but you're too sick to get around. That's why I went to the library yesterday!"

"What are you talking about?" Z asked.

"We'll go through this together, buddy, don't worry," Aysel said loudly. Z sensed Azra was in the room. Then there was a click on the other end of the line and a long beep. Z slouched on the floor staring at the back of Mrs. Dunnigan's olive-green couch. The fabric had long ago been clawed to shreds. Outside, they heard the bus screech to a halt at the stop, and then hiss and lurch away. The rain had stopped, but the sky was still dark.

And Mrs. Dunnigan would not be home. By now, the water would have come up and closed over her head, by now she would be far out in the deep salty clean sea. Z prayed there were no oil slicks near the coast. Z thought of the miles of water, so cold, and dark, and the sky above the sea gray, and shivered.

Aysel came over to get Z and they went on the bus and then walked, to a part of town Z did not know, and now Z sat on the stoop of the black house. In the yard there were a few tents set up covering the sparse yard and sidewalk, and someone had dragged a picket fence so it bordered the yard. The tents were empty; their occupants were inside with the other people who lived in the house. There was no more rain and the sky was drying out. Z was glad. They could feel it now when the rain fell on them. They were cold. They felt more cold lately, felt the absence of heat as a kind of ache, and even though that was probably better than being totally numb, or being in pain and falling apart, they didn't like it. The rain made the cold worse, so now that it was dry—maybe it would get better. It would have been warmer inside, but Z did not want to go inside. From inside they heard the voices of the meeting, a low mumble through the glass. Z knew it was important. It had definitely sounded political. Z was glad Aysel was meeting people, but the noise and the buzz and the intense sound of all those unfamiliar rushing hearts was too much when they went in with Aysel and it only took about ten minutes before Z had said they were going outside, to smoke. Z hadn't known why they had said that, but it seemed like a good cover story, and Aysel smoked now, apparently, and carried cigarettes around with her, so it was convenient to take one or two and just check out. The image of the waves coming up to Mrs. Dunnigan hit them again. All that cold water, the feeling of all that salt and seaweed, the joy in her eyes and the melting bones becoming one with the skin kept so long in a box. The bubbling breath of seals and the deep salt water after all those years of pretending.

It must be perfect joy, Z thought. I am happy for her. She can find a group of seals and go up north to the San Juans and frolic, and avoid boats, and eat salmon. There must be a great mystical beauty in being out at sea and waking and swimming in the surging waves watching the dawn. Z thought of the empty house with the cats in it, and the rent. Mrs. Dunnigan had left without telling them how to pay rent. Z knew she had a pension check that came every month, but Z wouldn't know what to do with it. She had said Z would be taken care of. By whom?

But then there was the question, how long would Z be

here to worry about it? The Anti-Monster league, or whatever they called themselves, could be watching the house.

"Hey," a voice said behind Z.

Z turned around. It was a boy. They realized after a second that it was the boy they'd seen over a month ago when he asked for a cigarette and directions. Z realized that the girl who had been with him was Aysel's Elaine. The boy smiled his weird smile and Z looked at his mustache as he lit his own cigarette.

"I saw you before," the boy said. "You said you didn't have a cigarette then. Started smoking?"

"Stuff happens," Z said glumly.

"Yeah," the boy said. He was looking at the scars on Z's forehead. "Did we exchange names? Someone said Aysel said your name was Z."

"It is," Z said. "I mean, not legally, but that's what I go by."

"I'm Chad," the boy said. "Same deal. What I go by."

Something clicked in Z's head. "I knew someone named Chad a while ago," they said.

"That's funny, because I had an internet friend from this town named Z." The boy smiled. "They were supposed to be older than you, though."

Z stared at him. "Wait," they said. "Wait."

"Did you listen to the Team Dresch tapes?" Chad asked.

"I did," Z said. They felt a series of sparks around their heart suddenly sink into them in a way that was painful. They had a vivid memory of lying with their headphones on in their parents' attic, clutching Chad's letter. The cassettes had sounded like an echo of an echo of the music because they'd been recorded on a tape recorder from somebody else's stereo. It had only been four months ago.

"What did you think?" Chad said. "They're a little corny, but I like what they're trying to do."

Z tried to exhale and felt the smoke catch inside them. "They seemed really cool. But I had to leave my tape deck and stuff when I left my uncle's."

"I thought you lived with your parents."

"They died," Z said.

"Shit," Chad said.

"Stuff happens," Z said. "It's not a big deal."

"Yeah it is. Stuff happens and you get weird forever," Chad said. Z felt him looking at the scars on their neck and wondered if he knew.

"I was already weird."

Chad had finished his cigarette and stamped it out with his foot. "Look, Z. I'm glad you're here. I know it's weird to see each other in person and you maybe didn't want that, but I want to be your friend or bro or whatever still. I'm no good at that stuff but I think you're a cool kid still."

"Thanks," Z said. It sounded dry but they were sort of dry-sobbing. They wanted to touch Chad, and couldn't figure out what to do about it.

"I think we all have to get out of town pretty soon. I don't know when I'll see you again, but I can write you."

"I'm probably not staying long either," Z said.

Chad looked at them seriously. "Is it that bad here for you?"

"How bad is bad?" Z asked. "Nobody's set me on fire yet."

"I guess that is the standard," Chad said. "It's hard to leave a place until it's literally killed you. But then again, you don't want to wait that long." He spat on the deck. "You sound old. I forget teenagers aren't dumb. I'm sorry if I ever treated you like you were dumb."

"Maybe we'll leave at the same time," Z said. "I can go with some of you guys."

"The cops are on us, probably," Chad said. "We won't all get busted, but werewolves right now aren't great road buddies."

"I want to stay in touch. Whenever you're online. I don't know when I'll be online all the time, but I'll write back."

"I can definitely say yes to that," Chad said.

They hugged for a second. Z wasn't sure who had moved first. It only lasted a second, and they didn't make eye contact. Then Chad slapped Z on the back and went inside.

Z stood up and, creaking, stretched. They walked into the weird narrow alley at the side of the house, where the mud was wet and thick, and balanced on a wooden beam that someone had thrown down, and took out one of the cigarettes Aysel had given them. They also took out the lighter with the little picture of Betty Boop on it. They wondered where Aysel had gotten the lighter. Their hands were able to bend. There was a collection of sighs that filled their lungs that seemed all at once to burst into the air.

The sirens started a long way off and got closer over the course of minutes, and you didn't notice that kind of thing right away; it was just a kind of echo, until it was right there on top of you. Z tuned out the sirens, because there had been so many lately. They thought about Chad. They focused on the cigarette, burning down at the low gray tips of their fingers. Then they looked up and there were policemen there, and four cars, with the lights flashing. Z dropped the cigarette into the mud. They looked up at the window. They could try to knock on it, to alert someone—but the door to one of the police cars was opening, and Z was pressing their body into the side of the house instead. And really it was times like that when you felt like a huge coward. Wasn't it? Z held themselves as still as they could. The police did not see them. They could hear everything, though.

14

The police had guns—you could see it as they crossed the blackened garden. Carmen threw the curtains closed and Josh looked around with an expression of panic. Aysel thought, It isn't pretend anymore, and then she froze up and didn't think anything except: Where is Z?

Aysel had felt really daring when she had run out the door yelling over her shoulder to Azra about how Z needed help with homework. She knew that Azra barely heard her, and that she was hardly intelligible, and in some part of her mind knew that Azra was going to worry about where she was, was probably going to pray for her, but the hurt that thought brought on hung where it was, far away from the present. Aysel's feet had splashed through puddles on the way to the bus and the wind had whipped her heart into a delicious feeling, a feeling of bright future. Even Z's somber dead face and the smell of liver and onions and cats in Mrs. Dunnigan's kitchen couldn't dampen her mood—on the contrary, it was wonderful, Aysel thought, to be watching Z pulling on red rain boots in the bright kitchen as the sky darkened outside. It was already night, really, and the clouds hung down thick and the sun was nearly set as they went out together and caught the bus. Cars passed in the night and Aysel rocked side to side in the seat of the bus, barely containing her smile.

The house had been full and there was the smell of food—rolls from a can that had been pulled apart clumsily and baked in the crusty rusting brown-black oven on a blackened cookie sheet, and vegetarian chili, because some of the wolves said they were vegetarian when they weren't in a moon and some of them even when they were. Alice had made the chili, and Aysel heard people call out compliments to her. There were bowls of chips that were a little stale but tasted fine, said Chad, when you dipped them in salsa. And someone had made big mugs of coffee for everyone; Aysel didn't know her name, but she had green hair.

There were the zines everywhere, and all of the art supplies that had been used to make them, all the pens and stencils and two or three typewriters and pieces of loose paper. A couple of wolves were lying around on the floor making drawings on paper, still, and the fat guy, Josh, was stapling copies of the zine. Aysel picked up one of the zines that was sitting on top of a pile and flipped open its gray cover. There was an image on the inside cover of several photographs of wolves, cut up and with the heads on human bodies, next to a little drawing of a turntable and a box of records and some beer cans and pizza, and underneath this was a table of contents. Aysel ignored this and flipped through the pages. She had read zines before and was used to them being slightly illegible and weird, and she sort of liked it when the font was really small, because it made you concentrate. Though it was true, in the dim light of the black house, with one lamp on in the corner and a lightbulb hanging from the ceiling, it was hard to read. But it was clear there were things in there that Aysel was going to have to come back to and read, like: "Punk Rock and Lycanthropy," "How I Survived Prison," "The Real History of Werewolves." There was a really grainy badly copied page that had a poem on it by Audre Lorde, and someone had made a border for it out of exclamation marks . . .

Aysel sat down on the floor and pulled Z down next to her and felt the crumbs from other people's snacks under her knees and didn't care; she handed one of the zines to Z and said, Read this, and Z had obediently opened it up and looked at it. Aysel folded her copy of the zine and stuffed it into her shirt pocket and stood up, because she had seen Carmen. Carmen's eyes widened in deep shiny delight—

"I'm so glad you could make it, Aysel," she said. "I hope you aren't going to get in trouble with your mom."

That made Aysel a little embarrassed, but she smiled. "You'll take care of me as well as she would," she said to Carmen. For a moment she really meant it—maybe longer than a moment.

Z went outside after about ten minutes and Aysel had thought that was fine, because Z didn't feel comfortable around so many people. Aysel thought Z maybe didn't feel like they belonged right now. But it was okay, because Aysel felt sure Z would see that they were a part of all this too, part of the movement that had to happen. The police brutality, the oppression was based on being a werewolf or homeless, and Z was luckier than a lot of the people here, but they felt the pain Chad and Carmen and everyone felt. Maybe it would take a couple of meetings, but they would feel it too. Aysel handed them her cigarettes and smiled at them as the door shut.

The meeting itself wasn't really all that comprehensible to Aysel. The people were all continuing a conversation they had started earlier, that much was clear. Of course it was about the two who had died during the full moon. Everyone was really tense, and Aysel thought she understood. A question was hanging in the air, and Aysel thought it had something to do with nobody knowing if they were safe anymore. Chad, who had talked a lot in the first part of the meeting, left and went onto the porch when someone tried to argue with him.

"What we have to ask," Josh said, "is how much our current strategies of organization are sufficient. At some point we have to be visible, and we have to take action that makes it clear that we refuse to be seen as monsters, or as diseased. We've been talking about imitating some of the strategies of Act Up. Matilda, you especially seemed to want to talk about that."

"That's not what I said," Matilda said. "Anyway, why are you saying *we*? You aren't a werewolf."

"Well, I thought that was what you were saying," Josh said. "Anyway, if we did do that, it probably wouldn't be an action centered in Salem, since there's so much risk. But if we persuaded some of the people down in Oakland and the Bay, like Jake's friends, that they should do an action with us, we might have enough numbers to make a national statement."

"What the hell would you have us do, a die-in where we all lie down in the street? A march on the capital?" Elaine said. It was the first time she had spoken.

"Well, I'm not saying the strategies others have used are going to work here—"

"Josh, most of us are illegally in Oregon. We haven't even been in the registration office in years. We're homeless, we're poor, and we're afraid. Police are everywhere trying to arrest us. Do you understand that?"

"That's exactly why we have to show that we're not defeated, that we can't be defeated, by doing something visible that has dignity. Something that demonstrates our humanity and shows that we're angry, but that we're controlled, organized, reasonable."

"Let some liberal do-gooder do that," Carmen said from a seat near the door, where she was periodically checking behind the curtains. "God knows there are enough of them in San Francisco. I'm with Elaine. We were talking about how to get people out of the state last week, and then two of us die and now you want to be more visible to cops? I still got a scar from the last time I was in a protest."

"Part of the point," Chad said suddenly, opening the door, "is being committed to change. Isn't that right, Josh?"

Josh looked uncomfortable. "I mean, Carmen has a point," he said. "I think it is important to make sure everyone is safe."

Aysel didn't understand anything about what was happening, but she was intrigued.

It was also clear that there were rules for who got to say what when, because Josh was taking up the most space talking, and it seemed like he was the president of whatever it was that they were trying to do, but after a while other people started talking too, without raising their hands or anything, and they would disagree with Josh or agree, and sometimes they would be loud, and there were some people who never said anything. Aysel knew some of them were the homeless people who were just here for the camp. She wondered if they had come, not because they liked werewolves or things that the guy named Josh liked, but because it was supposed to be safer than being downtown. Outside it was dark and cold and quiet and in the black house the yellow lights burned warmly and everything was so full of heat and smell and sound that Aysel knew she was a part of something.

And then the police came.

Carmen was the first one to notice. "Are those sirens?" she asked loudly, over Chad, who was talking about someone named Emma Goldman and someone else named Bakunin. Chad stopped mid-sentence, and the couple of people who were whispering to each other near the entrance to the kitchen also became quiet. Everyone listened, and sure enough, the sirens were there.

"They're getting closer," Alice said after a second. Everyone looked around uneasily.

"Maybe it's time to call the meeting," someone said. "Disperse."

"What do you mean, disperse?" a woman in the corner asked. "Where are we supposed to go?"

"We better move to the basement," a guy said who was sitting on the floor near Aysel. Aysel had not been introduced to him, but she thought he was Craig.

"We don't need to move to the basement and we don't need to stop talking. There've been cops all around for days. They don't know we're here," Josh said. There was a pronounced, careful calmness in his voice. But he said this softly, and Aysel could hear the sirens getting closer in the background. Everyone was a little tense.

"Maybe move just in case," someone said, and there was a general shuffle of standing. Matilda and Alice disappeared around a corner. Elaine rolled off the couch and rose up, looking at Aysel with concern.

"You might want to leave," she said. "I can't tell how close those sirens are. Everyone's getting a little nervy and weird anyway and this meeting isn't going anywhere."

"I like the meeting," Aysel said. "I like hearing people talk."

"Those sirens are really close," Carmen said.

Alice went over to the window and looked out. "Shit, you can see the lights a street over. They are coming here."

Aysel was left staring at Elaine for a second as around them everyone leapt from where they were and moved rapidly. A few people immediately raced for the back door, but more gathered around as Alice unlocked the door to the basement. Then Elaine grabbed Aysel's hand and pulled her toward the back door. Aysel looked over her shoulder, and she saw through the curtains that the cops were pulling up, and the lights were flashing, and they were getting out of the four cars, and they had guns . . . Carmen pulled the curtains shut, and ran for the back door . . . and some people had gotten into the basement, but some people hadn't, and one of the people who had gone down the stairs threw the door shut. Elaine managed to push Aysel into the kitchen and behind the corner into the hallway that led to the back door. Elaine and Aysel hunkered down there as the front door flew open. Aysel could see the reflection of the cops in the glass of the kitchen window.

And so Aysel thought: Where is Z?

"Freeze," one of the officers said to the four or five people who were still in the room. He was tall and blond in the dark reflection of the window and reminded Aysel of one of the actors who played soldiers in movies. Not the ones who died, because they could look like anything, but the ones who lived, who all had strong jaws and cheekbones and always had light hair and ruddy pale skin. This officer seemed to think he was a soldier, too, because he shot twice at the wall behind Chad's head as Chad raised his hands in surrender. Chad dropped to the floor and covered his head with his hands.

"Jesus, what'd he do to you?" someone shouted. Aysel looked over at Elaine. Elaine, still crouching, turned and looked at the back door. Carmen had gotten away through it and it was still standing slightly open, letting in cold air from outside. But if Aysel and Elaine stood up now, the police might see them, and they had guns . . . Aysel could tell Elaine was thinking the same thing she was. Both of them stayed very quiet. Aysel closed her eyes. There hadn't been any shots before the officers entered the house, and so they may not have seen Z. Z might have even gone home before the police arrived . . .

"This is suspected to be the site of a meeting for an illegal terrorist organization," the officer who had shot the wall said. "In addition, it has been determined that you are illegally squatting in this building. Everyone present is under arrest for suspect connection with the murder of Archie Pagan, and we have a warrant to search the building and confiscate any illegal materials we find."

"Like this thing," one of the officers said, from a part of the room not visible from the kitchen. Aysel knew the officer was holding a zine, even though she couldn't see it. "Just what the hell is this? Wolf Guts. Let's see, what's in here. This your magazine? For your little group? 'Destroy Capitalism, Up the Wolves,' says here. You all don't beat around the bush."

"Sounds about right," Blond Soldier said. "How 'bout that altar-looking thing in the corner? Five guesses what the hell's that's for. All these werewolves. Archie Pagan probably never knew what hit him, did he?"

"What the fuck," Chad said very loudly, and Elaine tensed up more until her veins showed, because he was running his mouth with all those guns around, "None of us had anything to do with that. We don't give a shit about Archie Pagan. We never attacked anyone, and everyone's coming after us."

The officer did not seem to be paying attention. He picked up a goblet. It wasn't an abnormal goblet, just the kind used to make household spells if you were old-fashioned. The wolf carving on it was unusual, but it didn't change anything about the magic. "Some kind of dark artifact. God, right under everyone's noses. What the hell were you planning to do?" This question was directed at the girl who had shouted when the officer shot the wall. The gun was now leveled at her head.

"We weren't—" she began.

"You haven't read us our rights," Chad said from the floor. "We've got the right to remain silent—" There was a yelp as one of the officers kicked him.

"You fuckin' better remain silent except when we're asking you a fuckin' question," the officer said. Aysel could feel Elaine tense up even more. "You're gonna shut your damn mouth, not bite anyone, and if you move a muscle I'm going to shoot your goddamn brains—"

"I'm unarmed," Chad said. "Look, I've got no guns. I don't have anything."

"Fuck," Elaine muttered. She grabbed Aysel's hand. "We're running for it first chance we get, okay?"

Aysel nodded, mute.

"Don't move," the officer shouted at the werewolves in the front room. He turned and said something quietly to a woman officer—all this in the dark reflection of the window. Elaine pushed Aysel back a little and shifted her position. She leaned out from around the corner very slowly, and Aysel saw her mouth something at Chad. Then Elaine braced and tightened her grip on Aysel's arm. Aysel's foot was falling asleep and she tried to tense the muscles in her leg so it would stop and she would be ready to go.

Suddenly there was a noise from the front room, and one of the police—a woman—screamed.

"There's something—a monster outside!"

There was the noise of a table overturning, and then a gunshot and the sound of breaking glass. Aysel couldn't see the source of it, but Elaine was already on her feet and opening the door, so Aysel only managed to turn around briefly and catch the slightest glimpse of what was happening through the back door as it swung wide. Z's disappearing form was retreating from the window, and Blond Soldier was jumping to open the door and chase Z. And Chad was getting up from where he had been on the floor, and there was nothing in his hands, but as he raised himself up he was shouting, loudly, incredibly loudly, words that weren't spells, not even curses, just insults. Chad was gesturing at the people against the wall to run—a few of them turned and ran toward a window, toward the kitchen—Blond Soldier was turning to look back inside, from the porch—

—and there was another gunshot, and the back door shut. Someone else had gotten out the back door and was running toward the street around the side of the house. Aysel and Elaine were in the garden, running, and they reached the edge of the garden and now Elaine was trying to push Aysel over a fence. This was a difficult task because Aysel, even if she felt very small right now, was as solid and large as she had ever been. Aysel managed to heave herself over and pulled Elaine after her. Then they were in someone's backyard, and a dog barked at them. Elaine and Aysel ran. Behind them there were more gunshots from the direction of the black house, and then shouting. The police knew that someone had left. The grass was wet and Aysel's feet were going to get soaked. Bushes from people's hedges scratched at both of their faces. They went through what seemed like a hundred backyards and dark neighborhood streets, Aysel's heart pounding in her throat.

"Did you see who they shot?" Elaine half said, half shouted over her shoulder. Her hair was wild and all over the place, surrounding her face in a haze of reddish-brown tight curls.

"The door had shut," Aysel gasped back.

Fear smells like sweat and it tastes like salt and iron,

Aysel thought, and there was a great sweaty blur in her memory for a little while as her feet thumped away beneath her, painfully—she had a rock in her shoe. She focused on Elaine, who ran mostly in front of her. Elaine had on really old messed-up hiking boots with brown and pink and maroon and green, the colors so bright you could see them in the dark.

They came to a settled stop once they were out of the dark neighborhoods, and there were streetlamps around them. By that time it was clear that the police didn't know how to pursue them. There had been the sounds of sirens for a little, but they had died away. Aysel was seeing dots because she didn't run very much. She heaved several breaths and then found she was starting to cry. She looked up and saw Elaine was crying too, though she seemed to have it more under control. Elaine hugged Aysel and Aysel let herself have three good sobs against Elaine's collarbone before she pushed herself back and looked around. They were next to the dumpsters in the parking lot of a strip mall Aysel vaguely recognized. There were only a few cars parked around. The stores were all closed except for one twenty-four-hour doughnut shop, the lights of which were flashing. Inside there was an old, sedate couple with two cups of coffee and a man at the counter reading the paper. It seemed enormously bright against Aysel's tears and the dimness of the parking lot. She breathed a little.

Elaine punched the chain-link fence around the dumpsters and screamed unintelligibly. Her arms flailed above her head and Aysel saw that she was cutting her knuckles on the fence. Blood was dripping down her hands. Elaine threw more and more of her body into punching the fence until finally she slipped on the gravel and fell over.

"Do you want a doughnut?" Aysel asked Elaine.

Elaine made a very forced-looking smile and said that that would be great. They went in. The old couple rotated their heads to look at them.

"An old-fashioned glazed doughnut," Aysel said, "and a coffee."

"And a maple bar and another coffee," Elaine said. Aysel noticed she was making her voice higher than it usually was.

The man smiled at them both, a little uncertainly. Aysel brushed her hair out of her eyes and searched through her pockets for a scrunchie. She looked younger if she pulled her hair back, and she felt she needed to appear innocent. The man put the doughnuts and coffee on the counter. Aysel paid. Elaine had left the credit card she had been using somewhere in the house. They sat in a window and looked out at the street.

"My mom thinks I'm at Z's house," Aysel said. "I said she could pick me up from there, that I'd call her. I don't even know where Z is."

"Z got away, I'm pretty sure," Elaine said with a certainty that was convincing if you didn't look her in the eye. Elaine was very good at avoiding eye contact.

"What time is it, even?"

"I don't know. Not past like, eight thirty, though. Maybe. It isn't that late."

"Late for me to be out." Aysel ate at the edge of the doughnut and thought about the fact that she'd eaten two yesterday too. Whatever. The police were trying to kill her. She could eat as many as she wanted. She felt a deep anxiety and knew that Elaine could see it in her face.

"Look," Elaine said, "I don't think they're gonna go after Z. They have like thirteen to twenty werewolves in that house that they're going to arrest or shoot. That's what they're going to be focusing on."

Aysel looked at Elaine and felt the tears coming to her eyes again.

They walked, slowly, in the direction of Mrs. Dunnigan's. There wasn't anything else to do, after all. Aysel had sniffed several times and managed to not start crying again. She touched her face again and again, though. The night wind was picking up and the new little buds that were appearing on some of the trees wavered against a dark blue-black clouded sky in the light of the streetlamps.

"You know, when I first came out as a young transsexual or whatever, Chad was the first person I felt comfortable talking to about it," Elaine said to a puddle a little ways ahead of them.

Aysel looked over at Elaine. She didn't know what to say. "Yeah," she said monotonously.

"He's trans too," Elaine said. "Which made me feel kind of safe. We were both in like, Oklahoma City and hanging out at this drag bar that let teenagers in sometimes, and someone who worked there was letting us sleep in the dressing room. And we just started talking to each other about stuff. All the transgender people we'd met before then were like these older people who were really careful and scared and wanted to be respectable, and who could *be* respectable."

"So you're like . . . a transsexual. I didn't know. I wouldn't have known. You're so . . ." Aysel stopped short of saying *pretty*. Elaine looked over at her and Aysel felt the devastating heat of her eyes. She could tell that Elaine thought of her as just a kid.

"I actually have a shirt that says 'Nobody Knows I'm a Transsexual,' but I forgot to wear it when we went to the movies," Elaine said. She had an edge in her voice.

"How did you know? Like, how did Chad know? Instead of just being gay," Aysel said. "I mean. I guess you're gay too, sorry. I mean how did you know?"

"We'd seen some talk shows." Elaine grinned, her face still tense and tears still on her cheeks. Aysel knew she was making fun of her.

"Oh," Aysel said.

"After I got out of the hospital and hit the road, I'd been couch-surfing in cities and been to a couple groups for *transsexual women* who were all in their thirties and like, voted for Bush. Also it was like Iowa so they were all white. They were getting potion treatments and magical alterations and had their driver's licenses all nice. They all thought I was really lucky to be transitioning so young. Which was ridiculous because I wasn't ever gonna be able to live normally. I hated them. Which is dumb. But Chad and I found each other, and realized we were both wolves, and I told him I was *transsexual,* and he told me he was a guy, and everything totally made sense."

"Yeah," Aysel said in the same sort of monotone she had used before. "You seem really close."

"Like, there's stuff I'll never understand about him, and stuff I'm never telling him about me. But we've been through a lot together. We've kept each other out of a lot of bad shit."

"Yeah."

"He's always been really dumb when it comes to police," Elaine said. "Which isn't to say I don't think a change of government would be nice, but he's into the spray-painting, the yelling, the believing in revolution that is actually gonna work. All of that kind of stuff. He's been in protests and stuff and gotten arrested, and half the time he's been like, high or whatever. I'm like, God, you're gonna get yourself killed, you asshole, and if they take you alive they'll put you in a women's prison probably, and he's like, whatever, let's light a dumpster on fire, I'm an idiot." She was looking at the sky now, and talking really loudly. She made to walk straight across the road when Aysel knew they had to turn, and Aysel gestured to try to get her attention.

"I bet he's fine," Aysel said. Her voice lacked conviction.

"I hope so," Elaine said, laughing. Her voice caught in her throat and she shivered. "I love him so much. Chad's such an ass." She shut her eyes. Aysel knew that she had heard the shot, too, and that she was under no illusions about the likelihood of Chad being fine.

"Z and I are like that," Aysel said. She regretted it at once. She was out of her depth.

"Really?"

"Not really. I mean, it's not the same thing. But Z isn't a boy or a girl. They say they're genderqueer. And I'm gay, and we're the only two in our school who are monsters. And I knew I had to stick with them and then we became friends." Aysel paused. "And I'd like, I'd die for Z."

"No, yeah," Elaine said, putting her arm around Aysel for a second and giving her a kind of half-hug. "That's what it is, what I'm talking about. You're on it."

"I love Z," Aysel said suddenly, quietly, surprising herself. She looked at Elaine.

"I understand," Elaine said.

"Not like, you know. I just really really want them to be all right. They're like, the first person who's meant something to me in a really long time. They're really cool."

"Yeah."

"I'm really worried they're dead. And for you, too— I'm worried Chad's . . ." Aysel trailed off.

"Yeah," Elaine said. "It would be really nice if that all hadn't happened back there."

Aysel felt a shiver run through her seeing the way Elaine's face was set. She looked tired and bleak and old.

They were nearing Mrs. Dunnigan's. The street was dark except for the light above the bus stop. There was a cold bleakness to everything. Aysel and Elaine went and sat out in front of the building, looking out into the dark together.

Suddenly something in the dark moved. Aysel's heart leapt as something that had looked like the shadow of a tree moved and became a humanoid dark shape. It moved slowly, limping slightly. Aysel jumped up from the cold curb. Next to her, Elaine started up and jumped to her feet.

"Aysel," the dark shape rasped, "you're okay!"

"Z!" Aysel ran forward and hugged Z. Z's skin was cold and clammy and damp. "You're okay, too."

"You don't have any cops following you, do you?" Elaine asked, looking down the street in both directions. She had jammed her hands in her pockets.

"No," Z said. "I was hoping to get them to follow me by scaring everyone at the window, but the two in the car who came after me couldn't see me in the dark or something."

"Night vision detects heat," Elaine said. "You're cold."

"That makes sense," Aysel said. "God, Z, are you all right?"

"I'm as okay as I'll ever be. What happened? How did you get out? Did other people get out?"

"We don't know," Elaine said. "They were there because

they were investigating the terrorist werewolf group that was behind the death of Archie Pagan. I don't think they were planning on letting anyone go."

"A couple people got out," Aysel said.

"God, I hope so," Elaine said. She balled up her hands into fists and kneaded at the edges of her eyes.

"I hope so too," Z said. They were shaking.

Z had the key on them. Once inside they all took off their muddy shoes and stood there for a moment, looking at one another. Z realized all the cats were still missing. The radiators were cold.

"I'll make like, tea," Z said. They looked over their shoulder. "You can both stay the night. I *think* we'll be safe here."

"Where's Mrs. Dunnigan?" Aysel asked. "It seems like it's too early for her to be asleep."

Z turned away. "She had to leave."

"Like, on a trip?"

"No, she left for good. She's a selkie. Someone sent her her skin in the mail today. The people who ransacked the bookstore after the rally took it from there, and then sent it back to her. It had been hidden in the attic from when her wife was alive."

"Holy shit," Elaine said.

"Yeah. I mean, she didn't have a choice. If a selkie knows where their skin is, you know, they gotta . . . go. It happened earlier. I didn't tell you because it's kind of a shock."

"No kidding," Elaine said.

"I mean, it's just one more thing that fell apart," Z said. "But it's whatever. At least she's like, going to be happier there maybe. If there are no oil spills."

The coil under the kettle rattled with the heat. Elaine and Aysel watched it. Z was staring out the window. Aysel felt a horror at the idea of Z in the place alone. At least I don't have to think about that tonight, since Elaine will stay here, she thought.

"I should call my mom," she said.

15

The news carried the story before eleven thirty. Z had left the TV on and had not slept—they wondered if it might have been a onetime event—and Elaine did not seem to have slept either, though she had remained motionless on the couch, facedown into the cushion almost from the time she came in the door. She spun around so fast when the news came on that she became tangled in her blankets and nearly fell to the floor. Z looked at her worriedly. They didn't know Elaine, and didn't know if they liked her, and here she was on their couch looking like she was about to cry. Z turned their attention to the news story. None of the werewolves were identified, but the anchorwoman (pink jacket) told the anchorman (bald spot) that fifteen werewolves had been taken into police custody and that three had been shot and were now dead. The raid was being saluted, at this early hour, as part of Charles Salt Sr.'s new police program to end monster violence in the city.

"Chad," Elaine mouthed. Then, louder, "Chad. They mean Chad. And two others. Jesus. He died trying to save us."

"Maybe not."

"Three dead. It's someone. And they were shooting at Chad."

"No," Z said. Elaine looked over at them. They didn't feel like explaining.

The anchorwoman said that the discovery of the terrorist organization raised more questions than it answered, and that the police investigation and a state of emergency would continue until it was determined what role the group had played in Archie Pagan's death and the assault on Ron Hardeback. In the interim, all werewolves in custody of the state would be interrogated and all registered werewolves within traveling distance of the city of Salem would have their records examined. Travel out of the state was prohibited for werewolves—which was usual—and for all members of a werewolf's family. Reporters were up late to cover the story, and looked visibly shaken and tired.

Elaine chewed at her lip until it bled.

"Chad's dead," she said. "They mean Chad."

Z looked around. "No."

"He was there and they were shooting and he was a dumb fucking asshole and he's dead."

Chad was dead. He was here and then he was dead. He was here he was here he was here.

At about one in the morning, there was a knock on the door. Aysel and Elaine started, and went to hide in the bedroom. Z braced for it to be the police, but it was Tommy. He was holding his school backpack.

"What are you doing here?" they asked, closing the door behind him.

"I went home but then there was a car in front of my house when I got close. It was the police. Someone tipped them off about something—the necromancy books maybe, or maybe that everyone thinks I'm a fairy, or that I was a patient at Archie Pagan's practice." He was panting. "I couldn't think of what to do so I hid for hours and then came here. They didn't see me."

"Do you think they know I have the books too?"

"I don't know," Tommy said. He looked up. "Who is that girl?"

"I'm Elaine," Elaine said, emerging from the bedroom and sticking out her hand. "On the run from the cops too, huh? What'd you do? I'm a werewolf."

Tommy and Z both stared at her.

"Is she—" Tommy looked to Z. "Can I trust her?"

"I don't know," Z said. "She's the one Aysel went to the movies with, though."

"I have forbidden books," Tommy said. "On necromancy and demons. I took them from the university library."

"The numbskulls at school say Tommy's a fairy," Aysel, also emerging from the bedroom, informed Elaine.

"Shit," Elaine said brightly. She looked down at Tommy. "Nice hair, by the way."

"Thanks," Tommy said. "Also, I think I should tell you guys. Before things get worse." He looked at Z.

"What is it?" Z asked. They wondered for a moment if Tommy had brought someone back from the dead.

"You should know, uh, I didn't tell the whole truth before. When I said I wasn't a werewolf. That's true, but I did get electroshock from Archie Pagan. I'm a shapeshifter."

Elaine and Aysel exchanged a glance. Z just stared.

"What do you mean?" Z asked.

"My dad took me to him. It was experimental and like, probably very illegal, usually that's not what happens with fey, but my dad said it worked for him. Archie did it for him too."

Elaine sat back down on the couch slowly. "God," she said. "I've known people who went to Pagan for years and never heard about any of that shit. You know that's crazy, right? That's way more dangerous than any of us thought."

"Yeah," Tommy said.

"Do you know, though?" Elaine asked. "Shapeshifters can't get their magic taken away like werewolves can. You guys are like way more fey than us. You're made of magic. If he zaps you he's just asking for like, a rift to open and for some kind of magical explosion to jump out from the fey world and neutralize the whole state of Oregon."

"I've never met a shapeshifter," Aysel said. "I thought they'd all left America or gone into hiding."

"Well, they have," Elaine said, gesturing to Tommy. "Clearly."

"He talked a little bit about the risks," Tommy said. "He sort of thought that people had that part wrong and that we were more like werewolves after all. I started shape-shifting into big scary monster things when I was like eight. Or switching around my body. My granddad was full fey, and my dad got electroshock and can't do magic. Which—Archie Pagan thought that proved his theory, so I went to him too. But we kept it hidden and stuff. As far as I know, all his other patients were werewolves."

Elaine shuddered. "What happened when he shocked you?"

Tommy looked down. "Mostly I would transform in the chair and then gradually I would like, feel worse and worse like my skin was bursting and I'd turn back into a kid."

Everyone paused to absorb this information.

"That must have fucked up your ability to like, transform when you wanted," Elaine said.

Tommy shrugged. "I didn't think about it for a long time, but probably. But I still can do magic pretty well. And I turned into animals when I was taking the books from the library."

"Have you ever like, exploded? In the chair?"

Tommy looked sideways at Elaine. "What do you mean?"

"Like lost control."

Tommy flinched. "Uh, yeah." He took a deep breath. "Uh, actually, uh." He brushed his hair back. "I guess I can tell you, right?" He gestured at the window. "Everything going on is because of me."

"What?" Aysel asked.

"Well, actually," Tommy said, "the, uh, the night that

Archie died, he like, was doing a session of electroshock with me. And I broke out of the chair as this big lion thing shooting electricity everywhere." He looked at Z, rather than anywhere else in the room. "And, well, uh, I killed him. He shot me first, with this silver bullet gun he had in case stuff ever went wrong, but it didn't do anything."

Aysel made a rasping noise, more choking than speaking.

Tommy raised his shirt slightly, and Aysel and Elaine leaned forward. Z looked away, but not before seeing the deep bullet hole under one of Tommy's ribs. "I didn't mean to. I felt awful when I turned back into myself and the pain stopped. But I couldn't figure out what to do so I hid his body in the woods." He shuddered. "So basically it's all my fault."

"You killed him? You killed Archie Pagan?" Z asked.

"It's why I was trying to bring him back. And why I wanted to help you with the potion, kind of. I mean, I like you and want you to be safe, but also, I wanted to know if I could bring him back."

Elaine shrugged. "I hate that kind of guy. He's better off gone."

Aysel was scowling. "I mean, sure. But Tommy, this whole thing is why werewolves are under attack right now, you realize that, right?"

"I know," Tommy said. "I didn't really think about it, or care, I guess, at the time. I didn't really know any werewolves personally. The only one I knew of was Mr. Holmes."

Aysel was clearly verging on rage and ready to explode, but this threw her for a loop. "Mr. Holmes," she repeated in a kind of haze.

"He was another of Archie's patients," Tommy said. "I saw him sometimes. He's totally nonmagical now, but he was still doing shock sessions three times a month until this year. Anyway, he sucks, so I didn't think about the fact that there are a lot of other werewolves around who would get blamed."

Aysel pointed to Elaine. "Elaine's friend is dead because of what you did. I should clobber you for him."

Tommy looked at Aysel. "Then do it," he said. Something unnerving and steely flashed in his eyes that Z had never seen there before. Aysel saw it too, and flinched. Z felt Aysel's magic and Tommy's at the same time inside them like two opposing floods.

Elaine raised her hands. "Whoa," she said. "It's not his fault. It's the fucking pigs that shot Chad. If it was a just country, Archie wouldn't have been doing shady electroshock and wouldn't have gotten himself into more trouble than he could handle, and the cops wouldn't hunt people down for nothing. In a just country there wouldn't be cops. Chill out, Aysel."

Aysel looked abashed.

"I do feel sorry about it," Tommy said. "I feel awful about it." He took a breath. "But it's over now, and I'm the one who has to live with it, not you. And I care about Z, and about you, and whoever your friends are, and I want to be your friend. And the cops are after all of us now."

"True," Elaine said.

Tommy sat down next to Elaine. "It's just like, hiding from now on I guess. Because if they found out, then I'm not even seeing daylight. It really is like Charley Salt and everyone said. They just put you in a silver box for observation. I'd have to leave the country to escape that." He ran his fingers through his hair. "God, it's late. I just want to go to bed."

Z looked at Aysel and Elaine. "I'm not sure it's safe here," Z said. "Mrs. Dunnigan had to leave. She—uh, she turned out to be a selkie."

"What?" Tommy asked.

"Long story," Z said.

"And the werewolf house got raided. Z might have been seen by the cops there," Aysel added. "And they're the only registered zombie around. The cops know where Z lives. Or they can look it up."

Z looked at Aysel. "Oh, right. Shit. Where should we go?"

Elaine pulled her hair back from her face and tucked it into her hooded sweatshirt. "I think we probably all have to leave town," she said. "The faster the better." She looked over to Aysel. "Except you, I think. Nobody saw you. I think you're safe."

"What?" Aysel asked. "No, I'll go too."

"No you won't," Elaine said firmly. "Maybe someday, maybe soon, but not now. You need to stick with your mom and not get found with us."

"I'm not sure if the police have found Archie Pagan's back room in his office yet, where he kept his records," Tommy said. He paused. "I mean, if they had found the records, they would have moved before now. I'd be arrested already, and so would all the other patients."

Elaine chewed on the inside of her cheek, looking at Tommy seriously. "I bet they've looked at the office already, though, if they've found evidence of him treating werewolves before. Maybe they have everything already and are just waiting to act. Maybe the werewolf house raid tonight was just the start."

"There's a hidden back room they haven't found yet," Tommy said. "Where he died. The room with the chair, and all the records on his werewolf patients. I know the police haven't found that yet, because that's where Archie Pagan died. If they find that, they'll realize a patient killed him in his office, and they'll know it wasn't Morris, or any of the wolves that were out in the forest that night. I think they could probably figure out it wasn't a wolf. There's been nothing about that in the news. I don't think they'd keep it secret if they knew."

"You're saying that if they find that back room, they'll also have all the information on anyone who ever went to him. All the werewolves. And they don't have that information yet." Elaine moved toward Tommy and took him by the shoulders. "Are you like, at least ninety percent sure about this?"

"I mean, I think the information they have is from whatever was in the front room. If they saw the back room and his real schedule, they'd realize that I was the last patient Mr. Pagan saw before he died. But they only came to my house after they learned about the stolen necromancy books."

"You're saying you think the information on all the

werewolves he treated is still there in the office? Just sitting there?"

"I think. Anyway, the cops don't have it yet."

"'Yet' being the key word here," Elaine said. She breathed out through her teeth. "Oof. I was all ready to go jump on a bus and go."

"We still can," Z said. "We should. They won't find the records tonight if they haven't looked yet."

"Are you chill with it if they find them after we're gone, and round up every werewolf and ex-werewolf in town?" Elaine asked. She looked at Z.

"What can we do?" Z asked. "I don't want bad stuff to happen to werewolves either, but what are we going to do now? We have to leave. You said so just two minutes ago."

Elaine turned away from Z toward Tommy. "Do you know exactly where Archie kept his records?" Elaine asked. "Could you get us in there?"

"Yeah," Tommy said.

"We'll break in, then." Elaine said. "We'll burn all the stuff. Then we'll skip town."

"All of us?" Aysel asked. Z knew she was thinking about her mom, and how Elaine had told her she wasn't going to leave town with the rest of them.

"You can go home if you want."

Aysel and Z exchanged glances.

"What about staying safe?" Aysel asked. "Like you were talking about, at the meeting before the cops came."

Elaine looked at Aysel. "Well," she said, "everyone's in

danger now. You're probably okay to come with us as long as we split right after we set the fire."

Aysel bit her lip, but she nodded.

Z picked at their fingernail. "It seems like a bad idea to try to do this right now, doesn't it?"

Elaine nodded. "It's as dumb as anything I've ever done. But we're gonna try."

"We have to do it," Tommy said. "I agree. It's over near the industrial park, in an office building next to the dentist. It isn't far." He looked at Aysel, at Z searchingly, as if to figure out if they thought Elaine was nuts. "If we walk it's maybe half an hour."

Elaine grimaced. "We have to do it. It's the difference between innocent people getting arrested or not." She looked over at Tommy. "As long as the shit we want to burn is still in it."

Aysel looked at Elaine with a mixture of concern and devotion. Z saw it and felt a mix of jealousy and fear.

It was near two thirty in the morning when they reached the street sign near the industrial park and Tommy had them all turn left. They broke in through a bathroom window. Elaine threw a rock which made a surprisingly solid crash for being so small. The glass splintered and broke, falling inward into the building.

"Jesus," Tommy said.

Elaine lifted herself through the window, her thin legs kicking against the outer wall. Aysel followed her, and Tommy and Z scrambled after. Z caught Tommy looking nervously over his shoulder.

The building was almost entirely silent. Aysel turned on the light so they could see what they were doing. The gray linoleum that had been laid at an obscure point in the past was mottled and broken in places, showing a strange brown underbelly of floor. As soon as Elaine was inside, she had taken off, and the noise of her footsteps could be heard climbing the flight of stairs visible from the bathroom door. The dust drifted in dim patterns down the hall as Aysel, Tommy, and Z followed slowly. Upstairs, there was the noise of Elaine rattling the handles of different doors.

"Will anyone else be in the building at all?" Aysel asked Tommy. They could all hear Elaine knocking on different doors.

"I don't think so," Tommy said. "Only one other office is occupied in this part of the building. It's a dentist office. The dentist was never here when I came to afternoon appointments. I don't think dentists are here this early, either." Tommy's voice sounded very high and reedy and a little like he was going to cry. Z thought how hard it must be to be in the place where he had come so many times.

"Well, that's good. Elaine would probably have made someone call the cops by now with the way she's thumping around."

"Elaine," Tommy called, "do you even know which is his office?"

Elaine's footsteps came thumping down the stairs again. "What?" she called back loudly.

Tommy led the others to the right office door. The group rocked on their heels in front of it.

"So what are we uh, looking for?" Z asked. "Like, I know incriminating documents, but how do we tell which those are?"

"We're just going to set fire to all of it," Elaine said. She leaned forward and tried the handle. Z thought it would be locked but it wasn't, and it swung open with a groan. Inside there was a little waiting room with a potted fern dying by a small window and a pile of magazines in a little wicker basket. At the other end of this room was another door with a placard saying *Pagan* on it. They all crossed to it. This one was locked and did not open when Tommy turned the handle.

"It's locked," Tommy said.

Elaine tapped the doorknob with her knuckles and hummed something. The door opened when she tried the handle again.

Z was not sure what they had been expecting, but whatever it was, the office was disappointing. The walls were a pale mint color that made the room seem somehow smaller than it was. It was mostly bare inside. There were only two chairs and a small bookshelf with some files on it. The plush olive-green carpeting covered the floor in a sort of mossy squalor.

"Not very much to look through, is there?" Aysel asked.

"Have they had it cleared out?" Elaine asked Tommy. "Was it always like this?"

"It's emptier. But there's the back room still," Tommy said. "Behind the bookshelf." He paused. "I don't know if we can open it," he said suddenly. "There's a spell, and I don't know it."

Elaine scrutinized Tommy. "Don't worry," she said. She slowly walked the length of the office, running a hand along the blank walls. She turned back toward the door. Z was surprised at how easily she had given up. Then Elaine suddenly turned and ran at the bookshelf headlong. For a second, Z was sure she had lost her mind, or her temper, or both.

"Elaine, what are you—"

There was a substantial thud as Elaine collided with the side of the shelf. The files that were still on it went flying. Surprisingly, though, the rickety shelf didn't fall over. Instead, one side of it shifted away from the wall, while the other remained anchored to the wall, almost as if it were—

"A door," Elaine declared triumphantly, raising herself from the floor where she had rolled after her assault on the furniture. "A secret goddamn door hiding a goddamn magic room." She stood and tried to pry the bookshelf farther from the wall. It was clear now that there was indeed an opening behind it. It was also clear that the shelf was very much more solid than it looked. Elaine was bracing her full weight against it and it was only inching very slowly outward.

"It seems like a pretty difficult door to open," Aysel said.

"Only to intruders. Whoever used it regularly probably had a password. But I'm not about to sit out here just because I don't know what it was," Elaine said. She muttered something that sounded like a series of expletives mixed with foreign words under her breath and a series of sparks shot along the length of the side of the bookshelf. It began to swing open more easily.

"You're like the goddess of burglars," Z said without thinking. "How many breaking-and-entering spells do you even know?"

"Enough," Elaine said, and pushed the door clear of the opening in the wall with a final volley of sparks. "My other magic is shit, but this stuff works."

"Holy shit," Aysel said as it became apparent what was inside the large room beyond the hidden door. She moved forward, and Z followed slowly.

There was no light inside and it was dim, but even with the narrow strip of yellow that came through the concealed door, it was clear that some kind of disaster had taken place. The space inside was in total disarray. Elaine went in first, and in a moment had found a light switch. All of them walked in. The first thing one's eyes were drawn to was the mahogany desk which had been broken in two in the center and which lay in separate halves on either side of the door. The contents of the desk drawers had been spilled all across the room—page upon page of torn and shredded yellow files spilled over every surface. There had at one time been several whole pieces of furniture in the office, but Z could not be sure what these had been, as the things lay in smithereens and splinters. In the corner of the room there was something which looked like a couch, but one couldn't be entirely sure. After a visitor took all this in their eyes would probably register the dark smears of black that stained the ceiling. Z knew these were blood. They looked over at Tommy. His face was very pale. His expression was unreadable. He caught Z's eye and swallowed audibly.

They examined the room for a while, moving about amid all the heaped trash. The room gave off a definite smell, like a crypt or a hospital. It was clear that the air hadn't circulated for some time. Z bent over and looked at the papers on the floor. Some of them were lease agreements, like the ones on the outside shelf. Others were pages that had been torn from books, shredded or crumpled as if between powerful claws. They looked over and saw Aysel holding the empty binding of a book called *Never the Moon's Child: Finding a New Life and Ridding Yourself of the Past*. She read the back of the jacket, made a grimace, and dropped it. Z looked back to the papers they were holding. They looked legal and vague, and Z wasn't sure what the pages were part of. Some of them looked like patient agreement forms.

"Burn everything," Elaine said, and picked up a piece of paper. A spark jumped from her hand to the page, and it caught fire, disappearing into cold ashes and then falling to the ground like dust. Aysel watched her, and then muttered the fire incantation while lifting a fat manila folder that had wedged itself under the desk. It caught fire much more dramatically.

Tommy was crouching under the window, sorting through a pile of yellow manila folders so shredded they resembled the curls of shredded paper used for shipping glass.

"My question is," Elaine said, "where's the chair? There should be an electroshock chair in here. Did you already like, rip it out of the ground?"

"Uh," Tommy said. "That's it, under the papers."

"What, this thing over here?" Elaine asked. She moved over to the lump in the middle of the room, covered in trash. "Z, help me clear it off."

Z and Elaine pulled the papers off the top of the thing, scattering them onto the floor. Z did not recognize it, though parts of it looked a little like an electronic keyboard their father used to own. It was turned on its side, and the bottom, which had been connected to the floor, had been ripped up at some point. It was made of metal and had a lot of buttons. Elaine made a few more efforts to clear off the rubbish on top of it, and its shape became clearer. There was a part like a chair or a couch. There was also a lot of wire, and straps which hung all along the sides of the thing, loosely. There was a bit on top that looked like the silver dome at hairdressing salons that women put over their heads when they were getting their hair colored, though it had more jutting electrical-looking pieces and appeared as if it was meant to fit a lot tighter around the head. The whole effect was extremely menacing.

"So that's what an electroshock chair looks like," Z said. As they said it, they saw Aysel clenching her jaw and looking very uncomfortable.

Elaine settled back against the broken desk and crossed her arms. "Too elaborate, really, since this guy was trying to be discreet," she said, slapping the button panel of the thing. "He should've gotten something smaller or less menacing. I think they even make little kits now that you can pack away in a cupboard, no need for all of these buckles and horrible metal thingies. Although maybe he felt like since he was only one person he needed to secure his patients a little more intensely. Who knows?" It was clear that the presence of the machine made her nervous, too.

"How does it work?" Z asked. "I've never understood that."

"It administers electric shocks to whatever poor shit has to sit in that chair. It induces small seizures. People use something kind of like it to treat normal-people mental problems. Stuff like psychosis and chronic depression. It reorganizes your brain, kind of. Even before they started using it for that, though, they figured out how to use it to block magic in things they don't think should have magic. Like, for instance, me." She turned over to Z. "I got zapped in one of these."

"Tommy, you got strapped into this machine, too, right?" Aysel asked.

Tommy was very, very pale. "Yeah," he said.

"I want you to know that that's bullshit," Elaine added, "I said it before but it is. Electroshock on fey doesn't work at all the way it does on werewolves. If your dad tells you he's nonmagical now, he's bullshitting you. Fey are made of magic. You can't get rid of it."

"He said he had a special method," Tommy said. "Maybe he was right. But I'm never getting in one of those things again." Suddenly Tommy started shaking. They all watched him. Z made eye contact with him for a second and then looked away; it was too deeply unsettling to see the frenzy in his eyes. They looked up, instead, toward the bloody ceiling. Tommy's eyes followed theirs and he gave a little shriek of a sob. Elaine gave Tommy's left shoulder a little tentative pat; he seemed not to notice. He put his fingers to his neck, as if checking his pulse.

"Tommy, let's get you out of here," Z said.

"He turned up the voltage really high." Tommy got up and walked over to the chair, and looked down at it. "And the chair came loose from the ground . . . And I was this big lion thing, I think. And then he had a gun, and he was coming toward me."

"Did you heal from that on your own?" Elaine asked. "Are the bullets still in you?"

"I pulled them out," Tommy said. "With magic." His voice shook. "Once the body was in the woods I tried to bury it. But I—I got upset and I transformed again and when I came to I was really—I couldn't think straight. I was scared. I didn't really think about it, to be honest. I just went home and left him where he was." Tommy paused and shut his eyes. "God. I hate myself."

Elaine moved forward and clasped Tommy's shoulders. "Tommy," she said, "I have hurt a lot of people. Everyone hurts people."

"But you haven't killed anyone," Tommy said.

"No, I haven't," Elaine said. "But I don't want you to think you're a monster, Tommy."

"But I still killed him," Tommy said. There were tears in his eyes again. It was clear that he didn't know what to make of Elaine's sudden willingness to forgive him. "I don't know what was happening to me. I couldn't control myself. And that's dangerous, isn't it? You all—werewolves know when you will transform and you can get away from people. You know days ahead when the change is going to be. I'm a demon. I could kill someone at any moment!"

"No," Elaine said firmly, her hands still on Tommy's shoulders.

"Aysel's necklace works on me. I can't look directly at it. I can't get too close to it without feeling weird."

"What?" Aysel asked. Her hand went to her necklace.

"I'm a thing, a thing that looks like a boy sometimes but really isn't anything, just a demon—"

"He shot you in the chest."

Tommy stared at her for a moment and then crouched on the floor, where he sat staring at his hands. Even Aysel, who had looked about ready to punch him earlier, now looked worried for him. She was hugging herself, looking between Tommy and the blood on the ceiling. Z knew how upset Aysel had to be about everything, and they knew she was as confused as they were about how to feel about everything. Z looked over at Elaine and stared at her until she looked up at Z. Elaine's eyes were red and opened wide; her eyebrows were furrowed. When she made eye contact with Z she blinked hard and shook her head.

"Let's set a fire, keep moving. They'll find the chair in the rubble, but whatever. The papers will be gone."

They all stood there then, looking at one another. A feeling of being deeply exhausted, washed out and raw, rose in Z and they could see that the others felt it too. Z looked at Tommy again, thinking of what he had gone through, and of the fear he must have lived with these last weeks. What would happen to him now? What would his life be like? They thought of what Elaine had said, that Tommy was a being made of magic. He had more power than any of them, then—more than Aysel even. It was hard to believe it of the tiny, skinny form curled like the bones of a mouse on the floor with his hair in his reddening eyes. He could tear the world apart if he was scared enough.

And he was connected now with the sigil on Z's chest.

Z was not able to think too long because suddenly there was a noise downstairs. Aysel seemed to hear it first; she looked up toward the door. Soon the sound reached the rest of them. It was the low ache of wood bending as someone walked down the hallway beneath them. Initially it wasn't clear if it was just the noise of the building creaking, but as the seconds passed it resolved itself into definite, distinct footsteps. Elaine, who had seemed distracted, heard it and froze, looking quickly around at them all.

"Shit," she mouthed.

The footsteps paused and a woman's voice called out, from down the stairs. "Hello? Is anyone there?"

"It's the dentist," Tommy said. He was getting to his feet unsteadily. "Who works downstairs. I've met her a couple times."

"Mr. Briggs?" the voice called. "Is that you?"

"Stay very quiet," Elaine whispered. She looked over at the door to the secret room. Z could see her puzzling over what to do. One could close the door, possibly, with a lot of work—but then they would all be trapped inside. In any case it was sure to make a noise. And the footsteps were now coming up the stairs.

The footsteps retreated just as Elaine looked ready to rush out and attack the dentist. Then, in the hallway, there was the sound of a phone being dialed. The dentist had one of those small new cell phones. After a second, her voice spoke again, this time low and confidential into the receiver Z imagined was pressed close against her face.

"Yes, hello, 911? I would like to report . . . a burglary. I think. The intruder may still be here. I'm at the Cloudburst Pines office complex in East Lancaster . . ."

16

"This is terrible," Aysel said quietly. "What do we do?"

"I'll distract her," Tommy whispered suddenly. He stood up, swaying a little. "She's seen me before. Then—I don't know—you all can go past if I can get her downstairs, or go out the window . . ." He said all this very fast, and walked quickly toward the door.

Aysel looked back at Elaine and Z. Elaine was clearly trying to think of a plan. Z merely looked paralyzed. Their eyes flicked over to Aysel and Aysel realized Z was not going to be able to move very fast. There was no way they would get out without being seen.

Unless Aysel did something.

Aysel shut her eyes and felt the well of wavering magic in a warm sphere. All the rage that had been building up for the last hour, and the fear, had fed quietly into it, the energy pent up and almost painful when one focused on it. Aysel knew she had the capacity for an immense burst of magic if she tried. But what should she try to do?

Tommy, meanwhile, had gone out into the main office, and then there was the sound of him opening the door into the hall.

"Hang on," the woman said, out in the hall, apparently into the receiver. Then, to Tommy, "Oh, it's you—"

"I'm sorry for startling you," Tommy said.

"I thought there were burglars," the woman said in an accusatory way. "The police are on their way. It's the middle of the night. What are you doing here? This is—this is Archie's office, isn't it?"

The 911 call had been placed. The police would be here soon. The only thing to do would be to try to make it easier for them all to flee and make sure that the woman wasn't able to tell anyone what had happened.

"I, um. I was coming to pick up some papers that were left over after Dr. Pagan died. Medical records," Tommy said. "I called uh, I called Mrs. Pagan, and she said that she would be here . . ."

"So late at night?" The woman sounded doubtful.

Tommy was silent for a second, and Aysel realized his story was going to crumble. She looked back again at Elaine and knew Elaine didn't have any idea of what to do, either. If only Tommy would shut the door to the office, they could try to go out the window. Aysel wondered how to communicate this to Tommy.

"No," Tommy finally said. "But uh, the door was open, when I got here, so I . . . I just went in and my papers and things were on the desk, so I picked them up." His voice got a little farther away. He was clearly trying to edge down the hall, and take the dentist with him.

"I thought I heard voices. Are you sure you're alone?"

Aysel was sure the woman was going to lean forward and look into the office, and she moved toward the door of the secret room. Indeed, the dentist's shadow fell across the door into the empty office. She was going to see them. Aysel closed her eyes and allowed a shard of her ball of frustrated magic to splinter and shoot toward the door. It swung shut with a slam that was too forceful to be natural.

"What was that?" the woman said, and her footsteps approached. She tried to turn the doorknob. Aysel pursed her lips in an instant and tried to remember the spell for locking. She couldn't remember the Latin, but she thought of what she wanted. Don't let her get in, she thought.

"Ouch!"

Aysel looked through the door to the secret room and saw that the doorknob in the outer office had melted into a silver, tarnished river of hot metal that was seeping slowly toward the carpeted floor. She blinked.

Behind her, she felt Elaine's breath suddenly on the back of her head. "Nice work," Elaine said quietly. "I was panicking."

"What is that?" the dentist's voice said, outside.

"There must be a security spell on the door," said Tommy, feebly. He was now stuck outside the room as well. They all would have to figure out how to get to him and get him away before police came. For now, though—

"The window, quick," Elaine said. Aysel turned around and pulled Z from where they were standing in the middle of the floor. To Aysel's surprise, they pulled away forcefully. Aysel felt the tendons in their arm strain and there was a chilling snapping noise as they staggered back. Z didn't show any sign of having noticed.

"We have to finish destroying the evidence and then hide the secret room," Z said. "Someone could be in danger otherwise. Tommy especially." They turned toward the mess.

Aysel shot a bolt of her angry-magic at a file cabinet containing most of the remaining papers, and it exploded. She shot another bolt at the electric chair. It buzzed with a purple electric glow and crumbled into dust and embers. Aysel was a little shaken by her own ferocity. "There," she said. "They're gone. Let's go." She grabbed Z's hand and pulled them toward the door. Outside, Elaine had removed the glass from the window with a spell again and had one leg over the side.

"Let's see if I can do this," she said, and disappeared over the ledge, her frizzy hair trailing after her, a rush of orange-illuminated light. Aysel rushed over to the open window. The wind blew the curtains back into the room. Outside, Elaine was standing upright about a foot above the earth, holding herself aloft with an anti-gravity spell Aysel recognized as a variation of one she had learned in elementary school. Elaine looked breathless as the purple force field broke and she dropped to the ground.

"You next," Aysel said, turning back to Z. "I'll help."

"Wait, the door to the room," Z said. "We have to close it."

"I'll deal with it," Aysel snapped, forgetting to be quiet. Outside the door, the dentist was pounding her fists against the wood. She seemed awfully brazen for someone who seemed to believe that burglars had invaded, Aysel thought. The door creaked against its hinges.

"Who is in there?" she called loudly. "You are trespassing—"

Aysel put all her strength into slamming shut the bookshelf-door to the interior room. The wolf inside her prickled up in her shoulders. She turned toward the entrance to the office that the woman was behind and felt the familiar crackle of static in her hair. Everything rushed at her at once, and she felt her eyes and face grow hot with it. Sweat collected on her brow. She had to be careful, doing so many forceful, wordless spells at once. If she didn't use caution, she would end up doing more harm than she meant to, unleashing all of her magic at once in a torrent she couldn't control. But this woman couldn't see them. Aysel knew she had to protect Z, and herself, but she couldn't remember any Latin—her brain was going blank. There was nothing to do but return her attention to the buzzing locus of magic in the front of her brain, and she gritted her teeth, and ran forward and kicked the door with a loud, languageless cry. Aysel wasn't sure exactly what this would do, and she was not prepared for what happened. As her foot made contact with the door, it burst instantly into a sizzling purple fire. On the other side of it, the woman screamed. For a second, Aysel stared with some horror at what she had done. Then she shook herself back to her senses.

"Come on, let's go!" Aysel said. She rushed forward and lifted Z over her shoulder, diving toward the window. The evening air hit their faces as they flew through it, and Aysel drank it in, filling her lungs with its sweetness, so sharp and refreshing after the hot, dead air of the dead therapist's room. She brought the swell of magical energy within her to her feet and sang the anti-gravity spell under her breath—*non deficimus, nec me in terra deorsum*—and landed, lightly. She looked back at the window they had leapt out of and saw smoke issuing from it. Aysel's fire was spreading.

"That's that," she said to Z, trying to be jovial. Her heart was pounding. Z looked at her with a kind of morose horror that made Aysel feel horrible.

"Where's Tommy?" Elaine asked.

"Still inside," Aysel said. "He was stuck on the other side of the door. I hope he can get out. I don't think it's a good idea for us to go back in. We have to get out of here."

"We can't leave Tommy," Elaine and Z said at once.

"I didn't say we should," Aysel said. She looked from one to the other, wondering how not to make them hate her while getting them both away from the burning building. "But we also can't all get caught. I think Tommy can take care of himself better than you think. He got away from the police twice already today."

"Thanks," a voice behind Aysel said. She turned. Tommy was disheveled, his pale hair mussed up at the back of his head. He smiled nervously.

"How did you—" Z began.

"Never mind, I'm sure we'll know in a bit," Elaine said. "Right now we have all our members assembled and are outside a burning building and the cops are on their way, so let's get the hell out of here. Can I hear an aye for support?"

They all ran. Elaine led the way. She turned and they all rushed through a kind of dirt alley behind a cluster of warehouses, between large metal dumpsters and the marked-up beige walls of the buildings. The security lamps which lit the parking lot didn't reach into the alleyways and for a second Aysel squinted from the loss of light, and stumbled. She was breathing hard trying to keep up, and out of the corner of her eye she could see Z stumbling. She remembered Z falling walking home from school. Even if the potion had helped them, Z wasn't going to be able to keep up this pace for long. Aysel decided to carry them again if they fell behind. Tommy, meanwhile, traveled fast, and had boundless energy. Elaine ran far enough ahead that there was always a danger of losing her, but she seemed to be determined not to let them fall behind. After they got out from the long alley between warehouses they found themselves in a neighborhood. Elaine turned away from the road that led toward a thoroughfare and took them, instead, toward a series of smaller residential streets. She had slowed to a walk—either because there was no way Z could keep up with her pace or because she thought they were safe. But she did not stop, either. The idea seemed to be to get as far as possible from the main road. Aysel looked over her shoulder only once, and saw a column of smoke rising into the sky behind them. She bit her lip and hoped that the dentist woman had the good sense to get out of the building. Hopefully, the police might think she had set the building on fire, for insurance fraud. She could now hear the distant wail of sirens. Aysel thought: This is the second time I have been on the run from the cops in a week. This time I actually set something on fire.

They came to a neighborhood park,with small, dilapidated pieces of beige playground equipment made of wood and metal pipes. There wasn't much light. Elaine turned and nodded to them and then looped her arms around a pull-up bar and brought herself up so she was sitting on it.

"We're far enough away now that I think we can rest," she said. Her face was dark with the blood that had rushed to it running, and she combed her frizzy hair out of her eyes with her hand. "I don't think the police will be looking at these neighborhoods for a while, and in the meantime we all need to catch our breath."

Tommy pulled his hooded cape up over his hair. "What did you do back there, Aysel? The building's on fire."

"I was trying to get her to stay out of the room. I just sort of . . . let something go." Aysel felt guilt pounding in her head.

"Hopefully they can't trace it back to us," Z said. They sat down grimly on the round-pebbled gravel and hugged their knees to their chest.

"Well, we're in for it either way," Tommy said. He grimaced. "It's probably time for us to get out of town as soon as we can."

"You have a point," Elaine said. "I definitely was not planning our break-in to have casualties." She looked at Aysel. "Not that we know that woman is hurt, of course, but she was definitely in for some smoke inhalation."

"Sorry," Aysel said, and felt a deep gloom settle on her shoulders.

"You were saving our asses, nobody holds it against you."

"All our asses except for Tommy, anyway," Z said.

Aysel looked at Z. They were glaring at her. Aysel found her throat had closed up. She choked for a second. "I wanted to get Tommy out," she said. "My magic just sort of—happened. I wasn't thinking."

"You trapped him in a burning building."

"He's alive, isn't he?" Aysel found her voice sounded angry, even though she didn't feel angry. She felt—scared. Z had never looked at her like that.

"Aysel's right, though, I can take care of myself," Tommy said loudly. "I didn't expect any of you to come back for me. I'm glad you all got out. And it turned out all right."

His casual smile made Aysel feel even worse than she had before. She knew he was sincere.

"We probably should have put someone on watch duty to make sure we could have avoided that whole thing. But we're alive. Live and learn," Elaine said. She sounded so flippant that for an instant Aysel felt reassured, until she remembered that they didn't know if the woman dentist had been trapped inside when the fire spread. Aysel thought about bringing this up, but she couldn't speak somehow. Instead she sat down on the gravel next to Z. In the ensuing silence she heard the noise of more sirens in the distance. She looked in the direction they had come. There was more smoke now.

"Jesus," Z said, looking at the smoke. "You set a fire, all right."

"I need to get home," Aysel said. "My mom will be pissed, but I can deal."

Z turned to look at her. "Yeah, you had better get on back *home*."

"What?" Aysel asked.

"Nothing," Z said, standing. "Nothing. Jesus."

"Are you mad at me?" Aysel asked. "Look, I'm sorry about the fire. I did it because I care about you. I wanted to protect you."

"And you've really protected me now," Z said. "All of us are so much safer now that you've committed arson. Time to go *home*."

"Hey," Elaine said. "Cool it."

"I'm not going to cool it," Z said. Their hands were balled into fists. They looked at Elaine hard with their dead yellow eyes. "Aysel has a mom to go home to and I have nobody, except her and Tommy and I guess you. Aysel and Tommy are what is literally keeping my body together but she doesn't even need me—"

"I want you all to be safe," Aysel said, her voice high.

"Aysel wants us to be safe! Great! What a wonderful girl! She can just go *home* at the end of the night, but she cares about the people who are out in the dark!"

"What the hell, Z!" Aysel shouted. "You don't think I'm scared? Police all over town, shooting people like me—"

"Oh, yeah, because you're totally the same kind of werewolf as the kids living in the woods, without parents, without shelter. The police are going after you for sure."

"I'm still a werewolf."

"You don't really give a shit if you get all of us killed. You just want to be where the action is."

Aysel felt tears come to her eyes. "That's not true! I care about you, Z! I care about Elaine! I care about Tommy!"

"We're a great plot twist in your suburban werewolf sitcom life," Z said.

"I love you," Aysel said to Z, and her voice broke. "I would die for you."

"We give you an opportunity to piss off your mom and light things on fire—" Z was shaking.

"Fuck you," Aysel said. The allusion to Azra stung, and she couldn't get past the hatred in Z's eyes. She still didn't feel anger, only misery, but she had made herself too vulnerable. She crumpled in on herself.

"Look, Z," Elaine said, "Aysel doesn't need to hear this shit right now. I understand you're mad, but getting all upset with one another is literally the last thing we can afford. We need to have one another's backs."

Z scrunched up their mouth. "Fine. Whatever." They turned around and began to walk away. "I'm going home to grab my necromancy stuff before we leave town. Elaine, Tommy, I'll see you there." They stepped off the gravel and into the grass and began, somewhat unsteadily, to walk toward the road.

"Jesus," Elaine said, looking at Z's retreating form. "I'm sorry that happened."

"Z didn't mean all of that," Tommy said to Aysel. "We all care about you, too, Aysel. You look out for people, you care about people. You're not a thrill-seeker. You put yourself on the line because you've got a big heart. Z knows that." He looked at her with his deep purple eyes and Aysel wanted to punch him, or gently touch his cheek.

"Yeah, right." Aysel looked at Tommy, thinking back to the last year. She thought of all the times she had ignored Tommy, all the days he must have left school and gone to be strapped to that terrible chair—

"It's true," Elaine said. "Look, this kind of fight happens all the time. Z loves you, too, Aysel, I know they do." She hugged Aysel, who was too surprised to hug back. "I'll talk to Z about it, okay?" She moved away and made as if to go. "And you'll see us again. But we have to get out of here."

Aysel watched them move away as a group. The tears came more easily now. She could barely see as she left the park, walking in the opposite direction.

Azra got home and found Aysel on the couch.

"Did you know I was out looking for you? For hours."

"Oh," Aysel said.

"I'm so scared for you. I just don't know what to do."

When Azra turned on the news, Aysel looked at her face to see if she knew Aysel had something to do with the fire. She didn't. The news station wasn't even a local one. It was national.

". . . five fire trucks and a perpetual rain spell eventually managed to subdue the blaze. The origin is magical, and it is widely supposed that the werewolf terrorist organization, now known as the Wolf Guts Group, is responsible. Documents found in a hidden room inside the building are badly damaged, but it seems likely the group acted with the intent to destroy evidence about a patient or patients previously treated by Archie Pagan, the local man recently murdered by werewolves. Pagan had worked to rehabilitate werewolves in the past, and potentially kept illegal personal records of this treatment. It is now thought that one of his patients took his life. Police are following a lead to locate a possible link to the incident of stolen necromancy and demon-summoning books at the Willamette library, as a charred pentacle was found inside the hidden room. Suspects include three teenagers spotted running away from the scene."

Aysel thought of the fire, and the clouds of smoke on the news, and how the fire looked smaller in real life, and the words about the police not being sure there were survivors. She thought about Tommy.

Her throat was raw and her nose stuffed up, but she couldn't bring herself to stand up to go to the bathroom for water or get tissues. The only position she could imagine being in was the one she had adopted on the floor, half under the bed. She wanted to keep crying, and she was sure she would have if she hadn't been worn out and if her voice hadn't given out after a long while sobbing to herself and her pillow. She was trying to be quiet so her mother wouldn't hear, and was sure she was failing. Aysel fell asleep with her eyes feeling swollen and her chest and body feeling hollowed-out and sore from crying. The streetlamp illuminated a thin strip of carpet and several cassette tapes and CDs that were strewn across her floor.

She fell asleep and for a while was calm, her mind blank. But then something stirred in her sleep. Aysel woke with a start. She hit her head badly on the underside of the bed and scrambled up to her feet, stumbling so that she knocked her small bed askew and nearly tipped it over. Her head ached. Her hair was in her eyes. Outside the window mist massed along the cold earth of the yard and the streetlamps shone dimly at the end of the street. She looked over at the clock. It was four thirty. She thought of Tommy and Elaine at Z's house, all together, and wished she were with them. Then, in a second, she wished she never had to see any of them ever again. For a guilty moment she regretted ever meeting them; her life would be so much cleaner if all she had to do was keep her head down and pretend not to be a werewolf, alone. But that was wrong.

Aysel stumbled again and sat down on her bed. She ran her fingers through her long hair again, and then in a moment had grabbed the scissors and was in the bathroom, turning on the light, looking at her puffy pink eyes in the mirror and holding the scissors to a long lock of hair. She cut several chunks at once, in a hurry, because in her sleepy state she knew she wouldn't be brave enough to do the job properly if she didn't make a big, dramatic gesture immediately. The hair fell to the floor in dark curls. She had cut in random, ragged directions with no sense or purpose, and the result looked as wild as Aysel felt inside. Aysel forced a laugh at herself in the mirror and splashed cold water on her face, and began again, more carefully. When she was done, she cleaned all the hair off the floor and put it into the trash wrapped in toilet paper. Then she drank four glasses of water in quick succession and threw herself down in her bed, on top of the blankets.

17

Z stumbled off, their cold hands shoved underneath their frigid armpits. The streetlamps lit the signs on every corner very dully, and it was several wrong turns and a good twenty minutes before Z could say with certainty where they were or what direction it was to Mrs. Dunnigan's home. Finally they were on a street they knew. There was a house with a tall hedge that stood as a landmark. They felt in their pocket for the key to Mrs. Dunnigan's apartment, thinking how empty and hollow the place was, how cold they were. They thought of Aysel for a second and blinked, hard, against the pressure of their scratchy eyeball.

At the end of the block, in front of Mrs. Dunnigan's building, there was a line of police cars. The lights on one of them were still going, but the others had their engines turned off. The door to the first-floor apartment stood open. Z stood and leaned against a mailbox for a second, then turned around and walked, as hurriedly as possible, back past the house with the tall hedge. Their legs were weak from running and their calves cramped painfully. Finally they gave up and sat down in front of someone's flowerless chilly hydrangea bush and curled into a ball. They were still in that position when Tommy and Elaine finally found them.

"There's cops in front of the apartment," they said, to Tommy more than Elaine.

"We saw," Elaine said.

"That's that, then, isn't it?" Z said. "We're all homeless now."

"I don't understand how they knew to come to where you were," Tommy said.

"I mean," Z said slowly, looking at the sidewalk between their feet, "Mrs. Dunnigan's store has been getting attention recently. Everyone in the city government probably knows she's the registered caretaker for the city's only zombie . . ." Z shrugged. "It was only a matter of time."

"Can you stand up?" Elaine asked. She reached a hand down toward Z. Z turned their head away, rolled awkwardly over, and propped themselves into a crouch. For some reason they still felt an aversion to having Elaine help them. But Z's knees were too weak to support them, so they fell over anyway. Elaine caught them under their arms.

"I can walk," Z said, but they couldn't. "Where are we going, anyway?"

"Here, just let me like, hold your arm or something," Elaine said. "Anywhere. We have to split. We need to get out of the town before sunrise."

"We can't," Tommy said. "We don't have a car. I don't have money for a bus."

Z, leaning awkwardly into Elaine, suddenly had an idea.

"Mr. Weber," they said. "We'll go to him." They felt a pang of doubt as soon as they said it—Mr. Weber had avoided them since the beginning of March. But they knew where his house was, and it wasn't far. If anyone they knew in town could be prevailed upon to help them at all, it was him.

"Who's Mr. Weber?" Elaine asked.

"He's the science teacher," Z said. "He's sort of friends with Aysel. He's the one who tried to break into the library for me, and got arrested." They took a couple of steps, supported by Elaine, and felt the necessity of clinging to her shoulder. "We won't make trouble for him, just ask if he knows a way out of town today or tomorrow. Or a transport spell. I'm sure he has a transport spell. He's a sorcerer."

"Okay," Elaine said. "I mean, my plan was just to hitchhike and then ask someone down the road to let us sleep in a Subway bathroom, so that's probably as good as my plan."

"How far is it?" Tommy asked. "Can you make it?"

"Not far," Z said. "Yes."

"Let me carry you on my back," Elaine said. "You weigh like forty pounds, my backpack was heavier than that. It's no problem."

"We'll go quicker that way," Tommy agreed. "No offense," he said to Z. "It's not your fault."

"Fine," Z agreed. Elaine hoisted them onto her back and hooked her arms under Z's knees.

"You don't actually smell that bad, for a zombie, you know," she said. "You kind of smell like metal and something on fire, but not like, dead animals."

"Thanks," Z said. "I used to smell worse."

"We're like, a two-thirds transgender, one hundred percent monster traveling group now," Elaine said as they started down the street. "That's cool. Or wait, I guess I shouldn't assume about you, Tommy. What's your gender?"

"What?" Tommy said.

"I just don't wanna assume. I know some shapeshifters who switch it up. Z, Aysel told me you were calling yourself like, genderqueer or something these days, right?"

Z was a little taken aback by the conversation. "I guess," they said. "Yeah." They tightened their hold on Elaine's shoulders.

"The words change a lot," Elaine said. "Doesn't really matter."

"Turn right at the end of the road," Z said.

Mr. Weber's house only had one light on, in a back room, with the window barely visible from the street. One light meant he was home. The group hesitated on the sidewalk in front of his house for a moment, wondering if they should go up one by one, or just send Z, or what.

"We look more suspicious, just standing out here," Tommy said. He had a point. They all walked up to the door, and Elaine unhitched one of her hands to knock.

There was a period of long silence inside. Then, the noise of footsteps approaching the door became audible.

Mr. Weber opened the door holding a ball of white fire in his hand.

"Holy shit," Elaine said.

"Who are you?" he asked. Then, seeing Z on Elaine's back, he started. "What's going on? Why are you here, Z?"

"Let me down, Elaine," Z said. Elaine folded her knees, and they held her arm and stood next to her.

"Tommy, why are you here?" Mr. Weber said. "I saw the police come to the school today. They called you on the intercom." He folded the fire back into his palm and grabbed the frame of the door. "What the hell is this?"

"Sorry, Mr. Weber," Z said. "The police are after us. Mrs. Dunnigan left and the police are at my house now. I'm liable for incineration. Tommy's—the police are after Tommy too. He was a patient of Archie Pagan's and they . . . think he's involved." Z looked at Tommy, who nodded.

"I was looking at the news. Someone set fire to Pagan's old office earlier tonight."

"Yeah, I heard," Tommy said, at the same time that Z said, "really?" They looked at each other.

"They say there are three suspects on the loose."

"You don't say," Elaine said, raising her eyebrows.

Mr. Weber opened the door wider. "Come in, fast. There's a monitor spell that sweeps this block every ten minutes, it got put in after I was arrested."

They all stumbled into his living room. Mr. Weber turned one of the lamps on and drew the curtains. "Stay away from the windows," he said.

"We don't want to make problems for you," Elaine said. "We're just trying to get out of town. Z thought you could help us, and we can't think of anyone else."

"Who are you?" Mr. Weber asked.

"I'm a werewolf," Elaine said candidly. Mr. Weber started.

"Are you with the group that got raided?" he asked.

"Loosely. My friend got shot," Elaine said.

"He was also my friend," Z said. Elaine looked down in surprise.

Mr. Weber put his hands to his temples. "How do you know my students?"

"I'm friends with Aysel," Elaine said.

"Oh."

"Normally I don't say the whole werewolf thing straight out, but I figure if I'm already running from the cops, and you know that part, why not mention it, you know?" She looked around the front room, the tidy couch, the teacup sitting on the table by the shuttered window. "We'll be out of your hair soon. We just want to know if you have any like, magic cool transport spell things to get us on our way."

"What happened today? How do—never mind," Mr. Weber said, looking at Tommy. "Don't tell me." He looked back to Z. "You said your guardian is gone?"

"She had to leave," Z said. They wondered whether to elaborate. "She was very sick."

Mr. Weber seemed to tremble a little, standing and looking at them all. Z did not feel fear coming off him in waves as they had when he told them not to ask any more about his arrest, but that could be because he had become numb, in a trance of horror. That happened.

"You don't have to help us," Z added. "Though like. Please don't call the police on us."

"Oh, hell," Mr. Weber said, breaking out of his frozen

silence. "I'm not going to call the police on you." He wiped his hand over the bottom part of his face, over his short beard. "But you might have made it worse for yourselves by coming here. I'm under surveillance. The monitor's probably going to see you when you leave. And I'm not sure I can . . ." he trailed off.

"Okay," Tommy said. "We'll leave out the back in a little bit."

"No, no," Mr. Weber said. "Let me just think. I'll make you all some coffee. Go back into the office by the bathroom down the hall. There's only one window and the monitor can't see it from the street."

The office, which had brightly painted blue walls, was a jumble of books and papers. There were photos of a younger Mr. Weber with six men Z assumed were his brothers. They had different face shapes but all had Mr. Weber's nose and ears. He looked like the youngest. Tacked above the desk was a yellowing card that said "Happy Rosh Hashanah" and had an image of a pomegranate in red and gold. One wall was covered entirely with tanks of lizards. Z recognized Leo. He evidently still was not well enough to return to school. There was only one chair in the office, so Z and Tommy and Elaine sat on the floor.

"I'm not sure this was a good idea," Z whispered.

Mr. Weber returned after a space of some minutes, carrying a tray with a thermos and four cups of coffee.

"It's instant," he said. "But it has caffeine in it. That's

something. You all are going to have a long night. You can take the thermos for your trip. I have another one."

"Do you have any ideas on how to get us out?" Elaine said. "There's gotta be a spell, right?"

Mr. Weber picked up the smallest cup and sipped from it. "Technically yes," he said. "The thing is, that kind of thing is pretty detectable. You need a massive amount of energy." He looked at Z. "I've been planning to go by myself, but I've had to plan carefully. The location I'm planning to take a portal to is the attic of a friend's house in Idaho. But I couldn't take you all with me. It would kill me."

"Is there any way we could put our magic together?" Z asked.

"Z could undo the necromantic spell holding their body together, and that would generate enough energy to transport you all and then some," Mr. Weber said. He looked at Z. "You've done something new, right? You're preserving yourself. You look different."

Z grimaced. "Yeah," they said. "Tommy and Aysel helped me cast it."

Mr. Weber shook his head. "That's incredibly dangerous sorcery to do with a werewolf's magic," he said. "It's a huge amount of energy." He shrugged. "If you undid your spell . . . all the magic in your body, and all the magic in the bodies of their casters, is bound to that symbol, and if you blasted it open by unlocking the sigil, you would all go to the moon or something, if you really wanted. Or turn this town into a crater. But I don't imagine that's high on your agenda, and there isn't really any other way for the three of you to put together that much energy."

"So we have to go nonmagically," Tommy said.

"Basically, yes," Mr. Weber said. "Unless you want to make a ruckus."

"That's the opposite of what we want to do," Z said.

"What I figure I'll do," Mr. Weber said, "is we'll cast a shield spell over my car, have you all hide in the back, and I'll drive you out to the Grayhound station."

Z, Tommy, and Elaine looked at one another. "I guess that makes sense," Tommy said.

"It's what I can do. Magic isn't going to necessarily help this situation," Mr. Weber said. "It could just kill us."

"Are buses running this late?" Elaine asked. "Also, we don't have any cash."

"I'll get your tickets," Mr. Weber said. He looked at Leo, in the tank. "Actually," he said, "not the bus. I'll put you on the night train toward California. That's safer. The train stops all of maybe two minutes and it would be very hard to get waylaid by the police. And then you can sleep."

"Honestly, that's way better than anything else we could have come up with," Z said. "Thank you so much." They tried to read his face.

Mr. Weber nodded, but he did not say "you're welcome" or anything. His eyes were dark and he was staring into the middle distance. "We'll get moving after the monitor goes by again in maybe nine minutes," he said. He looked at his watch. "Safer for us to get on the road sooner rather than later. Be ready to go out the back and get into my car. I'll cast a shield spell so you're invisible for a minute or so." He rose to his feet. "I'll go get the car warmed up."

Tommy, Z, and Elaine sat in silence with the lizards in the office and drank their coffee. Its heat scorched Z's throat, and they could feel peels of dry skin shaking loose from inside their esophagus.

"This seems too nice," Elaine said. "Is this a trap?"

"He's a good person," Z said. "He wants to help. He's just scared."

"I relate to that," Tommy said.

There was the noise of the door opening and closing, and the car starting up outside, its engine making banging, gasping sounds. Z put their empty cup down and looked into Leo the lizard's eyes through the thick glass of his cage. Z thought about where they would go when they got out of Oregon. They didn't have any identification and they couldn't go to a shelter. They could sleep in the woods, they thought, but then they had a vision of sitting in a tent with insects crawling over them, trying to dig into their skin. At least Elaine would be there, Z thought. And Tommy. Maybe. Or maybe they would all fight at some point and Elaine and Tommy would leave, and then Z would be alone.

When Mr. Weber came back in and gestured for everyone to move, Elaine reached down for Z and hoisted them to their feet. Mr. Weber clapped his hands and a pink bubble shot out around all of them. Their bodies became transparent. Mr. Weber nodded for them all to follow him, and they went out the back door and around the house to the waiting car.

╬

The backseat was covered in paper and a jacket was bunched up against one of the doors. Z tried to put it gently on the floor as Tommy and Elaine squeezed in next to them.

"Where is Aysel?" Mr. Weber asked suddenly, after he closed the door and shifted the car into reverse, looking behind through the rear window into the dark night. "She's good friends with you, Z, right? Is she safe?"

"She's at home with her mom," Z said. "She's not in danger."

"Well, that's a relief anyway," Mr. Weber said. The car swung back in a wide arc, its bumper pressed against the neighbor's hedge. His hands were shaking on the wheel a little, Z saw.

Suddenly a large blue light passed the car, on the driver's side.

"Shit!" Mr. Weber said.

A second after passing, the orb froze in midair and pivoted back toward the car. A beam of light shot out from it toward the back bumper of the car as Mr. Weber turned the corner. He hit the gas.

"Do you think it got our license plate?" Elaine said.

"Shit," Mr. Weber said again. "There's two monitors now. I saw one go by four minutes ago. They've increased surveillance." He ran through a stop sign, the car's tires bumping unevenly over the patched cement of the intersection. Streetlamps flashed by in the darkness. "This might be difficult."

"How do they even have the resources to do that?" Elaine asked. "This is a tiny town."

"National Guard got called in a while ago," Mr. Weber said. "I think they're borrowing tools and stuff from the Portland police too. Emergency and all that."

"I haven't seen an orb monitor since I was in LA.," Elaine said.

"They're cheaper to make nowadays," Mr. Weber said in a flat voice. "And the federal government authorized their use just after Bush got reelected in '92. Only a matter of time before small municipalities have some."

Z looked out the back window. The orb didn't seem to have followed the car around the corner. "We lost it," they said hopefully.

"It's not designed to tail us," Mr. Weber said. "It registers us and reports and goes back to its rounds."

"Oh."

The houses flashed by in the dark. They turned onto Center Street, and Mr. Weber's car suddenly gave a loud bang and a rattle. A light on the dashboard came on. Mr. Weber glanced at it and swallowed, and pressed a little harder on the gas pedal.

"This is a pretty old car," he said. "It does this a lot."

They drove for a minute.

"Mr. Weber," Z asked, "just in case I do have to undo the spell and release the energy, to save us, how would I do that?"

"Don't worry about it, Z," Mr. Weber said. "You won't. And if you did I think it would kill you."

"We're dead either way," Z said matter-of-factly.

"No we aren't," Elaine said. "We're escaping."

The car made another noise and shuddered. Mr. Weber stopped at a traffic light, and it made a final, wheezing kind of bang. When Mr. Weber put his foot on the gas pedal again, the car didn't move. There was a whooshing noise like it meant to move, but the wheels didn't turn. The car behind Mr. Weber honked its horn.

"Let's get out and push it," Elaine said, opening her door.

"Get back in here!" Mr. Weber hissed. "Nobody can see that I have people in my car!" The car behind Mr. Weber honked again.

"Why not?" Elaine asked, shutting her door. "It's not like the whole world is watching you and reporting to the Salem Police Department."

"That might be true," Mr. Weber said, "but—oh God." He looked up into the rearview mirror. Z followed his gaze and saw a police car, lights off, pulling around the corner. It was driving slowly, and Z saw the officer in front peering out his window at the stalled vehicle and the three or four cars now pulled up behind it, honking. One driver angrily hit the gas and raced past Mr. Weber with an enormous noise. The police car, apparently in response, pulled into the driveway for the gas station they were next to, and the officer got out.

"Here he comes," Mr. Weber said. "God."

"It's a Portland car," Elaine said. "It's not a local guy. He won't know you."

The officer came over to Mr. Weber's window, and Mr. Weber rolled it down.

"Some car trouble?" he asked.

"Yes, sir," Mr. Weber said. "It does this every few months. I was hoping I could turn her off and on again and she'd start up, that happens sometimes, but no go." He laughed awkwardly. "And here we're trying to get these ah, my niece and her friends home."

The officer nodded sympathetically. "It happens," he said. "I figure it's best to get her out of the road, though. If everyone can get out and push and you can hold her in neutral, we can put it in the parking lot here until your mechanic gets here."

"I appreciate it awfully," Mr. Weber said. He looked back with a certain degree of fear at the rest of them. "You heard the officer, everyone out! We're going to push the car off the road." He shifted into neutral. Z looked at Tommy and Elaine. Elaine shrugged and opened her door, and then went around the car to where the officer was. Meanwhile, the cars behind them one by one pulled around and sped by. Tommy got out too. Z tried to move but found that their knees weren't working very well. They decided to sit in the car unless someone specifically told them to do something.

"You too, Z," Mr. Weber said.

"Tommy, could you . . ." Z looked out at Tommy. He reached in and helped them out. They leaned against the car for balance, and Tommy shut the door. The two stood awkwardly next to Elaine and the officer.

"Pleased to meet you, officer," Elaine was saying, using a bright and sunny voice. "My name's Maureen Weber. My mom's been telling my uncle to get this thing fixed for years. Sorry for the inconvenience."

"Nice to meet you, Maureen," the officer said, smiling. "It's no problem. It's nice to try to help out around the town a little bit."

"You're one of the police they brought in from Portland or somewhere, aren't you?" Elaine asked. "For the emergency. This town is pretty small."

"Oh, yeah," the officer said. "There must be a hundred cars stationed around this town right now, twice as many orbs. It's good to be getting home. There'll be action tonight, with these arsonists and werewolves on the loose. Hear there's a missing zombie, too. It's a big mess."

"It's awful scary," "Maureen" agreed. She turned to Z and Tommy. "All right, let's help push this car!"

They all leaned into the dented back end of the car as Mr. Weber spun the wheel and held the car in neutral. Z was not contributing anything, and as the car had been their support, they found it hard to stay balanced as it rolled forward. They lost their footing and fell onto the cement curb of the sidewalk as the car rolled over the threshold into the gas-station parking lot.

"Oops," they said. Tommy bent to help them, but the officer got there first. His large hand closed around Z's own and pulled them up. They tried not to look up at him. Potion or not, they still looked very dead.

"Thanks," they muttered, and tried to turn away.

"You all right, miss?"

"Oh, yeah," Z said. "Just fell is all."

"Hey," the officer said, "no need to be scared of me. Huh?" He bent down slightly and looked Z directly in the eye. As he did so, the smile he'd held on his face slipped a little, and then froze into an expression of shock. Z knew he was probably looking at the stitches on their forehead.

At that moment, the hip radio on the officer's belt buzzed.

"Monitor 257 reports suspicious exit by resident under surveillance in Survey Zone 45," the little buzzer said. "Jeremiah Weber. Brown Honda Accord 1979, dent in back, license plate"—the voice rattled off Mr. Weber's license plate number. The officer, who had broken eye contact with Z and stood up, stared into space for a moment as he registered the voice from his radio and looked at the car.

"Hello, this is Officer Burton," the officer said. "I have that car here, it ran out of gas just before the gas station, it's immobilized. Three passengers in addition to the driver. Doesn't seem suspicious."

There was a buzz of static, and then a different woman's voice replied. "Resident lives alone. Relationship with passengers?"

"What's he under surveillance for?" Officer Burton asked, into the little walkie-talkie. Z looked over at Elaine, who was standing very still and watching the cop's face. She made eye contact with Z and jerked her head as if to say, Be ready to go, but Z could not run. Z couldn't even walk.

"He's a sorcerer. Attempted to break into Willamette restricted archives a while ago, is what I got here. Relationship to passengers?"

"Hey, young lady," Officer Burton said. "What did you say your uncle was driving you and your uh, friends to?"

"Oh," Elaine said. "Just home, you know. But it's okay, my mom can come instead."

"It's his niece and her friends," Officer Burton said into the headset. There was a minute of crackling, and then a response came through in the woman's voice.

"Can I have a description of the passengers?"

"Now, what's this all about?" Officer Burton asked. "They're just teens. They haven't got anything to do with whatever he did. His car broke down. Haven't we got bigger issues here?"

"A description of the passengers," the voice insisted.

"Uh, well, one's this kind of sick-looking small girl, one girl's . . . also small, long blonde hair in a bun, one's tall, black girl, or Spanish maybe, curly brown hair. That's the niece. Maureen Weber, she said."

"Resident has no blood relatives in Salem, according to this database," the voice on the other line said. "Hold the suspects until backup arrives."

"We live down in Albany," Elaine said quickly. "Not in Salem. Just moved a while ago to be closer to family, from Oklahoma."

"Okay," Officer Burton said, smiling at Elaine before frowning and turning away and muttering something into his headset. He looked back.

"All right, well, everything's on edge tonight," he said. "But you know, they want me to hold you all here and they're going to send some other people over, to check. Guess they think the arsonists today might have been teenagers, figure they'll follow up anything." He smiled. "But that's okay, it'll be sorted out. You can ride home with one of our officers."

"That's inconvenient," Elaine said.

"I don't figure you all have done anything to make you afraid."

"Nah," Elaine said. "We're totally innocent. But that's pretty inconvenient. Are we free to go?"

Officer Burton frowned a little. "You said you lived in Albany? You can't walk there."

"No, I was just asking. Are we under arrest for anything?" Elaine articulated this question with very sharp consonants. "If we aren't, I figure we'll walk over to Safeway, call my mom."

"I can't walk," Z said very quietly to Elaine. They were

managing to keep their balance standing, but they weren't sure how long they could keep that up. Elaine looked at them and her mouth drew in a line.

"I don't think—I think you had better all stay here," the cop said. "You're not under arrest, but just stay put a second. How about you go sit over by the gas station, wait it out. I'll talk to your uncle and maybe get some more answers as to what this is all about, and he can call a mechanic from inside the station."

"There's no phone in this gas station, it's been broken for like a year. He'll have to go use the phone by Safeway too. Small towns, huh." Elaine smiled a little. Z wondered if she was bluffing or really knew the station had no phone.

"Well, let us sort it out. We'll call your mom too."

"If I'm not under arrest, then I'm free to go make a phone call, right? I just want to let my mom know what's happening so she knows it'll be a little bit."

"Well, yes, that's fine, I guess," the officer said.

Elaine gestured to Z and Tommy. "I won't be gone long, I gotta look out for these nerds. I'm just going to use the phone over in Safeway if that's okay." She turned and quickly walked away, without glancing back to register Z and Tommy's surprise. Z wondered what Elaine meant to do. Was she leaving on her own?

"You go wait over against the side of the gas station," Officer Burton said to Z and Tommy.

They did as the officer asked. They waited ten minutes.

Mr. Weber went inside the store after a short talk with Officer Burton, and then came back out, looking around nervously. Then, from around the corner, three more police cars pulled into the gas station parking lot, lights off. The doors opened and six officers got out. They stood by their cars until one of them, a tall blond one, walked forward. These were officers from Salem, not like Officer Burton, and it appeared that for the moment they were in command. Z pointed to two of them, standing back by the cars.

"Those guys were there when the werewolf house got raided," Z said.

"Shit," Tommy said.

Officer Burton and the tall officer appeared to be having an argument. Officer Burton raised his hands defensively. It was not clear what he was saying. He pointed in the direction Elaine had gone, and asked a question. The tall officer turned and said something to the other cops, and two of them got back into their car and pulled out of the parking lot in the direction of Safeway. Mr. Weber watched all this with increasing alarm. As two more officers approached Z and Tommy, he looked as if he were about to spring forward to step between the officers and Z's ragged knees, but Z and Mr. Weber both knew that would be a stupid thing to do, so he stood near Officer Burton looking tense and wary.

The officers—a woman and a man—spoke to Z and Tommy.

"Stand up," said the woman officer.

Both of them stood and were spun around. There

were suddenly zip ties, pulled tight, around their wrists behind their back. The police officer seized Z roughly by the shoulder with the hand not holding Tommy. Z, not expecting this level of force, stumbled and fell to the ground. Their head hit the painted cement. Their face was tilted back toward the dark gray sky. Anyone who happened to be passing by at that moment would have seen Z's eye fall out of its socket and hang down their cheek.

"Undead," the officer articulated clearly, and kicked Z in the stomach. Z felt the world spin around them with the unexpected pain. They bit down on their own tongue. Fear like a ribbon of wire closed around their throat.

With their good eye Z could see the cashier inside the gas station standing at the window, watching this unfold. The noise of the road seemed to have flickered out into silence. There was a long pause as Z pushed themselves up into a sitting position, looking at the officer with their good eye. They stood slowly, deliberately, and faced the officer. The officer, still holding Tommy with one hand, reached and grabbed Z by the back of the neck. Her hand was so large that her fingers reached almost the whole way around. Z thought about how undead bodies were supposed to be able to leach magic toward themselves, and use it. They wondered how it was done. They remembered the passage in the necromancy book, about interrupting the sigil, breaking it open.

Mr. Weber, who was being handcuffed by the squad

car, suddenly tried to step forward, and cried out. His feet made a scuffle on the pavement as he was dragged backward by the shoulder of his coat and slammed against the side of the squad car.

"What you're doing is illegal," he said.

The officer turned to look at Mr. Weber, taking in the sudden widening of his eyes and the sheen of sweat across his forehead. His fists were clenched behind him. Through his palms Z could see white fire.

"I'm sorry?" the officer asked. She glanced over at the wall, and one of the two policemen who were now standing near the door began moving toward Mr. Weber. His eyes flickered over to the advancing officer and he swallowed. The fire in his hands evaporated.

"Brutality toward a suspect without any threat or hostility to the officer's person is illegal, and the choke hold you are putting on that child is illegal. The state included it in a measure against police corruption which passed three years ago in '94." Mr. Weber coughed and swallowed. "Initiative 5587. If I remember right, the old commissioner in Salem lost his job shortly afterwards."

The other policeman near Mr. Weber reached forward as if to restrain him.

"It is also illegal for you to use any force against me," he said. "I am not obstructing your work. I'm restrained and not resisting."

"Put him in the car," the officer holding Z's neck said. "Come on, both of you."

A gust of wind made the cold dry air hit Z's throat. Z felt their legs weakening under them and allowed themselves to lean against the officer leading them. The officer grunted in surprise and perhaps a little fear. The whole group moved slowly toward the cruiser.

"No," Mr. Weber said to the officer holding his hands behind his back, "I'm not going with you." He looked at Z and Tommy.

"I'm sorry, I have to go."

Z gritted their teeth. "That's okay, go," they said. "But help me undo the sigil."

"What?"

"I know you know how to do it!"

"Quiet!" the officer holding Z said. The officer nearest Mr. Weber moved to pin him down, secure him.

"Do you *want* to?"

"I don't think we have any other options!"

Mr. Weber looked at Z for a moment, and then nodded. "Brace yourself," he said to Z. "You have to be ready."

"Stop," the cop at Mr. Weber's shoulder said.

Mr. Weber opened his hand, which was still wrenched behind his back, and a sphere of bright fire glowed there. The officer at his shoulder put a hand on his gun. Mr. Weber flicked his wrist, and the fire flew toward Z's chest. It sat on the surface of their shirt for a second before being absorbed through the fabric. Z felt it burn along both sigils inscribed on their skin, and then had a sensation inside like something had broken or shattered and all the vague icy coldness left in their body was shooting out of their skin and a fire was replacing it, streaming toward them from all sides.

"What the hell was that?" the officer asked. "What the hell did you just do?" He drew his gun and pressed it against Mr. Weber's neck.

Mr. Weber opened his palms again, snapping his handcuffs into pieces. Only Z noticed. "I've been afraid too long," he said flatly.

"I need you to shut up," the officer said.

Mr. Weber looked at Z. "Just remember, I didn't want to destroy anything. I wanted to make things right."

The light shot out of his back in a thin bright spear and ran through the body of the officer behind him. The officer let out a shout and pulled the trigger of the gun. The gun went off, but Mr. Weber's head and neck were elsewhere. The light which had replaced his body expanded in a brief flash and dissipated, leaving a charred circle on the ground beneath the officer's feet.

"A portal spell. Burton, why did you not contain the area?"

"I didn't think . . ."

It was silent for a moment. The police were shaken. Tommy and Z looked at one another.

"Okay. Deal with that later," a woman officer called. "Man was a sorcerer. We weren't prepared. We weren't going to be able to apprehend him without a fight. He did something to the curse on the zombie. Get the suspects in the car."

"What's the evidence you're arresting us on?" Z demanded. They could barely speak over the rush of heat flowing into their body from the direction of Tommy and the policemen surrounding them.

"You were both seen in the vicinity of the burnt building yesterday, and censored materials were connected with your names. Necromancy. Demonology. Susan Chilworth, you are being apprehended as a revived life-form with no human guardian which has inflicted damage on private property, arson, destruction of evidence, and burglary. You have also been linked to attempted murder. Alondra Dunnigan has been declared missing and you are implicated in her disappearance."

"That's bullshit!"

"Mostly bullshit, anyway," Tommy said, making eye contact with Z. He looked mildly alarmed and Z wondered if he could feel the way his magic was flooding into Z's body like water out of a broken dam.

"We have reason to suspect this boy has stolen materials long missing from the Willamette library and may be, through the work of dark magic, associated with the Wolf Guts Group and complicit in the murder of Archie Pagan."

They were being guided toward the car.

"Reason to suspect!" Z said loudly, thinking, What would Aysel do? They felt the fire hot within them and could feel the faint hot resonances of the bodies around them, the hearts of the officers pulsing with their own blood and magic.

"Reason to suspect!" Tommy repeated. "What a bunch

of corrupt assholes. You were going to shoot Mr. Weber when he didn't do anything."

"Thomas Wodewose's father also confirmed earlier today that he is an unregistered magical being who has on several occasions transformed into uncontrollable monsters which caused him to fear for his life."

"He's fourteen!" Z shouted. Their eye was still dangling down their cheek. They felt the hot heartbeat of the officer nearest them and thought about merging it with their body, with the white fire Mr. Weber had put in them. They felt magic building up within them and preparing to burst forth. They hoped Tommy wouldn't be destroyed in whatever explosion happened.

"But they're right, aren't they?" Tommy asked. "Neither of us are human. I'm an unregistered magical being. And dangerous."

"Shut them up," shouted the police officer who had put on the zip ties.

"You need to loosen my handcuffs," Tommy said. The zip tie was too tight. His hands were turning purple. The police tightened Tommy's zip tie.

At the entrance to the gas station, more police cars were pulling in. Three, then five of them fanned out to form a circle around Z and Tommy.

The woman officer pushed her hand against Z's face, to push them backward into the car, and Z bit her. The officer yanked her hand back, and Z reeled in the other direction, their knees not strong enough to hold them. They slipped down to the ground, their cheek against the metal of the car. They felt Tommy next to them suddenly, his magic like a fire coming through the skin of their chest so hard it hurt. Z and Tommy looked at each other, and Tommy mouthed *What, now?* Z tried to remember what it had felt like to cast magic. They murmured the spell their mother had given them again, and felt Tommy's magic draw into them through the second sigil on their chest. It burned them and sent a rapid jolt of electricity out in a wave, a ripple.

Then, a blow came down on the back of their head.

18

Aysel woke up to a pounding noise outside at the window of her room. She sat up in a haze. It was still dark outside, and her feet were tangled in the covers. There was a dark figure at the window. Aysel's hair, short now, spiked up in a frizz around her head. As she threw her legs over the bed onto the carpet she gave herself an electric shock.

"Elaine?" she said, opening the window. "How did you get here?"

"Tracker spell I put on everyone earlier in case we got separated," Elaine said. "I figured we were going to."

"Oh," Aysel said. "Well. Hi."

"Hi," Elaine said, panting. She leaned over and propped herself on her knees and inhaled deeply. "Look. The police have Z and Tommy. We have to do something."

"What?" Aysel asked. "How?"

"There were police at Mrs. Dunnigan's place," Elaine said. "Here, get back from the window, I'm coming in."

Aysel took a step back, and Elaine threw a long leg over the sill and pulled herself into the room. She fell onto the floor with a jarring thump and looked around in the dark, trying to pull herself upright on the sill. Aysel went over to the wall and turned the light on.

"So they got you when you went back there?" Aysel asked. "How are you not dead?"

"No, not there. We went to what'shisface, Mr. Weber. Z thought it was a good idea. And he said he was going to drive us to the train station, but then his car broke down over in the gas station by Safeway and a cop was driving by and we all got busted. He got arrested too. Mr. Weber. Some—I don't know. The point is, I have no fucking—" Elaine made a weird noise, and gasped, and made the weird noise again. Aysel realized after a second that the noises were sobs. "I have no idea what to *do*." She hiccupped. "I can't figure out how to *save* anyone. And they're kids, and you're a kid, and . . ." Tears were coming down Elaine's face in big wet drops. She suddenly clutched both hands to her face. Aysel had cried so much in the last few hours that she found herself unable to now.

"We have to go right now," Aysel said. "To get them before they get back to the police station." She went around the bed and started to pull on her shoes and coat. "We have to run."

"Wait," Elaine said. "God. They're just going to arrest you too. Or shoot you. Or god knows. And then you'll be gone too. God."

"We have to go," Aysel said again.

There was a noise in the next room, where Azra slept, and the sound of feet on carpeted floor.

"Great, now my mom's awake," Aysel said. A moment later the door to Aysel's room rattled and Azra opened it and shrieked.

"Who are you!"

Aysel found herself shaking.

"I'm Elaine," Elaine said.

"Why are you in my house?"

"I'm sorry. I came here because the cops got me and Z and Tommy and I was warning Aysel." Elaine stood up, brushing her hands on her pants. "And running, because that's all I know how to do, or whatever. Or I don't know."

"Mom," Aysel said, "Z got arrested by police at the Safeway. It's about the werewolf gang thing, and about the Archie Pagan thing and the building that got burned earlier. My friend Tommy is there too."

Azra looked at Elaine, and then at Aysel. "This is happening now?" she asked. She put a hand to her forehead and looked at Aysel. "Where has your hair gone?" she asked as an afterthought.

"It's my fault," Aysel said. "I set the fire earlier. I have to fix this. I have to go to them."

"You can't," Azra and Elaine said at the same time.

"That's really dumb," Elaine said. "Stop, Aysel."

"Aysel," Azra said, "what is this? What have you gotten yourself into?" She moved forward, opening her arms to try to hold or restrain her. Her hands came around Aysel's shoulders.

Aysel pulled away from Azra, pushed past Elaine, and

jumped out the window without looking to see if Elaine was following.

Lightning formed in Aysel's hands as she ran. The flush of her cheeks felt like fire in the cold night and she felt inflamed through her knees and in her nostrils and in the back of her dry throat. She wanted to let out a cry of pure fire, and she thought she felt sparks gathering at the back of her tongue. Her feet hit the pavement and her hips ached and her feet hurt from the memory of all the running she had done just hours before. She could hear her mother and Elaine calling out behind her, yelling at her, and then fading as she rounded the corner.

Aysel did and did not want to be followed. She was worried she would be held back.

The breath that Aysel found as she slowed, seeing the lights of the gas station over the roofs of houses at the end of the block, was channeled immediately into a long, rumbling roar that interrupted her and made her stumble. When she fell she left a charred mark on the sidewalk, her hands and belly and knees smoking and blasting away at the pavement beneath her. Her arteries throbbed in furious jerks and her intestines lurched. Her teeth were chattering. Aysel threw herself forward and became aware, out of the corner of her eye, that she had left a flaming trail behind her, which in places had caught large sections of lawn and mailbox and moss and telephone pole ablaze, and in places had fizzled into black chars on the asphalt and cement. Everywhere, steam rushed up in her wake.

Aysel knew where Safeway was, and the gas station. She had walked there a lot. It took maybe ten minutes to get there. Aysel knew that if she was too late—but she wouldn't be too late.

When she rounded the corner to a spot where she could see the lights of the police cars, she was already winded, but in a way where there were sparks in her lungs and dancing purple before her and it only made her run faster. There was a circle of cars, a full wall blocking Aysel from immediately seeing what was happening. There were ten police officers total. Z and Tommy were visible near one of the police officers. Tommy was being pushed into the back of a police car. His hands were behind his back. Tommy's hair was coming out of the bun on his head and falling back around his shoulders. It took a moment to see Z, half crouched and half sprawled on the pavement. Their arms were bent at an odd angle behind their back, and a pool of black-green bile was spreading under their mouth. A police officer stood over them with a baton, watching them, tense. It was a moment before Aysel noticed the wound in Z's head was leaking blood.

Aysel felt a pulse of magic radiating out from her skin, involuntarily. It took her a second to put together that the pulse coincided with the tremors convulsing through Z. Aysel felt torn open, with all her nerves exposed. Any kind of restraint she had was gone.

Aysel started forward before she could stop herself. She had to get to Z. She did not think of hiding herself. She raced instead directly at the police officers, vaulting over the nearest car with fists raised, summoning magic as she went. She would destroy them. A fire burned in her nose, her teeth, her bones. It came from her belly, from the pit of tensed muscle over her spine, from between her eyes like a deep well of heat, the internals and externals all shaken by spasms, an iron burning. She would do more than she had ever done before, Aysel thought to herself. She saw Z on the pavement, among the black-booted feet, eyes open, not moving. Z's head looked like it was coming open. Aysel remembered that Z had told her the head wound was how they had died in the accident. It had been split open again. Aysel felt part of herself being pulled at Z, her magic yanked out of her solar plexus toward Z's bleeding head and the sigil on their chest. The rest of her was on fire.

Aysel screamed, in rage, and it felt like a wave cresting. There was pearly elastic grasping flame in her hair and at the tips of her fingers. Out of the corner of her eye she could see that there was already fire visible under her fingernails. The police officers turned and saw her. They tensed. Eight of them were men and two were women. Aysel prepared to release a spell in her hands that would blast them off their feet, send them spinning through the air. One of the officers must have seen that she had vicious fire in her eyes, must have seen the great depths to which she would reach to draw her magic out in violent force, because he shouted loudly.

"Hey, kid, stand back!" One of the policemen threw something up between Aysel and the car, like a shield. It was made of painful, pointed noise.

Aysel allowed herself to release a little of the fire welling between her fingers, and a pulse of blue energy radiated out from the glass shell in a shriek of noise that made one of the policewomen cover her ears. She looked over at the red and black and bloody wound which had opened, pouring darkness, at the crown of Z's skull. Aysel was now certain that she was going to kill them.

She let out a great cackle, but it might have sounded like a cough or scream. One of the police officers stepped backward and reached into a holster, pulling out a gun and pointing it at her, with both arms.

"Shoot to kill, she's a sorcerer."

The juice of the fire hit the police officer's face first and he escalated himself backward in a lurching path that defied the order and solid presence of each of his limbs. Another officer, one of the other men, raised a gun while one of the other officers scrambled away toward the cruiser she had come out of. Aysel spun around and threw a great flux of stippled hairy conflagration at her, and it caught her in the back. She went down and Aysel did not see her come up.

"Aysel!" a voice called from behind her.

Aysel turned.

The car that Tommy and Z had been led toward had

split along its seams into white fractured pieces of metal and there was nothing at the heart of it anymore, it seemed, only that glowing light like a sun except there was no sun. There was a rending sound as glass and piping and wires flew into the air and then hung suspended, spinning in organic shapes like succulents radiating from a central cluster. There was a great shrieking that filled the air, a pulse that came from the center of the light. It flashed and made Aysel blink hard.

"Tommy," she whispered.

Something inside Tommy had been released, or broken, or freed. All the components of the car he had been held against went rocketing away at top speed in all directions. A piece of fiery metal caught a fuel dispenser and blasted it open, and a fireball shot in all directions. The police dived out of the way. Aysel flinched, but when she opened her eyes she found herself untouched by the flame. One of the officers who was still standing was forced forward and fell flat on the ground, arms outstretched in front of him. A wave of heat rippled over the cement. It distorted Aysel's vision before it hit her and the officer. To Aysel it felt like a comfortable warmth. The heat smelled familiar, like firewood and the smell of almost crying. It sizzled on her skin. Aysel looked over at another officer. The cop was frozen, eyes wide, staring at the explosion, while covering part of her face with one hand. Her skin seemed to be blistering.

The white light faded, and there was no longer any car, and no boy inside of it. Instead, there was an enormous white beast standing on delicate feet in the midst of burning rubber things that had once been tires, which curled and fell like a shield around the body of Z. Two of the officers who were still uninjured pulled themselves to their feet and stared at it in consternation. The beast had a mane like Tommy's hair and dark eyes. Tommy was a great, white, goatlike, horselike thing with a single horn growing from between two flexible pointed ears, eyes flashing fire and sunlight.

The remaining police cars had caught fire in the blast of Tommy's transformation, and now formed a blazing wall between Tommy, Z, Aysel, and the remaining police officers. Aysel could see their dim shapes flickering through the haze. Several of them had their guns out. Aysel turned in a circle to look at them all. As she did so, she felt something whiz past her ear. She looked up and saw one of the guns pointed at her.

"Hands up, and don't move," the officer called out.

Aysel dropped to all fours and crawled, and the next bullet hit a car on the other side of the ring. She edged toward Z, her hands scraping the cement.

Tommy shifted, his shape jumping between forms. He was a great white bird, and then he was a boy hugging Z. Z was still sprawled on the ground spitting bits of black and green liquid onto the pavement. Aysel moved toward Z too. She undid the zip ties on Z's arms.

"We need to go now, now, now," Aysel said to Tommy in a low, panicked voice.

"I don't think we're going to get out of this alive," Tommy said. "Z's hurt. I can feel it in my chest—can you feel—"

"I feel it pulling on me," Aysel said.

Z turned their head toward his voice. Their eyes were screwed shut. "We are," they said. "We *are* going to get out of this alive." Then they bent and held their hand over their mouth and heaved again. Aysel did not want to watch Z's organs all come up through their mouth, and she shut her eyes. She remembered the first day she had seen Z's black guts empty themselves onto the pavement.

"Z, you're warm," Tommy said to Z, who looked like a corpse. Tommy trembled, and Aysel felt herself shake at the same time.

Aysel scrunched her eyes shut and then opened them again and bent town to touch Z. Their skin was hotter than hers. Their eye was hanging on a thread of muscle down their cheek, and Aysel pushed it back into the socket. Z shuddered as it popped into place, but didn't say anything.

"What the hell is happening to you?" Aysel demanded. "What's going on?"

Z's eyes flickered for a second and opened. They let out a retch and a stream of glowing green vomit, which collected on the pavement and steamed. Aysel felt herself breathe in deeply, the biggest gasp she'd ever taken. She bent down with Tommy and wrapped her arms around Z's shoulders. She felt like throwing up too, but instead swallowed sharply and scowled at the open wound in Z's skull.

In the middle of Z's chest there was a bright fire burning at the skin.

Tommy looked up. "Mr. Weber threw something at Z," he said, "and since then I've felt them kind of pulling at me. I think he was trying to set off their spell and release the magic so we could use it to get out of here. But if that's true, then they'll die, right?"

Z was breathing; Aysel could feel the inhale and the exhale. Aysel kept her arm around their shoulders. The blood was still dripping from the place the baton had hit them, and it covered Aysel's hands in black ooze. She felt like she and Z were melding into one being. Tommy was breathing in time with her. They shuddered with a violence such that Aysel thought they would break apart in their hands, and then they fell flat to the ground again, their face contorting.

"Don't die," Aysel said.

"I'm not going to die!" Z rasped. "You're not going to die either. Neither of you."

Aysel thought Z was about to throw up again, but then something else came out of their mouth—a bright green light.

"What's happening?" Aysel screamed.

The light was liquid, sort of, and poured out of Z in a fresh wave that did not smell of death. When it hit the pavement it sizzled and burned through it, and quickly formed an expanding pool. Z's hands were submerged in the liquid, and then the stuff spread and began soaking through Aysel's pajamas. It felt like cold water. Aysel looked at Tommy in a panic.

"Holy . . ." Tommy said.

He gestured, and Aysel saw that at the edges of the pool the cement was crumbling away and tendrils like those of plants were sprouting out of the cracks and spreading outward.

Aysel could see, where Tommy touched Z, the light spreading from his hands to Z. She looked down at herself and saw pulses of sparks shooting into Z's body. But neither Tommy nor Aysel had any control. Z absorbed it, and shook, and screamed, their face flaking, and they hit the ground with their hands, and the magic went through them and out again in a torrent that even Z did not seem to be able to direct or move.

The pool engulfed the whole circle between the cars in a matter of seconds and began to spread outward through the fire Aysel and Tommy had set, sending up a fifteen-foot-high shield of green smoke that filled the air above the gas station with an eerie glow. Aysel couldn't understand how it was all coming out of Z, who was still shivering in her arms like they had a fever that was breaking. As the watery light welled up, Aysel lifted Z and held them under their arms with their back against her. Sitting, she was submerged up to her hips. There was nothing to do but hold on.

"What the hell is that stuff?" Aysel heard an officer shout from behind the rubber-smelling wall of burning car.

A second officer responded by screaming. Aysel squinted through the haze and tried to make out what was happening.

It didn't quite make sense. Aysel and Tommy seemed to be protected from it, but everything else the spreading light touched floated like steam. Matter shook like shadows in the sun, and shrank back. The parts of the cars, for example. They fractured and split apart, and through the diminishing flames and steam they appeared to turn into something that looked like the material of a spider's web. The cars had been metal a moment before, but now they swayed like silk.

As the two officers moved toward Aysel, Tommy, and Z through the immaterial barrier, they turned into other things. The liquid spreading across the parking lot touched their boots and changed them. The tall blond one was the first. He dropped his gun with a splash and started back in shock. His arms became porcelain, or something that looked like fractured porcelain, and began to crumble. His other arm followed. Aysel sat in awe of the grass that was springing up from the wet earth underneath Z's body. Behind the car, the officer Aysel had thrown fire at was standing. She did not seem eager to advance toward them. This did not seem to matter. The light around Z was not a stable thing, and as Aysel watched it spread out toward the figures assembled around the perimeter of the glow. The grass and flowers that now sprang up from the pavement followed the light. The officer watched as the light came toward her, and stepped back, but too slowly. She turned into something that resembled condensation on the edge of a glass, and then dissipated and became a series of musical notes and mist. The world bent and space shifted and their forms changed, and flew backward in drops of dew. One of the men's badges had become a dandelion.

Distantly, Aysel heard the sound of the ocean.

The world rippled around Aysel and Z and Tommy. The light was still expanding dramatically. Tommy's form began to shift from a unicorn into a bird and then into a cat, a dog, a wolf, changing so quickly that one couldn't follow the shifts. There was so much light one could barely make out the edges of one's own skin. The grass that had come up from the pavement was getting longer. Aysel found she could smell the leaves, the crisp earthiness that crumbled under the roots of each plant. It smelled like the edge of the universe. It smelled like magic, but deeper, hotter, more star like.

Gradually, the fires Aysel and Tommy had set died out completely, submerged in a thick steam which obscured everything around the ruins of the gas station. Aysel felt herself closing her eyes against the steam. Her glasses were fogged up. Her skin prickled with a new sweat. When the air around her finally began to cool again she opened her eyes one at a time.

"Where did the road go?" Tommy asked before Aysel could say anything.

The heap of spiderwebs which had been the police cars lay spread out like deflated ashy tents in a circle around them. There was no sign of the police officers. There was also no sign that the place where the three friends were crouched had ever been touched by human habitation. Around the perimeter of what had been the parking lot, there was a ring of enormous trees. Branches and undergrowth were still sprouting from a glowing wetness that soaked the earth. In places, splintered cement had been thrown up in vertical projections among the proliferating roots. The shells of the gas-station fuel dispensers that still remained were now backed against the base of cedars.

Z spat a last green spark into the grass they were kneeling in, and reached out to grip Aysel's arm. They leaned against her.

"Help me stand," they said.

Tommy and Aysel both grabbed Z and tried to support them. They stood slowly, and swayed in the middle of the clearing in the black woods. The air around them smelled clean.

"What the hell did you do?" Aysel asked Z.

"I don't know," Z said. "I don't know. I wanted you all to be okay but I couldn't remember any spells, and I was just shaking. I had Mr. Weber undo the sigil so I could take magic from everywhere at once. I felt like I was tapping into you more. I hope it didn't hurt."

"This isn't even sorcerer-level magic," Tommy said. "That's something else. That was my magic. This was like the moment I was in Archie Pagan's chair and the power was turned up all the way. It didn't hurt but it felt like the same charge. I changed form without even thinking about it, like, five times. I was flickering. It was scary."

"It was like transforming but I wasn't transforming," Aysel said. "Everything else was."

"Sorry," Z said.

"No," Tommy said, "it's okay. Look what you did, though."

Z leaned their neck into Aysel's shoulder and she felt their blood through her shirt. "Guess we're really fucked up now, huh," they said. "This is next-level." They looked around. "Where are the police?"

"You made them disappear," Aysel said.

Off in the distance, an owl made a noise.

"Where are we?"

"I don't know," Aysel said. "I don't know if you moved us or if you changed where we were. But we could walk, and find out." She paused and squinted at Z in the dark. "If you can walk."

"If you lean against me I can walk," Z said.

Aysel hooked her arms underneath Z and propped their worn body against her. Tommy stood by for a second, and then moved forward and wrapped his arm around Z's waist. Their feet dragged against the naked green earth for a second and then they shakily found their footing again.

"Which direction should we go?" Tommy asked.

"I think any direction we move in will be okay," Aysel said.

They walked a little through the giant roots and the ruined cement and asphalt pieces, picking their way slowly along. It was dark, but Aysel felt nervous about casting a spell for light. Even if they were in a forest now, there was presumably an end to that forest, and on the other side was a town full of policemen and rioters and people who had watched the building Aysel had set fire to burn to the ground. The deep blue light was barely sufficient, but it had to do. The wind rustled in the branches.

"Do you smell something like the ocean?" Tommy said.

"I can't really smell," Z muttered weakly.

"I can hear the ocean," Tommy said.

"I heard it when you did your spell," Aysel said. She paused. "The ocean is better than sirens, though."

"I swear I hear the ocean," Tommy said. He grew quiet again, as if straining to hear. Aysel could feel the tightness of his hand on Z's waist as it pressed against her own side.

"This is really weird," Aysel said a few minutes later. They were lifting Z over a stump which looked as if it belonged to a recently fallen three-hundred-year-old tree. The farther the three moved, the less the forest seemed to have an ending. The roots grew large and violet blue-black. There were no signs of houses or power lines or even roads. Aysel shivered, in a wind that seemed all the colder for the recent heat Aysel had been in the center of. She whipped her head around and squinted for any sign of the familiar in the new growth of forest. Above the trees, she thought she could see a pillar of smoke rising in the distance, but with every second it seemed to be coming from farther off.

"Is that a stop sign?" Tommy asked, and pointed. All of them paused and looked. It was. It was embedded in the middle of an oak.

Z, their arm around Aysel's shoulder, started to laugh. "What if I made a forest that destroyed the whole town?" they asked quietly.

Neither Tommy nor Aysel answered. They looked at each other over Z's bloody head.

Suddenly in the underbrush behind them, Aysel heard something move. It was followed by a human shout.

"Who's there?" Aysel cried out, turning. "Who are you?" She wheeled around, letting Z fall against Tommy's skinny body. Tommy stumbled back from their weight and landed in a patch of ferns.

Aysel raised her fists. She felt too worn out to cast any more spells. She strained her eyes against the deep scratchy darkness.

"Aysel?"

Azra's hair was pulled rigidly back on her head. Her face was blotchy and worn-looking. She was wearing a housecoat over the suit she had worn to work; she had put on sneakers with yellow stripes on the sides. Her coat was covered in mud.

"Oh God, it is you," she said.

"Mom," Aysel said uncertainly. "How did you find us? What are you doing here?"

"We saw the light in the distance when we were two streets away. The fire. You left a trail of fire." She swayed, looking a little dizzy. "And then these trees began to grow. Are the policemen dead?"

"Maybe," Tommy said faintly.

Elaine appeared beside Azra, from behind a tree. "Holy shit, it's them," she said.

"You have to go back," Aysel said. "You have to go back home. You can't be here."

"Go back where?" Elaine said. "There is no back." She pointed behind her. "This goes on for miles."

"But you can't be with us," Aysel said, her voice getting hysterical. "We just set fire to a bunch of cop cars. We're wanted criminals. You need to get out of here, both of you."

"I can do whatever I like," Azra snapped. "I knew you were in trouble. I've been letting you get into trouble, letting you run loose and nearly get killed. I need to protect you. I need to be there with you."

"Mom, go home. Mom. Mom, you're not like me, you're normal, you can live a normal life!" Aysel found herself getting hoarse, and on the last word her voice cracked. "I'm a werewolf and have to run away my whole life, but you don't have to. You need to go. You need to go!"

"What's happening with your friend? With Zee? What is wrong with Zee?" Azra asked, looking over to where Z and Tommy were struggling to stand against each other.

"An officer hit them in the head with something..." Aysel didn't mention the bigger conundrum: Z was supposed to be dead and dry as bone, and shouldn't be bleeding at all.

"I'm fine," Z said. "I think I stopped bleeding when the light faded. It's just still wet."

Aysel and Tommy exchanged glances.

"Aysel, oh god, my baby, you should never have to see things like this. I am so glad they did not do this to you," Azra said. She scrambled over two lumpish roots to put her hands under Z's skull, near the place where the wound was.

"I'm really okay," Z said again.

"Police all over town and you think you can run away on your own? You and Zee and this boy all being accused of attacking police and who knows what else, with everyone up in arms? You think you would be able to save your friend on your own, while running from the police? You didn't think to ask if I could *help*?"

Aysel stared at her mother. "I didn't want to put you in danger. I don't know if we'll make it. But I couldn't risk the police coming to our house, and I had to try to help Tommy and Z, since Z has nobody and Tommy can't go home now, and I attacked a police officer—"

"If they caught up with you alone they would take you back to the station and burn you and I would hear about it on television. What do you think I would feel if that happened? Do you think I could just go on with my life?" She was tearing up. She turned back and moved toward

Aysel, engulfing her in a hug. "I am your mother, and I'm not going to let you act as if you have nobody in the world and have to fend for yourself. And I'm not going to let your friends grow up thinking that there are no people in the world willing to help them when it comes to a matter of crisis."

"You came and found us in order to save us?" Tommy asked. He still seemed to be trying to clarify the situation.

"That was the idea," Azra said.

"It looks like you guys are okay on your own, though." Elaine smirked. "Who did this bit with the trees? We should have done that part earlier." She knocked her hand against the trunk of the nearest enormous cedar. Her movements looked worn out, hollow. "Would have saved a lot of trouble. Cop comes up to you, bam, the cop is a tree. Everything is a tree." She paused for a second. "This is a mess of a day, isn't it?"

"Yeah," Aysel said. She felt drained.

"We're going to have to talk to each other, and be more honest," Azra said. "If we get through this alive. You and I need each other, Aysel, and I can't have you dying or leaving me. Think how my heart skipped when you were out and the werewolf house was raided, and then again when the fire—"

"Elaine and the others were just trying to hide out, and then we were only in Archie Pagan's office tonight because—" Aysel said. She looked at Tommy.

"Aysel, I wouldn't care if the werewolves were planning

to set fire to the White House. But I want to know about it."

Aysel bit her lip and looked at her feet. She could feel Tommy watching her. "I didn't know that's how you thought," she said finally.

"I have to cast my lot with you," Azra said. "And with your friends, now. This town isn't safe anymore. We all have to run, together. Your friend says there are places in other towns where werewolves are safer. I don't know what I'm doing, God knows, but I'm going to take you there."

"If we can ever get out of this forest," Z said from behind Azra.

They all looked around.

"I swear I smell the ocean," Tommy said again. "Do you think Z might have moved us? To the coast?"

"I definitely saw a mailbox back there," Elaine said. "In the middle of a bush. I'm not sure that's what happened."

Together, the group moved uncertainly forward again through the brush. Elaine hoisted Z onto her back and carried them. Azra clung to Aysel, and brushed her fingers through her short hair repetitively, as if Aysel was a small child again. It was almost annoying, but Aysel didn't stop her. Tommy trailed along next to Elaine, in the front.

It had been almost half an hour of walking when suddenly, in front of them, Elaine fell out of view. She let out a shriek and there was an enormous snapping of branches and crashing in the brush ahead of Aysel. Azra screamed. Elaine's yells grew slightly more distant, and then there was the sound of a splash. Aysel pulled away from her mother and ran to stand by Tommy at the point where Elaine and Z had fallen. They found themselves looking down into a ravine. At the bottom was a creek. Z had fallen off Elaine's back and was half standing against, half clutching a tree growing on the mossy fern-covered incline. Elaine, some distance below, was picking herself out of the water. She sloshed back to the shore.

"Fuck, that was a surprise," she said. "Woke me up, though." She held still for a second and then shook like a dog. Water droplets flew away from her in a great mass and then held themselves suspended in the air around her. Elaine pulled her fingers through her hair, now dry.

"We should follow along the banks of the creek," Tommy said. "It's got to lead us somewhere. If we really are near the ocean this is the surest way to find out."

A branch with a low-hanging leaf dripped water into Aysel's face as she slid as carefully as she could down to the bottom of the ravine.

The shores of the creek were barely wide enough to walk on, and Aysel and Azra could not walk side by side, but she felt her behind her all the time. Ahead of her, Z and Tommy were holding each other's hands. Z seemed to be gaining in strength the farther they went. Twice Aysel accidentally fell into the icy water of the stream, her feet slipping on the rocks. The second time she fell, she came up spluttering.

"It's salty," she said.

As they rounded the next corner, it became clear why. A roar, previously audible only to Tommy, overtook Aysel's ears too. The creek and the ravine opened up toward the lightening sky, streaks of pink cast across it from where the sun rose behind them. Under the sky lay the ocean.

"That's impossible," Azra said. "We were miles and miles inland."

"I think it's clear that nothing really is where it was before," Elaine said.

They picked their way down the last rocky incline and landed on the hard brown wet beach. The water crashed onto the shore, dredging up brown and green seaweed and leaving, on its retreat, open pores in the earth through which clams squirted. Aysel stood and looked out at it. It had been years since she had been to the sea. Z turned to her. The first light of morning illuminated their face.

"I think today is going to be better than yesterday," they said.

There was no sign of a road leading to the beach, but Azra said she could see a house on top of a high bluff in the distance, its western windows starting to gleam in the sunrise. At first Aysel could not see it, but when she looked harder she could spot a light on in one window.

"We need to go toward it," Azra said. "At least to find out where we are. Not all of us have to go up."

They walked toward the distant bluff.

Far out in the water, there were small black things bobbing in the surf. It took a moment, but eventually Elaine yelled that they were seals. Z's head whipped around and they stood a long time looking out at the animals.

"Do you think one of them could be Mrs. Dunnigan?" they asked. "She said she was going to do magic to protect me, from the ocean."

"Maybe," Aysel said.

The seals made no move to come ashore.

When they reached the bluff, they stood, for a while, looking at one another and the water. There was a staircase carved into the grainy stone, with one wooden handrail. The sun had almost made the entire sky orange by the time Z grabbed Aysel's and Tommy's hands and pulled them forward, and all of them began the slow climb.

ACKNOWLEDGMENTS

I first want to offer thanks to Leylâ Çolpan for offering invaluable information on the details of growing up in America as part of Turkish diaspora and providing me with ideas about how to think about magic and nationality, magic and religion, and magic and family. Leyla's own poetry and other writing has always been astounding and I was so lucky to have this input on my own book.

I would like to thank Mal Nair, Tom Phelan, Alaz Ada, Seph Mozes, Phoebe Weissblum, Destiny McEntyre, Constance Zaber, Sherwin Shabdar, Nathaniel Zanardi, Sami Brussels, Eden Staten, Luis Galvan, Stephen Ira, Mairead Case, Emily Lampkins, Vivyan Efthimiou, Chaya Klarnet, Sharon Adams, Kyle Lukoff, Micah Brown, Nicholas Shannon, and my mom for reading my drafts in whole or part at different points throughout the writing process and giving honest and invaluable feedback again and again, and/or for connecting me with spaces or people that allowed my writing to improve. Thank you too to those people who offered input and feedback who are not listed here. I love you even if I do not know more than your internet handles.

I want to articulate how lost I would have been without Cat Fitzpatrick, Jeanne Thornton, and Sanina Clark. I needed the intense and thoughtful work they put into helping me revise my manuscript. In 2016, Cat close-read my manuscript and helped me identify the things about trans communities before my time that I was leaving out and made me think about my characters' relationships and how to resolve them. Cat, who is doing important work to connect trans authors with audiences and also to teach trans fiction in academic settings, also worked like hell to help me find a publisher who would give me the support I needed. She connected me with Jeanne, a genius and workaholic whose confidence in my book kept me going even when I was sure it would never reach a broader audience. In 2017, Jeanne helped me plot the story more, brought up ways in which I was leaving side characters out, and helped me figure out the goals and motivations of people who I had not thought about. Jeanne brought my book to Seven Stories, where Sanina Clark read it and advocated for its publication. Sanina's painstaking editing and focus on timelines, character arc resolutions, and tiny details helped me make the manuscript a real book and worked to align the story in a way that made practical sense.

I would be extremely remiss if I left out mention of mentors and role models who encouraged me in my writing from a young age or who created work I liked and were kind to me when I brought it up to them. The following is an incomplete list of people I want to appreciate here, some of whom I knew well and some of whom I met once: Mrs. Sheehan, Jason Gacek, Janet Hubbard, Katherine Deneen, Sandra Rowell, Kirsten Bennett, Mattilda Bernstein Sycamore, Ned Hayes, Filiz Satir, Talcott Broadhead, Eric Fleming, my mom, Jane Yolen, and Sy Montgomery. I want to include a special thanks to Naomi Shihab Nye, one of my favorite authors, who, when emailed by a twelve year old ten years ago, corresponded with me about my vacation to my grandparents' house in Oklahoma for three weeks.

Finally, I want to thank Sebastian Blake Stott for reading the first thirty pages of a version of this story in 2013 and telling me it was good. Your encouragement stuck with me more than any other and kept me going with this project long after you were no longer part of my life. Rest in peace; may everyone who ever hurt you feel the weight on their conscience forever.

ABOUT THE AUTHOR

Hal Schrieve grew up in Olympia, Washington, and is competent at making risotto and setting up a tent. Xie has worked as an after-school group leader, a summer camp counselor, a flower seller, a tutor, a grocer, and a babysitter. Hir current ambition is to become a librarian. Xie has a BA in history with a minor in English from University of Washington and studies library science at Queens College, New York. Xie lives in Brooklyn, New York, and hir poetry has appeared in *Vetch* magazine. This is hir first novel.

ABOUT SEVEN STORIES PRESS

Seven Stories Press is an independent book publisher based in New York City. We publish works of the imagination by such writers as Nelson Algren, Russell Banks, Octavia E. Butler, Ani DiFranco, Assia Djebar, Ariel Dorfman, Coco Fusco, Barry Gifford, Martha Long, Luis Negrón, Peter Plate, Hwang Sok-yong, Lee Stringer, and Kurt Vonnegut, to name a few, together with political titles by voices of conscience, including Subhankar Banerjee, the Boston Women's Health Collective, Noam Chomsky, Angela Y. Davis, Human Rights Watch, Derrick Jensen, Ralph Nader, Loretta Napoleoni, Gary Null, Greg Palast, Project Censored, Barbara Seaman, Alice Walker, Gary Webb, and Howard Zinn, among many others. Seven Stories Press believes publishers have a special responsibility to defend free speech and human rights, and to celebrate the gifts of the human imagination, wherever we can. In 2012 we launched Triangle Square books for young readers with strong social justice and narrative components, telling personal stories of courage and commitment. For additional information, visit www.sevenstories.com.